D1052824

# OUT OF CHARACTER

*To Janice, for being with me every step of the way.*
*You're the best of them.*

*And to Malachy, who needs to run more laps.*

Quill Tree Books is an imprint of HarperCollins Publishers.

Out of Character

Library of Congress Cataloging-in-Publication Data

Names: Miller, Jenna, author.
Title: Out of character / Jenna Miller.
Description: First edition. | New York : Quill Tree Books, [2023] |
   Audience: Ages 13 up. | Audience: Grades 10-12. | Summary: When
   seventeen-year-old Cass lands the girlfriend of her dreams, she
   struggles to hide her secret online life where she role-plays fanfiction
   scenes with a group of internet strangers, and things get even more
   complicated when she winds up falling for her scene partner, Rowan.
Identifiers: LCCN 2022031707 | ISBN 9780063243323 (hardcover)
Subjects: CYAC: Secrets--Fiction. | Role playing--Fiction.
   | Interpersonal relations--Fiction. | Lesbians--Fiction. |
   LCGFT: Lesbian fiction. | Romance fiction. | Novels.
Classification: LCC PZ7.1.M576 Ou 2023 | DDC [Fic]--dc23
LC record available at https://lccn.loc.gov/2022031707

Typography by David DeWitt
22 23 24 25 26 LBC 5 4 3 2 1

First Edition

# OUT OF CHARACTER

## Jenna Miller

**Quill Tree Books**
An Imprint of HarperCollinsPublishers

# ONE

Mr. Tuttles would be the death of me.

We'd brought him home as a kitten ten years ago. I was seven at the time, and it was shortly after my neighbor Mr. Tuttles had died. Naming my cat after a crotchety old man who hated me more days than he didn't wasn't the smartest idea, but I'd never been good at letting go of things that were bad for me.

This wasn't the first time Tuttles had run away. I'd usually find him on the porch swing next door like he was trying to take the place of old-man Tuttles. Or he'd be hiding under a car or an equally hard-to-reach place out of cat spite. But he wasn't in any of his usual hiding spots. He wasn't anywhere.

"Tuttles!" I yelled, hoping that did the trick. It never did. He was a pain in my ass who showed up when it suited him, but I loved him too much to not look anyway.

A car passed, a few leaves fell from the maple tree in front of my house, and still no cat. My heart started racing. Knowing he always came back didn't mean something wouldn't prevent him from making it home. Something like a moving car. "Tuttles!"

"Come on, Cass! You'll wake up the neighborhood with your screeching!"

Tate Larson approached my yard from his house with a tired grin on his face, clearly proud of himself for the weak jab. As if we hadn't exchanged this same banter a hundred times over the years. My best friend was, simply put, beautiful. He was Black with warm brown skin, deep brown eyes, and a smile that was all teeth, and he shadowed my five-foot-five frame by almost a head. He and his mom had moved into human Mr. Tuttles's house a few months after the old man died and Tate's parents divorced. Being the only other kid my age on the block, we'd become friends immediately.

"Have you seen Tuttles?" I asked, meeting him between our houses and exchanging a fist bump out of habit, but I couldn't bring myself to smile. "I wouldn't be surprised if he curled up in your bed in the middle of the night, the ungrateful beast."

Tate snorted. "Not my fault everyone adores me. But no, he's not at my house. Want help looking?"

I groaned, not in the mood for a cat hunt when Tuttles was impossible to find. "No, thanks. He'll turn up. Always does." I looked around, willing my body to feel as calm as my voice sounded.

"For sure," Tate said. "In that case, is this a good time to talk about the weekend?"

Of course he was thinking about the weekend on a Monday. "Sure, let's hear it."

"Do you have plans?"

"You know me—always got a packed weekend."

He narrowed his eyes, smirking. "So Netflix, books, and waffles?"

I rolled my eyes, a smile finally forming. It was damn near impossible not to smile around Tate. "Obviously. You?"

"Rachel and Greg are coming over if you want to hang with us."

I groaned. Again. "Why would I want to do that?"

"Come on, C," he said, nudging me. "Just because you hate him doesn't mean *everyone* does."

"No, but they should," I muttered.

Greg Jensen was my first and only boyfriend for a few months in eighth grade. When I came out the next year, he reacted by dragging me online, which was a shitty way to start high school. The drama of it passed quickly enough because no one actually cared about my sexuality, including him, but it was hard to forget.

Tate shuffled his feet. "I know it's a sensitive subject."

"It's not *sensitive*. I can't help that he's an ass who never got over me wounding his fragile male ego because he's not my type."

Tate snorted, shaking his head. He and Dad were the only guys I knew who'd appreciate the words *fragile male ego*. "Look, I get it. He was the worst back then, but he's good people now. And he's on the team, so."

3

I knew it went beyond them playing football together. "You mean Rachel wants me to come over so someone can entertain Greg."

He grinned like a boy in love. "Yeah, maybe that too."

*Cue the world's most exaggerated shock.*

I didn't dislike Tate's girlfriend, but I knew it bothered her that Tate had a female best friend—even a lesbian who'd rather go without waffles for a month than see him naked. "Why invite him if you and Rachel want to hang out alone?"

"Because I'm trying to juggle everything at once," he said, scrunching his face. "Between football and senior year already kicking my ass and trying to give a shit about the people I give a shit about, it's a lot."

I nodded, understanding the feeling more than he knew. "We'll see," I said, which we both knew meant *hard pass*. Tate tried to involve me in his friend group, and I loved him for it, but it wasn't gonna happen. Some people weren't meant to be friends, and that's okay.

He sighed in defeat. "Fine, fine. But I'm heading back inside. Be ready in an hour or you'll miss your ride, fail the econ test, and have to deal with me lecturing you about the importance of your future or some other obligatory best-friend bullshit. No pressure!"

"I'll be ready, you goof," I said, shoving him playfully toward his house.

Retreating inside to my upstairs bedroom, I sat at my desk and opened my laptop. I had an hour and needed the distraction from a missing Tuttles. Multiple windows awaited me with messages related to the Tide Wars roleplay I comoderated.

I'd only ever been a fan fiction reader, not writer. But the concept of making a character from my favorite two-book series my own and using them to interact with other characters within new storylines excited me. It was like gaming, but with words instead of controllers or dice or whatever the hell people used to nerd out these days.

The roleplay had eleven people in it from across the country, but the Discord server labeled Home Base included my four closest friends other than Tate—Rowan Davies, Carina Moretti, Holly Stone, and Autumn Murphy. I'd met them online two summers ago when joining my first Tide Wars roleplay. I'd stumbled upon it while scrolling Tide Wars Tumblr tags, needing the distraction from my parents fighting *again*. The whole stranger-danger aspect made me nervous at first, but I'd quickly gotten sucked in. The more my parents fought, the more I relied on online life. And after a month of roleplaying, I couldn't imagine my life without my new friends and the fake world we inhabited.

When the first roleplay ended only a few months after I'd joined, Rowan and I decided to start our own, and the other three followed. We wrote scenes together either as a group with the larger roleplay we acquired through Tumblr or privately one-on-one, but Home Base was for out-of-character conversations between the five of us. The personal, real-world stuff. And maybe we sometimes used it to bitch about other characters—and the people playing them.

I clicked on Home Base to catch up on morning messages.

**Carina:** Can someone read my Yale essay? My dad says it's make-or-break, and I can't afford to break. It has to be perfect!

**Carina:** Ugh, I hate being on the East Coast. You're all probably sleeping.

Carina Moretti was a senior from Boston, on track to getting accepted to Yale for political science. She had Italian and American dual citizenship and was the only one of us in a real-life relationship. Tom frequently took priority over the roleplay, but most things in her life had taken priority over the roleplay lately. I couldn't remember the last time she'd started a conversation.

My shoulders slumped when I realized she'd reached out only for personal gain. Still, she was my friend, and I wanted to help. I swallowed the hint of bitterness I felt and replied before she could throw herself into a deeper panic.

**Cass:** Morning! Rowan is the essay expert, but I can look if you need more eyes.

**Carina:** THANK YOU, CASS! You're an angel.

**Carina:** Rowan, please say yes too.

**Carina:** But I need to go. Class is about to start. Love!

I clicked out of Home Base with a sigh, switching to one-on-one roleplay scenes on Discord. I'd shamelessly snagged one of the main characters, Aresha Petrovka, who was the pirate crew's captain, meaning I always had multiple one-on-one scenes going at once. As moderators, Rowan and I also got messages from people when they wanted to create a new character or if there was in-character or out-of-character drama to mitigate. Moderating a roleplay sometimes felt like babysitting, but it was worth it for the reward of writing amazing scenes and having friends who shared my love of Tide Wars.

I responded to the scenes that were waiting on me, ranging from Aresha helping a crew member who'd been injured to discussing provisions with a supplier—a needs-based role, not a regular character. Then I moved to the roleplay's Tumblr site, which mainly acted as a hub for people to apply and get added to the Discord server. There were also pages dedicated to available and taken characters with bios and a general timeline of where the roleplay was to date, helping newcomers decide if they wanted to join.

Our pinned post from day one welcomed me.

*Welcome to Tide Wars, nerds!*

*The roleplay picks up where Macy Whittier's books ended. In case you aren't obsessed enough to remember the duology's final line, it was: "We go home." Princess Aresha and her crew will begin their journey to Shiibka, Girishtova, so she and her brother, Prince Allain, can rebuild after being away for two years. Although the main enemy was defeated and the king and queen have been avenged, the crew will still encounter smaller, lingering enemies along the way.*

*Main plots are posted under each character on the*

*Characters page as a starting point, but PLEASE get creative and make them your own.*

*A few basic ground rules:*

1. *We aren't limiting how many characters you play or monitoring how often you're around (we all have lives), but we won't hesitate to call you out if you ghost for a long time. Don't leave your plot partners hanging. Communicate, etc.*

2. *We hope to avoid drama as much as possible, but if you can't figure something out on your own, talk to Cass. (Rowan is garbage at mediating.)*

3. *Any roleplay-wide plots should be run by the moderators (that's us!) first, since they'll most likely affect everyone. That said, send us your cute, fun, intense, and spicy ideas!*

4. *Honestly, that's it, but Cass prefers even numbers.*

   *Message us with questions, and apply to characters at your leisure.*

   *We can't wait to see you aboard soon.*

   *XoXo Rowan and Cass*

I grinned at the post, thinking of how far the group had come since the roleplay started.

Moving to the message inbox, I noticed a new person had applied to join. There wasn't enough time to dig into their information, character's bio, and plot ideas, so I left it unread. Rowan was the go-to for applications anyway. She had an eye for who would make a good addition, and I was the mediator who handled character and roleplayer drama. We made the perfect team. I couldn't do it without her.

A knock came from the other side of my door, and I closed the laptop right as Mom walked in. Her blonde hair was pulled back in an uncommon ponytail, and makeup was missing from her face, including her signature red lipstick and perfect eyeliner that bordered her round hazel eyes. People said we looked a lot alike, but they always left out the part where I was fat and she wasn't. The omission used to feel awkward, but now it annoyed me when people acted like obvious things didn't exist.

"Just making sure you were up," she said, a small smile on her lips.

I laughed. "You must've missed me yelling for Tuttles outside." My brows furrowed as I gave her a pointed look. "Did you leave a door open on accident?"

"I haven't been out, so maybe it was your dad," she said as she eyed my laptop. "Not doing anything questionable on there, are you?"

"Of course not." I tried hiding the inevitable flush of my cheeks for being called out. "Secret project. Will share eventually."

Guilt rocked me when her smile grew. I'd always been an A/B student in school, but my grades had started slipping last year. She and Dad assumed it was because they'd done a shitty job at hiding their growing tensions with each other. And that was a big part of it, but staying up late to roleplay instead of studying or doing homework didn't help.

"Well then, don't let me keep you from it," she said. "But don't get too into it and end up late for school. I know how laser-focused you can get."

"I won't."

"And don't worry about Tuttles. He always turns up when he's ready."

"I know, but school would go better if I wasn't thinking about him all day," I said, knowing I feared for my cat more than he deserved some days.

"Oh!" she said, her eyes widening. "Speaking of school, don't forget about your early-action deadline for UIC."

I groaned. "I know, Mom. I have, like, two weeks to get it in." I willed her to leave so I could wrap up a couple of scenes before school. UIC stuff was obviously on my mind, but it didn't matter this second.

"Another reminder doesn't hurt. Just like I'm going to remind you about Ursula. Halloween is around the corner."

"I haven't forgotten," I said. The costume we were almost done making together was going to be my best one yet. Sure, Ursula was Ariel's villain, but that didn't keep her from being a badass in her own way. I couldn't wait to make her my own. "We'll get it finished in time."

Mom nodded slowly. She remained in the doorway, her eyes locked on mine. "I'm really proud of you—you know that, right?"

"I know," I said again, smiling in the hope that she'd leave this time. Mom was one of my favorite people, but hovering made me nervous. "I'll see you after school."

"Yeah," Mom said quietly, absently, as she glanced around the room. She was likely thinking about work stuff or what to make for dinner or whatever else parents thought about that I didn't want to know. "See you."

I opened my laptop after she left, staring off into the void of my secret life. My parents didn't know anything about the roleplay or my online friendships. They didn't need to know how much time I spent away from the real world.

After trading in ice-skating lessons for playing *The Sims* in middle school, I became all too familiar with gaming addiction. In the beginning, I'd invite Tate over to play with me, but soon he was more of a watcher than a participant and gave up trying to join. Before long, I was bailing on plans with him and other friends to game. I'd stay up late and sleep in on weekends. When that extended to sleeping in on school days, missing assignments, and failing tests, my parents took the game away. Everything settled down after that.

Then my parents started fighting last year, and it became too much for me. So I found a way to cope.

Not only was the past addiction an issue, but the parents also didn't trust internet strangers in general. If they found out about the roleplay, they'd worry unnecessarily about stranger danger, me falling back into my old ways, and my grades. And that would lead to them feeling disappointed in me for not talking to them, which would lead to them blaming each other and fighting more, which would lead to no technology, no roleplay, and an even shittier senior year.

I refused to let any of that happen. I wouldn't give up my nerd friends.

And my grades weren't *that* bad.

Before I could send another roleplay reply, a horn sounded from outside. I looked at the clock, and sure enough an hour had already passed. And I wasn't ready. Fuck. It was yet another morning of getting behind because of online life. I couldn't keep doing this to Tate.

I texted that I'd be right out before rushing to get ready, throwing on jeans and a green hoodie over a Tide Wars T-shirt. After knocking my twenty-minute morning routine down to three, I grabbed my phone and backpack and ran downstairs for a granola bar and bottled coffee drink. I raked a hand through my messy hair on my way out to his truck when I heard my name.

I froze at the sight of Taylor Cooper approaching me, my ginger loaf of a cat in her arms. Gods, she was beautiful. Her pale skin contrasted against her dark-brown bluntly cut bob with a side shave. She had more piercings on her left ear alone than I'd have in a lifetime, and her large blue eyes pierced my heart in a swoony way. She looked almost exactly like Rowan's roleplay character, Roux. It was perfectly normal to crush on someone who looked like my online character's fictional ship partner.

But it wasn't just that. Taylor was *cool*. Not like popular cool, which was totally different. Being around her made people feel like they were floating—or maybe that was just me. She was a pansexual gamer, in newspaper club with Rachel, and nice to everyone in an adorably snarky way. And she worked at Spyhouse Coffee, my favorite Minneapolis coffee shop. Not that I knew anything about her.

Locking eyes with Taylor, I immediately forgave Tuttles for running away.

"Is this one yours?" she asked when I didn't say anything.

"Yes," I said, relieved and nervous at the same time. What if Mom came out and embarrassed me? What if Tate hollered something as a joke that made it obvious I liked her? I didn't know which possibility was worse. "Where'd you find him?"

"On my route to school a couple blocks over. He was playing with a leaf on the sidewalk."

A nervous laugh escaped me as she shuffled Tuttles into my arms, and he was purring. I didn't blame him. "Sounds like him. But how'd you know he was mine? Or where I live?"

"So many questions." A swoonworthy smile formed on her lips. "I went to a party at Tate's house last year and heard him mention you were neighbors." She shrugged. "And your cat's kind of a regular on your Insta."

I blinked. Taylor Cooper followed *my* Instagram? Or she at least popped by it enough to know about Tuttles. This information hit me in a new way. I obviously kept a casual eye on her life, but I didn't realize she did the same to me. "He's the star of it, honestly. Thanks for finding him."

"You got it." Taylor's gaze lingered on me for a beat before she nodded toward an SUV on the street where a man sat with the windows down. "Anyway, my dad's waiting. See you around?"

This moment was either a stroke of fate or a cruel joke. Probably a cruel joke, because fate sounded made up. Either way, it was over before I could let it sink in. "Yeah, see you."

"Cool." She winked at me before walking away.

The simple gesture turned my body into mush—something I wasn't used to. I watched her go and waved to her dad in thanks before securing Tuttles in the house and rushing to Tate's truck. "Sorry about that," I said as I hopped in and buckled my seat belt.

"Don't be sorry," Tate said as he backed out of the driveway. "But Taylor Cooper. *Damn*, C." He let out a low whistle.

I immediately turned scarlet. "Shut up," I said, swatting his arm. "She found Tuttles. It's not a big deal."

"Uh-huh. You've only been into her since you knew you were into girls. But sure, it's not a big deal."

"Okay, maybe it's a big deal, but I don't want to overthink it."

"I'll say no more."

I knew there was a hidden *for now* buried in that statement but left it alone. "And sorry for the delay. Girl shit, et cetera."

"Yeah, your just-woke-up look must've taken hours," Tate said, not unkindly. "But it's all good. We leave twenty minutes early for a reason."

*Me.* I was the reason. And the worst part was that he didn't know why. Like my parents, Tate knew nothing about my roleplay life. Netflix, books, and waffles were really all he thought I did on the weekends—unless I had plans with him, of course. And he wasn't technically wrong, but my free time was spent online more than anything else.

I was an out lesbian who didn't hate my fat body, yet *this* part of my life was a secret. It would be one thing if I was ashamed of it, but I wasn't. Roleplay had entered my life exactly when I needed it—my own little safe haven. And maybe it had become more than that, but it wasn't *dangerous*.

As much as I hated keeping the secret from Tate, I knew it was for the best. He'd been around for the whole *Sims* addiction drama, and I didn't want him thinking this was the same thing. I didn't want him to worry. And considering how close our families were, I knew he'd tell my parents about it if he ever had a reason to think it was a problem. So he didn't need to know.

I pulled out my phone as Tate sang along to a daily Spotify mix, both of us aware I'd gone into my own head. Home Base had a few new replies.

**Rowan:** Thanks for the voluntold, Cassidy Williams.

**Rowan:** I'll read the essay, Cari, but only if you stop second-guessing your genius.

**Rowan:** Off to school. Love!

Rowan Davies was my roleplay comoderator and online bestie. She lived in Chicago and was a senior like me. Also like me, she wanted to go to the University of Illinois Chicago next year for English. Our characters were a ship, which basically meant we constantly had a scene going together. And unlike me and our characters, she was straight.

I knew the *Love!* mockery was frustration and hurt talking because Carina wasn't around much anymore, but I couldn't help but laugh. I opened our private out-of-character server.

**Cass:** You're an asshole, Rowan Davies. Love! ;)

"What's that grin for?" Tate asked.

"Cat meme," I said, instantly hating myself for how easily the lie slipped out. I put my phone away to focus on him, trying to calm my face as if smiling over a friend's snark were a crime. I'd wanted to tell Home Base about this morning's encounter with Taylor—because of course they knew all about her—but it could wait until after school.

Rachel, Tate's girlfriend, was waiting in the parking lot when we pulled up. She had a lot of friends, but she didn't need a girl posse at her side to look confident or get noticed. On top of being in newspaper with Taylor and on the volleyball team, she also volunteered at a women's shelter a few days every month.

"Good morning, Cass," she said politely as we approached, holding her hand out to Tate. Her long brown hair fell perfectly down her back, and her minimalist makeup look was flawless.

Tate took her hand and looked back at me, grinning. "See you in econ. Don't choke."

"Don't die," I retorted, smirking back at him before heading into the building to brave my weekday nightmare—the no-phone zone. I didn't hate school, but most of my classmates had friends to talk to throughout the day. For seven hours every weekday, I was completely cut off from 80 percent of my friend group, and the other 20 percent was usually with his girlfriend or in a different class. I also hated small talk with people I wasn't close with, and that was a major component of high school. Disappearing wasn't an option here.

By the time economics rolled around, I was mentally exhausted. There was a special place in hell for teachers who scheduled tests on a Monday, and Mr. Blake was no exception. He was the kind of teacher who gave you a chance to rewrite a paper using his feedback on one draft, then turned around with opposing feedback on the next draft. He was also the head football coach, so he loved students like Tate and tolerated students like me. But taking econ meant I got out of taking history class, which I loved since the biased American perspective was grating.

"Pencils out, everything else away," Mr. Blake said, looking at a few students pointedly.

Tate shot me a similar look before wiggling his eyebrows and facing forward.

I wanted to die at the thought of another potentially failed test. But it was my own fault.

I really needed to stop roleplaying after midnight.

[Tide Wars group scene]

**Cass:** Aresha looked out across the length of her ship as the sea carried them closer to home. Her peaceful but mighty country had been ravaged by a madman and his followers, by magic and darkness. She took in the faces of her crew, knowing she wasn't the only one who'd lost something. But they'd defeated the enemy at sea, and now was the time to return to whatever life waited for them on land. Only this time, she and her brother, Allain, wouldn't be alone. "Our journey will be long, and new threats await us on our route," she said, addressing the lot of them. "But I promise that no matter what path led you to this ship, you are all welcome in Girishtova as heroes and friends. As you have promised me your lives, loyalty, and love, I now promise you shelter, nourishment, and comfort. My home is your home until your final day or until you wish to leave. No matter which path you choose, you have my deepest gratitude."

**Rowan:** ((Great speech, Captain. Warn us next time you plan on writing a novel.))

**Autumn:** ((I love Cass's novels!))

**Cass:** ((I hate you, Champ. And thanks, Autumn!))

**Rowan:** ((Sounds fake, but nice try!))

**Holly:** ((LOLOL))

# TWO

I wandered to the bleachers after school for Tate's football practice, feeling forever out of place among the scattered girlfriends and one boyfriend. I didn't *need* a ride home, since the bus system existed, but considering how disgusting the bus was and how obnoxious people on it acted, I kind of did. And any opportunity to embarrass Tate was a win.

Sitting away from the others, I pulled out my phone to check Home Base. Holly Stone, one of my four online friends and a junior from Las Vegas, had shared an awkward scene reply she'd gotten from another roleplayer. Everyone in the roleplay was in high school, so the servers were mostly quiet during the day, but I could usually rely on a few replies after school.

**Cass:** Awkward scene, Holls!

**Cass:** Also Tuttles snuck out this morning and Taylor Cooper found him?

I watched a couple of football plays, not wanting Tate to tease me for giving zero fucks or being glued to my phone. By the time I looked back at the Home Base server, Holly was all over my news. She was no doubt in her last class, sitting at the back, twirling her long blonde hair, risking getting her phone taken away. A true rebel wrapped in a short, thin frame that was 75 percent sass. But that was to be expected from someone who roleplayed to spite her mom. And I admired anyone who did things out of spite—except Tuttles.

**Holly:** GIRL, WHAT?!

**Holly:** wait wait WAIT

**Holly:** THE Taylor Cooper? The one you've mentioned a hundred times?

I laughed at the dramatic response, my cheeks warming. My roleplay friends knew almost everything about my life, including my crush. Something about airing my anxieties behind a screen was easier than confronting them in real life. Couldn't imagine why.

**Cass:** I only know one Taylor Cooper.

**Cass:** And I don't talk about her that much!

**Holly:** SURE ;)

So maybe they all knew about how she looked like Roux. And maybe they all thought it was perfect that I crushed on a Roux look-alike in my real life *and* had a ship with the character Roux in my pretend one.

But I didn't talk about her *that much*.

The fifth member of Home Base, Autumn Murphy, joined in.

She was our sweet summer child from Tacoma—a true cinnamon roll with curly red hair and freckles. Her parents homeschooled her, and she always managed to wrap up in time to join us. She claimed this was because sophomores had it easier, but I could see her doing the same thing in two years. Like me, she was very dedicated to roleplay life.

**Autumn:** This is exciting! How did she know it was him?

**Cass:** She recognized him from my Insta!!!

**Holly:** Girl, she's been creepin'! Tell us everything!

**Cass:** That's pretty much it. We had to get to school and Tate was waiting, so she left.

**Holly:** I'm disappointed you didn't make out as a thank-you

**Autumn:** LOL

**Cass:** Her dad was in the car! And Tate would've never stopped teasing me. AND she doesn't know I like her.

**Holly:** Would've been clear after kissing her, just saying

I felt chills at the thought of kissing Taylor Cooper. No matter how much or how long I'd crushed on her, I never dipped my toes in the fantasy pool. But now I couldn't stop thinking about it. Would her lips be warm? Would I brush my fingers against the shaved part of her head? Would we pull each other close and never let go? Would I have the courage to do any of that in real life? Roleplaying that kind of stuff was one thing, but with Taylor it would be . . . well, *real*.

Mr. Blake's whistle jolted me from my dream state. I cleared my throat before returning to my phone, and it hit me that only three of us were messaging. Carina's absence wasn't a surprise since she put academics, extracurriculars, and Tom before the roleplay these days, but it was weird that Rowan hadn't chimed in with a witty or snarky comment. Looking into it more, I noticed she'd replied like normal in Home Base this morning and had responded to the roleplay-wide server a few minutes ago. She was clearly available.

I messaged our private server.

**Cass:** All good, Champ?

I watched a few more plays and yelled something obscene at Tate to embarrass him and make the team laugh before looking back at my phone, my smile fading.

**Rowan:** All good.

It was not *all good*. When I wrote *Champ*, she wrote *Captain*, and vice versa. Always. No exception. Aresha and Roux called each other those nicknames in the Tide Wars books, and we'd carried it over to the roleplay and with each other despite us obviously not being a ship.

Something was off.

I wanted to ask if she was sure, but a yell from the field pulled me away again. The team started chanting some nonsense as if it were a real game. After a beat, I noticed Greg Jensen looking at me from the fifty-yard line—no, *winking*. Unlike Taylor, his eyes had no effect on me. Just like his tall, fit body, smirky smirk, and short blond hair had no effect on me. I smiled brightly in return and flipped him off, and he barked a laugh before focusing on the team again.

"Asshole," I muttered.

The rest of practice was spent switching from the football field to my second life. Roleplay scenes picked up as more people got home from school and extracurriculars. But Rowan didn't send anything else to our private server or Home Base, and I talked myself out of sending my paranoid question. She'd probably gotten busy with life and missed my news, but the growing pit in my stomach said otherwise.

Something was *definitely* off.

A hand waved in front of my face, and my head shot up. Tate was standing there, already showered and changed into normal clothes. When did that happen?

"Cat meme again?" he asked, grinning. "Or are you texting Taylor, your romantic heroine? When's the wedding?"

"Texting, but not Taylor," I said as I tried to stop my face from burning. No such luck. "Are you ready?"

"Yes. Let's go, girl in love."

I rolled my eyes and followed him to his truck, so many thoughts swarming my head that they almost made me dizzy. Tate must've sensed my overactive brain mode because he turned up Childish Gambino after starting the truck. I let it drown out the noise in my head, but after a few minutes I was back to checking Home Base.

**Carina:** Cass/Rowan, I emailed my essay. Be honest, I can handle it. Thanks in advance!

**Autumn:** Miss you, Cari!

**Carina:** You too, girl

**Rowan:** Essay received.

**Carina:** When do you think I'll have it back?

**Rowan:** You'll get it when you get it.

**Carina:** But like what day?

**Rowan:** A day later for every time you ask.

**Carina:** Rude but okay, thanks!

I checked my email, and sure enough her essay was in my inbox. I was tempted to make her squirm a bit and pretend I didn't get it, but that would result in a dozen more messages about faulty email systems and telling me to check my spam folder as if no one in the history of time had ever thought to check their spam folder.

**Cass:** Also received! I'm sure it's brilliant, but I'll get back to you within a few days. Don't obsessively check your inbox like I know you want to!

**Carina:** THANK YOU! That's all I needed to hear.

I put my phone away after that so Tate didn't bring up Taylor again or ask who I was talking to. I felt bad enough for dodging the question this morning—and every other time it had come up over the last sixteen months. But the moment I didn't have to worry about my parents shutting down my support hobby was the moment I'd tell Tate everything.

That day couldn't come soon enough.

Mom was standing by her car when Tate parked in his driveway, and her eyes locked on mine. She had the same disheveled look as this morning, and I knew right away she hadn't gone to work.

"What's up with her?" Tate asked.

"No idea," I said slowly, watching her retreat into the house as my stomach knotted. "Text you later?"

"For sure," Tate said, ruffling my hair and opening his door.

"Rude!" I shoved him before getting out of the truck and walking across our yards to my house, the mid-October leaves crunching under my feet.

Whatever reason Mom had for skipping work, I hoped to gods it wasn't something serious. People took days off. Perfectly normal.

"What's up?" I said after getting inside and setting my backpack down. "Is everything okay? Are *you* okay?"

"I'm okay," Mom said, smiling faintly. "How was school? Your test?"

"Fine," I said vaguely, frowning at her faraway look. "Mom, what's going on?"

"Let's sit down."

My palms started to sweat as I found a spot next to her on the couch. Being told to sit down was a classic red flag in every TV show, movie, and book it appeared in. Whatever was going on, it wasn't good.

If she wasn't sick—shit. She knew about roleplaying. I must've left my laptop on when I'd gone to school that morning. She'd found out about me talking to "strangers" online and assumed my grades weren't perfect because my addiction issues had returned.

And she was going to take away my laptop and phone and ground me until graduation. I clasped my hands together and tried not to fidget as I waited for my inevitable punishment.

"I don't know how to tell you this," she said. And then she started crying.

Whatever *this* was, it definitely wasn't roleplay related. I wanted to feel relieved, but I was too busy worrying. "What is it?" I asked, resting a hand over hers.

Through her fast blubbering, I made out the words *met someone* and *moving to Maine* and *sorry, sweetie*. And then she pulled her hands away, burying her face in them.

My heart cracked as my brain tried to digest. None of it made sense, but the point was made. She was leaving us. I knew she and Dad were having problems, but I never expected *this*. "What do you mean you're moving?" I asked, my mouth dry. "What about Dad?"

What about *me*?

"Dad and I have been unhappy for a long time," Mom said, raising her head again to look at me, her tear-soaked hands taking hold of mine. "We agreed to get a divorce."

The weight of her words sank in as tears started trickling down my cheeks. "I don't understand. Obviously you've been fighting, but you don't just give up and move across the country because of it."

Mom frowned as she started to wipe away my tears. "I know this is a lot to take in right now, sweetie, but I promise it's for the best."

"How can it be for the best if we're not together?" I asked weakly, pushing her hands away before standing, everything tightening inside me. A thousand questions filled my head, but looking at her made me feel sick. I hugged myself as I stared across the room, shutting down. "Who is this man?"

"His name is Colin," Mom said after a pause. "We met online."

Her words couldn't have punched me harder. After warning me for years about all the weird strangers to avoid on the internet, she was leaving us for one. It made my own secret laughable. A part of me wanted to throw my online life back in her face, but I wouldn't. She didn't deserve to know about one of the few joys I'd found since she and Dad started fighting. I'd never tell her another secret again.

I vaguely heard her stand behind me and say something about needing to get on the road. "I'll call you every week," she added. "Every day. Whatever you want."

I didn't want. Mom was the parent I relied on for everything kids relied on their parents for. Dad was in high demand as a surgeon at an area children's hospital, meaning he'd spent more time with other people's kids than with me when I was growing up. We got along well, and I loved him, but he worked a lot and didn't know me like Mom did. And now with little explanation, she was leaving—just like that. There were no words to string together that would convey the agony I felt. The betrayal. As far as I was concerned, our relationship was dead. I gave the slightest of nods and walked to the door, opening it. "Drive safe," I said quietly.

The urge to run to Tate's house, cry for hours, and let his mom cook me one of her delicious meals was strong, but the thought of walking across the yard exhausted me. Instead, I ignored Mom's words and avoided her eyes, waiting until she left the house and drove away before collapsing onto the couch in a fresh fit of tears.

Tuttles barreled down the stairs seconds later, howling at the front door as he pawed it—like he knew she'd left for good. Giving up after a minute, he jumped onto the couch and curled up with me in an uncommonly comforting way. "I'm sorry, buddy," I mumbled into his fur.

After getting in some much-needed snugs, I pulled out my phone. When Rowan's dad had died unexpectedly in February, I was the first friend she'd called, even though we'd known each other for less than a year. I'd stayed on the phone with her while she cried and talked about him. And despite something still feeling off between us, she was who I needed in the moment.

"What's up, Captain?" Rowan said after a few rings.

Hearing her voice and my nickname almost made me forget why I'd called. "My mom—she left."

"What do you mean? Left where?"

"She's gone," I said a little louder as tears returned. "I guess my parents decided they're getting divorced, and she's driving to Maine to live with some random man from the internet."

"Oh gods," Rowan said, her tone thick with shock. "Do you want me to egg her car when she passes through Chicago? Or send poisonous cookies to her new address?"

She clearly knew humor was my brand far more than sympathy. "Both sound very tempting, but no. She's not worth the eggs or the energy."

"Good point." She was quiet for a moment. "But seriously."

"Can we roleplay until dinner?" I asked, my voice shaking. The last thing I wanted right now was to live in the real world. "Please?"

"Until dinner *and* after dinner, I'm your girl," Rowan said. "I'll get on my laptop now."

"You're the best."

"No, *you're* the best, Cassidy Williams. See you online."

A weak smile formed. We had our nicknames, but she was the only person who called me by my full name. It was a comfort. "See you online, Rowan Davies."

After hanging up, I loaded our private server on my phone, too emotionally wrecked to go upstairs for my laptop. I didn't move from the couch until the door opened sometime later.

"Hey, kid," Dad said, his tone cautious as he took off his shoes and stepped into the living room. "I meant to get home sooner, but there was an emergency surgery that lasted a few hours. I should've taken the afternoon off. . . ."

I tuned out the rest as I took in his tall frame, green eyes that matched mine, and salt-and-pepper hair. We couldn't exchange our usual brief pleasantries, and our new reality hurt too much. But we'd have to face it eventually. "Why didn't anyone tell me the truth sooner?" I asked as my eyes shifted back to my phone. "I deserved to know."

"You did." Dad joined me on the couch, and I curled up to give him space. "I didn't know she was leaving today. We were going to tell you together soon, but after you'd left for school this morning she texted to tell me she'd be gone by the time I got home. Between the short notice and the surgery . . . well, it doesn't matter. You deserved better."

"Yeah, I did, but what I deserved doesn't really matter anymore," I said, letting out a sigh. No matter how mad I was at both of them for keeping this from me, I knew blaming it all on Dad wasn't fair. He wasn't the one who'd left. And I wasn't the only person Mom had screwed over. "I'm sorry she ruined everything."

"Me too," Dad said, his hand finding mine. "But we'll get through this together. I'll figure out a better work schedule so I'm around more."

I looked at him for a moment before refocusing on my phone. He'd never had the kind of job where he could switch everything up without issue—that's why things were how they were. "You don't have to do that."

"I want to," Dad said, squeezing my hand. "I know I haven't been the most present parent, but I don't want to miss any more time with you than I already have. Let me do this for both of us."

Being seventeen, I felt fully capable of handling things on my own, but hearing that he *wanted* to be around was a comfort I wouldn't give up. Us not being close over the years didn't matter anymore. He'd stayed, and right now that meant more than anything else in the world. "Okay," I said quietly.

"Okay," he repeated. "Have you eaten?"

"Not yet," I said. Mom had always been the dinner maker because of Dad's weird schedule. He probably didn't know where to start, and I hadn't worked up the energy to move, let alone think about food. "Leftover totdish?"

Tater Tot hotdish, aka totdish, was a Williams family staple. Mom had made it last night, which now made a lot of sense. It was like she knew we'd need it tonight. I wanted to hate her for that, but she was right. It was the only meal that would help numb my pain.

Dad smiled sadly, nodding. "Leftover totdish," he agreed. "I'll heat it up. Want to find us a movie to watch after eating?"

I couldn't remember the last time we'd watched anything together. And as much as I wanted to spend the rest of the night crying, I wouldn't pass up Dad time. "Will do. Thanks, Dad."

I stared absently at my phone after he left the room, unable to stop thinking about Mom's mystery man. Not only had she cheated on Dad, but she'd done it with someone from the internet. Ever since they'd let me go online without parental controls a couple of years ago, the constant reminder was to not let strangers in. Our new reality made two things clear.

One, Mom was a fucking hypocrite.

Two, I could *never* tell Dad about my online life.

[Private conversation between Cass and Rowan]

**Cass:** My mom called. It was really awkward.

**Rowan:** Ugh! What did she say?

**Cass:** She made it to Maine and misses me. And she wants to come back for Christmas.

**Rowan:** Do you want her to?

**Cass:** No idea, but I said okay because I didn't know what else to say.

**Rowan:** Did she say anything else about leaving?

**Cass:** lol of course not, that would just make sense! She acted like everything was fine, like we all agreed this was how life was gonna be now.

**Rowan:** That's such bullshit.

**Rowan:** I'm serious about the poisonous cookies, you know. I'll do it.

**Cass:** Oh, I know you will. If Christmas is a disaster, I'll consider it. Thanks, Champ.

**Rowan:** Anytime, Captain. <3

# THREE

I didn't go to school the rest of the week. Being the best friend that he was, Tate said all the right things in response to my major life crisis before letting it drop. Instead of asking about my daily feelings, he delivered my school assignments and gave me space, and his mom brought over a few meals and desserts as if someone had died.

In a way, someone had.

Other than forcing my way through homework and Carina's essay, I was aggressively unproductive—unless you count roleplaying for hours every day as productive.

Sunday night, Tate showed up after dinner with a tray of Halloween-themed treats and an eager smile. "I come with gifts," he said after I opened the door. "And an invitation."

I eyed him for a moment before taking the tray, moving aside to let him in. "Go on, then," I said, selecting a pumpkin cookie and taking a bite.

"Friday night. Halloween party at Greg's house."

As if on cue at the mention of Greg Jensen, I groaned. And because in my depressed state, I'd forgotten all about Halloween. My favorite holiday. "Why can't someone else host Halloween? And why can't you accept that Greg and I aren't gonna be friends again?"

"It's not about Greg," Tate said. "It's about wanting you to get out of the house. I know you're going through something right now, C, but you should be around people, not shut away." He rested his arm across my shoulders. "Remember, I've been through the whole parents-divorcing-and-living-several-states-apart thing. Meeting you and other people really helped when I moved here. I just want you to be happy."

Considering I spent every available second roleplaying, he had no idea how often I was around people—in theory. Who needed in-person interactions when the real party was online? Still, I got his point. But that didn't mean I was ready to play along. "Let's make a deal. I'll watch *Hocus Pocus* at home, and you'll go to the party knowing I'm having fun."

Tate narrowed his eyes, clearly not impressed but also not in a position to argue. "Fine, deal. But I need a costume for the party, and you're the expert. Want to go to Target after practice tomorrow and help me find something? Rachel said nothing scary or bloody this year."

I chuckled, remembering how much Rachel had hated his elaborate zombie-football-player costume last year. "I guess I can use my expertise to help you find a costume that won't disappoint your girlfriend."

"Solid, you're the best," Tate said, grinning. "I need to get back to homework, but let me know if you change your mind about the party. It's gonna be killer."

If *killer* meant Greg Jensen doing a keg stand and people being fake nice because I was football star Tate Larson's best friend—hard pass. "I'll let you know. Thanks for the cookies."

Tate saluted and left without another word. I watched him jog home before a few laptop pings pulled me back to roleplay life.

The rest of Home Base knew about my mom leaving by now. Holly had reacted with shock, rage, and threats, and Autumn was her usual sweet self. Carina sent two messages to thank me and Rowan for the essay read before disappearing again, no doubt missing my big life update. We all understood her need to focus on other things, but having her around less and less stung after everything that happened with my mom.

But Carina or not, I needed my online friends more than ever, and I was grateful most of them weren't going anywhere.

My first day back at school was depressing the moment I entered the Halloween-decorated halls. I'd normally be talking Tate's ear off about how excited I was for spooks and candy, but those days were gone. Halloween had always been a Mom-and-Cass thing. So instead of beaming through the halls this year, I wanted to rip every ghost and fake spiderweb down.

I was in the middle of grabbing a few things from my locker over lunch when Taylor Cooper stopped beside me. "Hey, Cass," she said, a grin on her lips. "How's your cat?"

My heart flailed as I took her in, the moment in front of my house feeling like another life. But at least she didn't know about my mom. The last thing I wanted was to explain my recent trauma to my crush. "He's good. Thanks again for rescuing him."

"Anytime." She played with the hem of her plain black T-shirt, hesitating. "I've actually been trying to get the courage to ask you out sometime. Finding your cat felt like a sign, but I haven't seen you around school since and didn't want to just show up at your house." She laughed a little, shaking off her rambling, which didn't feel like her. She'd always been chill and collected. "Anyway, Greg Jensen is throwing a Halloween party on Friday. . . ."

Snippets of her words registered as my eyes moved from hers to the slightly chapped lips she bit when she focused on something—or was nervous, apparently. It didn't click that she'd stopped talking until her teeth found her bottom lip, and I looked back at her expectant eyes. "Sorry, what about the party?"

"Do you want to go with me?"

No part of me had wanted to go to Greg's stupid Halloween party, where someone could throw up or spill alcohol on me. Or both. It was my ultimate nightmare. And there was the fact that I was vetoing Halloween this year because of Mom.

And I would've said no, but all the feels had taken over. Pounding chest. Dry mouth. Heart eyes. I'd always been comfortable letting my Taylor crush be just that, but I couldn't pass up the chance to see what *more* was like, even if it was scary. "I'd love to go with you."

"Dope," she said. Her shining eyes lingered as her smile grew. "I gotta meet some friends for lunch, but let's firm up details later this week?"

"Yeah, dope," I echoed. A shocked expression stayed on my face as I disappeared to the bathroom to message Home Base, my heart fluttering in a way I wasn't used to. What the hell was happening right now?

**Cass:** Taylor Cooper asked me out to a Halloween party?!?!

I wanted to tell Tate, but I was too awkward to deal with a big reaction in the halls. Instead, I hid in the library over lunch and crunched last-minute knowledge into my brain for a test I hadn't studied for. But I couldn't get Taylor out of my head.

My jumbled head didn't settle down after school. I had to meet with a few teachers who wanted to tell me how sorry they were to hear about my mom and were there if I needed anything. Apparently, Dad had called the principal to explain why I'd missed school last week, and news had traveled. Super.

The only thing worse than the conversations was knowing Dad had never called the school until now. Mom had always been my caller when I got sick or something came up. She'd signed all permission forms for school outings. She'd attended most of the parent-teacher conferences. I was grateful to Dad for stepping up in the parenting department, but he could've not started with giving my teachers permission to pity me.

I met Tate in the parking lot, waiting until we were in the privacy of his truck before I told him about Taylor. I left out the part about Greg's party for now—because baby steps.

"That's huge, C!" Tate said, reaching over to squeeze my shoulder as he let out a whoop. "How do you feel about it?"

"Excited and sick at the same time? Is it possible to be both?" I clasped my hands together, watching the houses as we passed, many of which were littered with Halloween lights and decorations. My house should've been full of both, but instead we hadn't bought candy yet. Really, that should've been my first clue that something was off with Mom. And the totdish. And the lack of them noticing how much time I'd been spending online. All of it, really.

"I mean, it's you. Of course you're overthinking it already," Tate teased. "But *sick* seems a little dramatic, even for you."

"I know, I know." I paused. "But do you really think it's a good idea to go on a date right now? My mom *just* left, and I'm not exactly in a healthy brain space."

"Maybe not, but this could help," Tate said, shrugging. "A shitty thing happened, and you have a right to feel everything you're feeling. But that doesn't mean you can't have a little fun and be around someone great. And it's not like you didn't like her until today. I've been waiting for this for years, personally. You deserve this."

My heart warmed at his words. Anyone who stereotyped jocks would eat their words when meeting Tate Larson. "Yeah, good point," I said, looking at him. "But can we not make a big deal about this? I'm still processing, and I don't want to overthink it more than I already have and risk canceling."

Tate saluted. "You got it, but let me know when I can. I'll have my mom bake a cake."

I snorted, swatting his arm. "You're ridiculous. But thanks, good of you to volunteer your mom for the task."

"Anything for you, C," he said, grinning. "And she'd say the same."

"I know. You're both the best." I squeezed his forearm in thanks before checking Home Base, hoping to push away the part of my brain that was screaming at me to not ignore my grief. They were already on top of my news.

**Holly:** Yessss, girl!!! Amazing!

**Rowan:** Great news, Captain! Happy for you.

**Autumn:** Cass! I'm so happy for you!

**Holly:** We'll make sure our scenes are full of extra drama for you to come back to. I have several ideas.

**Cass:** lol appreciate it, thanks, fam

**Autumn:** I'll be around off and on if you're serious, Holls. Need to hand out vegan candy while the parents are at a vegetable charity.

**Holly:** Lol big yike. At least it's better than my mom. She's asked me to "hit the Strip" with her and her stupid

boyfriend because that's obvi what I want to do. HARD.
PASS!

**Cass:** Gross

"Hey, phone addict, we're here."

My head shot up at the word *addict*. "Sorry," I said, smiling sheepishly. "Let's find you the best costume ever."

Apparently, we weren't the only ones looking for last-minute swag. Entering the Halloween section, people of all ages were tearing through the plethora of options to find the perfect original costume that wasn't actually original—thanks, mass production. Fortunately, Tate didn't care about that. He just needed something *good enough* for his girlfriend.

"What's Rachel's costume?" I asked.

"I'm not allowed to know." Tate snorted, no doubt reciting her words. "She wants to surprise me. Honestly, I'm shocked she didn't insist on a couple's costume."

"Probably because you would've suggested a football and goalpost."

"How'd you know?"

I looked at him, on the verge of apologizing when his frown cracked into a grin. "Ass," I muttered, continuing through the aisle and nearly getting knocked over by a tiny human who'd zoomed by. "Do you have any ideas?"

"Isn't that why you're here? You always have the best ideas."

"Yeah, for myself. I've never had to think beyond fat-girl costumes, which is why I've always made my own. The selection is garbage." I grabbed a nearby costume and held it up against my body. "Like this. One size fits *all*? Hardly."

Tate sighed. "Okay, clothing companies suck, we know this. But I have no doubt you'll think of something perfect for me. You're a genius."

One of the many things I loved about Tate was how he didn't respond with the typical *You're not fat* comment other people had on reserve for moments like this. As if it was a compliment to lie. As if *fat* was truly an insult. Tate had never cared about my size, but he also knew better than to play into the norm of trying to make me feel better about something I didn't *need* to feel better about. Not that I owed anyone an explanation. Opening my mouth wouldn't stop some people from being the worst.

I grinned. "Okay, flattery will get you everywhere. But take a picture of this first. For science, or something."

Tate snorted, taking my phone after I unlocked it. He captured a couple of poses, then paused. "Who's Holly?"

My eyes widened. "What?"

He tapped the screen. "She messaged you—"

"Don't snoop!" I snatched the phone from him, immediately shutting off the screen.

"Who's Holly?" he asked again, smirking now. "Should Taylor be worried about another girl already?"

I nudged him before turning to put the costume away and resume the hunt. "Holly is a friend."

"What kind of friend? Because we don't know anyone named

Holly, and if you're being catfished by some creep at school or have a weird follower on Insta—"

"Tate!" I laughed to cover the panic I felt. "You and Rachel watch too much TV. I'm not being catfished, but I *am* allowed to have other friends. And I don't go snooping in your phone, so can you drop it? Please?"

Tate held his hands up in dramatic surrender, his raised brows telling me he wanted to ask more. "Okay, sketch city. Back to costumes. I'm open to any and all ideas. Nothing is off the table."

The internal panic subsided as a slow grin formed on my lips. "You really shouldn't have said that." Several ideas instantly came to mind that would send Rachel into a rage. I rejected a few mediocre-at-best costumes on the rack before remembering I owed him more information. "Also, speaking of needing a costume, my Taylor hang is at Greg's Halloween party."

I didn't think it was possible for Tate's smile to get any bigger. "Why didn't you lead with that earlier?" he asked. "People don't go on a date to a Greg party unless they're seriously interested. This is huge!"

"Don't make it a thing!" I said quickly, unable to hide my tomato cheeks. "She didn't *technically* say the word *date*, and I don't want to get my hopes up. Maybe she'd thought of me because she didn't want to go alone and assumed I had no plans."

"Needing someone to go with is when you ask a friend, not someone you go to school with who's a total catch," Tate said in a singsong voice, bouncing on his heels. "But yeah, sure, no hopes will get up."

I groaned. "Pretend I didn't say anything."

"Can't. I'm involved now. What're you going as?" He clapped his hands together. "Oh! Your Urs—"

"No," I snapped before he could continue. "Not that."

"Why not? You'd look killer! Leagues better than anyone else."

"Mom and I were in the middle of making Ursula when she *knew* she wouldn't be here to help me finish it," I said, feeling sicker as I thought about my costume. "We'd spent weeks on it, all so she could bail in the eleventh hour. And if I wear it, it's like saying what she did was okay, and it's not. I *can't* go as Ursula, Tate."

I didn't notice my tears or shaking voice until Tate's arms were around me in a tight hug. "You're right. I'm sorry," he said, rubbing a hand over my back. "Won't bring it up again."

My eyes locked on a kid who was gaping at us, and he ran the second he was found out. Great, now I was the crying girl who scared children at Target. After wiping away tears, I pulled back with a strained smile and distracted myself with more mediocre costumes, Tate doing the same in solidarity. "Thanks, best friend. But let's focus on you impressing Rachel. What's something she's into that's not obvious like showing up as a sexy volleyball or newspaper?"

Tate snorted, fiddling with the fabric of a Batman costume before looking back at me. "Girl Scout cookies," he said, smiling fondly.

I rolled my eyes, nudging him. "Cookie costumes are off the table. People will either want to eat you or argue with you about the best flavor, which is obviously Thin Mints. Pick something else."

"Caramel deLites, and you're no fun," he said, quiet for another beat before clapping his hands together. "Oh! She's really into Sherlock Holmes. Like, *really* into him to the point where I refuse to watch it with her."

"Which one?" I asked. "Movie Sherlock, BBC Sherlock, or Netflix Sherlock?"

"Yes. All of them."

Rachel never ceased to surprise me. "Okay, that's easy. But we won't find anything we need in this aisle. Come on, Sherlock Tate."

After Target and a trip to the thrift store, Tate had everything he needed to be the best Sherlock Holmes that Minneapolis had ever seen. I had him swing by Culver's for to-go burgers, fries, and shakes before heading back to the neighborhood, knowing it hadn't yet clicked that Mom's absence made Dad responsible for feeding us.

Tate badgered me with questions about Taylor for most of the ride and said he was happy for me at least three times. But sure, we were *not* overthinking it. "You're the queen of the world, C!" he yelled as I walked toward my house. I didn't dare admit it out loud for fear of it all being a joke, but I felt like the queen of the world.

A nervous, terrified queen of the world.

Dad turned off the news when I entered the house. "Ah, my favorite grease bomb delivered by my favorite child."

"Keep your voice down." I handed his shake to him on my way to the dining room. "Don't want Tuttles to hear you talking like that."

"Favorite daughter, then. Thanks for looking out for me."

"It's what I do," I said, as if our new situation was normal.

We settled at the table, and I let us get a few bites in before approaching my other reason for gifting him with food. "So I'm going to a Halloween party Friday night. Can you drop me off at Greg Jensen's house?"

Dad looked up from his meal, surprise on his face. He wasn't the only one. "Greg Jensen. Haven't heard that name in a while."

"I know," I said. "I'm attending somewhat reluctantly."

"I'll say," Dad chuckled, narrowing his eyes. "Is this an event I should be worried about?"

"It's me, so I doubt it," I said, smiling a little. "But you're the parent, so it's your call."

Dad nodded as if it now hit him that yes, he was indeed the parent in this situation. "You can go, but wouldn't you rather ride with Tate? I assume he's going?"

"He is," I said slowly, not wanting to bring up Taylor just yet. "But I don't want to third-wheel with him and Rachel." And I knew if I started the party with Tate, I'd use him as a support the whole night.

"Fair. In that case, I'm happy to drop you off. It's your senior year. You should be out having fun, making memories, et cetera."

I laughed quietly. He probably worried that my only friend was my neighbor. Getting out in the world sometimes wouldn't kill me if it meant easing Dad's concerns. And being around my crush was a perk, even if the idea of dating her gave me heart palpitations. I'd never dated a girl before, or anyone in high school. It was a lot more pressure than in middle school. Maybe I wasn't up for the task. But I wanted to at least *try*. "Agreed. And thanks in advance for the ride."

"I was actually thinking about that today," Dad said. "I'm not against being your chauffeur, but we should get you a car soon."

I blinked. Was he serious? "I distinctly remember you and Mom dramatically agreeing that me having a car gave you nightmares."

"Oh, it does," he said, chuckling. "But college is in less than a year, and you should have a handle on driving by then in case you end up somewhere you'll need one. And it'll make you feel obligated to come home sometimes to visit me." He shrugged. "The no-car thing was more of your mom's decision anyway."

*And she's not here.* He didn't need to say it for me to know where his head was at. "I mean, it's the next logical step since I've had my license for a year," I said, not wanting to focus on the Mom part and cry for a second time today. "I should bring Culver's home more often. Thanks, *Cool Dad*."

His brows shot up. "Cool Dad?"

I grinned. "Yeah, it's what I'm calling you now. Congratulations on moving up in the world." The proud look on his face told me to never admit it was a joke. And really, a new car *did* make him pretty damn cool.

"Thanks, I'll try to live up to the name," he said, pausing to drink his mint shake. "Do you know what kind of car you'd want?"

"Something that won't die on me for at least a few years and doesn't look like complete garbage," I said, knowing next to nothing about cars. "I trust you."

Dad nodded, his smile warming. "I'll figure something out." We finished eating in silence before he stood. "I need to get a little work done. You good?"

Seeing him gather his trash reminded me of another inevitable conversation. "Well, we're almost out of groceries. And we need laundry detergent and cat litter. Probably a few other things too."

His face fell. "I'll go tomorrow after work," he said, his voice quiet, ashamed. "I'm sorry, kid. Still filling in some blanks here."

"Don't be sorry," I said quickly, not wanting him to feel bad about it. "No one's starving. It's fine."

"That's no excuse," he said. "Will you make a list of anything you need and some meal preferences?"

"Of course," I said, smiling a little. "Even my menstrual products?"

Dad gave me a look that said *I cut people open for a living.* "Yes, whatever you need. If my cart sends me into a shame spiral, that's what self-checkout is for."

I laughed as he ruffled my hair, feeling lighter. "Thanks, Cool Dad. Go finish work stuff. I'm good."

Dad grinned all over again at his new nickname as he disappeared to his office.

After throwing away my trash, I went upstairs. My eyes lingered on a closed door at the top—Mom's old crafting room slash guest bedroom. I used to go in there daily for one thing or another, but now the space felt cursed. My body pulled me in and to the closet without my brain's consent. The Ursula costume hung in the front, the black and purple of the dress poking out. My stomach turned at the sight of it.

I didn't know when. I didn't know how. But at some point, Mom had finished sewing the costume. And of course it looked perfect. I didn't know if this softened the blow or made it worse.

Mom and I had our things. Before Tate got a truck, she drove me to school every morning on her way to work, giving us eleven minutes of *us* time. We bitched at the news and overall state of the world in our pajamas while eating nachos on nights Dad worked late. We talked to Tuttles in comical voices while pretending he was a regal king, stealthy ninja, or dramatic pirate in past lives. And we always, *always* made my Halloween costume together.

All of that was gone now. Tuttles's occasional spiteful escapes had turned into a replacement hobby since Mom left. He'd bolted out the door—or at least tried to—every day in the last week. I knew he was looking for her, but I didn't have the heart to tell him she wasn't coming home.

Unlike what she'd said during our last conversation, she hadn't called every day. Other than the one brief call to tell me she'd made it to Maine and was excited to visit for Christmas, I hadn't heard a word from her. I hated how much space she took up in my head. I hated that every noise on my phone made me hope it was her. I hated how much I'd overthought all the things she'd given no thought to before putting herself first and leaving.

I shoved the costume deeper into the closet and went to my room, settling at my desk and pushing Mom from my mind. I had a paper to write for English and a French quiz to study for, but I moved to my Tide Wars life first. There was nothing new on Home Base, but Autumn had private messaged me.

**Autumn:** When did Cari last reply to your scene?

**Autumn:** Sorry, I know you're going through a lot. Here if you want to talk. <3

I knew she meant it. Autumn was the sweetest person I'd ever met—online or off. Her heart was in it every day, and I loved that about her.

**Cass:** Thanks! The distraction is welcome. Her last scene reply was about two weeks ago.

**Autumn:** Okay, thanks. We had a big scene going that I want to finish before the next group scene. Having a ship with her is frustrating!

**Cass:** But also worth it?

**Autumn:** Ugh, yes, totally worth it. Allain is a dreamboat!

I laughed quietly. Allain was one of the other main characters in Tide Wars, and my character's brother. And he was Autumn's biggest plot since he was in a serious relationship with her character, Hypernia. Unfortunately, Carina was likely on her way out within the next year because of college, and Autumn showed no signs of slowing down. Rowan and I intended to keep things going in college, but we couldn't predict other people's dedication.

> **Cass:** LOL yes! Also I'll reply to our scene but need to start an essay after. Might have to ghost until tomorrow.
>
> **Autumn:** No worries! Good luck. And I'm beyond excited about your date news!
>
> **Cass:** Thanks, friend! <3

I spent the next half hour replying to scenes. Aresha was the captain, but she was also nineteen, so my scenes were usually a mix of professional correspondence and sassy shenanigans. Most of her sass was reserved for Roux, but Rowan hadn't replied to our scene despite being active elsewhere, including accepting a new character application from this morning. I decided not to nudge her, assuming she was busy, and instead posted to the main server to see when people were free for a group scene.

After catching up, I opened a Word document to start my essay on Jane Austen—the original queen of soft snark. The classics didn't woo me like they did some people, but I *loved* Austen. Writing about her didn't feel like homework, especially when my teacher let me write about why certain characters were obviously queer. By the time I'd completed a moderately successful first draft, Rowan had replied to our private server.

**Rowan:** Congrats again on your date, Captain! I know parties aren't your thing, but try to have a good time. What are you and Tate going as this year? I assume Ursula is out?

A small smile tugged at my lips. Of course she'd know I was already nervous about the party scene, and I loved when she asked about Tate. It was an easy in for me to jokingly tease about having a stranger crush on him.

**Cass:** Correct! I don't know what I'm going as yet, but your boyfriend is going as Sherlock Holmes to impress his other girlfriend.

**Rowan:** Man after my own heart.

**Cass:** You know it!

When she didn't respond, I returned to Austen land, relieved I had fictional dances to write about instead of giving my brain space to panic over a first date—or whatever it was.

[One-on-one scene between Cass and Rowan]

**Cass:** Aresha paced the room, feeling beyond foolish. The lilac gown Katrin had picked out pushed her chest up in an uncomfortable way, and she was sure she'd stop breathing soon. And her hair! It looked abnormally perfect. She missed her captain's gear. But if she was going to charm a possible ally in their home, she needed to look like a member of the royal family she'd been born into. "I look ridiculous in this purple monstrosity," she said, huffing out a sigh.

**Rowan:** ((Of course Holly had Katrin give Aresha a boob dress!))

**Cass:** ((lol right?!))

**Rowan:** Roux was enjoying this far too much. Of course Aresha would be offended by her own beauty. But she'd have to swallow it. They needed Count Taraklea's support and supplies if they were to return home safely. "You do. Nothing like my pirate queen. You'll pull this off perfectly."

**Cass:** Aresha stopped in front of Roux and sighed again. Loudly. "I despise you."

**Rowan:** Roux grinned and stepped up to Aresha, tapping her nose. "No, you do not."

# FOUR

By Friday, I was a ball of nerves. I'd never been on a date-like outing with a girl. Minneapolis was a generally accepting community when it came to the gays, but I'd never put in the effort to ask a girl out. And none of them had asked me out—until now. Greg was the last person I'd dated, and going to a Marvel movie in the eighth grade that his mom dropped us off at barely counted.

Taylor Cooper had some kind of mysterious allure and charm that made even straight girls pause. And I was a total nerd catch, obviously, but I'd never expected the badass gamer barista to want to hang out with me.

In short, I was in *way* over my head.

I also hadn't come up with a better costume idea. The more I thought about Ursula, the madder I got. It might've been a Mom-and-Cass thing, but it was *my* costume. I'd come up with the idea. I'd found the inspirational design. Yes, she'd helped with the sewing, and yes, she'd finished it, but it was mostly me who'd brought it to life. And after everything she'd taken from me, I wouldn't let her take Ursula.

Tonight, I was reclaiming the sea witch.

Dad helped me with the light purple body paint and dress zipping after I'd sprayed my hair white and added a ton of product to make it stand up wild. I could see him looking at me in the mirror as I finished my makeup. "What?"

"Nothing," he said, chuckling. "You look really great. I'm glad I'm here to see it."

I smiled, willing myself not to get emotional and destroy the paint. Dad had rarely seen my costumes in action over the years since he was always working. And while that had hurt at the time, I was happy to have him here now. "Me too."

"I'll go start the car. Take your time."

I nodded and grabbed a tube of bright red lipstick as he left, applying it before stepping back to take everything in. We'd done our best, and I wouldn't let the fact that Mom could've somehow made it look better ruin my night.

After saying goodbye to Tuttles, who'd hissed at me in response, wanting nothing to do with Ursula, I got into the car. My anxiety returned, and I texted Home Base while Dad drove.

> **Cass:** I'm gonna throw up. What if this date is a disaster and I can't show my face at school ever again? What if it's not a date!?
>
> **Rowan:** I told you she'd overthink it.
>
> **Cass:** ROWAN DAVIES

**Rowan:** ILY

**Holly:** OMG, Rowan, staahhhp! You'll do great, Cass! She asked you out. You're a catch!

**Autumn:** What Holly said. You've got this! Be yourself.

**Cass:** Thanks, fam <3

**Autumn:** What's your costume??

**Cass:** I couldn't think of a new idea, so I'm wearing Ursula.

**Holly:** Huh?

**Rowan:** Ursula. The last costume she worked on with her mom.

**Holly:** Sorry, we don't all have the best memory like some people

**Rowan:** Forgiven.

**Autumn:** How do you feel about that, Cass?

**Cass:** Not great. But it's my best costume to date, and I didn't want my mom to ruin this for me too. I'm choosing to rock it and hope for the best.

**Holly:** You'll crush it! Have fun! And don't forget to mention your cool online friends to Taylor. I'm excited to DM her on Insta and gush about you! When you're ready, of course.

**Rowan:** Damn, Holly, no pressure.

**Holly:** I said what I said!

**Autumn:** LOL! Have fun, Cass!

My heart raced at Holly's words. I hadn't thought about the fact that I could test out my secret obsession—I mean hobby—on someone who didn't know about my past addiction and who wouldn't tell my dad. It was worth considering, but I wanted to survive the night first.

**Cass:** Thanks, all! TBD on the gushing ;)

For the first time in a long time, I resisted responding to my roleplay scenes and put my phone away. Tonight, I had other plans. Halloween was the grand ball, and Ursula was my pumpkin. Or my fairy godmother. Whatever.

Dad and I had a lengthy, heated conversation about the best Halloween candy—obviously Reese's, *not* candy corn—until he parked in front of Greg's house. "Here we are," he said, smiling a little. "Have a good time, and keep an eye on your cup."

I couldn't believe my dad was sanctioning drinking. Mom never had to deal with this situation, but I knew she would've felt uneasy about me being anywhere near alcohol away from family. But I wanted to go, so I wouldn't remind him how non-parental his comment sounded. "Thanks, Cool Dad. I'll call you when I'm ready to leave. Have fun eating your boring-ass candy corn."

"Hey!" Dad laughed, likely caring more about me dissing his favorite candy than my language. "You know I will. Let me know if you find Ariel."

It took me a moment to realize he meant the mermaid. *Dads.* "Oh, you'll know. I'll have stolen her voice." I wiggled my eyebrows dramatically before getting out of the car, texting Taylor and Tate that I'd arrived. And then I braced myself for the nightmare worse than the no-phone zone at school—fraternizing with my peers.

Greg stood at the door greeting people, music booming inside behind him. His Dracula costume had a dramatically popped collar that made him look extra bro-ish. Awesome.

"Dope costume," he said after taking me in, his vampire teeth on display. "Always knew you were a witch."

"Always knew you sucked," I said, patting his chest.

His face fell immediately, and he cleared his throat. "Where's Tate?"

"I didn't come with Tate." I stood a little taller, which was still several inches shorter than him. "I have a date."

"Huh." He looked around before leaning in. "Did your imaginary friend from third grade come back or something?" he whispered.

I rolled my eyes and pushed past him, refusing to acknowledge that he remembered Renaud. "She'll be here. Thanks for hosting!"

"I didn't invite you!" he yelled after me.

"Eat glass!"

Being in Greg's house after years of avoiding his street was surreal, but at least I still knew my way around. My palms sweated as I walked to the kitchen, my nerves on high alert as people perceived me—well, Ursula. I started mixing a drink as if I were an expert, but in reality I'd only had a glass of wine a couple of times with Mom. And there was that time Tate persuaded me to try cheap beer mixed with Hawaiian Punch in middle school. Do not recommend.

"I don't think this is gonna work out."

I turned to see Taylor wearing a blonde wig and a tight-fitting Zelda costume, her smirky smirk immediately turning me to mush. If I wasn't a Zelda fan before, I was now. Sign me up for Saturday night gaming. "Um, what do you mean?"

"The drink you're making will burn like hell and taste even worse." She took the cup and dumped it out before starting to mix a new drink. "Allow me."

"Thanks," I said softly, still staring at her. So chill. "I like your costume."

"Back at you," she said, glancing at me. "Love the hair and paint. You went all out."

I didn't want to love the compliment since Mom had something to do with it, but Taylor didn't know that. I hadn't published my trauma on my social accounts, and I was hardly someone people gossiped about. As far as Taylor knew, I had two parents who loved me at home. And for now, that was enough. "Thanks, I made it."

"That's amazing," she said, looking at me in awe. "Wait, did you just make it this week, or did I take you away from other plans?"

"No other plans," I said, her gaze making me feel warm. "I was gonna wear it when passing out candy, and this is better, so."

Taylor chuckled, returning to drink mixing. "I hope so."

"Yeah," I said quietly, feeling increasingly nervous when all I wanted to feel was relaxed for once in my life. I'd told myself I wouldn't be weird tonight, but my curiosity got the better of me.

"So I have to ask, why did you ask me to hang out? I'm obviously glad you did, but it seemed random. I mean, we aren't exactly friends."

"No, but we're friendly," she said, shrugging. "And I've always thought you were cool. And funny when you decide to join the conversation." Her eyes lit up as she cracked another smile. "Like when we watched *Little Women* in English last year, and you said Jo had more chemistry with a doorknob than with Laurie."

I laughed at my own joke as if it were hers. I couldn't believe she'd remembered that. It was a dramatic comment, but I'd made my point. "Jo's obviously queer. I'm prepared to die on that hill."

"Agreed." Taylor handed me the new drink, biting her lip for a beat. "And I maybe asked Rachel about you in newspaper. She talked you up and said I should ask you out, and finding your cat kind of solidified everything."

Jo March, Rachel, and Tuttles came together to make this happen. And I couldn't think of anything witty to say about it. "Rachel probably wants more alone time with Tate. She doesn't think I'm that cool."

"Maybe not, but *I* think you're cool. That's all that matters, right?"

My face was on fire. Thank gods it was painted. "Right. And I think you're cool, too."

"Good. Now that that's settled, want to wander? See what people are wearing?" She held out her free hand.

I hadn't held a hand in a long time, and mine suddenly felt

clammy again. That had happened every time with Greg too. I'd later assumed it was because I wasn't interested in guys, but now it seemed to be happening purely out of raging nerves. I smiled it off and took her hand, feeling the warmth of her nonclammy skin. She was cool, calm, and collected. I envied her. "Let's wander."

She led us from the safety of the kitchen into the throng of partygoers, hip-hop music blasting overhead. I drank as we slid between bodies that were flirting, gossiping, and touching each other in ways that were foreign to me. I drank more after we sat on a large L-shaped couch, taking it all in. Mom's last act of selflessness before leaving was making the dress less puffy than I'd originally imagined. "You'll want to sit at some point," she'd said the day we'd discussed it.

At least she'd been right about one thing.

I turned toward Taylor after a moment to see her looking back at me, a smile on her lips that I couldn't place. People never looked at me like that. I was tempted to message Home Base and ask what it meant. No doubt Rowan would know. She knew everything. "What?" I asked instead, pushing Rowan from my brain.

Smooth.

"Nothing, I'm just trying to figure you out," she said loud enough to hear over the music. "You're usually quiet at school, but now you're wearing this badass, sexy costume. And I obviously love it, but I didn't expect it."

Gods, did she say *sexy*?

Was seventeen too young for a heart attack?

And I knew exactly what she meant about school. "School is

that place I have to be but don't want to be. It's always felt kind of suffocating with all those people around. I usually keep to myself." And there was the part about only having one friend there.

"Wait." Her knee brushed mine as she shifted closer. "If that's true, why are you at one of the biggest parties of the year?"

"Because you invited me?"

"You're sweet," she said, tucking a loose strand from her wig behind her ear. "But we could've done something else. I don't want our first date to suck because you're uncomfortable."

"I'm not uncomfortable now," I said, brushing against her knee in return. *Boldly.* But only because she'd officially confirmed it was a date. "I mean, I'm not gonna turn into the life of the party, but it won't kill me to get out of my comfort zone."

"Thanks for doing it for me." Taylor smiled a little more. "But we can keep things chill. Want to judge other people's costumes?"

It sounded like a low-key, easy way to gauge her opinions on things. Because I didn't know *everything* about her. Casual observation, Instagram, and other people's comments didn't tell the full story. "Yes, definitely."

"Great." Taylor drank more as she studied the crowd. "Oh! Look at the Marvel trio."

I followed her gaze and saw three girls from our grade dressed as Thor, Hawkeye, and Black Widow. "Okay, I know we're on a date, but female Thor is crushing it."

She laughed, nudging me. "Agreed, and I wouldn't hate being Hawkeye's bow."

I grinned, glad she played along. "It's settled. The trio gets first place."

"No, just the duo. Black Widow's pants aren't tight enough. She's not even trying."

"Fine, fine, just the duo."

I looked around for our next victims when two girls stopped in front of us with big grins on their faces. "Oh my god, your Ursula costume is killer!" one of them said.

"Thanks," I said, blushing under my face paint. A moment's glance told me exactly what their costumes were, but Taylor spoke before I could compliment them and fangirl appropriately.

"Your costumes are great too. Pirates?"

"Yes and no," the other girl said. "We're Aresha and Roux from the Tide Wars books. It's a little niche, but this one is obsessed, and I get the appeal." She nudged the other girl, who laughed. "Cool Zelda costume, by the way."

"It's Link, but thanks," Taylor said, her tone shifting. "I guess my costume is a little niche too."

The girls laughed, not noticing. "For sure," the Aresha-dressed girl said distractedly as she noticed something across the room. "We better carry on, but have fun!"

"You too," I said, practically giddy as I watched them go. Tide Wars had a small cult following, but I didn't know anyone outside of the roleplay who loved it enough to dress up like the characters. I wanted to chase after them and get their names, maybe tell them about the roleplay, but that would involve abandoning my date, so

I focused on Taylor instead. "They were nice. Do they go to our school?"

"No idea, but how do people not know the difference between Princess Zelda and Link?" She sighed, sounding annoyed. "And real talk, those books aren't that great. I couldn't get through the first one. But their costumes were still cool."

I stared at her as my brain tried to piece her words together. Taylor didn't like Tide Wars. The books weren't long, but she couldn't even get through the first one. How was that possible? She obviously didn't have to like everything I liked, but this was a jab. And she didn't know it. "They were cool," I agreed quietly. "And sorry, but I thought you were Zelda too."

"It's whatever," Taylor said, nudging me. "And oh my god, look at Tate and Rachel."

My eyes followed until I saw Tate in his Sherlock costume. Rachel stood next to him dressed as—also Sherlock. "Oh my god," I echoed, relieved by the hilarious subject change.

"Come on, I spy a couple of detectives," Taylor said, grinning as she stood, the Link/Zelda dilemma apparently behind us.

If only I felt the same about Tide Wars.

I followed her, thinking once again that Tate and Rachel were disgustingly perfect for each other. "Sherlock," I said in greeting to Tate before looking at Rachel. "Sherlock."

"Isn't it the best?" Rachel said, beaming as she wrapped her arms around Tate's middle. "Tate surprised me with my favorite character, having no idea I was doing the same. What are the odds?"

"Boyfriend of the year," I said, smiling more at her excitement. The part where I'd helped Tate create the look didn't need to be mentioned. "Nice work, Sherlock Tate."

"Thank you, thank you," Tate said, bowing dramatically before looking at Taylor. "Solid costume choice, Cooper."

"Thanks, *Larson*," Taylor said, smirking back at him. "Unlike you two, Cass and I obviously planned our costumes. Link and Ursula are a tale as old as time."

Tate tilted his head, narrowing his eyes for a moment. "Good one," he said.

I giggled at the clearly missed sarcasm and Disney reference. "Do you two want to judge costumes with us?" I asked before I could remind myself I was on a date.

"Sounds fun," Tate said, wrapping an arm around Rachel. "But we're in for flip cup."

"We're flip cup champs, can't miss it," Rachel said proudly. "Do you two want to play against us?"

Tate barked a laugh. "C doesn't drink like that."

"I don't, but that doesn't mean I wouldn't," I said, giving him a look before focusing on Taylor. "You decide. Costume contest or drinking game?"

"Oh, definitely drinking game," she said immediately. "We have all night to judge."

I smiled at her gratefully. I didn't want to pass up a chance to be at a party with my best friend, but I didn't want Taylor thinking I was pushing her aside either. Now I understood what Tate dealt with when trying to include me and Rachel on plans together.

A few rounds and too much beer later, I accepted that flip cup wasn't for me. The drink from earlier had been strong, and the added beers made me a lost cause as I failed to flip anything. Taylor carried our team, but we were no match for Team Sherlock.

After accepting defeat and watching other matchups for a while, Taylor pulled me back to the living room, where people were dancing. Most of my moves were busted in my bedroom while cleaning, but I had Taylor and the alcohol coursing through my veins to keep me going. Before long, I was flailing like a chaotic sea witch and loving every second of it.

What felt like minutes turned into hours, and Taylor's curfew approached. Mine probably did, too, but Dad and I hadn't gotten that far yet. We texted our parents for rides and said goodbye to Tate and Rachel before going outside. The party carried on as we sprawled on the cold grass in Greg's yard. By some miracle, I'd survived the night without embarrassing myself *or* throwing up. And bonus—no one else threw up on me either.

"This was fun," Taylor said, turning onto her side to look at me. "Thanks for braving other humans for me."

"Thanks for inviting me," I said, mimicking her movements. "I had fun too." It wasn't a lie, though I was still an internal mess over her Tide Wars comment. But I shut that shit down and focused on her face, committing every inch of it to memory as if tomorrow would prove it was all a dream. Weirder things had happened.

"Good," Taylor said.

And then she kissed me. My first girl kiss. I froze for gods knew how long before I found the courage to kiss her back. Her lips were soft, her body warm against mine, and my heart was no doubt ready to burst from the thrill and anxiety of it all. I forced away thoughts about me being a trash kisser or her being too badass for me.

Everything was fine. I was a catch. I was a catch. I was a catch.

She wrapped an arm around me as we slowly made out on the lawn of my ex-boyfriend's house. Her other hand found my purple face, and it smelled faintly of the alcohol she'd poured earlier. My hand moved to her wig, tempted to remove it and brush my fingers along the shaved part of her head. If this was how kissing felt, I didn't want to do anything else ever again. And maybe the alcohol was making that dramatic declaration for me, but still, I meant it in the moment.

The distant sound of a car horn snapped me out of it. A few more honks made me realize it was for me. I'd already forgotten about texting Dad for a ride, and my phone was on silent. And he could clearly see us. Perfect. I wasn't dying inside or anything.

"I better go," I said, my body a thousand degrees despite the almost-freezing temperature outside. My racing heart and tingly body made no attempts to relax as I tried to force my wide smile down a couple of notches. But it was no use—I had *zero* chill. "You good? Need anything?"

Taylor looked back at me, out of breath and grinning. "I'm good. My mom will be here soon. See ya, Ursula."

"Yeah, see ya!" I shuffled to Dad's car and climbed in, fumbling as I buckled the seat belt. "Hey."

"Hey yourself."

I didn't dare look over as he chuckled and started to drive. He'd always supported my coming out and being who I was, but that didn't mean I wanted him to see me kissing another human. "Did you have a good night?" I asked.

"Not as good as you, I'd imagine."

I groaned. "Can we not talk about this right now?"

"We don't have to talk about anything. But before we go into silence mode, I have something for you. The bag at your feet."

Of course I hadn't noticed it. I leaned down to grab the bag. Pumpkin-shaped Reese's. Mom hadn't bought trick-or-treating candy *or* my pumpkins this year. "Thank you," I said quietly, my heart happy and sad at the same time. "You're simply the best."

"You're welcome. Also, I'm all for you hanging out with friends, but let's not make drinking parties a regular thing. School needs to be your focus. Your grades last year weren't like you, and I doubt everything with your mom is helping."

He wasn't wrong, but he knew only the half of it. "It won't be a regular thing," I said, not trusting myself to say more words. Trying to sound somewhat sober was a monster of a challenge. And a headache was kicking in, so silence was my friend. How did some people do this every weekend?

I looked out the window, taking in the night's memories. I'd braved a Greg Jensen party and survived. I'd played a drinking game and hadn't felt like a loser after losing. I'd drunkenly danced without throwing up. I'd risked hypothermia to make out with my crush. I was drunk in the car with my dad, and no one was yelling about it. And my entire body was humming with joy for the first time in a long time.

To my ultimate surprise, life in the real world wasn't as horrible as I'd imagined.

# FIVE

I was in the middle of folding laundry on Sunday when Dad called for me. By the time I made it downstairs, Taylor stood in his place, hands behind her back and a grin on her lips. In that moment, I was relieved I'd just changed out of my cat pajamas.

"Hey," I said slowly. "Did I miss a text?"

Her smile warmed the room. "No. I was out shopping with my mom and—here."

Everything slowed when she bit at her bottom lip and presented an elaborate bouquet of flowers. The various shades of purple popped among the few flowers that were colored black. "Ursula flowers," I said after taking them in.

"Do you like them? Are they too much?"

"No." I looked back to meet her eyes, flailing inside. "I mean no, they're not too much, and yes, I like them. Love them, actually."

Relief flooded her face as she stepped closer. "I didn't want to wait until tomorrow to see you."

I'd never gotten flowers from anyone who wasn't family. Chills covered my body as my brain struggled to keep up. I knew how to be a girl with a secret crush, but I didn't know how to be a girl with a crush who liked me back. A part of me had been convinced our date would end horribly and there'd never be a second one. Instead, there were hand delivered curated flowers.

I realized I had to say something. "Um, do you want to stay, hang out for a bit?"

"I do, but my mom is waiting for me in the car, and I have a shift at Spyhouse soon." Taylor's eyes remained locked on mine. "But before I leave, I was kind of hoping you'd agree with me that there's something here, and maybe we can do something about that?"

"There's something here," I agreed, taking a small step toward her. The fangirl in me developed major heart eyes over this moment as my socially awkward side had a thousand ideas for ruining everything. I tried pushing the latter down. "And what would we do about that? Do you mean more kissing?"

Taylor let out a quiet laugh. "I mean, yeah, kissing is great. But I was thinking bigger—like being girlfriends."

"Are you sure?" I asked before I could help it. "I'm—well, you're really cool. And I had a lot of fun at the party, but you're *really* cool."

"I'm not that cool." She set the vase on the coffee table before her hands found mine. "And I'm sure. I want to date you and kiss you when I see you and rescue your cat whenever he needs rescuing."

"He needs a lot of rescuing." I glanced at our hands, biting the inside of my cheek. "I've never had a girlfriend. I might suck at it."

"I'm willing to risk it if you are," she said, squeezing my hands.

Being someone's girlfriend wasn't on my senior-year bingo card, especially right now, but this incredible girl was asking me to be hers. And I'd liked her for far too long to let Mom trauma and my chaotic brain win. "Yes."

Her brows perked up. "Yes?"

"Yes, I'll be your girlfriend. And go on dates. And kiss you when I see you. All of it."

Her lips were a magnet that pulled me in until mine were pressed against them. Our arms wrapped around each other, and I felt the weight of something heavy disappear. The panic was eased, my thoughts locked away for a moment.

We kissed until her phone rang, and she pulled back to answer. "Hi, Mom."

I could hear her mom enough to make out her words. "We have to get the groceries home. What are you doing in there?"

"Kissing my girlfriend."

My cheeks warmed as her mom paused. "Happy for you, sweetie, but the ice cream is going to turn the trunk into a lake if we don't get moving."

"Be right out." Taylor hung up, looking at me with an apologetic smile. "Gotta go. See you tomorrow, girlfriend."

"Yes," I mumbled as she kissed me again, pushing down the nerves that threatened to explode. I could do this. I could handle Mom leaving and juggle my roleplay life while having my first girlfriend. It would be great. "Tomorrow."

I picked up the flowers once she left, staring at them for gods knew how long before hearing a throat clear behind me. Dad had returned. "Hey."

"Hey yourself," he said, grinning like a goof. No, *I* was the one grinning like a goof. "Was that the girl I saw you kissing at the party the other night?"

My face started flushing immediately at the reminder. "How many girls do you think I go around kissing?"

"How should I know? I'm only your dad."

I rolled my eyes despite being unable to stop smiling. "That's the only girl I've been kissing. And I won't be kissing anyone else, because she's my girlfriend now."

His eyebrows shot up. "Your girlfriend?"

"Yeah," I said slowly, immediately thinking about Mom and how me dating someone could affect him so soon after his marriage ending. "Is that okay?"

"Of course it's okay," he said, resting a hand on my shoulder. If he was thinking about Mom, too, it didn't show. "You're seventeen. You should have a girlfriend."

I relaxed at his words. "I should. You're absolutely right."

"But since she's your girlfriend, you need to leave your bedroom door open when she's here. You might call me Cool Dad now, but I'm not *that* cool."

I was no longer relaxed. What happened behind closed doors wasn't something I was ready to think about yet. "Got it, keep the door open. But don't make a big deal about it, okay? Drawing attention will make me overthink it."

"Consider the subject dropped. Now go be productive or something. You've got school tomorrow."

"As if I could forget."

I was not productive. My brain wouldn't stop thinking about school the next day. Taylor and I would be a *thing* there. People would *see us*. And the last thing I wanted was to get bombarded with questions from people who didn't give a shit about me—as if my dating life was any of their business.

After eating dinner with Dad and temporarily freeing myself from panicking, I returned to my laptop. Since roleplaying had entered my life, I'd never taken two days off from it. While the temptation to check in a dozen times had been strong, pretending to be someone who lived in the real world for a couple of days was refreshing. But I'd missed my online life something fierce.

Home Base had speculated whether my date had killed me or we'd run away together. Instead of adding to the dramatic conclusions, Rowan reminded the others that I was allowed to take a break. Thanks, Champ.

**Cass:** Hope everyone had a good weekend! I come bearing news: I have a girlfriend!

**Autumn:** YAY CASS!!

**Holly:** OMG DIIIISSSHHH

**Holly:** And welcome back to the nerd herd!

**Autumn:** Yeah! We missed you!

I typed a recap of the party, leaving out Taylor's reaction to the Tide Wars costumes. Not because it didn't matter, but because I didn't want them getting a negative opinion when there was a lot to like about her. My cheeks warmed as I added the part about kissing.

**Cass:** And then this morning she showed up with Ursula-themed flowers and asked me to be her girlfriend.

**Holly:** And then you kissed some more?!

**Cass:** EXACTLY

**Holly:** YAAASSS! This is the best news!

**Autumn:** Send flower pics ASAP. Congrats!

I grabbed my phone and noticed Taylor had texted me a while ago.

**Taylor: Can't wait to see you tomorrow, girlfriend! ;)**

Panic made a home in my head all over again, but I managed to force it down enough to text back a quick *You too!* I then sent a picture of the flowers to Home Base.

**Autumn:** OMG cuuute I love them!!

**Holly:** Don't turn into Cari and forget about us now that real life is busier!

**Cass:** I'm not going anywhere. <3

**Holly:** Good. Does Taylor know all about us now?

I groaned at the question I'd been dreading since shutting down the idea of telling Taylor about the roleplay. Lying to my friends was not something I wanted to do, but it would be harder telling Taylor the truth. Our relationship was new and fragile, and I didn't want to risk it ending before she could get to know me outside of my internet life and the books she didn't like.

**Cass:** Not yet!

**Autumn:** Aww why not?

**Holly:** Uh yeah, why not? We want to brag about you to her!

**Carina:** Don't rush it, Cass. Tom doesn't know about the RP either. No one in my life does.

**Holly:** CARINA! This is brand-new information! What would Macy Whittier think!?

**Carina:** It's not that big of a deal?

**Rowan:** I'd say it's a big deal to start a new relationship off by lying about a big part of your life, but maybe that's me.

**Holly:** lol agreed! And you've been RPing for five years, Cari! What do they think you're doing every time you hop on Discord?

**Carina:** I'm not on Discord around them, problem solved.

**Holly:** omgomgomgomg

**Rowan:** My friends know about the RP and all of you and I LOVE that. No shame here.

**Carina:** I didn't say I was ashamed, but whatever.

I couldn't find words. And it wasn't lost on me that Rowan had replied only to debate Carina, saying nothing about Taylor. I'd read over the conversation twice by the time Carina sent me a private message, which was shocking on a number of levels.

**Carina:** Seriously, Cass, don't let them bully you. Keeping this little hobby to myself was one of the best decisions I've made. People wouldn't understand. Don't feel bad if you decide to keep it to yourself too.

**Cass:** Thanks Cari.

**Carina:** You got it, girl. Talk soon. xx

Not knowing what else to say, I left it there. Carina was one of those people who always seemed *right* about things—well, except for being minimally involved in the roleplay this year. She was also the only other member of Home Base in a relationship. For now, I'd trust her judgment.

I was about to click out of Discord to start homework when Rowan messaged me.

**Rowan:** Hey. I'm obviously happy for you, but I also know you're going through a lot right now with your mom. Is jumping into a relationship really a good idea when you have other feelings to process? I know how easy it is trying to fill a void, and I don't want that for you.

I read the message multiple times. Rowan and I always had each other's backs, but something about her message made me feel ashamed, like I was letting her down. And I hated how well she knew me.

**Cass:** Thanks for the concern, but I can't help the terrible timing. I've liked her for a long time, and I'm not turning her down just because I'm mad at my mom.

**Rowan:** Okay, Captain. I'm here if you need anything. <3

**Cass:** Thanks, Champ. <3

Instead of calling it a night, I let roleplay scenes suck me in for nearly an hour before getting through as much homework as I could handle and passing out. I'd been in such a Taylor daze that I'd forgotten about it over the weekend. And of course my brain thought to jump online before making progress in my academic life. Kudos, me.

The next day at school didn't go anything like I'd thought—or feared—it would. Other than a couple of Taylor's friends waving at me in the hall, no one knew or cared about the new couple at school. It was the same as every other day, at least until Taylor showed up at my locker in the afternoon. "Hi, girlfriend."

Her bright smile sent my heart floating, and I pushed down Rowan's words about filling a void. My eyes fell on the chunk of hair slightly in front of her face, and I forced myself to leave it alone. "Hey, you. What's up?"

"Not much, just here to kiss you."

Oh gods. We'd never kissed around people, at least not knowingly—thanks, Cool Dad. I swallowed, looking around for a beat before back at her. "Yeah, sure. You can do that."

She giggled quietly, stepping closer. Our eyes met briefly before her lips pressed against mine. It had been only twenty-four hours since our last kiss, which felt both like lifetimes and seconds ago. I wanted to stay locked in this moment forever.

"Get a room!"

I yanked back, seeing Greg looking proud of himself. A couple of football guys nudged and cheered him, but Tate gave him a hard shove before jogging over. He'd been shocked and thrilled when I told him the news—shocked because I never dated and thrilled because obviously. At least *he* didn't ask me if I was filling a void. "I hear we'll be seeing more of each other, Cooper," he said as we bumped fists.

"Right, I guess dating Cass means dating you, too, huh?" she teased, grinning back at him.

"Something like that," Tate said as the bell rang. He gave the team a salute before looking back at us. "Well, carry on. See you after practice, C."

"See you," I said, focusing on Taylor after he left. "Want to hang out after school? I'm sure Tate wouldn't mind giving you a ride home."

"I have to work," Taylor said, scrunching her nose like it was the most inconvenient thing in the world. "But I'll text you?"

I nodded, feeling a small relief. I had to catch up on school reading. And roleplay scenes. "Yeah, sounds good."

"Cool." She kissed me again quickly before we rushed off to class.

As I walked into French, it hit me that I'd fallen asleep last night before I could get to my assignment. It was a two-page essay all in French, so not something I could half-ass in the minute I had before Madame Thomas asked for it.

I squeezed into my uncomfortable desk and pulled out a piece of notebook paper, writing my name at the top and *Demain, je suis désolé* in the middle. I really was sorry, and we both knew turning it in tomorrow meant docked points, but it was better than nothing. I handed it to the person in front of me, who snorted at my words and passed it up.

When it got to the front, Madame Thomas did a quick flip through the pages before landing on mine, locking eyes with me. Those few seconds told me everything I needed to know: I would for sure lose points for this, and she was disappointed. I mouthed another apology, and she offered the slightest of smiles and head-shakes before moving on.

That was two strikes this semester for her class. I'd lost count of strikes with her last year in French 3, but it wasn't good.

The small joy I'd felt at having a girlfriend at school after kissing Taylor in the hall quickly vanished. If I couldn't get my shit together academically, no amount of girlfriend time would make up for my school-related anxiety.

[One-on-one scene between Cass and Rowan]

**Cass:** "And you're sure this is what you want?" Aresha asked. She knew it was possible to give up her throne. Allain would make a great king, after all, and she could see herself boarding her ship again for more adventures. Her heart had returned home, but she'd go anywhere with Roux.

**Rowan:** Roux stepped up to Aresha, taking her hands. "I don't think you understand how this works. I made a vow to remain loyal and stay by your side through anything when joining the crew. Those weren't just words to me."

**Cass:** Aresha smiled a little, squeezing Roux's hands. "I know, but we're talking about something different now. You aren't a member of my crew anymore. You're my partner, my family, and my equal. You decide our future as much as I do."

**Rowan:** "My vow stands," Roux said, inching closer. "Captain or not, you are my truest love, and I will follow you until my last sunset."

**Cass:** ((Wow, I'm feeling things! How are you so good at this?))

**Rowan:** ((It's a gift. And you make it easy.))

**Cass:** ((Aaaawwwwweeee))

**Rowan:** ((Shut up and reply))

# SIX

A blue Subaru Crosstrek was parked in the driveway when I got home, and my immediate fear was that Mom had shown up unannounced with her boyfriend. My heart raced as I called Dad.

"What's up, kid?" he said after a few rings.

"Do we have company?" I asked.

"No, why?"

I sighed, relieved and—admittedly—disappointed. I should've known it wasn't her considering she'd called me only once, but a part of me hoped things would somehow get better. "There's a really nice Subaru in the driveway."

"I said I'd find you something," Dad said, his voice casual with a hint of excitement. Before I could reply, he stepped onto the porch, a proud grin on his face.

I hung up the phone, walking to meet him as I blinked in disbelief. "This is for me?"

"Yes. Why are you so surprised?"

"I don't know. I guess I assumed it would be a while before I got one."

"It was on my priorities list," Dad said, shrugging. "It's a couple years old, but it has low mileage and will help you feel secure during the winter."

His thoughtfulness tugged at my heartstrings. It meant more than I could put into words. "Thanks, Dad," I said as a start, pulling him in for a hug. Neither of us were big on hugging, but that fact had gone out the window lately. "It's perfect."

"I get it right sometimes," he chuckled, hugging me back. "And I know I said I wanted you to have something for college, but this car is also a reward for all the hard work you've been doing. Don't think I haven't noticed your light on later at night."

I wanted to throw up, and not because he was acting sentimental. While I intended to commit more to school, my actions hadn't followed. It felt like I was falling down a deep pit—like the scene in the second Tide Wars book where Aresha fell into a pit and had to face an enemy. Except my enemy was myself. "Thanks," I said again, owning my cowardice instead of admitting to reality.

"Want to go for a test drive?" he asked, oblivious to my internal dilemma. "Get dinner?"

I forced a smile, wishing I was more excited. "Yeah, for sure."

He handed me the keys. "Let's roll."

I drove to Wakame, our favorite sushi restaurant in Minneapolis. I took my time getting used to the feel of the vehicle and internally obsessing over how in love with it I was. I'd been so in my own head the whole drive that it didn't hit me that Dad was quieter than normal until we were seated at the restaurant. We ordered a feast of spring rolls, miso soup, and a combination of maki rolls before I brought it up. "You have something to tell me."

Dad narrowed his eyes. "How could you possibly know that?"

That was a yes. "I've kind of lived with you my entire life."

"Touché." He paused to drink a little water, no doubt trying to hide his forming frown. "Your mom called. It sounds like she won't be able to make it for Christmas after all."

I blinked, taking in his words as the wreckage found a home in my heart. Mom had sounded so excited about being here for Christmas when we'd talked last. And now she wasn't coming, and she'd used Dad to relay the message. Maybe that was why she hadn't called after the first time—she'd never intended to come. "Did she say why?"

"She didn't. I'm sorry, kid."

Taking in his tired, sad eyes, I remembered this wasn't happening only to me. My mom had left me, but his wife had left him. Them being separated and heading to divorceland didn't automatically erase the anger or pain or whatever he felt that he kept to himself.

"Don't be sorry," I said, trying to stay calm. "But speaking of Mom, what's going on with all the . . . divorce stuff? Do I need to have a role at all?"

"No, that's nothing for you to worry about," he said, his frown deepening. "Not unless you want to go live with her. We assumed you wouldn't want to be pulled from school, and I didn't like the idea of you living with a stranger, or away from me in general, but if you want to live with your mom—"

"I don't," I said quickly, not wanting his brain to linger on that possibility. "Even if she'd asked me to go with her, which she didn't, I wouldn't have gone. This is my home. *You're* my home. I'm not going anywhere."

Dad was quiet for a few seconds, his expression softening. "Good, then there's nothing you need to do. Having you here while things get figured out is more than enough."

I nodded, desperate for him to be right. Nothing felt like enough most days. "So after Christmas, you'll keep your work trip as planned, and I can stay here and hang out with Tate's family." Dad's seminar at another hospital overlapped the dates Mom was supposed to visit, and I doubted that kind of appointment was easy to reschedule.

"You're not spending Christmas break away from family," he said, waving off my response. "I'll cancel the trip. It's fine."

"No, it's not." My eyes met his, and I forced down the tears that had wanted to spill since the second he'd told me the news. If I broke, he'd feel terrible, and no good would come from that. And I wanted to be able to show my face at Wakame again. "You're not the kind of person who cancels their commitments, and I'm not the kind of person who'll let you. So I'll go to Tate's. His mom will love it, and we'll have a great time."

Dad let out a deep sigh. Even with Mom a thousand miles away living her best life or her truth or whatever the fuck she was doing, she still managed to mess things up for us. "I appreciate what you're doing, but let me be the parent. If you really want me to go on my trip, you're coming too. You can explore the city while I'm teaching, and we can find something fun to do after. How's that sound?"

I was about to insist again that I'd be fine here, but then I remembered his work trip was to Chicago. Rowan lived in Chicago. We'd always talked about meeting up eventually, which I'd always assumed meant college. The thought of meeting an online friend for the first time filled me with anxiety, but I'd make an exception for Rowan Davies. Every amount of internal flailing would be worth it. "I'm in."

Relief spread across his face. "Good. And we'll only be there for a couple days. You'll have plenty of friend time over winter break—maybe see that girlfriend of yours."

Beets. My face was instantly beets. "Yeah, great."

Dad chuckled, looking at me for a moment. "We'll be okay, Cass. And personally, I'm looking forward to having some us time on Christmas."

I knew what he meant. The holidays were chaotic every year because Mom ran around making sure everything was perfect, and she always inevitably roped me in to help. We usually celebrated with her family, something we definitely weren't doing this year. And despite wanting to call and scream at her for bailing, a part of me was relieved we'd have a stress-free holiday for once. "Me too, Cool Dad. And you're absolutely right. We *will* be okay."

He matched my smile as the soup and spring rolls arrived, followed by the maki rolls minutes later. We spent the rest of dinner talking about the various places he thought I'd enjoy in Chicago based on his many work trips there over the years. I made a mental list of art museums, Millennium Park, Chinatown, and the pizza places he was convinced would beat anything I'd ever eaten in Minneapolis.

I didn't mention Rowan during the conversation, since he didn't know she existed. But if Rowan was free to meet up, I'd be smart about it. We'd choose somewhere public where I could make a fast getaway in the extremely unlikely event that she was actually some forty-year-old man with a long-game fetish and a skill for sounding like a teenage girl on the phone.

After dinner, I went to my room to feel the weight of Mom's decision and how I'd handled everything up to this point. I'd never yelled at her or attempted to make her understand how messed up and selfish it had been to leave. I was passive aggressive, sure, but that was a love language in Minnesota—not the same as real honesty.

The fact that Dad was trying made me want to believe that we really would be okay. But if everything would be okay, why was I sobbing in my room while Phoebe Bridgers's *Punisher* album concealed any potential noise? If everything would be okay, why did I feel a heavy weight in my chest? If everything would be okay, why was Tuttles purring comfortingly against me as I curled up in bed?

I wasn't okay yet, but telling Mom that wouldn't make a difference. If she'd cared about my opinion, she wouldn't have left with no warning. She wouldn't have put herself first without considering me. But she *did* put herself first, and time was proving how little she cared. The more I thought about it, the more I realized how many things had been about her. Making costumes with me so she could brag about her talents to anyone who'd listen. Bitching at the news to her daughter, the sounding board. Driving me to school to look like the good, caring parent while knowing she was going to leave me.

Had it all been a lie? Were Dad and I some kind of stepping-stone to a better life? Maybe I'd never really known my mom until the day she'd left. Or maybe she had actually been a good parent and just did a shitty job of handling a shitty situation, as humans do. Whatever the truth was, our past life was dead, and I didn't want to give the universe the satisfaction of watching me cry over her anymore. If I could control anything, it was how I moved on. I had Dad, Tuttles, my friends, roleplaying, and my girlfriend, and that was more than enough.

Quiet sobs took over my body for nearly an hour before I couldn't keep it up, my body shaken with exhaustion. After calming my tears, I turned on my laptop to feel the sweeping relief of my online life that only existed in part because of my parents fighting. If anything, I could thank Mom for that.

I stared at the various roleplay servers of one-on-one scenes and out-of-character conversations waiting for me. Normally, I'd go down the list until I was completely caught up, but all I wanted to do was talk to Rowan.

**Cass:** My mom bailed on Christmas.

She replied within a minute.

**Rowan:** Shit, seriously?! I'm about ten seconds from asking you for her number to scream at her.

**Cass:** She's not worth it.

**Rowan:** Damn right. What can I do? Want to get on the phone?

**Cass:** Thanks, but I'm trying to move on. And I have some good news.

**Rowan:** Lay it on me.

**Cass:** Cool Dad is going to Chicago the weekend after Christmas for work, and I'm going with him. I'll have most of a day free if you want to hang out?

My hands started shaking halfway through typing the news. What if she said no? Or what if she said yes and it was a disaster?

**Rowan:** First, let me check my calendar.

**Rowan:** Second, shut up. Obvs we're hanging out!

The ache I felt over Mom dissolved as I let out a relieved breath. Now I just had to make sure it wasn't a disaster.

**Cass:** Yaaasss!

**Rowan:** I can't wait!!!

In less than two months, I'd meet my online best friend in

person for the first time.

I was thrilled.

I was *terrified*.

When we'd met online, Rowan and I had quickly bonded over our Midwest niceties and pocket snark—her pocket being much bigger than mine. She was the first roleplayer I'd told about being a lesbian, and the first one I'd shared my phone number and Instagram account with to be "real friends"—her words. Talking to her was like talking to myself. She always knew where my head and heart were at.

I was still broken over Mom, but having someone in my life who could stitch me back up with a handful of responses was a gift I didn't feel I deserved.

[One-on-one scene between Cass and Rowan]

**Cass:** Their final night of battle filled Aresha's head as she found a lingering piece of her enemy's ship under the main deck's stairs. After almost two years at sea, it was really over. They'd won. But she couldn't fight her anguish. "I wish my parents could've been here to see this," she said, looking back at Roux.

**Rowan:** Roux nodded, smiling gently. "They'd be so proud of you, Captain. I have no doubt." Her smile dissolved as she thought about her own parents. Traitors.

**Cass:** As if reading her mind, Aresha considered what this victory meant for Roux. "Your parents would be proud, too," she said, reaching to take her hand.

**Rowan:** "I don't want to talk about their pride," Roux snapped, but she didn't move her hand away. "They betrayed Girishtova and your parents. They don't deserve to be considered."

**Cass:** Aresha frowned. "They made a mistake and put their faith in the wrong people. It's human to be steered off course."

**Rowan:** "You're only saying that because it's me."

**Cass:** "Maybe. Doesn't make it any less true." Her lips formed a soft smile. "You're allowed to miss them, you know."

**Rowan:** "I know," Roux said, letting out a stubborn huff. "Doesn't mean I want to."

# SEVEN

A new routine started after getting the Crosstrek. I drove myself to and from school, giving Tate more time with Rachel in the morning. I brought Taylor to work some days and hung out while she made coffee for the evening crowd. Dad agreed to that plan only because I promised to focus on homework there. And sometimes I did. Other times I got swept up in my nerd life.

The week before Thanksgiving, I was driving Taylor to work when she reminded me of our upcoming days off from school. "What's your family doing for Thanksgiving?"

I bit the inside of my cheek, unsure how to answer. My family took turns spending Thanksgiving with my mom's side in Fargo and hosting my dad's side at our house. The former obviously wasn't happening, and the latter sounded depressing. Family pity over an absent parent would be pure hell, and I was sure Dad agreed. "I don't think we have plans. Why?"

"My parents said you could all could come over for it, if you want. We have a big extended family, so it gets pretty loud, but it would be the perfect cover for us to hide out in my room until dinner. And my parents want to meet yours."

My parents. What a concept. "It would be me and my dad," I said after a beat, knowing we hadn't gotten to that part yet. Taylor told me all about her family and friends and pretty much everything during our first few weeks of dating, but I'd failed to do the same. She hadn't pried, but I knew she didn't like my lack of openness. "My mom isn't around."

Taylor's face fell. "Oh god, I'm sorry. I didn't know."

"She's not dead," I said quickly, realizing how it sounded. "But she won't be there. She lives in Maine." I shrugged, willing myself not to cry. Mom should be around to help me through navigating my first girlfriend, but she wasn't. Add it to the list of things she was missing out on.

Taylor paused before reaching over to take my free hand. "In that case, my parents will be excited to meet your dad."

"Same," I said, relieved she didn't ask more about it since it was still a sensitive subject, and no amount of telling myself I was done with my mom would change that fact anytime soon. Apart from family, only Tate and Rowan knew the *full* story.

"So you'll come?" Taylor asked after another pause.

The thought of meeting her entire family made my insides twist, especially after dating for only a few weeks. But I desperately wanted a distraction from Mom being absent for a big holiday— even a bullshit one like Thanksgiving. "Let me make sure my dad hasn't been secretly planning something for us. If he's in, I'm in."

"Cool." She let go of my hand and started playing with my hair, something I was growing more and more used to despite it making my heart race and my hands clammy every time.

Taylor was really nice and cute and fun, but something continued to hold me back from fully relaxing around her and letting her in. I wasn't ready to overanalyze it, mainly because I was sure it was "new territory" flailing, so I focused on the road instead in the hope that it would help me tune out Mom thoughts and relax.

"I want to meet your dad more officially, too," Taylor continued after a moment. "We didn't really talk that day I came over."

"You mean the day you asked me to be your girlfriend?"

"Yeah, that one."

I grinned at the memory, parking in front of Spyhouse Coffee before turning toward her. "You'll meet him more officially. If not at Thanksgiving, then soon."

"And Tuttles. You know, post-rescue."

As if I needed the reminder that other than on Halloween, we'd hung out only at school and Spyhouse Coffee. And we hadn't been on an official date since becoming girlfriends. Dates required staying off technology for hours, also known as not roleplaying. It wouldn't kill me to take a night off. Maybe. "Want to come over the weekend after Thanksgiving? We could eat dinner and watch a movie with Tuttles."

"Are you asking me on a date?" Taylor asked, batting her eyes.

"Yes, loser, I am."

"I'll have to think about it. I have many suitors, you know."

I snorted, having no doubt dozens of people fawned over her. "Tell them you're busy with your girlfriend."

She nodded, her smile growing as she leaned closer. "I think I can do that."

Her lips met mine, and I kissed her back as another twist of anxiety hit me at the idea of meeting her entire family. "Okay, get out of here," I said after getting in a couple more kisses. "I have to go tell all my friends how great you are."

"Sounds like a full-time job," she said. "Send Tate my regards."

"I will." A fresh knot of guilt replaced my anxiety. As far as Taylor knew, Tate was my only friend. But between what had happened at Greg's party and wanting to get used to a new relationship first, telling her about my online friends felt less immediate. And if Carina hadn't told Tom about us, I could wait a little longer to tell Taylor.

I made a deal with myself that I could check roleplay scenes after getting halfway through my English essay. Some classes were better than others as far as grades went, and doing well in a few was better than sucking at all of them.

I'd barely scratched the surface on writing when Dad checked in. "Hey, kid. How's the essay coming along?"

"Slowly, but it's coming," I said, relieved I wasn't lying about homework for once. Instead, I was nervous about Thanksgiving. But it was either ask him now or put it off forever and pretend we couldn't go. "Do we have Thanksgiving plans? Taylor's parents invited us to their house. They want to meet you."

"That sounds engaging," he said, which was Dadspeak for thinking it sounded like fun. "Count me in."

"Are you sure?" I asked, part of me hoping he'd say no. It wasn't that I didn't *want* to see Taylor—I just knew this would turn into a big deal. It would mean more than our casual, no-pressure dating. "I know it's not our normal, and it's okay if you're on call and it's too much."

"I made sure not to be on call this year," Dad said, smiling a little. "And honestly, this is perfect. I was going to suggest ordering a pizza and watching a movie so I didn't burn the house down with the big meal, but this sounds better. I'd like to get to know your girlfriend and meet her parents."

"Yeah, but her *whole family* will be there," I added, my hands fidgeting. "That's a lot of pressure."

Dad gave me a knowing look and stepped farther into the room. "Would it help you if I said no?"

"Yes? No. I don't know." I groaned. "Isn't this all happening really fast? Meeting her entire family after less than a month?"

"No matter what anyone else says, life doesn't have a set timeline," Dad said. "Don't think about how long it's been. If you want to go, let's go. If it doesn't feel right, we'll go back to the pizza plan, or whatever you want. I'm sure Taylor would understand."

Something held me back from an automatic yes, but I didn't know what. It was probably Mom-related, which made me want to go out of spite. But what if my brain was telling me no for another reason? And if I said no, would that ruin everything? I didn't want to disappoint Taylor, but shouldn't I be honest?

"I'm overthinking it," I said after a pause.

"Doesn't sound like you," Dad said with a Rowan-like sarcasm that made me laugh immediately.

"No doubt," I said, groaning again. "Okay, let's go. I'll ask Taylor what we can bring." It's something Mom would've done, which I hated, but it was the polite thing to do.

"Good call." Dad's smile didn't quite reach his eyes. He'd no doubt had the same thought. "Well, I'll leave you to it. Dinner will be ready soon."

My focus was officially zapped after he left. I texted an update to Taylor before opening my roleplay servers—you know, since I was already taking a break. Home Base was thrilled and jealous about the upcoming Chicago meetup, and that news had quickly overshadowed my having a girlfriend.

I didn't mind. The less they mentioned Taylor, the less they'd think about me not confirming that she knew about them. Rowan had brought it up in private how shitty it was that Carina kept us a secret, which basically meant she thought *I* was shitty. Or she would think that if she knew I *still* hadn't told Taylor about her and everyone else.

It was best not to talk about my girlfriend too much.

**Holly:** My mom surprised me last night with the worst news ever! She's marrying that douche canoe Glen on Thanksgiving with an Elvis! I'm not kidding! WHY!?

**Rowan:** Should I coordinate a sabotage mission?

**Holly:** Thanks, but she'd just find another one like him.

**Holly:** It's so tacky! And she wants me to wear this turquoise monstrosity that looks like something from an 80s prom. Not a compliment!

**Autumn:** I'm sorry, Holls!

**Cass:** Ugh, the biggest of douche canoes. Sorry, friend!

**Holly:** Thanks! But someone share good news. What's everyone doing for Thanksgiving?

**Rowan:** Stuffing my face with delicious food. Going to Millennium Park to people watch at the Bean. Shopping with my cousins. The usual American dream.

**Holly:** LOL love it

**Carina:** My grandma is visiting from Italy, and we're taking her to NYC that weekend.

**Holly:** You're alive!

**Carina:** Ha ha

**Autumn:** That sounds fun, Cari! And it'll be a regular weekend for me. My family remains morally against Thanksgiving.

Tuttles launched himself onto my desk as I read over the replies. "So much for not talking about Taylor," I told him before starting to type. He swatted a pen in response.

**Cass:** I wish everyone was morally against Thanksgiving. Dad and I are going to Taylor's house. Her whole fam will be there. Like, all of them. It's fine. I'm fine.

**Holly:** Damn, girl, you win!!

**Autumn:** Yay Cass and Taylor! OTP <3

**Rowan:** You know the bigger deal y'all make about it, the bigger deal Cass will make about it, right? Don't give her a panic attack.

**Rowan:** Also, hope everyone enjoys their plans! Especially Cassidy Williams, who has a date on Turkey Day with Taylor and her entire family, who will want to know everything about her. No pressure.

I groaned loudly, causing Tuttles to jump down and scurry out the door. "Sorry!" I yelled after him before responding in all caps in Home Base, my palms starting to sweat.

**Cass:** ROWAN DAVIES!

**Rowan:** See? She's panicking.

**Cass:** Wouldn't you!?!?

Dad called for dinner, so I went downstairs to fill a plate and tell him I had a lot of homework to finish before returning to my room. I switched between Home Base and one-on-one scenes while I ate, my homework going untouched.

Taylor texted me back to confirm Thanksgiving plans, and an endless pit of nerves returned as I thought about what Rowan had said. But I wouldn't back down. Our plans were better than sitting at home with nowhere to go and a heart full of bitterness over an absent parent. Mom had spoiled enough of my senior year already. I wouldn't let her spoil this too.

[Unfinished one-on-one scene between Cass and Carina]

**Cass:** Aresha looked between her brother and the sea. A calm returned to the water, gifting them a moment without chaos. They'd been through many storms, and for the first time in a long time, she felt at ease. But she feared she was alone in that. "What are you thinking?" she asked.

**Carina:** Allain had known the question was coming. Despite his sister being the one constant his entire life, they oftentimes had to pull information out of each other. Their losses ran deep, but they acted like they couldn't bear to show their pain to each other. "I'm worried about what we'll find when we get home," he admitted, glancing at her. "Do we even have a home to return to?"

**Cass:** "You know we do," Aresha said, meeting his eyes. "Mother and Father's remaining supporters confirmed as much."

**Carina:** Allain's brows raised. "And you believe them?"

**Cass:** She focused on the water again, letting out a slow breath. How well he knew her. "We don't have a choice," she said finally. "We can't stay at sea forever. That wasn't the plan."

**Carina:** "No, but it sounds better than going back to a castle of ghosts and memories I'll never be able to shake,"

Allain said, a shiver running up his spine. All that blood, and the screams . . .

**Cass:** Aresha turned toward him, resting her hands on his shoulders. "We'll face it all together. And I promise you we'll make Girishtova safe and prosperous again. Whatever it takes."

**Cass:** ((Also, we miss you. Hope everything is okay.))

**Carina:** ((Miss you, too, girl. And all good, just busy. I'll reply to this scene soon, promise.))

**Cass:** ((No worries! <3))

# EIGHT

On Thanksgiving morning, I woke to a purring turkey next to my face. "Good morning, Tuttles," I mumbled before climbing out of bed to start the pumpkin and apple pies—another Mom-and-Cass thing I'd bitterly leaned into this year since I didn't know what else to contribute.

Baking had always been a stress reliever for me. I liked playing with dough, experimenting with ingredients, and seeing the finished product of something I'd made. Family members always said I got into baking because of Mom, but I didn't think hobbies needed to *come from* someone else—sometimes they just *were*.

And fine, maybe I used to love baking with Mom too.

After pulling the pies from the oven and leaving them on the counter to cool, I faced my next dilemma: how to be a girlfriend on a holiday in a house full of strangers. After tearing through my closet twice, I settled on a soft, light gray sweater and black leggings. Not trying too hard. Not sloppy. It would have to be good enough.

Dad was in the kitchen by the time I returned, holding two wine gift bags, a bottle poking out from each. "I wanted to contribute," he said, his shoulders tensed. "Do you think they'll like them?"

Was Dad more nervous than I was? "I'm sure they'll love them. Very thoughtful." I giggled when he relaxed and went to secure the pies in a box along with a small cooler of ice cream and whipped cream. "You have the address?"

"I do. Nice neighborhood."

I groaned. "Of course you stalked them."

He gave me a pointed look. "Being prepared is not the same as stalking. It's good to visualize your surroundings."

I did that all the time with the seating situation at restaurants to know if I'd fit, but I decided that was different. "Whatever you say, stalker."

He opened the door. "Are you done harassing me?"

"For now." I flashed him a big grin on my way out the door. "Let's go!"

I tapped my lap the entire fifteen-minute drive, growing more and more nervous with each passed traffic light and turned road. Why had I agreed to these plans? Gods, Taylor and I hadn't even been dating for a month yet. Was I ready for this? I took out my phone to get advice from Rowan or Tate, but Dad parked before I could find the words. After collecting our contributions from the back, we headed up the driveway.

"Thanks again for coming," I said as we stopped at the door, Dad ringing the bell. "I know this isn't our usual."

"From now on, our usual is whatever we decide it is," Dad said, smiling down at me. "And maybe I'll have a chance to share some embarrassing Cassidy stories."

"I take it back. You can go home now."

He barked a laugh as the door opened, cutting him off from a very Dad remark. Natalie Cooper wasn't the woman you expected to see when entering Taylor's house, but only because I thought Taylor was so damn edgy and cool. Her mom had long blonde hair and a smile that said she wished her daughter had been in cheerleading instead of newspaper. And Taylor recently told me that her mom had gotten one look at Greg Jensen at a football game last year and said, "I wish you'd date a kid like that."

She'd have to settle for his ex-girlfriend instead.

"You must be Cassidy," she said politely. "How nice to meet you. And Dr. Williams, welcome."

"Thank you, Mrs. Cooper, nice to meet you, too," I said, hoping my smile didn't show how unprepared I felt.

"And please, call me Marcus," Dad said with ease and his usual charming surgeon smile as he lifted the wine bags. "I don't know your thoughts on wine, but I brought a couple bottles."

"How sweet, thank you. Come on in." She took the bags, leaving me to deal with the awkward pie box by myself.

We followed her as chaos unfolded around us. Kids ran

through the house. Football blasted from the living room, and voices shouted at the TV as if the players and referees could hear them bellowing about *their team*. Making it to the safety of the kitchen, I saw Taylor's dad standing next to an older woman. I nodded in greeting before setting the box down and putting the cold items away.

"Marcus, Cassidy, this is my husband, Dave," Mrs. Cooper said. "And this is his mother, Roxane."

"Good to meet you both," Dad said as he shook Mr. Cooper's hand. "Your home is very festive and lively."

Mr. Cooper laughed. "No shortage of chaos around the holidays, I'm afraid. But Natalie *insists* on hosting every event, so here we are."

When I turned back to the group, Grandma Roxane's eyes were glued to me. I forced a polite smile and stepped up to her. "Hello. I'm Cassidy, Taylor's—"

"I know who you are," Roxane said, a pursed smile on her lips as she looked at her son. "David, honestly, today is for *family*."

"Roxane," Mrs. Cooper said firmly before looking at us, her attempt to laugh it off falling short. "I'm sorry. She's not used to special guests. You're both very welcome."

I felt frozen, my head full of Grandma Roxane's words, and her tone. I knew I'd have to muster up some charm to get through meeting a large family, but I didn't realize I'd have to add shielding myself from judgments to the list. Or maybe she really was unhappy that *anyone* outside of family was invited. And if it was such a stretch to invite us, I wondered why Taylor had in the first place. "Thanks. Where's Taylor?"

"In her room," Mr. Cooper said, inclining his head. "We can keep your dad company if you want to head up."

"Just keep it PG," Dad said.

"Dad!" I felt a current of heat flood my face. So generous of him to wait until this moment in my life to embarrass me. My eyes moved from him to Mr. Cooper. "I'm leaving the door wide open."

Mr. Cooper chuckled, looking at Dad. "Good one."

"Thanks, I thought so," Dad said, grinning.

"Dads," I muttered, escaping their jokes and Grandma Roxane. The staircase's handrail was lined with garland and lights, and the walls had an occasional festive snowman or Santa print littered among family photos. I paused at a picture of young Taylor on a boat with a little fish she'd caught, a front tooth missing from her bright smile. She was adorable, but I couldn't imagine her fishing today, or wearing an all-pink outfit with what looked like glittery sandals. The sound of children running and yelling below brought me back to the present, and I carried on upstairs.

Stopping in Taylor's doorway, I saw her standing in front of a full-length mirror, smoothing her hands over a knee-length red velvet dress. A pile of clothes filled the floor of her closet, and she had a couple of coffee mugs and papers strewn across her desk. Posters and art from her favorite games and bands littered her light gray walls, as well as pictures with friends and family, and one with me.

Her expression wore a hint of uncertainty, barely enough to notice. I was intruding on a personal thought, but I couldn't turn back now and face Grandma Roxane alone. I knocked on the doorframe to get her attention.

All doubt fell from her face as she beamed back at me. "Hey, you made it!" Her arms were around me within seconds. "How's everything downstairs?"

"Well, Grandma Roxane is a delight," I said dryly, hugging her back.

"Oh god," she groaned. "Sorry if she was rude. She's the worst sometimes."

"She wasn't rude . . . exactly. Just had a telling look about her."

She pulled away, her nose scrunched in annoyance. "Sounds like her. I'm sorry."

"It's fine," I said. "And my dad has already embarrassed me, so he's having a blast." For once, I wasn't being sarcastic. Dad didn't hang out with a lot of people, so I'd allow him to make jokes at my expense if it meant having fun around other adults.

"That's very *dad* of him," Taylor said, chuckling.

"Totally." I paused, unable to hide what I'd seen a minute ago. "Are you okay? You looked off when I walked in."

"I'm okay." She sat on the side of her bed. "I've been a little nervous about today. Not all of my family is accepting of me having a girlfriend. And they'll be Minnesota Nice about it, of course, but still."

I nodded, finding truth in the assumption that her grandma was the type to call me a *friend* instead of *girlfriend*. "Why didn't you tell me?" I asked, sitting next to her.

"I don't know." She sighed, pausing. "Sometimes it's easier thinking everything is gonna happen how I want it to. Today was supposed to be special. I wanted to show you off and have them like you as much as I do."

I wanted to feel upset for not knowing what I was walking into, but I also felt bad for her. Coming out hadn't been that hard for me, but I knew my experience wasn't the only experience. I'd seen enough stories online to know that no matter how little my dad used to be around and how hurt I was over my mom leaving, I was lucky to have parents who accepted me without a second's hesitation. "A little warning next time would be nice," I said, nudging her knee with mine. "Also, I hope they don't like me as much as you do, or we might have a problem."

"True. No one is allowed to like you as much as me," she said, her hand finding mine. "And I'm sorry for not telling you sooner. If it helps, my grandma is by far the worst of them."

"It helps a little," I said, meeting her eyes. I wanted to push Grandma Roxane's stare from my memory and talk about something else.

"Maybe this will help more," Taylor said. And then her lips pressed against mine. Every reminder that our families were downstairs slipped away as I kissed her back. After several kisses, we moved fully onto the bed, my back resting against the comforter.

Taylor pressed against me, and her hands were everywhere. This was new territory, and my body locked in place as my heart pounded—and not in a fluttery, romantic way.

"They're kissing!"

Taylor grabbed a pillow and whipped it toward the door. "Get out!" she yelled at a cackling, retreating boy I assumed was a cousin.

Taylor's dad was in the doorway by the time we stood. "What's going on in here?"

"We kept it PG," I said, my eyes immediately widening at my abysmal response.

Mortified, check.

Mr. Cooper stared at me. And then he stared some more. And then he barked a laugh. "I like this one, Taylor. Keep her around." He left before I could officially die in front of him.

"We kept it PG," Taylor said slowly, narrowing her eyes.

"I panicked!" I whimpered, my face no doubt a shade of red that wasn't adorable. "I don't know how to do this."

Any of it. I didn't know how to do any of it. But if Taylor agreed, she didn't let on. She took my hand, planted a swoonworthy smile on her lips, and tugged me gently toward the door. "Come on, let's go eat. You're gonna do great, and they'll love you."

I didn't know if I was more worried about Grandma Roxane and the rest of the Minnesota Nice clan or the fact that getting closer to my girlfriend felt wrong. Either way, I followed along in silence, desperate to survive the day.

*Gods protect me.*

Thanksgiving dinner was awkward—unless there was a better word for the younger cousins making kissy-faces at us, Grandma Roxane shooting Christian bullets at me, and an uncle asking Taylor about some boy she'd dated last year as if it would make her less queer. But the food was amazing, our dads hit it off like old friends, and everyone loved my pies. And Dad *loved* Taylor. They bantered like it was natural and teased me like people who cared about you tended to do. I allowed it for the sake of my own survival.

We left a couple of hours after the meal with full bellies and enough memories to keep us going for a while. Dad offered to host Taylor and her parents on Christmas Eve since they celebrated with their larger family on Christmas Day, and they accepted immediately. And just like that, I was officially locked in for Christmas with my girlfriend and her parents.

It was fine. I was fine.

After settling in for the night at home, I hopped online to find a couple of one-on-one roleplay scene replies, but nothing from Home Base. Carina was busy living it up in NYC. Holly was becoming someone's stepdaughter. Autumn was probably watching movies or doing something to keep herself busy until new replies came in.

And then there was Rowan.

I messaged our private server to check in.

**Cass:** How was the Bean?

**Rowan:** It was glorious and sad. How was Taylor's fam?

**Cass:** They were mostly nice, but that Grandma Roxane put the fear of gods in me.

**Rowan:** Gotta love those grandmas.

My eyes focused on the word *sad*. Rowan didn't admit to negative emotions easily, so I knew it meant something big. I called her before I could convince myself it wasn't my business.

"What's up, Captain?" she said after a few rings.

"Why was the Bean sad, Champ?"

She didn't reply.

"Are you there?"

"I'm here," she said, clearing her throat. "When I was little, my mom got super overwhelmed one Thanksgiving because of all the family she had to cook for, and my brothers and I were being too loud. So my brothers went to play with my cousins, and my dad took me to Stan's Donuts and then the Bean. We devoured doughnuts and people watched for as long as we could stand the cold, making up little stories about where everyone lived and why they were there. And then it became our tradition." She paused. "My cousin offered to go with me this year, but it didn't feel right bringing someone else. Honestly, nothing feels right without him—even this stupid holiday. It was the same with Halloween."

"What about Halloween?" I asked, confused.

"One of the old theaters used to have a movie marathon, and my family started going together once my brothers and I got too old for trick-or-treating. But it didn't feel right going without him, and my brothers weren't in town anyway."

I knew she'd gone to a movie with her parents last year, but I never knew it was a *thing*. And this year I was too wrapped up in myself to think beyond my own plans. "I'm sorry. I should've been more considerate."

"You didn't know. And you've had a lot going on."

I still felt bad, but obsessing about it wouldn't help. "What would make you feel better?"

"I don't know," she said. "Tell me more about Thanksgiving."

"It was weird," I said, curling on my side. Tuttles jumped up to snuggle against me as if I was the one hurting. "My dad had fun, but I felt like I was on display."

"And gods forbid you get any attention."

"It wasn't a *good* kind of attention," I corrected. "It was people with their fake smiles and silent judging. And then my dad invited Taylor's family over for Christmas Eve, which is a much bigger deal than Thanksgiving."

"Damn, that does sound pretty heavy," she said. "A lot of pressure."

"So much pressure! And everything is moving fast—maybe *too* fast." I sighed. "I like Taylor, but maybe you were right. Maybe I'm trying to fill a mom void. Or maybe there's something else going on. I don't know."

"Don't let me get in your head," Rowan said. "I'm worried about you, always, but that doesn't mean you shouldn't have a girlfriend. And . . ."

"What?" I asked when she didn't continue.

"Have you talked to Taylor about any of this? Does she know how you feel?"

"No," I said slowly, standing up to walk around my room—a habit when on the phone. "But it's not like any of this is bad, you know? It's just new. And fast. And scary. And I'm probably just overthinking like I always do."

"Yeah, maybe," Rowan said, pausing. "Sounds like you owe it to her and yourself to keep giving this a try and see how it goes?"

"For sure," I said. "That makes sense."

"And if it still feels off after a while, you should talk to her."

I groaned, knowing she was going to say that. "Yeah. Yes, you're absolutely right."

"Happens sometimes."

I grinned, and a comfortable silence took over as I heard her soft breathing against my ear. I felt a little better, but I wasn't sure she did. Having a girlfriend made me slightly busier than normal, but I was determined to not be like Carina. My online friendships meant the world to me, and the roleplay itself would have to lose all its players before I'd stop participating. "Hey, Champ?"

"Yes, Captain?" she said.

"You're one of my favorite people in the world, and I can't wait to hang out next month."

"Back at you, Cassidy Williams."

I could feel her smile through the phone, and I beamed in return. "Good."

There was another pause before Rowan spoke again. "I should get going. My cousins like being ridiculously early for Black Friday shopping. Try telling them that it's all online now."

I stopped pacing, frowning at the abrupt change, but I wouldn't keep her from family time. She deserved it. "No doubt, and sounds good. Go get those deals."

"I will. And try not to overthink everything we talked about."

How well she knew me. Again. "No promises, but I'll try."

After hanging up, I returned to bed and moved an arm around Tuttles, letting the weight of a long afternoon and a full stomach pull me under for a nap.

[One-on-one scene between Cass and Rowan]

**Cass:** Aresha laid back on her bed with a sigh. "We need to keep our heads on straight."

**Rowan:** Roux laughed quietly as she moved over Aresha, straddling her waist. She slowly started untying her pants. "The only action we've seen in weeks is people shooting at us. We're going to stop talking about our possible deaths for one night so I can have my way with you."

**Cass:** Aresha lifted her head to watch Roux. It had been a while. Too long, really. "Are you making demands of your captain? Some might consider that a crime."

**Rowan:** "I'll take my chances," Roux said, her fingertips slipping between fabric and skin before pausing. "Or would you like me to stop?"

**Cass:** Aresha's heart skipped a beat, and the thought of a potential enemy attack disappeared. "No," she whispered, every cell in her body humming. "Don't stop. That's an order."

**Rowan:** "I'll be making the demands tonight, Captain." Roux leaned down, capturing Aresha's mouth in a heated kiss.

# NINE

The first week of December was full of snow, snow, and more snow. And roleplaying. Having a snow day was unheard of for Minneapolis schools, but the fluffy flakes wouldn't stop. I cozied up by the fire both days with my laptop, Tuttles, and snacks while Dad braved the roads to work.

I thought my date with Taylor would get canceled, but the snow stopped in time for the plows to catch up that weekend. We agreed to order in pizza and watch a movie, and my heart started racing the moment everything was confirmed. Things could've gone further on Thanksgiving had her cousin not barreled into her room and interrupted us. But whatever the reason, I hadn't *wanted* things to go further. Or did I but was scared? I groaned and texted Tate.

**Cass: Can you come over? Need advice.**

**Tate: Don't you have a date?**

**Cass: Later. Please?**

**Tate: Be there in 10**

**Cass: THAAAANKS**

I left my pillow nest to make homemade hot chocolate, pacing the kitchen while everything melted together. By the time Tate walked in, the drinks were on the table with extra whipped cream and chocolate syrup on top—just the way we liked it. "Thanks for coming over."

"Sure thing," Tate said, bumping my fist with his before sitting across from me. "What's up?"

I studied him for a few seconds. "Do you remember when you kissed me in ninth grade?"

He nearly choked on his hot chocolate. "Uh, yeah," he said through a cough. "You don't really forget something like that, C. Why?"

Freshman homecoming was a different time that lived between me dating Greg and Tate dating Rachel. It was before Tate joined the varsity football team, before my crush on Taylor. We'd been dancing close to a slow song, talking about being each other's favorite person, and then he'd kissed me. And then I'd ruined the vibe he thought we'd had going by coming out to him.

I wrapped my hands around my warm mug. "How did you know you wanted to?"

"It felt right in the moment," Tate said, shrugging. "I obviously read things wrong. What does this have to do with needing advice?"

I sighed, the weight of dilemma pressing down on me. If

anyone could help me talk through this, it was Tate. He'd been my friend longer than anyone else, and apart from my roleplaying life, he knew everything about me. "When I was at Taylor's on Thanksgiving, her cousin caught us kissing. But if he hadn't, I think it could've turned into . . . well, more than that."

"Damn, C." Tate grinned, nudging my foot under the table. One look from me made it click that this wasn't positive, and he cleared his throat. "I mean, do you *want* more to happen?"

"I don't know," I whined. "I mean, I like her, but I've only ever kissed her. And you, technically. I don't know how fast we should be moving, or if I want to move faster."

"Don't forget you've also kissed Greg."

I kicked him under the table. "I've only kissed the people I choose to remember kissing."

Tate snorted, shaking his head. "Fine, fine. But honestly, go with what feels right. You don't *have* to rush into anything just because it seems like she's ready for more. And trust me, she's probably as nervous as you are."

Nothing about those hands or lips had been nervous. "I don't know about that. Taylor's dated a few other people, and the way she acted was like it wasn't new territory. And that's obviously fine, but that's not me."

"But you're her girlfriend. No matter how much experience she has, she hasn't done any of this stuff with *you*. Rachel wasn't the first girl I hooked up with, but I was nervous as hell when we did."

This was news to me. "You were?"

"Hell yeah." He grinned. "But don't tell her that. I have an image to uphold."

"Wow, okay," I laughed, kicking his foot again. "And thanks. That makes me feel better."

"Good." He drank back more hot chocolate before standing. "I'm leaving before you can talk yourself out of this date."

"If you must," I said, sighing dramatically. "Thanks again for coming over."

"Anytime, C. Thanks for the hot chocolate. Best in town."

After he left, I showered, changed into leggings and a long sweater, and returned to my roleplay safety zone. Living in a fake world of pirates, adventure, and fictional relationships was exactly what I needed to calm my anxiety.

In the most recent group scene, our characters docked in a port town, giving Aresha more opportunities to barter and cause trouble with enemy pirates. She was supposed to do that with Allain, but Carina never showed up despite promising she'd be there. And she didn't reply when a couple of us texted to make sure she was okay.

I buried myself in the depths of my second life for the next few hours, taking breaks to make more hot chocolate and pour over Instagram posts from Home Base. Seeing their faces made me feel like we were hanging out in person.

Holly was still mad about having a stepdad, and her grimace in every wedding picture proved it. Autumn's feed had a picture of her holding a baby alpaca at a recent farmers' market. Carina had added multiple posts of her NYC trip, and I tried not to care about the picture she'd added with friends the night of the group scene. Rowan shared a few pictures with her cousins and a selfie at the Bean, a doughnut from Stan's in her hand. The caption read *Miss you, Dad*, and my heart hurt for her all over again.

My current scene with Rowan had taken a scandalous turn as Aresha and Roux tore each other's clothes off. It wasn't the first time they'd done this, but it hit me in a new way now that I had a real-life girlfriend. Roleplaying the occasional steamy scene with Rowan felt natural, but the idea of doing anything close to that with Taylor made me feel numb. I was sure it was because writing something and actually doing it were two very different things, and real-life affection was new and scary. But what if it was something else?

The doorbell rang, snapping me from my online stupor and intrusive thoughts as I realized the time. Taylor was here, and I hadn't finished getting ready or ordered the pizza. *Shit.* I shut my laptop and opened the door, my anxiety revving up all over again. "Hey. Sorry, I'm behind on life. Tuttles and I curled up by the fire and lost track of time."

"It's all good," Taylor said as she walked in. "I hope pizza is still happening."

"Yes, let's order that first."

"Let's do that second." She pulled me in for a kiss without another word.

For a handful of seconds, my anxieties were quieted, but they kicked back in the moment we stopped kissing. Would she take Dad being gone as a sign that we could do more than make out? Was that the point of the date? Was I supposed to know that and initiate something? *Oh gods.* "Uh, let me order the pizza, then I can give you a tour?"

"Yeah, sounds great," Taylor said, moving to the couch where Tuttles had ended up.

I watched them for a moment, a small part of me hoping Tuttles didn't get attached like he'd done with Mom. If I messed up this girlfriend thing, I didn't want him to resent me. I shook the thought away and called Carbone's, slowly pacing the living room as I ordered chicken Alfredo pizza and Italian fries.

Tuttles followed along as I showed Taylor around the house and told stories of random memories. The banister I slid down once that resulted in a sprained wrist. The dent in the hall from moving the desk into my room. The only corner Tuttles would sleep in for the first six months we had him. The window Tate climbed through when trying to be a movie best friend but failing miserably because he scared the shit out of me and got a heavy book thrown at him.

"That's very you, and very him," Taylor teased at the last story. She sat on my bed, a light smirk on her lips. "Is he gonna do that today? Or are there any cousins lurking around that I should know about?"

My heart started hammering immediately. My smart, funny, nerdy, adorable girlfriend was sitting on my bed, and I was a mess.

"No to both," I said, my mouth dry as I sat beside her. "But the pizza will be here soon."

"Yeah, in like twenty minutes."

"Yeah."

When neither of us said anything else, she turned to kiss me, her hand moving to my cheek. My clammy hands clasped together tightly on my lap as I kissed her back, and I tried not to fidget. We continued like that for several seconds or minutes—I couldn't function enough to know the difference—then she slowly pushed me back against the bed. Her eyes locked on mine for a beat before she kissed me again, deeply. The calmness that came with kissing disappeared as her hand moved under my shirt to explore my body, and I pulled away the second she touched my chest. I'd written enough roleplay scenes to know what came next. "Can we slow down?"

Taylor moved off the bed, putting distance between us. "I'm sorry."

"Don't be," I said quickly, my head on fire. "I'm not ready for all of this. I don't have experience like you do."

She blinked, her face falling like I'd slapped her. "How much experience do you think I have?"

"I don't know," I said, fumbling my words as my fingers twisted together. "You've dated other people, and I've only dated Greg Jensen in middle school."

"So dating a handful of people means I have loads of experience?" she asked, her eyes narrowed. "What the fuck, Cass?"

"I'm sorry, that came out shitty," I said, grasping for the right words, my brain struggling to keep up with the moment. "I just don't—"

"Don't what?" she asked when I stalled.

"I don't want to have sex with you!" I blurted, surprising us both as my voice raised. "I'm sorry, but I'm not ready for all that."

Taylor stared back at me. The adorable smirk I'd swooned over for years was long gone. "I wasn't trying to have sex with you, but that's good to know," she said quietly. "Is this a forever thing, or a right-now thing?"

"I don't know." I looked down at Tuttles, who'd been spying on us from the floor. Rude. "I've never had to think about this kind of stuff until now."

Her silence killed me. What did this mean for us? She wasn't pressuring me, but I knew she wanted more. And I hated that I wasn't there with her yet, but I also knew this was too important to pretend to be ready when I wasn't.

"Thanksgiving together was fast," Taylor said finally. "I should've realized that sooner, and it was a bad move not to warn you about my family in advance." I opened my mouth to respond, but she cut me off. "Don't. I know it bothered you, and that's fair. So let's slow down and figure this out together. We can take Christmas off the table and have a low-key gift exchange instead, if it'll help."

A weight lifted from my shoulders. It hadn't clicked how much the thought of Christmas together was causing my anxiety to spiral until she brought it up. "Are you sure?"

She nodded, a hint of a smile returning. "I'm sure. But I hope you at least like kissing me, because it would really suck if you didn't."

I laughed quietly, taking her hand. "I like kissing you."

"Good." She squeezed my hand. "And from now on, don't assume something about me—just ask. Like, I'm not a virgin, but I also don't have a scrapbook of scandalous sex stories. We can take it as slow as you want, but be honest with me about it, okay?"

"Okay, that's fair," I said, my cheeks warming. "And I really am sorry. I was overthinking, but that's no excuse."

"It's okay." She squeezed my hand again. "Let's go back downstairs. Tuttles is creeping me out."

I looked back at my cat, who hadn't moved in several minutes, chuckling. "Yeah, he's known for being the worst. Takes after me."

"Don't talk about my girlfriend like that."

I smiled as she kissed my cheek, my brain calming again. We returned downstairs, and I immediately wanted to tell Home Base and Tate everything. Instead, I continued into the kitchen for soda. Pizza arrived shortly after, and we devoured it as we watched Christmas-themed Netflix movies and cuddled with Tuttles, making fun of the cheesy one-liners and pretending not to cry at the emotional scenes. Nothing more was said about what did and didn't happen in my room.

Taylor's dad showed up exactly four hours after dropping her off. After a long hug and a quick kiss, Taylor left and I returned to my pillow pile. Tate texted before I could get comfortable.

Tate: So?

Cass: Hi, stalker! Shouldn't you be with your own girlfriend?

Tate: Whatever. What happened?!

Cass: Nothing

Tate: You don't have to tell me anything but I'm here if you wanna talk

Cass: That's just it . . . nothing happened. I'm not ready.

Tate: Nothing wrong with that! Wanna hang tomorrow?

Cass: Always, but I think I need a me day

Tate: Heard! Monday, then

Cass: Monday, then :)

I opened my laptop, immediately feeling at home with myself as I poured over responses from the last few hours. I clicked on my server with Rowan, tempted to ask her for Taylor advice since consulting best friends was apparently the thing to do in these situations. Instead, I moved to our roleplay server and continued writing a saucy scene with my best friend that I was afraid I'd never be ready to share with my real-life girlfriend.

Another shoe dropped a little over a week later when Carina messaged Home Base. Other than her recent failed promise to attend a group scene, she hadn't been around since before Thanksgiving break.

Carina: I GOT ACCEPTED TO YALE!!!

I stared at the message for gods knew how long before

standing, realizing my mistake.

In the chaos of Mom leaving and putting my little remaining energy into roleplaying and Taylor, I'd forgotten to submit my UIC early-action application. Instead of getting a result that week, I had one chance left to apply during the regular round.

I didn't *need* to apply early, but this was yet another thing I'd planned with Mom that she'd taken from me. We'd talked about celebrating my early acceptance with a weekend in Chicago to tour the campus and city. But she'd made other plans, so none of that would happen. At least not with her.

On top of that, school had turned into a bigger disaster than normal. I'd recently handed in four assignments late and failed an econ quiz. And I kept having school-related dreams. Forgetting my schedule. Going to the wrong class. Not knowing where my locker was with all my stuff. Showing up to school and standing in an empty hallway because I'd missed everything.

No matter how happy I was for Carina, it changed everything. Our roleplay was slipping further from my control the longer it went on. And it wasn't only Carina—a couple of other girls in the roleplay had ghosted lately. Rowan and I were committed to keeping things going in college, but what if it didn't survive that long? What if Carina leaving meant the end of the roleplay?

A part of me knew it would be for the best. I couldn't mess up in college like I'd been doing with high school, and not locking myself away to roleplay constantly would help. But I probably wouldn't have Tate or Taylor nearby to keep me in the real world.

I'd have Rowan if I got in to UIC, but that future felt uncertain now too.

Suddenly out of breath, I realized I'd been pacing my room for several minutes. My heart was pounding, and I felt sick. I left Carina's message for later so I could eat with Dad, knowing I wouldn't tell him about this. Mom had always been the college future go-to, and I didn't want to worry him since there was still time to apply to UIC.

After finishing dinner, I returned to Home Base to face the news.

**Holly:** Yaaasss girl! Congrats!

**Autumn:** I knew you would! Proud of you. <3

**Rowan:** Get out there and be excellent. Nice knowing you!

**Carina:** Shut up! I'm not going anywhere.

**Rowan:** Yet. ;)

This would hit Autumn the hardest. They had their character ship, but they'd also become really good friends—like a less-amazing version of me and Rowan, because biased. But this news confirmed that Carina would call it quits on roleplay life soon, and Autumn would be left without a ship partner. Either someone new would apply to play Allain, or we'd have to decide what happened to him and help Autumn's character, Hypernia, move on.

Pretend life had so many complications.

**Cass:** Look out, Yale! Thrilled for you.

**Carina:** Couldn't have done it without you girls!

**Cass:** lol we did nothing. It was all you.

**Carina:** Are you kidding? This RP has helped me so much. You're all such a big part of my life and mean a lot to me. <3

No one said it, but we were all thinking it. If we were such a big part of her life, why did we all know it wouldn't last? Whether it was in a few weeks, months, or next fall, Home Base would go from five to four. We were happy for her, but it was hard to accept how replaceable we felt.

Rowan sent a message to our private server.

**Rowan:** Can I call bullshit for a second?

**Cass:** She probably thinks it's true? But yes.

**Rowan:** BULLSHIT!

**Rowan:** I'm thrilled for her, obviously. She deserves it.

**Cass:** But?

**Rowan:** But this sucks! I know she'll disappear eventually, but this feels like confirmation. And it's shitty. And I feel bad for Autumn. And I'm still mad about her telling us we're all a secret, you know?

Oh, I knew. I thought about it every time Taylor was mentioned in Home Base or a private one-on-one server. I thought about it every time Carina's name came up. I thought about it every time Taylor asked about my plans and the answers I gave instead of the truth when I wanted to roleplay instead of hang out. I thought about it so much that I couldn't think of a day where I *didn't* think about it.

I let out a few slow, deep breaths before typing, my hands shaking.

**Cass:** I know. It def sucks, but at least the rest of us aren't going anywhere?

**Rowan:** Nothing will keep me from exchanging snarky comments with you, Captain.

**Cass:** That's all I needed to hear, Champ.

**Rowan:** Anytime. But speaking of people not being around, I have to go buy a couple more Christmas presents.

Shit. I hadn't shopped for anyone yet. Roleplaying and winter storms and girlfriend time and school pushed that kind of stuff from my brain.

**Cass:** Thanks for the reminder!

**Rowan:** I'm choosing not to judge your lack of planning and tell you good luck instead.

I called Tate and ordered an emergency friend outing. He was the only person I could depend on for spontaneous shopping, and we didn't exchange Christmas gifts, so I wouldn't have to hide anything from him.

If only buying presents would make me feel better about missing my early-action deadline, Carina's inevitable departure, or the throne of lies I was sitting on. Or how Carina slipping away felt like losing my mom all over again.

[One-on-one scene between Cass and Rowan]

**Rowan:** Roux sat up in bed, guiding Aresha's head to her lap so she could massage it. "What happened this time?" she asked, her voice groggy from sleep.

**Cass:** Aresha hated how real her nightmares felt. And she hated that they woke Roux too. She wiped the tears from her face before telling her yet another horrific story. "We were at a ball at the palace. I was the age I am now, except my parents were alive, and everything looked as it always had. Then the floor beneath them started on fire, and everyone else in the room carried on like everything was as it should be. My parents' screams echoed throughout the room, and they begged me to save them. But I couldn't get to them, and they burned right in front of me."

**Rowan:** Roux listened as she gently rubbed her fingers over Aresha's scalp. Sometimes the nightmares plagued her for days on end, and sometimes she didn't have one for weeks. But no matter how often they happened, Roux wanted to always be there to help Aresha through it. "I wish I possessed some kind of magic to make it all go away," she said, her voice gentle.

**Cass:** "Your fingers are magic enough," Aresha said before closing her eyes. "I don't know how I survived before they came into my life."

**Rowan:** Roux laughed tiredly at her words. "Only my fingers? I'm no good to you otherwise?"

**Cass:** Aresha smiled slowly, unable to let the terrors consume her for long with Roux around. "Maybe a little, but I'd hate for you to get a high opinion of yourself."

**Rowan:** "Too late for that, I think," Roux said, grinning proudly.

# TEN

After a week of barely surviving prebreak tests, finishing my shopping list, and making a variety of baked goods for home and Dad's work, it was Christmas. Taylor suggesting we hold off on celebrating together had made me feel better, but she was still coming over to exchange gifts. For the first time. No pressure.

I was a disaster.

I looked at the dress I'd bought during holiday shopping—hunter green with long lace sleeves. I didn't wear dresses often, but after seeing me stare at it for a full minute and call it pretty three times, Tate said I *needed* to buy it, and that was that. I added a pair of black tights, the diamond earrings Dad had given me when I'd turned sixteen, and red lipstick. It would be only me and him for the meal, but I wanted to look nice anyway. And I didn't want to let Mom's absence ruin the holiday, even if I'd had a mild panic attack over it that morning.

She still hadn't called me since that first time, not even on

Thanksgiving. I didn't need to wait until the end of the day to know she wouldn't be calling today either.

But it was fine. We were moving forward. We were okay.

Roleplay life always slowed during the holidays, but that didn't stop me from checking in after getting ready. All it took to calm down was a single message from Rowan Davies.

**Rowan:** Happy Merry Whatever, Captain. Hope you have a good one with Cool Dad. <3

My eyes lingered on the heart. It was a casual addition, but it always felt genuine coming from Rowan. I'd finally picked up on the trend that losing her dad made her emotional on big holidays, and I wished I were already in Chicago to be there for her.

**Cass:** Back at you, Champ! Give your mom extra hugs today. <3

My own heart skipped a beat when the doorbell rang. "I'll get it!" I yelled to Dad on my way downstairs, opening the door to reveal a rosy-cheeked Taylor. The falling snow outside had stuck to her hair and eyelashes. Everything about the moment hit me with a feeling of nostalgia, like we'd been here before.

"Hey, you," I said, stepping aside to let her in. "Merry Christmas."

"Merry Christmas," Taylor said, taking off her coat to reveal a velvet dress—similar to the red one she'd worn at Thanksgiving, except it was green like mine. It was exactly how Roux would dress if Tide Wars were a modern, contemporary series. She looked beautiful.

"Merry Christmas, Taylor," Dad said from behind me, peeling me from my daze.

"Back at you," Taylor said, grinning in return. "And my parents say the same."

"Back at them," he said, no doubt thinking he was cool by using her words. "Dinner will be ready in about fifteen minutes, if you have time to join us."

"Thanks, but my mom has everything started at home. And my dad is waiting in the car, so I'm not staying long." She gave me a look, silently asking if he knew why we'd changed our plans, but Dad spoke before I could elaborate.

"He knows he can wait in here, right?" he asked, looking disappointed. He'd had so much fun with the Coopers on Thanksgiving, especially Taylor's dad. But if he wanted to hang out with his new bestie, he was on his own for now.

Taylor grinned. "I think he's taking advantage of the silence while he has it."

Dad chuckled at that. "Touché. Well, I'll leave you girls to it."

Taylor held up my wrapped gift once he'd left. "Ready for this?"

"When you ask me like that, I don't know," I teased, nodding to the stairs before leading us to my room, not wanting Dad to overhear in case I said something ridiculous. We sat on my bed, our gifts between us. "Who goes first?"

"You," she said immediately, practically bouncing. "I'm excited about this one."

"No pressure, then, cool," I said, smiling a little to hide the forming anxiety. After unwrapping the box and digging through tissue paper, I pulled out a framed cross-stitch. It was us. Well, it was Link and Ursula with a heart between them. *TALE AS OLD AS TIME* was written below them. It took a moment to remember her saying that to Tate about our fake couple's costume at the Halloween party.

"Do you like it?"

I nodded, my growing smile impossible to contain. "I love it. Probably the best gift I've ever gotten. Thank you."

She let out a breath and smiled shyly, which was not like her. "You love it? Really?"

"Really," I said, forcing myself to ignore how clammy my hands felt. Maybe I should look into that. "I didn't know you cross-stitched."

"It's a hobby," she said, shrugging. "But I'm glad you love it." She gave my thigh a light squeeze before picking up her gift. "My turn?"

"Yeah," I said, my lips turning downward at the knowledge that her gift far exceeded mine. "Sorry, I'm not really crafty."

"Don't be sorry." She unwrapped her gift, her smile widening as she took out a *Fortnite* T-shirt and a framed picture of us from Thanksgiving. "This is awesome! Something framed totally counts as crafty. Thank you."

"You're welcome."

We looked at each other for a moment before I leaned in and kissed her. Ever since our date, I almost always had to make the first move. Not that it ever went far, but I hated feeling like she thought she'd done something wrong.

Taylor pulled away after a few more kisses, her smile slowly fading as something else caught her eye. "I didn't know you liked Tide Wars."

"What?" I looked in the direction of her gaze to the poster on my wall, which had been there for a few years, and my stomach dropped. I'd forgotten about it the last time Taylor had come over, and apparently she hadn't noticed it then. "Oh. Yeah. I do."

"I'm an idiot," Taylor said, groaning. "I was such a jerk about it on Halloween. Is that why you haven't mentioned it?"

One of the reasons, yes. "You didn't know," I said, taking her hand, not wanting her to feel bad. It wasn't like she'd meant to bash something I was obsessed with. It was unintentional bashing. Totally different. "And you're *not* an idiot."

"I feel like one." She bit her lip for a few seconds before looking back to me. "But hey, I read most of the first book in middle school. I could try again and give it a proper chance."

"You don't have to do that," I said quietly, shaking my head.

"It matters to you, so I *want* to," she said, squeezing my hand and smiling hopefully. "Can I borrow the books?"

There was no greater joy in the world than sharing your favorite book with someone you care about. But a part of me worried she'd still not like it, which was worse than her not wanting to read them again. "Only if you're sure."

"I'm sure."

"Okay," I said after a pause. Walking to my bookshelf, I pulled out the paperback versions of the books—because no one, *no one*, got to read *any* of my signed books. I handed the duology to her with a small smile. "It's my favorite series, so be gentle."

Taylor nodded as she took them. "Fair warning, I'm the slowest reader on the planet. It might take me a while to read. Is that okay?"

"Yeah, I can be patient."

"And if I don't love them, please don't break up with me."

"No promises there." I grinned to show I was kidding. Mostly. Hopefully.

Taylor laughed before pulling me in for another quick kiss. "Worth the risk if it means bonding over one of your favorite things." Her eyes roamed my face, and she bit her lip again for the briefest of moments before pulling back suddenly. "I should go. Don't want to keep my dad waiting."

I let out a breath as she pulled back, the flutter I'd felt over her eyes on me dissolving. "Right," I said. I'd forgotten about her dad and pretty much everything that wasn't us in this moment. "Thanks again for the gift. It's the best."

"You're the best."

"No, you," I said seriously, not feeling like the best.

I had an opening to build on my Tide Wars interest by mentioning roleplaying, but the words wouldn't come out. And maybe I didn't want them to anymore. Maybe Carina really was onto something when she'd said people wouldn't understand. Liking a book series wasn't the same as playing a character from said book every day with strangers. But at least Taylor was willing to read the books. She was bound to love them after another try. She *had* to love them. And until I told her the truth, it would be enough.

We returned downstairs, and I held our gifts and the books as she pulled on her boots and coat. "We're still on for the New Year's party, right?" she said.

Another Greg Jensen party. I wasn't as hesitant to go to his house after Halloween, but it sucked that no one else wanted to host. And there was no way in hell I'd volunteer. "Yeah. We'll only be in Chicago for a couple days."

"Cool. You'll love it. There's a ton to do—and a lot of chill coffee shops for when you're over the crowds. I'll text a few recommendations."

Despite how little I'd let her in, she understood my needs perfectly. Perk of having a barista for a girlfriend. "Great, thanks. See you next week."

"See ya." She kissed me quickly, collected the books and gifts from my arms, and left.

I lingered in the doorway, waiting until she was in her dad's SUV before locking up and meeting Dad in the kitchen. "Look what Taylor made me," I said, holding out the cross-stitch.

He took it, chuckling after a moment. "Must be an inside joke, but I like it. The things people make these days are impressive. Tell her nice work."

"I will," I said, feeling extra proud of my crafty girlfriend.

I helped him set the table and bring everything to the dining room. We'd agreed to make a smaller version of our usual Christmas dinner—ham, corn casserole, mashed potatoes, gravy, seven-layer salad, and lefse.

The food was the only part of Christmas that was the same as past years. The house wasn't full of family. Mom wasn't here to nag Dad to put up lights. She wasn't here to put together the "Santa" stockings for Christmas Day. She wasn't here to insist on blasting themed music throughout the house. Dad and I were both grateful for the last one, but it didn't make up for the reality.

But it was fine. This year was for simplicity and healing. After that, we'd make our own traditions together, sans horrible music.

After eating, I checked my phone out of habit. Nothing from roleplay life, but Tate had sent a picture of him and his parents. Despite being divorced, they got along well. Tate didn't get to see his dad a lot, so I was really happy for him, but I couldn't ignore the ache of not having both of my parents with me.

And then I tapped on Taylor's name, reading the message she'd sent minutes after leaving my house.

**Taylor: I can't wait to start the new year with you! ;)**

I smiled at her words, for once not feeling like an immediate disaster. Something about a new year gave me hope that whatever funk I'd been in would go away. I'd finally get back in the school groove. I'd learn to better manage my two lives. I'd have my awesome, patient girlfriend and best friends who endlessly gave a shit about me. I'd graduate, go to college, and figure out how to keep everyone I cared about in my life without sacrificing my grades or anything else that mattered.

Easy.

**Cass: Me too. :)**

Dad and I exchanged presents after that. Like Taylor, he got a framed picture of us from Thanksgiving. I also gave him a doctor-themed coffee mug, keeping it simple since my money came from him anyway. He gave me a few decorative things for the Crosstrek, a Tide Wars tote bag, a shirt that said *Macy Whittier Fan Club President*, and a too-generous gift card to the Mall of America so I could buy stuff I really wanted—his words.

We wrapped up the festivities by drinking hot chocolate and watching *Let It Snow*, one of my favorite holiday movies. Seeing other teenagers struggle during the holiday season with Dad and Tuttles made me feel grateful that Christmas was less chaotic this year.

But it wasn't lost on me that Mom really didn't call.

# ELEVEN

Dad and I flew to Chicago the next night. I was officially in Rowan's city, but I had to wait one more sleep before seeing her. After checking in at the hotel, Dad made a work-related call while I went through my messages. Autumn and Holly talked on Home Base about how jealous they were. Carina said nothing since she'd ghosted again after her Yale news. I clicked on my private server with Rowan.

> **Rowan:** Excited to see you tomorrow! I have the best day planned.

Warmth consumed me, shutting down the paranoia I'd had about her being a different person face-to-face. Rowan Davies was incapable of being fake or lying—unlike me.

At least my excitement was real.

> **Cass:** I can't wait!

> **Rowan:** You still good to meet at Stan's?

> **Cass:** Um, yes, I need to try these doughnuts.

**Rowan:** They'll change your life! So will the Bean.

**Cass:** I'm counting on it.

I looked up to see Dad staring at me. "What?" I asked.

"You tell me," he said, chuckling. "Actually, don't. You have a look about you, so whatever you and Taylor are talking about, I don't want to know."

"Smiling isn't a crime," I said, though I was unable to stop my cheeks from flushing. No matter how guilty I felt about keeping my online life a secret, I'd let Dad think the *look about me* was because of my girlfriend to keep the truth safe.

I left shortly after Dad the next morning, bundled up in a black coat, gloves, and boots. The bridge by the hotel overlooked Lake Michigan, and I lingered long enough to take a few pictures before walking down Michigan Avenue to Stan's Donuts.

Minneapolis had tall buildings, but something about being smack in the center of Chicago made me feel at one with the world. People were everywhere around me, minding their own business as they headed to unknown destinations. The monstrous buildings gleamed down at me like a welcoming party for my future life—granted I got into UIC, of course. Still behind on that front, I made a mental note to apply after getting home.

I was about to text Rowan when she stepped out of Stan's. Every noise and movement around me stopped. A couple of inches taller than me with an average build. Black hair in a messy bun. Fair, tawny skin that glowed despite the near-freezing temperature. A light smirk that I could paint in my sleep. Minimal makeup. Red coat. Light-washed jeans. Black boots. She was real—everything like her pictures. But there was something else I couldn't place. I thought I knew everything about Rowan Davies, but in that moment there was a mysterious side to her, one that I was sure I'd eventually understand.

"Captain," she said fondly as she pulled me in for a hug, oblivious to my internal monologue. "I can't believe you're here."

"I can't believe it either, Champ," I said, feeling a chill at saying our nicknames in person.

Rowan was real.

She stepped back and gave my cheek a quick pat as if to confirm I was also real before opening the door. "Come on. It's freezing, and I'm starving."

Walking inside, we were immediately hit by sugary smells of deliciousness. A closer look revealed standard doughnut flavors plus options like lemon pistachio, birthday cake, and Nutella banana. If heaven existed, it was Stan's Donuts with Rowan Davies. "How is this real?"

"If you think this is impressive, wait until we get pizza later."

"No, I mean *all* of this," I said, looking at her. Her eyes were a rare, unique shade of gray that could only ever belong to one person in the world. Seeing them up close gave me goose bumps. "You, specifically. We're actually meeting in person, and it's not weird. And you're exactly who I thought you'd be." And somehow, so much more.

"There's plenty of time for it to get weird," Rowan said, wiggling her eyebrows dramatically. "And did you really expect someone else?"

"No," I said a little too loud and fast. Maybe it was a weird, though not in a bad way. It was weird in the way of something exceeding your expectations when you didn't think it was possible. In the way that a single minute with someone makes you think they've been there all along. In the way you wouldn't know what to do if they weren't there anymore. "But I was mentally preparing myself for that small possibility."

"Of course you were, overthinker," she teased. "But here we are, looking like our pictures and about to consume some damn fine doughnuts. Consider it a win."

"It's a huge win," I agreed, letting my brain relax as I looked back at the bakery case. Focus, Captain. "So, doughnuts. What do you recommend?"

"Almost everyone I know who's been here loves the Biscoff pocket, but nothing compares to lemon pistachio, in my opinion."

Between the smells and colors and flavor types, it seemed impossible to choose wrong. "In that case, count me in for lemon pistachio."

"Cool. Coffee too?"

"Yeah, but I can order it."

"Not a chance, Cassidy Williams," she said, taking my hand as a light grin formed. "You came all this way. I won't have you paying for a damn thing. Happy Christmas."

The warmth of her skin trickled up my arm. "We agreed, no presents," I said, too distracted to come up with a better response.

"Don't care."

I groaned quietly before my lips curved into a smile. "Thank you. This is perfect. I love it. Most generous of you."

She squeezed my hand before letting go and focusing on the menu, her grin lingering. Once it was our turn, she ordered two lemon-pistachio doughnuts, a Biscoff Pocket, and two coffees.

"You'll confuse my taste buds," I said after she finished.

"Your taste buds will have to deal," she said. "The pocket is worth trying, but lemon pistachio is far superior."

"You spoil me, Rowan Davies."

"Only the best for my best," she said, her eyes lingering on mine before she stepped away to collect the goods.

There were no words for this moment. Meeting was inevitable, but not even my overthinking brain could've predicted how natural it would feel hanging out. I started picturing college—decorating our walls with Tide Wars swag, going to events together, helping each other study, making the same friends, and staying up for late-night roleplay group scenes with junk food.

A loud group of kids entered Stan's, snapping me from my fantasy. Rowan had started toward a table, but the kids gave me an idea and I reached out to stop her. "Let's take them to go instead."

"Why?" Rowan asked, her eyebrows arched. "What are you thinking?"

"We just got doughnuts, and we're going to Millennium Park

next," I said, shrugging. "It might not be Thanksgiving, and I might not be your dad, but if you want to live your tradition with someone who cares, I'm here."

Rowan looked at me, and for a moment I thought she was going to say it was the worst idea I'd ever had, but then her gentle smile told me otherwise. "That sounds perfect, Cassidy Williams. Let's do it."

"Cool," I said, relieved. "Lead the way."

We walked a block to the park, Rowan's smile lingering the entire time. She explained how in the summer several types of flowers bloomed, and occasionally there was an outdoor concert. Passing an area labeled Chase Promenade immediately made me think about *promenading* in *Bridgerton*, which was technically what Rowan and I were doing.

We stopped in front of our destination a minute later—the iconic Cloud Gate sculpture, also known as the Bean. The massive silver mirror in the shape of a bean reflected the large buildings behind it and people in front of it, including us. "This is incredible," I said, staring at it in awe.

"Right?" Rowan said, letting me take it in for a moment before leading us to a bench. She took the doughnuts out of the bag and ripped the Biscoff Pocket in half to share. "Welcome to Chicago, Captain."

"Many thanks, Champ," I said, picking up my doughnut in cheers. "Here's to hoping all meals here are this nutritious."

"Yes, nutrition is obviously at the top of my priorities list," she said sarcastically, tapping her doughnut against mine before taking a big bite and looking out at the people.

I laughed, glad she'd planned everything. Being fat meant being judged for liking the same less-than-healthy foods as most people. It didn't matter that I also liked healthier foods—eating a doughnut or slice of pizza meant I was unhealthy and lazy to the average nonfat onlooker, which was really messed up.

I was an introvert whose main hobbies included Netflix, roleplaying, and snuggling my ungrateful cat—eating only salads and counting calories wouldn't change that. And if that made me lazy and unhealthy, I could live with that opinion. What I couldn't live with was hating my body. I'd known from a young age that being fat made me different from other people, like how being a lesbian made me different. People thought and said all kinds of things about both, but there was a difference between them judging me and me judging myself. No matter what anyone else thought about me, I refused to be someone who hated myself for being who I was or how I looked. Period.

Rowan didn't care about any of that either. She knew what I liked to eat and rolled with it. No judgments. No comments. No weird facial expressions. She was equally supportive of me being a lesbian. She'd called me her hero for knowing myself like that, and for once she wasn't being sarcastic. I loved her for it.

Watching people together, we came up with several scenarios for why they were at the Bean. One couple had just gotten engaged and was in the city to celebrate. A group of friends was spending as much time together as possible before graduating and heading off to different colleges. An older woman came here every Saturday to walk the entire park and make friends with passing dogs. And then Rowan decided one man was a secret agent gone rogue and he was planning on using a Marvel-style gadget to shrink the Bean and steal it.

I snorted. "You're ridiculous."

"I'm serious!" Rowan said, her eyes shining. "We better get a closer look before he takes it and it's lost forever."

"So dramatic." I shook my head before popping the rest of my doughnut into my mouth and standing. "Let's go before the world ends next."

"That's the spirit," Rowan said, nudging me before approaching the Bean.

"We have a sculpture garden in Minneapolis, but nothing this level," I said after getting a good look.

"That's because you live there," Rowan said, nudging me. "Most people who live here don't pay attention to the Bean, but I love it. You know about my Thanksgiving tradition, but I also came here a lot this summer to people watch. Sometimes I'd photobomb."

I smiled at the image, but as we stepped closer to the Bean, I could see through its reflection that Rowan wasn't smiling. "Why photobomb?"

Her shoulders slumped as she looked at the ground, quiet for a moment. "My mom doesn't like to talk about my dad dying. And my brothers had already moved away by then. I guess photobombing made me feel like I was part of those families, even if I didn't know them."

I frowned, an ache building in my chest. Rowan rarely mentioned her dad after the night she'd cried on the phone. And she didn't talk about her family in general other than the occasional comment about Black Friday shopping with cousins and updates about funny things her mom did or said. "I didn't know you did that."

Rowan shrugged. "There's a lot you don't know about me."

Her reflection turned toward me, and I shifted to meet her eyes. "You know you can tell me anything, right?"

"I know," she said, her expression softening. "But there's no sadness or pity allowed today. You already made me feel things over eating doughnuts at the Bean, which I adore you for, but the quota has been reached. Let's focus on being tourists."

I knew all too well that some things were better left alone—at least until the right time. She'd say more when she was ready. "Do you want to photobomb families?" I asked.

"Not today," she said, grinning now. "I have my fam right here."

"Aw!" I said dramatically to avoid drawing attention to the fact that her cheesy line meant the world to me. "Okay then, fam. Let's do this."

We took a series of ridiculously posed pictures on her phone before smiling for the last few, then she brought us directly under the Bean to do it all over again. We finished as a gaggle of girls stared us down as if we were trespassing on *their* Bean. Rowan waved at them, giggling when two of them rolled their eyes. "I need a break from the cold. Ready to look at some art?"

I nodded, my shivering body grateful for the idea. "So ready."

We linked arms and promenaded toward an inclined walkway that led to the Art Institute of Chicago. The only thing I knew about it was that it housed the painting Cameron stared at in *Ferris Bueller's Day Off*. Dad didn't make a lot of time for movies, but he'd always been a sucker for John Hughes.

"Thanks for coming to my city," Rowan said as we started up the walkway. "Even if it was so your dad didn't feel guilty about leaving you home alone."

"I knew it was only a matter of time before we met," I said, looking at her. "And now that we have, and no one is a serial killer—"

"*Yet.*"

I nudged her. "You should come to Minneapolis so I can show you my city."

"Obviously I'm in," Rowan said, her smile widening. "When?"

Considering the invitation hadn't been planned, that was a good question. I took out my phone to look at my calendar as if I had a life. "I'd say my birthday, but it's a couple weeks before spring break, so that probably wouldn't work for you with traveling."

"Damn, I was going to suggest best friend prom dates," Rowan said.

I stopped, her words hitting me with a forgotten reality. "I can't go to prom," I said.

"Okay, obviously I was teasing," Rowan said.

"No, I mean I can't go at all," I said. "My mom and I were going to make my dress together. And it's not like it was with Ursula. I'd had that mostly finished, but the prom dress doesn't even have purchased fabric, let alone any work done. And I can't just buy a dress. We had a plan. We were going to—she—"

"Hey," Rowan said, her voice soft as she rested her hands on my shoulders. Her touch made me realize I was almost in tears. "You don't have to explain anything to me. And I'm sure Taylor will understand when you tell her why you can't go."

"But prom is such a big deal," I said, groaning at the image of me telling Taylor I wasn't going to prom. I didn't envy future Cass.

"Yes, but it's not everything," Rowan said, gently rubbing my shoulders. "A good girlfriend would understand, and Taylor sounds like a good girlfriend."

"She is," I said, letting out a slow, deep breath.

Rowan nodded. "Good, then it's settled. And as for visiting you, I can make your birthday work. I'll ditch school that Friday and head back Sunday. I *never* miss school, and my mom would let me skip for my best friend's birthday. What are your plans for it?"

Another good question. Another deep breath released. "No idea. I used to have friends over or go bowling or something, but Tate is my only Minneapolis friend these days. And Rachel, by extension."

"And Taylor."

"Yes, Taylor, too," I said, like it was news to me that Taylor was also a friend and not just a girlfriend. "But I could make plans with them another time."

"Or we could all hang out together," she said, her brows raised as a smirk formed. "Unless you want me all to yourself?"

Yes. I desperately wanted to keep my two lives separate, but Rowan didn't know that. Caught between a lie and the truth, I'd have to think of an explanation without explaining anything. Another future Cass dilemma. "We could have a little gathering at my house or all go out for dinner or something. But I don't want you to feel left out since you wouldn't know anyone else."

Rowan rolled her eyes, but her smile lingered. "I'm sure you'll find this impossible to believe given my snark and biting wit, but I'm actually good with people. I won't feel left out."

"You're right. I do find that hard to believe."

"Shut up." She nudged me again before dropping her arm from mine. We entered the museum, paying at the lobby before going in. "Okay, I know you're here to relive *Bueller* for your dad, but there's more in this museum worth checking out."

"Like what?" I asked, not doubting it.

"Uh, like Van Gogh. Picasso. Monet. Cézanne. Warhol. Dalí. O'Keeffe. Renoir. Do I need to continue?"

"You might want to. I'm not impressed by that list." I was beyond impressed.

Rowan turned to me—probably to bite back with some

snark—but one look from me caused her to grin all over again. "Captain," she said simply before walking away, her endearing tone lingering in my head.

We explored the museum for hours, and I recognized more art than expected. *American Gothic. The Bedroom* and Van Gogh's self-portrait. *The Old Guitarist.* And, of course, the *Bueller* painting, which I stared at Cam-style like the millions of tourists before me. Rowan took a picture of me doing it because I knew it would make Dad laugh.

After the museum, we walked toward Lou Malnati's for pizza. My phone dinged on the way, and I saw that Rowan had tagged me in an Instagram post of Bean pictures. The caption read: *Hanging out with the best of them.*

"Love the pictures," I said, my body warming. She always knew exactly what to say.

"Had to document your very first trip to Chicago," Rowan said. Her eyes widened. "Oh gods, I just realized! Your next trip here will probably be to tour UIC. Can you believe it?"

"If they accept me," I noted as I commented on the pictures with *You're the best* and two heart emojis, my own heart thumping with each tap. I still couldn't believe I was standing next to Rowan, let alone commenting on a picture she'd taken of us. "But if my grades continue to suck, I'll be lucky to graduate."

"Then get your shit together and it won't be a problem," she said. "You deserve to have all your dreams come true. And selfishly, I want to go to college together."

"I obviously want that, too," I said, a pit slowly forming in my stomach at the reminder that I really did need to get my shit together. "But it's easier said than done."

She stopped walking, touching my arm so I'd do the same. "Explain?"

I didn't want to spend our day together talking about my problems, but I had a habit of spilling everything to Rowan. Talking to her was like talking to myself. "It's like when you start down a path that you know isn't good for you, but you keep doing it because it's the only thing keeping you going."

"Not doing your homework keeps you going?" she asked.

"No, the roleplay keeps me going. You and the rest of Home Base keep me going."

Her head tilted slightly as she frowned, no doubt trying to piece together my nonsense. "But we're not good for you?"

My throat started to feel dry. "Not *you*. Never you. I mean it's not good for me to roleplay as much as I do or put online stuff before school stuff."

"Then take a break, or sign off earlier on school nights."

I sighed. "It's not that simple."

"Why not? Carina is absent ninety-five percent of the time, and you know I'm offline by a certain time when I have a test or a big project due. Same with Holly, even if she pretends to be too cool for academics."

"I know, but it's hard for me to flip that switch. I can't be *kind of* into something." My voice started shaking as my jumbled nerves caught up with me, and I let out a deep breath before continuing. "It's like addictive personality—all or nothing. I can't miss a group scene. I can't stop replying to one-on-one scenes just because it's bedtime. I've gotten slightly better since Taylor came along, but all that's done is add more time away from school."

Rowan was pulling everything out of me without trying. But I needed to let it out, and I knew she genuinely wanted to listen. "Ever since my parents started fighting more openly, I needed to fill my time to keep from overthinking more than I already did. And then my mom left, and that hole—I hate giving my brain time to remind me how not okay I am. So I keep busy with people who care about me. Home Base is my family. And I hate feeling needy, but I need you."

I didn't realize I was crying until Rowan's thumb brushed under my eye. "How can I help?" she asked.

"I don't know." I huffed another shaky breath as she wiped away the remaining tears. "I'm sorry. I didn't want to get into all of this today."

"No, but I'm glad we did." She linked arms with me and continued on—fair, because the cold had sunk in while we'd been standing there. "I basically did the opposite when my dad died. I didn't want to let anyone in."

"You let me in," I said.

"I did." She paused, the weight of silence heavy on my chest. "I could've gone down a dark path, and I wanted to, but you pulled me back that night on the phone. And yeah, the roleplaying has helped, too, but it wasn't everything." She squeezed my arm with her free hand. "It can get addicting, and I'm sorry it's affecting school, but it's not your entire life. I know we give Carina shit for not being around, but we still care about her. And you're *not* her. You genuinely want to be around, and you don't care what people think. If you need a night or week or however long off from online life, take it. The roleplay will be there when you get back, and if it's not, we'll survive. But no matter what, your friends will be there. *I'll* be there. Okay?"

"Okay," I said, releasing another deep breath. "Thank you."

"You got it." Her eyes stayed on mine for a moment before she stopped in front of Lou Malnati's. "Serious question. Are you ready to be forever changed by pizza?"

I took in her face, which was lit with enthusiasm. Despite all the emotions, this had been the best day I'd had in a really long time, and I was with one of my favorite people. I grinned back at her. No matter what came next, I was all in. "I'm ready."

[Home Base conversation]

**Holly:** Dying to hear about Chicago!

**Autumn:** Yes, tell us everything! Are you having the best time?

**Holly:** Are you both real people or is someone a secret serial killer?

**Holly:** My vote is on Rowan

**Autumn:** LOL!

**Autumn:** But seriously, hope it's the best time! <3

# TWELVE

We returned to Millennium Park after sharing a swoonworthy cheese deep-dish pizza. Rowan said she had a surprise for me, and my heart fluttered when she revealed it.

"Ta-da!" she said, turning back to me with a mischievous smirk on her face. I didn't know how I'd missed it before, but an ice-skating rink was situated on the level below the Bean.

She'd remembered.

Last year, Home Base had been talking about favorite winter activities, since most of us lived in colder climates. When Carina said she loved figure skating, I'd told them that I used to skate but had quit lessons after failing Basic Three level because I couldn't perfect the bunny hop. And because they'd made me wear a horrendous heart-shaped valentine costume that said *BE MINE* on it during an event. I hadn't been on the ice since.

"You realize I haven't done this since sixth grade, right?" I said in an attempt to hide how much it meant to me that she'd retained an offhand comment and turned it into a memory. "Do you want me to fall on my ass or something?"

"No, but that would be funny," she said, winking. "What I really want is for you to reconsider doing something you once loved."

Leave it to Rowan Davies to have the perfect reason for doing something I never thought I'd do again. I stared at the families, friend groups, couples, and solo artists as they moved around on the ice. It wasn't packed, but we'd be far from alone.

Reminding myself I was all in, I smiled. "Okay. Let's do it."

"Great attitude," Rowan said, patting me on the back. "Maybe you'll make it to Basic Four."

I gasped out a laugh. "Fuck you! And I'm not doing a bunny hop. I'll consider it a win if I don't fall and take you down with me."

"Challenge accepted."

After putting on rental skates, Rowan took my hand and slowly guided us onto the ice, assisting in my not-falling goal. We moved at a glacial pace for a couple of minutes before she spoke. "Why did you stop skating?"

I shrugged, glancing at her. "You already know why."

She stared at me pointedly. "You wouldn't quit because the moves got harder."

Damn, she was good. "I hated my body when I was younger," I said after a pause, looking at the ice again to focus—and to avoid *that look*. "My parents never got on my case about food or exercise, but my mom was always dieting despite being thinner, and her comments about herself really messed with how I viewed myself. And when I was in figure skating, the other girls were a lot smaller than me. They could bunny hop and I couldn't, and I was convinced it was because I was too fat—like my body was never going to let me get that tiny amount off the ground without punishing me by falling."

"But you don't think like that anymore," Rowan said, her tone softening. "What changed?"

"*I* did. When I realized I was a lesbian, I vowed to never hate myself for being different. And then it clicked that's what I'd been doing my entire life with my weight. I'd tried dieting, and all it did was make me feel miserable. And I think I'd tried hiding my sexuality in the beginning without realizing it, and obviously that didn't work either. It was suffocating, and lonely, and over time I became more comfortable, and I stopped thinking negatively about myself."

I realized we'd come to a stop near the edge of the rink, other skaters passing us with ease. Rowan was staring at me. There was no judgment on her face, but for once I couldn't figure out what she was thinking. "What?" I asked after the waiting started to feel like an ache.

"Nothing," she said as her cheeks reddened, probably from the cold. "I'm sorry you went through that. For what it's worth, I get it. Not in the exact same way, of course, but I think a lot of people our age go through some kind of identity crisis or imposter syndrome or whatever. It's like we're all suffering through something, but no one talks about it. And you're right, it does feel lonely."

I wanted to know what that meant for her, but I knew she'd tell me when she was ready. "Exactly. If only everyone our age was this great at talking about their feelings, we'd solve a lot of problems."

Rowan's eyes remained on mine as she laughed quietly. "Let's not get carried away about gross things like *feelings*," she said, nudging me gently before skating off.

After I'd quit skating, I was sure I'd never step foot in a rink again, but there I was. I'd missed the feeling of steel against ice. I'd missed thinking I was graceful despite having little grace. I'd missed being involved in something I loved despite it being hard. I'd missed fighting for something I wanted.

I stared after Rowan, feeling a warmth creep up my face as her words echoed in my ears. I was consumed by the sound of her laughter. The way she glided across the ice. The lingering feeling of her hand in mine. The way she'd remembered something so seemingly insignificant and turned it into everything. The chills I got when she called me by my nickname. The way her smile had lit up the entire block when she'd stepped out of Stan's. The way the mysterious side of her wasn't a mystery at all. It was something else, something so much bigger. My eyes widened as every moment flooded my brain, heading straight for my heart.

Oh, *shit*.

We skated until our toes started to feel numb—not that I was able to focus enough to enjoy it. All I could do was internally panic over how I totally had a crush on my best friend.

And I couldn't tell her.

For one, Rowan was straight. She'd respond perfectly about my feelings if she ever found out because that's how she was, but it could still make our friendship awkward. But also—and more importantly—I had a girlfriend. It was new and scary, and I worried about us having different levels of experience, but none of that erased the fact that I liked her.

Even if I didn't, I could never be with Rowan Davies.

So it was decided—I wouldn't say anything. We'd stay friends, and I'd get over the feelings thing and focus on my girlfriend. Everything would be fine.

"What's up?"

I blinked a few times before looking at Rowan. We were back in our boots and heading toward the hotel, and of course she knew something was going on.

"I don't want today to end," I said like the coward I was. At least it wasn't a lie. "Thanks for showing me your world and taking me skating."

"You're welcome," she said slowly, not pushing it, though I was sure she saw right through my response. "And speaking of showing our worlds, tell me what I need to know about me seeing yours."

"What do you mean?" I asked.

"Like, what do your friends think about roleplaying? Do they think we're all weirdos, or do they think it's cool? And what did they think about you meeting up with a real-life stranger today?" She shrugged. "I'm trying to figure out if I need to be extra charming or what it'll take to convince them I'm seminormal and a total badass."

I'd normally answer with a snarky comment, but how could I? My body threatened to collapse in on itself as my heart started racing. "I didn't tell anyone I was meeting up with you," I admitted quietly.

She stopped abruptly, confusion written all over her face. "Why not?"

"It would've been a lot to explain."

"Would it?" she asked, her eyebrows raising. "You could've said you were meeting up with your roleplay bestie. That's what I told my mom. Sounds pretty simple to me."

"It's not, actually," I said, clasping my hands together to feel grounded enough to let out the truth. "No one in my life knows about the roleplay."

"What?" Rowan's face fell. "I thought you'd told Taylor about us a while ago."

Her pained look broke my heart. I wanted to run, but I couldn't hide this from her anymore. If she was going to visit, she needed to know everything. "Last time it came up in Home Base, I said I hadn't told her yet. But that doesn't mean I *never* will."

"Well, I guess that makes sense since it's a new relationship," she said. "But obviously Tate knows. And your dad." When I didn't say anything, she groaned. "I can't believe this. After everything we talked about with Carina—you know how much it bothered me that she keeps us a secret. But you've been doing the same thing this entire time."

"It's not like Carina's situation," I said, as if that made it better. "She clearly has some hang-ups about her image. You know I don't care about that shit."

"I thought you didn't, but now I don't know what to think. Why else would you keep something like this a secret?"

"I have my reasons."

"Like what?" she pressed.

Looking at her face—those eyes—I knew I had to tell her *everything*. "My parents have always been weird about internet strangers, and then my mom left us for someone she met online. And before that, I didn't tell them because if they knew it was part of the reason I sucked at school the last year, they would've made me stop because—" I shuffled my feet. "I mentioned my addictive personality earlier, but this isn't the first time it's affected my life. I got addicted to gaming after quitting ice-skating. It really freaked my parents out, freaked *me* out, and they made me stop. And I know if I tell my dad about roleplaying, he'll think it's the same as my gaming addiction and take my phone and laptop away. And Tate knows all about the gaming thing, too, and would tell my dad out of concern. But roleplaying isn't like the gaming—it's not as bad. I have a handle on it."

Rowan's eyebrows furrowed. "Do you, though?" she asked.

"Yes," I said firmly. "And I could technically tell Taylor, but that's a whole different problem."

"Why?"

I groaned at the memory. "We saw these girls on Halloween wearing Aresha and Roux costumes. She told me she'd hated the first Tide Wars book, and I panicked. And now it's easier not telling her. And between that and my mom leaving—I don't want to lose anyone else."

We stared at each other for several seconds before she exhaled slowly. "How did I not know about any of this? I thought we told each other everything."

"We do," I said, my heart sinking at her words. "Almost. But this thing is really hard for me to talk about, and I didn't want to upset you."

"I think it's too late for that," she said, shaking her head. "I've never hid roleplaying from anyone in my life. My dad always thought it was badass I was making a fictional world my own, and with friends. He encouraged it, sometimes read scenes and gave me new things to think about, like I was writing a book or something."

"And that's awesome," I said genuinely, not wanting to take that from her. "But it's different for me. My offline life was crumbling, and I needed somewhere I could breathe. I didn't want to blend this amazing new thing with the world that constantly reminded me life was disappointing. And then Carina convinced me not telling Taylor was the right decision, and for some reason I believed her."

Rowan blinked at the latest admission. "You took Carina's advice over talking to me?" she said quietly. "So you *are* embarrassed by it. By us."

I frowned, stepping closer. "No, that's not what I'm saying."

"You don't have to," she said, stepping back. "It's pretty obvious."

"That's not fair."

"Isn't it?" Rowan asked, every inch of her face lined with hurt I'd caused. "You say we're all like this little found family, but no one else in your life knows about us. Isn't that kind of messed up?"

"Rowan—"

"Isn't it?" she asked again, her voice raising, shaking.

"Yes, okay?" I said, my heart pounding as I spiraled. "You're right. It's messed up. But it has nothing to do with being embarrassed."

"Then what did you plan on telling people when I visited? Who would I be to you?"

"I don't know," I admitted, my brain not getting that far. "I guess I could say you're a church-camp friend or something."

Her eyebrows shot up. "You went to church camp?"

I grimaced at the memory of Jesus songs and childhood bullies. "Yeah, once. It was awful."

The fact that Rowan didn't smile or make a joke about it was proof enough that I'd severely messed up. "So you would've asked me to lie about how we knew each other and never told them the truth?" she asked.

"I didn't have it all planned out. But yeah, I guess so, at least for a while."

Rowan stared at me for a few agonizing seconds. "I won't lie for you. And I won't ask you to out this part of your life, so I guess it's probably best that I don't come in March."

My heart sank. "Are you serious?"

"Yes, I'm serious!" she yelled, surprising me. She wasn't a quiet person, but I'd never expected her to yell at me. I'd never expected to hurt her to a point where yelling was valid. "I won't be someone I'm not."

People were staring as they passed, but I tuned them and the sounds of passing cars out as I focused on Rowan. I wanted to take back everything I'd said to make her smile again, but I also knew I wouldn't tell everyone this thing about me that I wasn't ready to share. Suddenly, I wished my feelings for her were my only dilemma. "I'm sorry, Rowan. I really am."

"Yeah, me too," she said, wiping at her cheek as a tear fell. "You know, for someone who just talked about not hating herself for being different, you're going to a lot of trouble to hide this thing that's not a big deal. You might think you have good reasons, but you're hurting people, and they don't even matter enough to you for them to know it."

My mouth opened in shock, and she blinked back at me like she knew she'd gone too far but wouldn't take it back. "I'm gonna go," she said, walking away before I could find the words to make this right. Frozen almost literally in place from the cold, I watched her retreat as my own tears threatened to spill. What the hell just happened?

I ran to the hotel after that, making it to the room before the crying unleashed.

The rest of my first trip to Chicago was trash. Dad knew something was off immediately, but he didn't try to force it out of me. We ate burgers that night and visited Chinatown the next morning before our flight home. I'd originally wanted to stay longer, but I was relieved to get home, curl up with Tuttles, watch Netflix, and stare at technology.

I didn't reach out to Rowan. Part of me hoped she'd message our private server or get back to our current scene, but in reality I knew better. I'd caused a rift, and it would take time before she'd let me fix it.

That didn't stop the others from mentioning the trip. I read the messages from Holly and Autumn, the joke about Rowan being a potential serial killer making me feel sick considering I was the one who'd serial-killed our friendship.

**Cass:** Sorry to disappoint, but we're both real people, no killers

**Cass:** And I had the best time!

**Autumn:** Yay! I'm so happy

**Holly:** Seconded. That's awesome!

**Holly:** Now we need a group gathering. Do your parents believe in planes, Autumn, or is there a moral code against them?

**Autumn:** I think planes are on the approved list. Save your shock.

**Holly:** Can't because I'm SHOCKED.

Pretending everything was okay was a special brand of torture, but what I'd written wasn't a lie. I'd had the best time—at least until the end. Spending time with Rowan Davies came as easily as breathing, and I was kicking myself for messing it all up.

At least I hadn't made it worse by telling her about my feelings.

I hoped our fight didn't ruin things for everyone else. Carina being around less was a shitty-but-expected reality, but we couldn't lose Rowan. *I* couldn't lose Rowan.

[Unfinished one-on-one scene between Cass and Rowan]

**Cass:** "What were you thinking?" Aresha yelled as her hands worked quickly to clean Roux's stab wound. If she stayed mad about someone trying to kill her, no other emotions could slip out.

**Rowan:** Roux let out a shallow laugh. "You act like this is the first time I've almost died for you, Captain. For the record, it's not."

**Cass:** "I cannot lose you," Aresha said firmly, her voice shaking. "You are not allowed to leave me, not for any reason. Do you understand?"

**Rowan:** Roux met her eyes, groaning at the sharp pain that came with being healed. "Understood. I'll let them kill you next time."

**Cass:** "Thank you," Aresha said, as if it were some kind of compliment.

# THIRTEEN

New Year's Eve arrived, and I forced myself out of my roleplaying and Netflix stupor to get ready. By the time Taylor and her parents picked me up for the party, I'd curled my hair, put on makeup, and changed into a sparkly black dress.

I texted Tate on my way out to let him know we'd be at the party soon. We hadn't talked much since his dad had been in town for Christmas and I was busy feeling like shit over Rowan, but I was excited to see him and catch up.

"How was Chicago?" Taylor's dad asked once we were on our way.

"Good, thanks," I said vaguely, smiling at him in the rearview mirror. "It's a really cool city."

"It sure is," he agreed before launching into a story about a trip he and Taylor's mom had taken there before they got married.

But I couldn't focus on it. My head was wrapped up in all the things I hadn't said about my trip—all the things I *couldn't* say.

And then Taylor's hand found mine, and I jumped, accidentally knocking it away.

"Are you okay?" she asked, concern etched on her face. "You've been acting weird since getting back."

"Have I?" I asked, my nerves prickling.

"Yes. All of your texts have been delayed, and short." She leaned in to talk more quietly—not that her parents were paying attention as they swooned up front over memories. "Did I do something wrong?"

"Of course not," I said, taking her hand now like that would prove it. "I promise this isn't a you thing. But I don't really want to talk about it, if that's okay. Tonight is for fun."

Taylor bit her lip, but she smiled it off. "You're right. Tonight is for fun. But I'm here if you want to talk at some point, okay?"

"Thanks." I smiled a little and squeezed her hand before looking out the window.

I was a fraud. Logically, it was the perfect night for telling her about my secret life so we could go into the new year with full honesty, but it didn't *feel* right yet. I hoped it would change after she finished reading Tide Wars—and when my Rowan feelings subsided.

As if I had any control over that.

I shoved unwanted thoughts aside as we stopped in front of Greg's house, and Taylor's mom shifted to look at us. "Have fun, girls. Text when you're ready to leave." The glow of her smile made me feel like she knew something I didn't, and I tried pushing that aside too as I got out and followed Taylor to the door.

We squeezed through the crowd and got drinks before Taylor led us to her best friends. Fynn was Black and gay, and he had one of the most charming smiles I'd ever seen. June was white and bi with purple hair, but she dyed it different colors regularly. They were both in newspaper with Taylor and Rachel. I knew them from the classes we'd been in together over the years, but like Taylor, I'd always thought they were too cool for me in a nerdy, queer trio kind of way.

I tried keeping up with their conversation, but I didn't understand the inside jokes. And my mind was elsewhere. Rowan had told Home Base about going to a party with her cousin who was in college. Despite her not speaking to me or responding to our unfinished scene, I hoped she got in a few drinks, danced, made friends with people who were better for her than me, and had someone to kiss at midnight.

Okay, maybe I didn't actually *hope* for that last one, but she deserved it.

I checked my phone, but Discord and Instagram didn't give me the result I wanted. No word from Rowan. No new pictures. Nothing.

"Cass?"

I blinked, my eyes shooting to Taylor and her friends. "Sorry, I'm here. What's up?"

"I was saying I can't believe we've only been dating for two months," Taylor said, smiling a little. "It feels like longer—in a good way, obviously."

"Oh, for sure," I agreed, pausing to drink whatever concoction she'd put together for me.

"Maybe that's because y'all were crushing on each other forever," June said, nudging Taylor.

"That's totally it," Fynn agreed, grinning. "This girl used to talk about you *all the time*."

"Shut up, it wasn't all the time," Taylor said, flushing.

"It happened frequently," June agreed. "Still does."

"*And* I spent months convincing her to ask you out," Fynn added proudly, standing taller. "You're welcome."

I laughed nervously, as if Taylor's friends would see through me at any moment and call my ass out for being a terrible girlfriend. "I'm glad you were there to guide her. I have zero game, so if Taylor hadn't made the first move, we wouldn't be together."

"A travesty," Fynn said solemnly, resting a hand over his heart. "But here we are."

"Here we are," Taylor echoed as she held up her drink. "Cheers to me for doing something about it. May we all survive high school and face the real world together."

Her friends cheered as I tapped my drink against hers, wishing I had something cute or complimentary to say, but nothing landed. I forced a grin and drank more instead, my insides twisting as I thought about her words.

Why did college feel so far away? What if Taylor and I ended up in different states? How could we face the real world together from a distance when I could barely keep it together in the same city? And if I still wasn't comfortable getting physically closer to her by college, would she even want to be with me?

They went back to talking, this time about *Fortnite*, and I looked at my phone to check on Rowan's life again and see if Tate had replied. Nothing. I texted him again before looking back at the others, nodding along.

We spent the next couple of hours talking to more of Taylor's friends, drinking, and dancing, but Tate never showed up. I almost called him when he finally texted to say they weren't going to make it. He didn't reply when I asked why.

By the time people started counting down to midnight, Taylor and I were dancing in the middle of a packed living room. I had trouble meeting her eyes, my mind stuck on my besties. What was going on with Tate? And how long was Rowan going to hate me? And what was she doing right now? Was she about to kiss some college guy who had his arms around her? Was he looking into those eyes that made me want to—

Taylor's hands rested on my face, and I snapped back to the present to hear her counting down from five with everyone else. The world slowed as her gaze locked on mine, and she leaned in closer as midnight struck. "I love you," she said before kissing me.

I kissed her back out of instinct, but the rest of me was frozen. When we pulled away, Taylor had a look about her that I'd remember for the rest of my life—like I was her entire world. But she couldn't have said what I thought she'd said. We weren't there yet. It was too soon. It was all too soon. "You what now?"

She rested her forehead against mine. "I said I love you. I tried saying it at Christmas with the cross-stitch heart, but I was so nervous I couldn't form the words. So I'm saying it now." She giggled. "Thanks, alcohol."

My sweet, thoughtful, cool girlfriend deserved only the best, and I couldn't give it to her. Of course I liked her, but I didn't *love* her. And the expression on her face made me think about the odd look her mom had given me in the car. Had she known this was going to happen? Obviously she couldn't have prepared me for this, but damn, a better hint would've been nice. I could've had more time to spiral over what to say.

"Cass?"

I blinked, realizing I had to say something. "You're great."

Her smile faded as she stepped back. "That's—thanks?"

The combination of noise and alcohol and Taylor's confession overwhelmed me, and I felt hot. "Can we go somewhere quieter?" I asked.

Taylor looked mortified, but she nodded and took my hand, weaving us through the crowd until we were in a guest room that was miraculously empty.

"I'm sorry," I said, knowing I should speak first. "I've never said those words before. And it was unexpected. I mean, I thought we'd agreed to take things slow."

"I know we did, but I can't help how I feel," Taylor said,

frowning. "And I'm sorry I sprung that on you. Please tell me I haven't scared you off. I don't want to lose you."

No matter what was going on in my head with Rowan, I didn't want to break up with Taylor. And her feelings complicated things, but it wasn't *bad*. I stepped closer, pressing my forehead to hers as if I could transport us back to the midnight countdown for a do-over. "I'm not going anywhere," I said. "And thank you for being honest, but I'm just not there yet. If liking you is enough, then we're good."

"It's enough," Taylor said quietly.

"Good."

We lingered together for a moment before Taylor pulled back, taking out her phone. "I'll have my parents come pick us up. It's getting late."

Pretending I wanted to stay longer wouldn't land, and no part of me blamed her for wanting to leave, so I nodded. "Yeah, a ride sounds good. Thanks."

After Taylor's dad confirmed they were on their way, we navigated through the party and put on our coats. A pit formed in my stomach as I watched various couples dance and make out, blissfully happy. That should've been us, but instead I barely let my girlfriend touch me, and I continued to keep secrets. And through it all, she was damn near perfect.

I didn't deserve her.

The cold air hit us as we stepped outside, and a light snow was in the process of coating Greg's yard. My eyes moved to the tree where Taylor and I had first kissed, and I wanted to go back to that night for a fresh start. I could've explained everything about Tide Wars and roleplaying. I could've told her about my lack of experience so she knew what she was getting into before feeling too much. I could've saved her the pain I'd caused tonight when I didn't tell her I loved her too.

Instead, we stood in silence on the steps, waiting for a car that would take us away from the house where she'd declared her love and I'd broken a piece of her heart.

Lights were on when I arrived home, instantly triggering my paranoia. Cautiously, I unlocked the door and went inside. Dad was sitting on the couch in the living room, tapping his phone. No, *texting.* "I thought you had to work," I said after letting out a deep exhale.

Dad instantly turned off his screen, clearing his throat. "I said I couldn't drive you tonight. I didn't say anything about having to work."

He looked nice—like, not-dressed-to-be-hanging-out-alone nice. And his cheeks were flushed. I knew exactly what it meant because my cheeks did the same thing. "You've been drinking."

"If you're allowed, I think I am too."

*"Dad."*

"You know, I'm glad you were responsible tonight by getting a ride, but I don't love the image of a tipsy daughter, so let's calm the parties for a while, yeah?"

"Of course," I agreed easily. "But back to the point. Wherever you were out drinking tonight, shouldn't you still be there? It's not even one."

He shrugged. "I wanted to be here when you got home."

Okay, adorable dad moment, but something else was going on. My eyes widened. "Wait, were you on a *date*?"

Looking immediately guilty, he patted the spot beside him. "Sit with me?"

"You were *totally* on a date!" I sat, pushing aside my Taylor guilt in favor of this conversation. "Tell me *all* about it."

"You don't think it's too soon?" he asked, smiling sheepishly. "The divorce isn't final quite yet, and I don't want to put more on your shoulders."

"No offense to our shitty situation, but I think if Mom can move across the country to be with someone else, you're allowed to go on a date. Stop stalling and tell me things."

"There's not much to tell," he said, shrugging. "If it turns into something serious, you'll be the first to know. But I don't want to rush into anything."

I rolled my eyes at his adult answer. I'd expected to feel something negative when Dad moved on because it would solidify the already-known reality that my parents were never, ever getting back together. Instead, I was relieved. And happy—*so* happy. "I expect details the moment it becomes serious. And I have to meet her to approve before it gets *too* serious."

"Obviously," Dad agreed, chuckling. "But speaking of dates,

how was yours? Did you keep it PG?"

I groaned. "You really shouldn't ask that kind of question. But yes, it was *very* PG." I played with the fabric of my dress, pausing. "She told me she loves me."

"Wow," Dad said, quickly covering his surprise with a smile. "That's great, honey."

"Yeah." I looked down at my hands. "I didn't say it back."

"Do we not want her loving you?"

I leaned against the couch with a heavy sigh, not knowing where to begin. "I don't know. I thought taking Christmas off the table meant we could slow things down a bit, but that obviously didn't happen. And I know you can't help feelings, but I feel terrible for not being on the same level. I mean, is something wrong with me?"

"Not a single thing," he said, resting an arm across my shoulders. "Some people move through the motions at different speeds. I told your mom I loved her months before she said it back."

"You did?" I asked, not sure why that surprised me.

He huffed a laugh. "Oh yeah. Scared the hell out of her too. But we got through it, and we had a really good thing for a really long time."

"I don't know if this is helping the way you think it is," I said, resting my head on his shoulder. "But thanks. I feel a little better."

"All that matters," he said, kissing the top of my head. "Now I think it's time for us to both get some sleep."

"You want me to go upstairs so you can go back to texting and grinning like a kid," I teased, pulling back to shoot him a pointed look.

"Okay, guilty," Dad said, proving me right as a wide grin hit his face.

"Fortunately for you, I'm exhausted," I said, standing. "Good night, Cool Dad."

"Good night, kid."

I plucked Tuttles from the stairs on my way, depositing him on my comforter. After changing and washing my face, I curled up in bed with my laptop. One of the roleplayers who had four characters and was always complaining about something had sent me an out-of-character message about another roleplayer offending her. Having no fucks to give about that tonight, I clicked on Home Base.

> **Autumn:** HNY, Cari!
>
> **Autumn:** HNY, Ro and Cass!
>
> **Holly:** It feels like we're in a different world from them for these next couple hours. Should we stage a riot in past year?
>
> **Autumn:** I thought you were going to a party?
>
> **Holly:** Plans changed. I'm taking advantage of having the house to myself since step-douche always hogs the TV. And I opened his expensive scotch. He owes me.
>
> **Autumn:** For what?
>
> **Holly:** Existing
>
> **Autumn:** lol have fun and be safe!

**Rowan:** Harpy now year! Im drnks

**Holly:** Proud of you!

**Autumn:** Be safe, Ro! And Cass!

**Rowan:** LOL shes fine.. always perfeect

**Rowan:** Perefct Cassidy Williasm!!

**Holly:** Getting awk Rowan. I'm going to focus on my movie and scotch. Night, all <3

I read Rowan's replies multiple times. We hadn't spoken since Chicago, and *this* was how she wanted to handle it? She probably needed more space, but I was calling her before I could fully rationalize it. Sounds of music and other people filled my ear a few rings later. "Hello?" I said after a moment.

"Hello yourself," Rowan said, a slight slur in her voice.

I could picture her drunken state—leaning against a wall, hair all over the place, smiling like a goof. But imagining her this way felt wrong. All of it felt wrong. "Why did you call me perfect when it was clearly a dig?"

"Because you are!" Rowan yelled over the music. "Or you think you are. Why else would you pretend none of us exist?"

"I already told you why."

"And I call bullshit. You're either embarrassed or don't want us in your real life—just like Carina."

I sighed, not sober or awake enough for this. "I wouldn't have met up with you last week if I didn't want you in my life. And I'm sorry for hurting you. That's the last thing I wanted."

She must've gone into a different room, because the music

became less jarring. "Do the others know they're a secret?" she asked.

"No, you're the only person I've told," I said, feeling sick all over again thinking about the look on her face when I'd told her everything. The hurt. The disappointment. The tears. "I really am sorry, Rowan."

"Being sorry doesn't change the facts. I—ugh! You matter to me. People in my life know all about the roleplay and Home Base. Why is it hard for you to let us be a part of your life? You say we're best friends, but *are we*?"

"Of course we are," I said, desperately wanting her to believe me. "You're not some random person, okay? You're so much more than that. But it's complicated."

"Why? What about this is complicated?"

"I don't know how to explain it more than I already have."

"Well, that's perfect," Rowan said, her voice shaky. "Happy fucking new year, Cassidy Williams."

The line went dead. Rowan Davies hung up on me, and I'd made her cry. Again.

The obvious solution was to tell everyone the truth and deal with whatever came next, but I wasn't ready. And I couldn't let this part of my life out for someone else. It needed to feel like the right decision for me, and it didn't yet. I couldn't risk Dad taking my safe haven away.

Still, it gutted me that I'd hurt her.

Tears formed as I tried calling her back. I was full-on crying by the time her voice mail picked up. "I'm sorry," I said before hanging up and sobbing into my pillow.

Whatever happened next, I needed to get over my feelings. I was close to choking on all my secrets, and I wouldn't let this one ruin my relationship with Taylor or the shred of hope I had for getting Rowan back in my life.

Tate came over the next morning for waffles—a New Year's Day tradition since we were eleven. He wasn't off the hook for bailing on the party, but something told me I wasn't the only one in need of best friend time.

"What happened last night?" I asked as we fist-bumped in the doorway. "Why weren't you at the party?"

"Good morning to you too." Tate walked by me to take off his boots. "Rachel didn't want to go, so we kept it low-key at her place instead."

Seriously? "That's not an answer. We'd planned on meeting there."

He let out an exasperated breath. "I'm sorry for disappointing you, C, but this has nothing to do with you."

I blinked, taken aback at his annoyed tone. I'd heard it a number of times over the years, but never directed at me. "I didn't say it did, but I was hoping for a little explanation. Last night was a lot."

"It was a lot for me, too," Tate said, nudging his boots aside as he looked back at me. "So who's going first?"

"You talk. I'll start the waffles."

He followed me to the kitchen and sat at the island, quiet for a beat. "Rachel is starting to get nervous about the future, like college and everything."

"All the more reason to kick back and enjoy the present," I said, trying to sound optimistic. It didn't land.

Tate snorted. "I tried that approach, but it only upset her more. College is eight months away, and she's already obsessing over the what-ifs. She's set on California, and I'm obviously staying here."

I nodded, knowing he'd already been accepted to the University of Minnesota with a football scholarship. "That's rough." I looked back at him, feeling like there was more. "You didn't break up, did you?"

"No, but it's starting to feel inevitable. And I'm not ready. I love her, you know?"

I did. It took years for me and Rachel to warm up to each other after she'd moved here in ninth grade, but Tate had been into her immediately. And college would change things for everyone, but I didn't want that to mean the end of their relationship. I couldn't picture him being with anyone else. "I'm sorry, Tate. I hope you figure it out."

"Thanks, C." He went into his own head for a moment. "Anyway, distract me. Tell me your thing."

"Right, my thing." I went back to mixing the batter. "Taylor told me she loves me at the party last night, and I didn't say it back. And I'm kind of freaking out about it because I don't know if I'm just not there yet or if something else is going on. I mean,

I had a crush on her for years. You'd think I'd love her back, but when she said it, I froze. Maybe I don't know what love feels like, but I know it's supposed to feel bigger than a crush."

"And this doesn't?"

"Exactly. And she said it was fine I didn't say it, but I hate feeling like I'm letting her down."

"All you can do is be honest with her," Tate said after a pause. "If you're not there yet, that's cool. But if it's bigger than that and you don't think you'll ever love her, tell her. Neither of you should be stuck in something if it doesn't feel right."

I groaned, the pit in my stomach growing. "Gods, you're right. I like hanging out with her, and the kissing is great, but it's like something is holding me back from being all in."

"Maybe this has something to do with your mom," Tate said, holding his hands up when I narrowed my eyes at him. "Listen, I'm just saying. You started dating Taylor, like, five seconds after she left. And I'm not judging, but that's a lot at once. Maybe letting her in and trusting her is hard because your mom ripped open a wound that hasn't healed yet."

This wasn't the first time I'd considered the possibility, and I knew there was some truth to his words. But even though the timing had been a void-filling factor, I wasn't convinced my feelings—or lack of—were related to it. "It's not that. I'm healing fine, and Dad and I are moving on. He had a date last night."

"Damn! Get it, Dr. Williams."

"Tate!"

"Sorry," he said, laughing quietly. "I'm glad you're both moving on. And if you say Taylor stuff isn't mom-related, then okay."

His tone said something else, but I didn't want to linger on it. "I need to figure out what I want before I make things worse."

"And when you do—"

"Be honest, I know," I said, groaning at the reminder of how many things I'd kept secret from Taylor already. "Thanks, Tate."

"You got it. Now, are you gonna stir that batter all day or what?"

"Shut up and take the juice out," I said, smiling as I started the first waffle.

Tate was right; I needed to be honest with Taylor. At least about some things. The rest I'd need to think about, but I *would* think about it. She deserved to know me better, even if I wasn't ready to share everything yet.

# FOURTEEN

First-semester finals came and went in mid-January, and I was half-convinced I'd failed everything. After a late-night roleplaying session with Autumn, I'd slept in and missed my econ final. Mr. Blake had generously allowed me take the final later that day, but I dreaded the result.

I added the missed final to my growing list of senior-year fails, including skipping several gym days to roleplay in the bathroom and failing a handful of quizzes and small assignments because of a one-on-one or group scene that kept me up late. I'd also lost my standing as the girl people tried to cheat off of in French after too many wrong answers.

Shutting off my second-life brain had been harder than I'd hoped, especially after I started staring at my phone even more in case Rowan reached out. Other than the occasional roleplay response—no doubt wanting to keep up appearances for the group—she never did.

When Mr. Blake asked me to stay after class on the first day of second semester, I officially started to panic. Econ had been replaced by government, but I still had to deal with Mr. Blake. I was exhausted from staying up late roleplaying the night before, and his disappointed expression made it worse. It was like he could smell my guilt the moment I'd entered the room.

"Here's the thing, Miss Williams," he said once the room had cleared. "Last semester was pretty abysmal for you. Your grades will post after school today, but I wanted to let you know you got a D in economics."

I stared back at him, unable to believe what he'd said. Okay, I *believed* it. My head had been in the wrong place when taking the final, and I hadn't done stellar otherwise. As someone who'd gotten all As and Bs her first two years of high school and a few Cs junior year, this was horrifying. The only saving grace for college was that I'd crushed my ACTs over the summer. But there was a chance that wouldn't be enough anymore.

"It's a passing grade," Mr. Blake continued when I failed at words. "But I'm concerned. I know you want to go to college, but your lack of effort tells a different story. And most of your other teachers feel the same. So what's the deal? Is stuff still off at home, or is it something else? Your girlfriend, maybe?"

I'd already been through a parade of teacher sympathy after Mom left, but his second comment put me on edge. "My girlfriend has nothing to do with my grades."

He looked at me for a moment as if he could stare a confession out of me. "Regardless, I'm going to tell you what I've told the boys on the football team. The person you're with now isn't who you'll be with five years from now. They aren't worth throwing away your future."

Instinct told me to defend Taylor, but that would result in more questions I didn't want to answer. "Respectfully, sir, who I date isn't your business."

Mr. Blake sighed, no doubt tired of my bullshit. *Same.* "You probably don't care much about what I do here, Miss Williams, but it's my job to make sure you graduate and move on with your life, whatever that means for you. I don't want you to fail, but if things continue to escalate, you're on track for getting held back—meaning no graduation."

My eyes filled with tears as his words sank in, shame flooding me. "I'll try harder," I said, looking at anything that wasn't him. "I want to graduate and go to college."

"That's what I'd hoped you'd say." He held out a tissue box, continuing after my shaking hand took one. "If you're serious about working harder, we'll figure something out. But I won't let you slide through if things stay the same as last semester. Understood?"

"Yeah, understood." I dabbed at my cheeks, mortified for crying in front of him. But I'd needed to hear that. "You really want to help me?"

Mr. Blake laughed, shaking his head. "I'm not a villain, Miss Williams. I believe in second chances. And whatever is going on in your life, I hope you figure it out. You're a smart kid, and I want you to succeed. Really."

I'd always assumed Mr. Blake was one of those jock teachers who wanted to relive their football glory days and used teaching as a way to do it. I'd never expected him to genuinely give a damn—even if only so he didn't have to teach me again next year. Gods, I didn't want that either. "Thank you, sir," I said, exhaling. "I appreciate it."

"Don't get too excited," he said as he opened a drawer to rifle through it. "The school will need to call your dad and make sure he's updated on everything."

I knew there'd be a catch. It made sense since Dad had talked to the school about my absences last semester, but that didn't mean I was ready for a big talk with him. "Yeah, for sure. Thanks for the warning."

"You got it." He pulled out a late pass slip and signed it for my next teacher, handing it over with a small smile. "Now get out of here and let me enjoy my break."

I nodded and escaped to my next class, hoping this was the last of my awkward teacher talks. It was time to get my shit together—for real this time.

As if the day hadn't been uncomfortable enough, life dropped another bomb on me after school. I met Taylor at the Crosstrek to drive her to work, and she greeted me by practically shoving her phone in my face. "Who's this?" she asked, her breath fogging in front of me because of the cold temperature outside.

I looked at it, my heart breaking all over again at Rowan's Instagram picture of us at the Bean. It amazed me how happy we looked when I'd managed to mess it all up hours later. "My friend Rowan," I said, trying to play it cool despite dying inside.

Taylor frowned. "You didn't mention hanging out with some-one in Chicago."

I handed the phone back, scrambling for an explanation. "How did you find this?" I asked instead.

She blinked. "Seriously? You hide some girl from me but want to know how I found out about her?"

"I wasn't *hiding* her," I said defensively, but of course she had a point. "And she's not *some girl*. She's a friend."

A part of me thought if Rowan were interested in girls, she could maybe be more than *just a friend* one day, but that wasn't the reality we lived in. And I didn't want Taylor getting the wrong idea when I was trying to make us work.

"People don't hide friends," Taylor said. Her eyes boring into mine made the seconds feel like hours, and my hands started to sweat. "Is this why you started acting weird after Chicago? Is she the reason you don't love me?"

I quickly shook my head. "What happened on New Year's has nothing to do with Rowan. We got in a fight when I was there, and it threw me off for a while. But none of that had anything to do with you."

"What did it have to do with, then?" she asked, folding her arms across her chest.

"She found out that no one in my life knew about her, and she got upset. I messed up. And obviously I messed up with you too. I'm sorry."

Taylor's eyebrows arched. "Why wouldn't anyone know about her? How do *you* know her?"

"Church camp."

The words were out before I could say the ones she deserved to hear. I had yet another chance to come clean and trust her with an important part of my life, but instead I made the same mistake all over again.

"Church camp," Taylor repeated slowly. "I didn't realize you were religious."

"It was a long time ago." I made a face. "It's not exactly something I go around bragging about, you know?"

"Yeah." Her eyes continued to linger on me as they narrowed. "And you promise you're just friends? Nothing happened in Chicago that I need to know about?"

"I promise," I said firmly, knowing that much was true. What happened in my brain couldn't be controlled, and I wouldn't let that ruin our relationship.

Her shoulders slumped as she looked at her phone. "Okay, well, we should get going. I can't be late for work, and it's freezing."

I wanted to ask if we were okay, but I took the subject change as good enough. No matter how risky it was, hiding my double life and a crush I wouldn't pursue felt like the right decision for now.

I didn't want people asking how my roleplay was going or if I was talking to my nerd friends every time I sent a text. I didn't want them knowing it was the only thing holding me together most days since my mom had left. And I didn't want them to accuse me of being addicted when I knew my talk with Mr. Blake had kicked me into gear.

Keeping it to myself was worth the risk.

It *needed* to be worth it.

After dropping Taylor off at work, I went home to figure out how to deal with Dad. Since nothing would prevent that disappointed-parent look, I made spaghetti and garlic bread for dinner and waited for him to dole out my punishment.

We ate in silence for most of dinner; then Dad cleared his throat. "I heard from the school today. They're concerned about your grades and unexplained absences last semester. Why didn't I know about any of this? And did you really miss your economics final?"

Where to start?

"I slept in the day of the final, but Mr. Blake still let me take it," I said, releasing a deep breath in the hopes that it would keep me from crying. Uncomfortable situations almost always resulted in tears. "The rest is . . . a lot to explain."

I met Dad's eyes, expecting something angrier than the actual look on his face. He was worried. "You got two Ds and two Cs, kid." He paused. "This is about your mom, isn't it?"

"Yeah," I said quietly, knowing it wasn't a lie. Mom wasn't to blame for my actions, but she still had a role in it all. "I've been pretending her leaving wasn't a big deal, but it was, and school kept getting pushed aside because of it."

"I tried not to hover, but maybe I should've," Dad said. "What would help? Do you want to talk about it, or speak to a professional?"

"Talking to someone might help," I admitted. "But I'm not ready yet. Is that okay?"

"It's more than okay," he said, a small smile on his lips. "Say the word when you're ready and we'll figure it out."

"Thanks," I said, quiet for a moment. "So what's the next step?"

"I've been thinking about that, and first we need to get you back on track with school stuff," he said. "How are you feeling about college applications?"

"Um, not great, considering I still need to send them in," I said, frowning as another wave of shame hit. "I'm sorry."

"Don't apologize," Dad said as he took out his phone. "It's your future, not mine. But I'd love to know you're going after what you want, and I know that involves college. So we're going to try staying positive. Remind me where you're applying?"

I let out a breath, feeling lighter already. I should've talked to him about this weeks ago. Months, really. "My for-sure schools are UND, U of M, and UIC. And then I picked a couple state schools nearby."

"I'm touched you might want to stay close to home."

I knew he was trying to make me feel better, but it also meant a lot that the idea of going to school in the area made him happy. "Don't get all sappy on me, Cool Dad, or I'll have to rethink the nickname."

"I couldn't bear it," he said dramatically. "But yes to state schools. Your grade average and ACT scores should be enough for most of your list, but let's not get *too* cocky." He looked at me after a pause, his eyebrows furrowed. "About U of M . . ."

"Yeah?"

"Applications closed January first."

"Are you sure?" I asked, my stomach knotting. "I thought I had more time."

"I'm sure," Dad said, showing me his phone long enough to confirm what he'd seen before going back to digging. "I'll check the others."

"Thanks." My heart started racing. I was sure I'd written down all the dates correctly. But that's what I got for thinking I could figure out all of this by myself. If Mom hadn't left, she would've had every due date added to our shared calendar with multiple reminders. She wouldn't have let me hang out with anyone or linger online until everything was submitted. And if *I'd* acted like I needed a parent instead of having Dad think everything was handled, he would've been on this sooner.

"UND and UIC are still open, and I know the other Minnesota schools are," Dad said after a moment, looking at me. "Oh, kid, it's going to be okay."

I didn't realize I'd started crying until he wiped at my cheek. "I feel horrible," I said, my voice shaking as the tears kept spilling. "You've worked so hard to give me a nice life, and Mom worked hard to make sure I was focused. And now I'm letting you both down, and she's not even here to be disappointed!"

"No one is disappointed in you, Cassidy. Come here."

We stood, and Dad engulfed me in a tight hug, brushing his

fingers through my hair while I cried on his shoulder, beyond embarrassed. "We'll look into this better after dinner, make sure you get everything figured out," he said. "And I'm not disappointed, but I *am* worried. You know I just want you to be happy. And I know your mom wants that, too, even if she's not here to say it."

"She has a funny way of showing it," I mumbled against his sweater, knowing it was easier to put this on Mom than to think about anything else.

"Another problem for another day," Dad said, pulling back after a few more seconds to look at me. "We'll get you through this, okay? I'm here. And deep breaths."

I nodded, letting out the deepest of breaths and wiping away the lingering tears. "Okay. Thanks, Dad."

"You got it, kid."

We returned to our chairs to finish dinner, but I couldn't stop thinking about what I'd done. "I can't believe I missed the date for U of M. Tate's gonna kill me."

"He'll be fine," Dad said. "Nothing we can do about it now."

He was right, of course. All I could do was focus on the other schools and hope for the best. "I promise to work harder on school stuff. Mr. Blake already scared me into that decision after telling me about my grade last semester."

"I'm not big on fear tactics, but hey, whatever gets the job done," Dad said, looking thoughtful. "Also, this isn't meant to upset you more, but you're definitely grounded."

Honestly, I'd *hoped* he'd say it. Someone needed to be the parent, and he was better at it than he realized. "Yeah, that's fair. How long?"

He clearly hadn't considered that part yet. "A few weeks? Give you time to get serious about school and see where you're at with grades."

"As long as I'm free by Valentine's Day, I can live with that," I said. "Taylor would come for us both if I canceled."

"Can't have that," Dad said, chuckling. "But yes, it's a deal. If things look good, I'll unground you by Valentine's Day."

"Perfect," I said, pausing. "And to be clear, what exactly does being grounded mean? Can I drive Taylor to work after school, or should she figure that out with her parents?"

"I'd hate to throw a wrench in the Coopers' lives, so you can drive her," Dad said. "But no lingering. No hanging out with friends. I want your phone after dinner every school night until you finish homework. And school stuff only on the laptop, no social media or whatever you kids do online these days."

I nodded along to his list. I didn't *like* any of it, but it was what I needed right now. "What about weekends?"

"Once your homework is done, you can have free tech rein."

So it wasn't a complete hiatus from roleplaying, but like Rowan had said in Chicago, people would understand my reduced availability. "Okay," I said. "Can the grounding start tomorrow? I promise to get started on my homework, but I want to let a few people know I won't be on my phone as much."

Dad nodded. "Deal. Go alert the masses. I need to make a few work calls, but I'll check in before bed to make an application plan."

"Thanks, Cool Dad," I said, reaching over to squeeze his hand before escaping to my room. I texted Tate and Taylor to generally update them, saying I'd explain more at school the next day. Then I opened my laptop to message Home Base.

**Cass:** Sorry I've been MIA today. First-semester grades came back and weren't pretty. I'm like 90% grounded, and I won't be online much for a few weeks. Please keep the troops in line, and don't let me get too sucked up in RP life once I'm back. School needs to come first. Love y'all! <3

**Holly:** No worries, girl! You got this!

**Autumn:** Sorry to hear about everything. You'll be missed, but we understand! <3

**Rowan:** Do what you need to do. We'll be here when you get back. And I guess our scene can wait until you're back. I GUESS.

A smile tugged at my lips at their replies, despite feeling like I was letting them down. But it was the right thing to do. I'd needed a break for a while to clear my head and refocus, so I was grateful to Dad for pushing me in that direction.

And no matter how long I was gone, Rowan was right. My people weren't going anywhere. And maybe she'd need more time before we were back to normal, but the fact that she'd replied when it mattered told me everything would be okay.

[Unfinished one-on-one scene between Cass and Rowan]

**Cass:** Aresha stood outside the palace, her hand clinging to Roux's as she took it in. The massive white structure made her feel as small as it had when she was a child. "Here we are," she said quietly, her voice barely loud enough to hear over the wind.

**Rowan:** "Here we are," Roux echoed, her eyes focused on Aresha. She knew this would be a lot for her. "Let's go inside."

**Cass:** Aresha continued to watch the palace as if it would come to life and swallow her whole. "I don't know if I can," she said, her voice sounding far away. "We left so quickly that night. Maybe it's better if I don't go back to that world. Captaining a ship doesn't make me a queen."

**Rowan:** "Yes, it does," Roux said firmly. "It means exactly that. You fought to get back to your people. And I refuse to let you give up now just because you're scared."

**Cass:** "Of course I'm scared," Aresha admitted, her eyes widening. "I'm terrified. Leading a crew doesn't compare to leading all of Girishtova."

**Rowan:** "Then use that fear," Roux said. "Use it as you've always used it. And trust me and the rest of the crew to help as we've always done."

**Cass:** Aresha glanced at Roux. The falling snow was starting to stick to her hair and eyelashes. She looked beautiful. "I hate that you're always right," she said, to cover up the fact that she wanted to kiss her and for-get all about her fears.

**Rowan:** "Someone has to be," Roux said, grinning gently as she squeezed Aresha's hand. "Come on. Let's put you on the throne, my queen."

**Cass:** ((You should start calling me that.))

**Rowan:** ((I'll consider it.))

# FIFTEEN

I didn't know how to be a girlfriend on Valentine's Day. Having free time after finally submitting all my college applications and getting caught up on homework, I decorated a homemade card and coupons redeemable for two free movies of Taylor's choice. We rarely agreed on what to watch when hanging out, so it sounded like a nice gesture. Other than that and dinner plans, I was at a loss. Anything more might make her think my feelings had skyrocketed into the love category, which they hadn't. So coupons would have to do.

The doorbell rang as I ate breakfast, and I hoped to gods Taylor hadn't decided to surprise me before school. If she had something massive planned, there was no way my coupons would compare. I reluctantly answered the door, my eyes widening at the person on the other side.

"Cassidy!" Mom pulled me in for a hug before I could register what was happening.

Valentine's Day was another Mom-and-Cass thing. When I was growing up, kids had to bring valentines for the entire class, but she'd always said I was her *only* valentine. She and Dad had their own plans, of course, but her handmade cards and cookies always made me feel like it was all about us.

And she had the *nerve* to show up on this day of all days.

I pulled out of her grasp. "What are you doing here?"

"I came to see you," she said, as if it were the most natural thing in the world. "I've missed you so much."

I'd waited every day for her to call in the beginning, but after she'd bailed on Christmas and used Dad to tell me, I was done. Missing her was one thing—I could live with that. What I couldn't live with was her thinking showing up unannounced after ghosting was a solid parenting move. "But what are you *doing here*? I haven't heard from you in months."

Mom ignored my question and stepped inside, smiling broadly. "Everything looks exactly the same."

"How'd you expect it to look? It's a house, not a toddler."

She laughed. "I've really missed your sense of humor."

I blinked at the audacity. *"Have you?"*

Mom opened her mouth to reply, but Tuttles barreled into the room and rubbed against her legs with multiple chirps. "Look who it is!" she said, picking him up. His purr rattled immediately.

Traitor.

I wanted to believe she was here for a good reason, but I felt too sick to stay. Like, physically sick. And I wouldn't risk crying on the adorable outfit I'd put together for Taylor—light gray sweater with a heart on the chest, knee-length red skirt, and black tights. I'd even curled my damn hair and put on makeup *for school.*

Fortunately, I had an excuse to bail. "I gotta go to school. Whatever this is will have to wait."

"I was thinking I'd call you out from school," Mom said, oblivious to all my emotions as she pet Tuttles. "Have a girls' day."

"It's my senior year," I said, forcing back the many things I wanted to say, knowing every line of defense would come out wrong. "We can talk after school if you're still here."

"Of course, I'll be here," she said, as if I had no reason to wonder.

"Right." I left my cereal unfinished and grabbed my backpack before pausing at the door. "Does Dad know you're in town? Because you don't live here anymore, so it's kind of weird letting you hang out here all day."

"I'll call him after you leave," Mom said, not getting my point. "Have a good day at school, sweetie. I'll see you later."

"Right," I said again before leaving, the door slamming behind me.

I parked in the school's lot and closed my eyes, taking slow, deep breaths to calm down.

What was Mom doing here?

It wasn't about Valentine's Day. She wouldn't come all this way without notice because of a day when we used to make heart-shaped cookies and dance to cheesy romance songs. No, she wanted something. I could feel it deep in my bones.

A knock on my window brought me back to reality, and I opened my eyes to see Taylor on the other side, red-faced from the cold.

"Hey," I said after rolling down the window. Was it possible to look chill after being caught doing breathing exercises? "What's up?"

"I hope you aren't nervous about today," Taylor said, a hesitant smile on her lips. "I promise we're only doing dinner. No big surprises."

If only I could go back to an hour ago when my panicking was because of my first Valentine's Day with my girlfriend. "It's not that," I said, pausing. "It's my mom."

Taylor's relief was quickly replaced by concern. "What about her?"

I didn't want to get into it, but I was already keeping too much from her. "She randomly showed up this morning after bailing four months ago, and I've only talked to her once since then. And I think she's still at my house, waiting for me to come back and hang out with her like nothing happened. And I have no idea what to do. And I'm kind of freaking out a little bit."

Taylor's frown deepened, and she opened my door. "Get in the back seat."

"Why?"

"Just trust me."

I did as she said, not having the energy to question her or over-think it.

She got in on the other side, patting her lap before pulling out her phone. "Lie down. I'll massage your head."

Though still confused, I listened. "Why?"

"My mom does this for me whenever I have a really bad day. It's always helped." One of her calming coffeehouse playlists started playing.

"I don't want to be late," I said, not wanting to risk more school issues and abusing Dad's trust.

"We can miss homeroom. This is more important." Taylor's hands rested on my head, her fingers gently massaging my scalp as they moved through my hair.

"Okay, you're right," I said quietly. Within seconds, my eyes were closed. This was exactly what I needed, but I couldn't shake the familiarity of the moment.

"I'm sorry about your mom," Taylor said after a minute. "How are you feeling?"

We rarely talked about serious stuff, mainly because I never let her in. But I needed to talk to someone, and she wanted to listen. Like always, she wanted to be there for me, and it was time I let her.

"Not great," I said, hugging myself. "She'll always be my mom, obviously, but I was finally starting to accept that she was out of our lives. I don't know how to let her back in, if that's even what she wants. I didn't stick around long enough to find out why she's here."

"If it helps, you reacted better than I would've," Taylor said. "I would've screamed at her, probably broken something."

"You're a rare gem on a beach of passive-aggressive midwesterners, Taylor Cooper."

"A really cold beach."

I laughed quietly, thinking of the freezing temperature outside. "The coldest."

Silence filled the car again. "So four months ago," she said eventually, her tone softening. "Did she leave before our first date? Is that why you didn't go to school that week?"

"Yeah," I said, frowning at the memory of Mom breaking my heart. "It happened after school the day you found Tuttles. She told me she and my dad were getting divorced, and she was moving to Maine to be with another man. And the worst part is I didn't see any of it coming. My parents had been fighting for a while, but I never thought she'd leave me like that, you know? We were close. Or at least I thought we were."

"I'm really sorry," Taylor said. "What she did was selfish and shitty, and I'm sure it had nothing to do with you."

"That's the problem," I said, letting out a breath as tears sprang from my eyes. "I was never considered. She found a new life and left me here to pick up the pieces."

Taylor moved a hand from my hair to wipe under my eyes. "I hate to say you're better off, but you are. You have people here who love you and would fight for you in a second. Don't let her take that away." She paused. "Also, we don't have to hang out tonight if you need to talk to her. Now that you're done being grounded, we can be cute together another time."

I smiled a little at her thoughtfulness but shook my head. "I'm not bailing on our date for her. We can't help it she showed up unannounced."

Her hand moved back to my hair after catching a few more tears. "We can't, but you'll always wonder about it if you don't hear her out."

I considered that before groaning, knowing she was right. "Okay, fair. Another time sounds perfect. Thank you."

"You're welcome."

As Taylor twirled a strand of my hair, it suddenly clicked why this was familiar. Roux massaged Aresha's head whenever she had a nightmare. And it wasn't just that and Taylor's appearance that reminded me of Roux. Both of them were thoughtful, loyal, funny, and adorable. Roux had rescued Aresha on many occasions, and Taylor had rescued my cat which, okay, wasn't the same, but a girl can pretend.

Was I living part of my roleplay character's life by dating Taylor? Was that what had drawn me to her in the first place? And was me not being like Aresha what kept me from being a better girlfriend? Or was it that she didn't like Tide Wars? Or was it Row—

*No, stop that.* I couldn't think about Rowan right now. Not on Valentine's Day when I was with my girlfriend, who just canceled plans she'd been excited about for weeks so I could focus on me.

"Random subject change, but have you started reading the Tide Wars books yet?" I asked after a minute of overthinking.

"Not yet," Taylor said, her fingers stopping for a beat before continuing. I could hear the frown in her voice. "Sorry, things have been busy with the holidays and school and work."

"Don't apologize," I said, remembering what she'd said about being a slow reader. "This reminds me of the two main characters. One of them has really bad nightmares, and the other one massages her head to help her calm down."

"Aw, that's adorable," Taylor said, giggling. "We're straight out of a romance series."

I noted the sarcasm and tried not to let it bother me. "It's more than a romance series."

"Oh, really? Well then, enlighten me, Tide Wars nerd."

Shame pinched me. Maybe if I'd properly gushed about it at Christmas, she would've finished them by now. Maybe we'd already be gushing together, and she'd know about the roleplay. Maybe talking about it now would help nudge her toward reading them sooner. "It's about coming together to fight a common enemy. It's about never having enough time. It's about survival. It's about found family. And yes, there's romance, but it's not *only* about that. And the main couple—wait, never mind. Spoilers."

"Wow."

I shifted to look up at her, noticing a light grin on her face. "What?"

"I didn't realize you were a bigger nerd than me."

"Shut up!" I whined, nudging her.

She laughed, resting her hand on my cheek. "I promise to start reading them soon."

"Thanks," I said, hope filling my chest. "I think you'll love them. Macy Whittier is a genius. She has other books, too, if you like Tide Wars."

"Cool. But remember our agreement," she said, her thumb brushing against my skin. "No breaking up with me if I don't love the books."

"Deal." My eyes lingered on hers, feeling us moving in a positive direction. The warmth of her smile and softness of her hand made me want to lean up and kiss her, but I remembered where we were and how I couldn't afford to be late for first period. "We should go inside."

"Yeah," Taylor said quietly, moving her hand away so we could get out.

Once inside the school, I kissed her quickly before rushing to first period. After arriving at my desk seconds before the bell, I couldn't stop thinking about how great Taylor was for wanting to make me feel better. But I also knew no head massage or perfect words would help.

The only person who could fix this was Mom. And after the last four months, I didn't feel too confident she was here for me.

Dad's text after school confirmed my fear: Mom hadn't left yet.

**Cool Dad: I heard from your mom. Call me if you want me to**

**come home or need anything. Love you, kid.**

My heart sank. I didn't want to do this alone, but I needed to. Plus, I wouldn't let Mom ruin the date he had planned tonight.

**Cass: I'll be fine. Enjoy your date! Talk when you get home. <3**

I gripped the steering wheel the entire drive as I talked myself into being alone with Mom. My legs forced their way into the house after I parked in the driveway, the familiar smell of cookies smacking me in the face. I'd never felt so distrusting of cookies until now.

"Hi, sweetie," Mom said as I entered the kitchen. "I thought I'd get an early start on the cookies, but the frosting is all you. I hope you're up for our special pizza."

We were *those people* who made heart-shaped pizza to go with our heart-shaped cookies. It was cute—until now. "Sure," I said, feeling as unprepared for this as I had this morning. I thought I'd find the right words by now, but all I'd found was more pain and confusion. "I'll start the frosting."

"Perfect, thank you." Mom hummed along to her playlist of terrible love songs as she pulled another batch from the oven. We carried on that way for several minutes—her moving around the kitchen like she still lived here, me mixing frosting and feeling like a stranger in my own home. It was torture.

And then she slapped her hand on the counter as if she'd had a revelation. "I forgot to tell you: I saw those Ursula pictures on your Instagram. You looked *amazing*. I'm so glad I decided to make the dress less puffy."

Did she want a thank-you for finishing the dress before leaving us? Because that wasn't going to happen. "Dad made it a success. Couldn't have gotten all that paint on without him."

"That was nice of him," she said, scrunching her nose. "I'm surprised he wasn't working for once."

My eyebrows shot up, and it took everything I had not to scream. "I'm not. He's been very available."

"Huh." She looked lost in thought for a moment before shaking her head. "Anyway, you went to a party, right? Was it fun?"

"It was." The feeling of sickness from this morning returned. What was she doing? Was this our new way of bonding? Bringing up *my* memories like she'd had any part of them? Saying shit about Dad like I'd agree? "You should've been there."

Mom rested a hand on my arm. "I know, sweetie." She gave me a light squeeze before letting go, grinning suddenly. "Do you remember the year we got distracted by singing and dancing and forgot to add flour to the cookies?"

"Yeah," I said shortly. "They were disgusting."

"They were *awful*! But they weren't as bad as the *many* waffles I've burned over the years."

My hands gripped the edge of the counter. I couldn't take it anymore. The joking and reminiscing and pretending were too much—I really would scream if it didn't end soon. "Mom," I said, willing my voice to sound firm when I knew tears were inevitable. "Why are you here?"

"I already told you. I missed you and wanted to see you," she said, her tone casual like it made perfect sense. "Am I not allowed to do that?"

I shook my head, turning to face her. "Not without warning."

Mom sighed. "You're right. I should've called first. But I have some news and wanted to tell you in person. You remember Colin, right?"

I blinked. No doubt this had to be awkward for her, but honestly! What a question. "If you mean the man you ran off with, yes, I remember."

Mom's frown deepened, and she cleared her throat. "Yes, well, he asked me to marry him last weekend, and I said yes. But I wanted to tell you first, and you deserved to find out in person, so here I am."

I stared at my mom as years and years of positive memories washed away. Making costumes together. Baking cookies. Playing with Tuttles. Vacations. Drives to school. Her being proud of me when I came out freshman year. All of it vanished as I took in her words. She was getting married and officially starting a new life without us. It wouldn't get more real than this.

"Please say something," Mom said when I didn't respond.

Anger replaced any hurt I felt, and I was done holding back. "Don't you think you should finalize your divorce before getting engaged to someone else?" I asked, laughing bitterly. "And honestly, Mom, I don't know why you're even telling me. We haven't spoken in four months. You could've moved on with Colin and saved yourself a plane ticket."

Mom looked stunned, but she kept talking anyway. "I know this is a lot to take in right now, sweetie, and I know things haven't been handled the best, but your dad and I—"

"Because they weren't handled at all!" I said before she could make an excuse. "What you did was *wrong*, Mom."

She paused, letting out a deep breath. "You might not understand this right now, but life isn't always as simple as right and wrong. I was suffocating with your dad for a long time."

I turned away, blinking back those inevitable demon tears. "Were you suffocating with me?" I asked, choking out the words.

"Of course not! I love you *so much*." She stepped in front of me, resting a hand on my cheek as the other wiped away tears she'd caused. "I hope we can put all this nasty business behind us and move on. I want you to be in the wedding."

I met her eyes, taking in her words. I wanted nothing more than to have both of my parents in my life again—and to be happy about it—but that wasn't reality. We hadn't been that family for a long time. It just took her leaving for me to realize it. "I can't be that person for you anymore."

"Cassidy—"

I stepped away from her touch, shaking my head. "You were my entire world. I *needed* you, and you left me here like it was the easiest decision you've ever made. And you haven't given a shit since. If you thought empty promises and a single phone call to talk about yourself were enough to keep me waiting around for you, you're wrong. And you don't get to dig on Dad about not being around when he's the one who stayed."

She reached for me despite looking like I'd slapped her. "Cassidy—"

"No!" I yelled, moving back more. "I'm done. And the best thing you can do for everyone now is leave."

Mom's face flooded with fear, like she was finally taking me seriously. "You can't mean that. I'll come back tomorrow when your dad is here, and we can talk about it together."

"We're not bringing Dad into this," I said. I wouldn't let her talk shit about him one day and hide behind him the next. "Please. I want you to leave."

Seconds passed as we stared at each other. She was waiting for me to apologize, to take it all back and say she was right like I used to do when we disagreed. But this was bigger than anything else we'd been through. And she hadn't bothered to own her actions, let alone apologize.

After a grueling silence, she conceded. "You have my number if you change your mind."

"I won't," I said.

Mom left the kitchen without another word. I followed her to the door, watching as she put on her coat and boots and grabbed her purse. Her eyes met mine, and for a moment I thought she was going to say something, but instead she turned and walked out. I waited as her car door shut with force. I waited for her to come back and do the one thing I desperately wanted her to do—apologize, mean it, and make things right.

I waited until she was gone.

Dad knocked on my door later that night. I wanted to pretend I was sleeping, but more than that I wanted to see him. "It's open," I said loud enough for him to hear, my voice strained from hours of crying.

"Hey, kid." He sat on the edge of my bed. "Where's your mom?"

"Don't know, don't care," I mumbled, my face half-buried in my pillow.

"Want to talk about it?"

*No.* I sighed, sitting up after a moment. "Mom's getting married."

"Yeah, she mentioned that."

I frowned. *Of course* she'd told him. "But you're not even divorced yet."

"We are, actually," Dad said, looking guilty. "I'm sorry for not telling you sooner, but it happened when you were getting the rest of your college applications in and figuring out school. Not that this is the right time to tell you, but you deserve to know."

So it was official. We'd never be a family again. I thought I'd spiral when it was finalized, but all I could feel was relief. Mom could keep doing whatever she was doing, and Dad could move on. "Thanks for telling me," I said quietly, realizing Mom had tried to earlier. But I'm glad it came from Dad. "And I'm sorry."

He shook his head. "I know things have been messy around

here, but you're the last person who should be sorry. *I'm* sorry for not being around more for you two. And I know she's sorry for leaving you."

"But that's the problem. She's *not* sorry. She didn't apologize. She waltzed in and acted like nothing had changed, and I lost it. So don't apologize for saving lives. She made this mess, not you."

"She did, but it's not that simple," he said. "I gave up a lot of time with you both for longer shifts and career advancements. Saving lives or not, that wasn't fair. And that didn't make it okay for her to leave you, but we hadn't been happy for a long time. Even if she hadn't left, divorce was inevitable. But you know what?"

I wiped away tears that had slowly returned. "What?"

"I'm glad we have each other," he said, smiling a little. "I've learned to live without your mom, but I don't want to learn to live without you."

My heart swelled, and I smiled to cover other emotions that threatened to rush to the surface. "Wow, that's pretty damn cheesy. But thanks, back at you."

He chuckled. "Happy to hear it."

I looked back at him for a moment before remembering his plans. "How was your date?"

"You know, it was pretty good," Dad said vaguely. "I think there will be another one."

At least Mom showing up hadn't ruined *everything*. "Good, I'm glad."

"Me too," he said, patting my leg before standing. "I'm going to take care of the baking tornado that swept through the kitchen, but there's leftover pasta in the fridge if you want it."

He understood my love language. "Yeah, I'll be down in a minute."

Dad nodded and left me with my thoughts. I didn't know if I'd made the right decision in kicking Mom out, but it was better than pretending to be happy. I had to protect my heart.

[Tide Wars main server message]

*Attention, nerds!*

*The votes are in, and we're doing a group scene this Thursday at 7 central. Setting is a local tavern, a.k.a. be prepared for shenanigans and at least one fight. It doesn't look like Cass or Carina will be able to make it, so we'll pretend the royal siblings are off doing royal sibling things.*

*And you know what they say—when the captain's away, the crew will play!*

*XoXo Rowan*

# SIXTEEN

Focusing on anything after seeing Mom was damn near impossible. I told Tate everything the next day, and we spent Saturday eating waffles, drinking hot chocolate, and watching Star Wars. Other than that and driving Taylor to work, I rarely saw either of them. I put most of my limited energy into school, determined not to mess up again.

After a couple of weeks of silence, I returned to my online life. I'd been around off and on during my grounding period, but nothing like I was used to. A collection of messages waited for me in Home Base, but only Holly and Autumn had sounded worried about where I was. Rowan replied as if it were normal for me to disappear, which was so far from the truth that it was offensive. But I knew it was her own lingering hurt talking.

**Cass:** I'm here! Sorry for ghosting. My mom showed up without warning on Valentine's Day and threw everything into a spiral. And I found out she's engaged, so I'll be joining Holly in the Unwanted Stepdads Club.

**Cass:** What have I missed?

**Holly:** NOOOO THE WORST CLUB!

**Holly:** And sorry about your mom. Wanna talk about it?

**Cass:** Short version: She acted like everything was fine and wants me to be in her wedding. And she didn't apologize. I said no and told her to leave.

**Holly:** Damn, girl, that's heavy! But good for you.

**Autumn:** Sorry to hear, Cass! Sending hugs. <3

**Cass:** Thanks, friends. I feel a little bad for kicking her out of the house she raised me in, but I didn't know what else to do.

**Autumn:** You did the right thing!

**Holly:** Agreed! As for what you missed, we had a group scene last week and planned another for next Monday. Can you join?

They'd all done a scene without me. I'd needed the break, but I still felt a certain way that no one had tried texting me. Then I remembered the person who usually texted me still wasn't speaking to me, and my heart sank all over.

Taylor had a Spyhouse Coffee shift on Monday. I'd planned on doing homework there, but she'd be working anyway. It wasn't like bailing on real plans. I could get homework done between dinner and the group scene. And I refused to miss another group scene. Aresha and I wanted to be there for our crew.

**Cass:** I'm in! Did I miss anything big in the last one?

**Holly:** We killed off Roux and Allain. Aresha needs to find a new lover and brother.

**Cass:** Good one

**Holly:** Thanks, I thought so! But you missed nothing. We pretended Aresha and Allain had family shit going on. All good!

**Cass:** Cool, thanks. I'll catch up on scenes now and promise to be around more.

**Holly:** You do you <3

I switched between roleplay scenes and an essay on Shakespeare's history plays for the next few hours, pausing only to eat dinner with Dad once he got home from work. It was almost nine when my phone rang. I stared at Rowan's contact picture—her standing under the Bean with her tongue sticking out—before answering. "Hello?"

"I hate your mom."

I smiled a little, relieved she was acting like herself. "Hard same."

"Also, I'll be there."

"Where?"

"Minneapolis. I'll take the train in for your birthday weekend. If I'm still invited."

A jolt went through my body, and I stood up to start pacing. "*Of course* you're invited. But don't come because you feel sorry for me. You have every right to be mad at me. And I really am sorry about everything."

"I know," she said, letting out a sigh. "And yes, I'm still a little mad, but you're my best friend. You were there for me when my dad died—more than anyone else in my life. Let me be there for you. Let me meet your friends and dad and see your world."

I smiled hopefully. "You mean it?"

"I mean it. And my mom already said I could go, so you have to say yes."

"Okay, yes, of course!" I bounced a little excitedly. Then reality kicked back in, and I stopped walking. "I haven't told anyone about the roleplay yet."

"I figured," Rowan said. "I can be your church-camp friend for now, but don't make me be that person forever, okay? I want us to be ourselves and be able to talk about our nerdy obsessions and our other friends without having to find a Jesus way of saying things."

"I don't think there's a Jesus way of talking about Tide Wars," I said.

She snorted. "Exactly. So I'll cover for you this time, but eventually I'd like to be your nerdy online friend. Okay?"

"Yeah, okay. That's fair."

"Perfect! So I'll book a train ticket and send you the deets."

"I guess I can pick you up and let you stay at my house," I said, grinning now.

"You better," she said. "Now get back to school shit. Good night, Captain."

The mention of my nickname after almost two months was a

symphony in my ears. I hadn't realized how badly I'd needed to hear it until now—to hear Rowan's voice. "Good night, Champ."

After hanging up, I found Dad in his office. "Have a minute?" I asked, hoping his good mood hadn't changed since dinner.

Dad looked up from his laptop and smiled. "Oh, I think I can spare a minute," he said, nodding toward a chair. "What's up, kid?"

I approached the desk and sat across from him. "My birthday is coming up, as you know, and I want to have a little party," I said. "Like, Taylor and Tate and Rachel, maybe a few other people. Nothing big, just dinner and movies or something."

Dad's eyebrows raised. "You know, I thought we'd go to dinner and at best you'd maybe hang out with Taylor or Tate. But a party. Huh."

"We can still go to dinner," I said.

"It's not that," Dad said. "I'm just surprised is all. And happy to hear this plan. You should absolutely have friends over. I'll make plans so you don't have me hanging around embarrassing you."

I laughed, shaking my head. "You don't have to do that," I said, a token Minnesota Nice response that meant I wanted him to but wouldn't say it.

"I'll plan a date night, so everyone wins," Dad said. "Just let me know what you need for the party and we'll get it settled. But nothing out of control, okay?"

"Of course," I said easily. "It'll just be a few people. Also—"

"I knew there'd be more," he teased. "Go on."

My eyes lingered on him for a moment. After everything Dad had done for me this year, he deserved the truth, roleplay future be damned. But I couldn't bring myself to tell him. The lie I'd fed Taylor was the only option if I was going to stay consistent and ensure Rowan was able to visit. "I've started talking more with an old church-camp friend lately, and I want to invite her for my birthday. But she doesn't live here, so can she stay in the guest room that weekend? Other than the party and sleeping, we'll mostly be out exploring, so you won't have to change any plans or work stuff you might have going on. You won't even have to cook. I'll take care of everything."

"What's her name?" he asked.

"Rowan Davies."

The seconds ticked by as he considered it, his expression unreadable. The summer I'd gone to church camp was the same year Dad had a lot of work advancement and was gone a lot. He wouldn't remember any of the friends I'd made, let alone who I'd kept in touch with. And now he was probably feeling guilty for not knowing anything about that time in my life, which made me feel even more guilty for lying to him. But the words were out, and I wouldn't turn back now.

"I don't see why not," he said finally. "You're old enough to handle hosting company, and honestly, I'm just glad you're spending more time with friends. I've been a little worried my daughter would be a hermit at college."

I laughed quietly, though I felt sick. "Good one. Thanks, Cool

Dad." I pushed a smile as I stood. "I have an essay to finish, so I'll leave you to your adulting."

"Don't stay up too late," Dad said. "Love you."

"Love you too."

I returned to my room and let out another deep breath once at my desk. There was plenty of time to feel like the world's worst daughter for lying, but for now I had a date with Shakespeare. Pulling up my essay, I spent another hour on it before finishing. And for once, I didn't hop on Discord to check on roleplay life before bed.

Returning to my online life made it easier to get back to my in-person one—like I couldn't have one without the other. Halfway through driving Taylor to Spyhouse Coffee for a shift, I decided to bring up the Rowan news. "You remember my church-camp friend, right?"

"You mean the one you met up with in Chicago and didn't tell me about?" she teased, nudging me. "I remember. What about her?"

I smiled sheepishly, knowing I'd never live that one down. "Well, we were talking last night. It sounds like she's gonna visit for my birthday, so you'll get to meet her."

An uncomfortable silence took over, and I glanced at Taylor. She was looking out the window, suddenly far away. "Did you hear me?" I asked.

"I heard you," she said, pausing. "I thought you were having a small party at your house for your birthday."

"Yeah, but what's one more guest?"

"We won't get any alone time or cute girlfriend moments if you're playing host the whole weekend."

I laughed at her wording. "I'm sure she can fend for herself when we're having cute girlfriend moments. It'll be a fun group thing like it would've been anyway. You and Tate will love her."

"Okay."

I frowned, knowing her well enough to know something was off. "You don't sound very excited about it."

"Because I'm not," Taylor said, her biting tone slapping me in the face. "I know you've had a lot going on, and I understand, but I've hardly seen you since you were grounded. We're just getting back to normal, and now the one weekend we're supposed to spend together is going to be full of other things. This isn't what we planned."

"Well, it's *my* birthday," I said, my annoyance instantly matching hers. "So it would be cool if *I* got to decide what to do for it."

"And how do you think this makes me feel, Cass?" she asked, her voice raising slightly. "First you keep this girl a secret, and now she's coming all the way from Chicago for your birthday."

"I'm allowed to have friends," I said defensively, my hands gripping the steering wheel as I tried to stay calm.

Taylor's eyes narrowed. "Friends don't look all adorable and close in pictures online for everyone to see."

"Don't they?" I said as I stopped at a light. "You and June take pictures like that all the time, and I don't say a damn thing about it because I trust you. And June isn't straight. Rowan is. So I think if I'm not freaking out about *that* friendship, you can chill the fuck out over mine."

She blinked, my words surprising us both. I knew it wasn't fair to be mad about this when I felt a certain way about Rowan, but also she had no right to tell me how to spend my birthday. She looked like she wanted to say something, but the light turned green and I focused on the road again.

A few minutes passed as the latest Phoebe Bridgers album drowned out my thoughts. Taylor didn't say anything until I parked at Spyhouse.

"I'm sorry, Cass," she said softly as she stared at her lap. "I was really excited to take you out for dinner as a surprise. But you didn't know, and I shouldn't have taken that out on you or her. Of course you can do whatever you want for your birthday."

My palms started to sweat as I felt a bigger deal brewing in the pot of well-intentioned plans. "Why didn't you mention any of this until now?" I asked.

"You said your only plans were the party and something with your dad on Sunday," she said, shrugging. "We don't get to hang out much, and I figured you'd let yourself take a break that weekend. It seemed like the perfect time to surprise you."

I sighed, torn between remaining angry and feeling like the worst girlfriend ever. "I'm sorry, Taylor. I wish I'd known sooner so we could have made a better plan. But I rarely see Rowan, and we just started talking again after a stupid fight."

"I get it," she said, looking at me. "You don't have to explain. It's fine."

It didn't feel fine. "I can't tell her not to come now," I said. "I want her to meet you and Tate. And if it helps, we can get brunch on Sunday. She leaves in the morning, and my plans with my dad aren't until later."

"That does help." Taylor rested a hand on my thigh. "We'll do friend stuff on Saturday and brunch on Sunday. No problem."

"Perfect," I said, covering her hand with mine. "So we're good, then? No more thinking I have a second girlfriend or anything?"

Taylor laughed, rolling her eyes as her cheeks flushed. "Yeah, we're good."

"Good," I said, smiling hesitantly. "Because you're thoughtful and adorable, and I don't like fighting with you."

"I don't like fighting with you either," she said, making a face. "It was weird, right?"

"So weird," I said, relieved we could joke about it—even if I was still panicking. "And I promise you'll like Rowan."

"I'm sure I will," she said, turning her hand to squeeze mine. "Thanks for the ride. I'll see you tomorrow."

I let everything sink in as she disappeared into the coffee shop, hoping to gods my birthday wouldn't be a total disaster.

[One-on-one scene between Cass and Rowan]

**Cass:** Aresha's hand slipped from Roux's as she entered the royal palace. Now that she'd finally arrived home, she had to see the throne room where they'd held their final ball. The last place she'd seen her parents alive. She moved past broken chandeliers and paintings littered with dust and cobwebs until she was standing in the middle of the room that had haunted her for years. Everything had been stolen or was broken or dirty, except for the two thrones, as if time had preserved them. Her feet led her forward until she was seated on her mother's chair. Her fingers traced the arms, trying to remember what her mother had been wearing the last time she'd sat there. The nightmares rarely showed her in the same dress. Regardless, Aresha knew that before everything had crashed down on them that night, they'd been happy.

**Rowan:** Roux followed in silence, keeping a close eye on their surroundings in case someone was waiting for them. But they were alone. She stood in the throne room that she herself had seen before, but it meant little to her compared with Aresha. She watched as her captain sat on the throne like it was made for her. In a way, it was. "What's our next move, Captain?" she asked, after giving Aresha a moment alone with her thoughts.

**Cass:** Aresha's eyes snapped back to Roux, past thoughts slipping away. She had the present to think about, and the future. She sat a little straighter in her seat, thinking of her mother's mannerisms and what a true queen would do. "We rebuild."

# SEVENTEEN

Rowan arrived in less than an hour, and my brain was chaos.

After telling Tate and Rachel the news, they'd insisted on coming with me to get Rowan from the train station. Much to my relief, Taylor had picked up a Spyhouse shift for a coworker. Introducing everyone at once would've been a lot for me to handle.

One step at a time. One introductory lie at a time. No big deal.

"I'm so screwed," I muttered to myself.

I jumped as the Crosstrek's passenger door whipped open. "Happy one day until your birthday!" Tate said as he practically jumped in, bumping my fist with his.

"Yes, happy almost birthday," Rachel said after climbing in back. "Can't wait to meet Rowan. What did Taylor say about this secret friendship?"

I backed out of the school parking lot and drove toward the train station, my nerves jumbling at the memory. "She wasn't thrilled, mostly because she'd made surprise plans for us that needed to change. But I think they'll get along great. You all will."

"No doubt," Tate said. "I still don't understand why you didn't tell me about having a Jesus friend, but okay." He flicked my arm with his finger.

I rolled my eyes the way someone would if that story had been the truth. Tate had forgotten most of my church-camp stories by now, but that didn't make the lie any easier for me to swallow. "I know. I'm sorry for being a shit friend."

He snorted. "You're not a shit friend."

I really was, though.

"Okay, but back to the good stuff," Rachel said, smirking at me in the rearview mirror. "What if Taylor and Rowan get along *too well*, you know? Imagine the drama."

For once, there was something I *didn't* have to overthink. "If anyone needs to worry about Rowan charming someone, it's you. She asks about Tate all the time."

"Does she really?" Tate asked, jumping when Rachel punched his arm. "Ow!"

I grinned, feeling victorious. "She does, but it's not in *that* kind of way. It's her brand of humor. And because she knows you're my bestie."

"It better not be in that kind of way," Rachel grumbled. "I'm not above violence."

"Yeah, my arm is aware," Tate said, rubbing it like she'd actually wounded him. "But tell us more about her, C. Is she actually religious? Will she judge us for drinking tomorrow?"

I laughed at the image. "She's as religious as I am, so not at all," I said. "And she won't judge you for anything. She's good people."

"Solid. Tell us more."

There was a lot I could say about Rowan Davies, like how she was one of my most favorite people in the world, or how she'd made my heart flutter that day in Chicago. Instead, I told them about how she also wanted to go to UIC for English, and how she was good at ice-skating and loved junk food. Safe stuff.

"You better not replace me if you both end up at UIC," Tate said.

I didn't want to think about that until I found out my fate within the next few weeks. "No one could ever replace you, Tate Larson."

"Damn right."

"Do you think she's hot?" Rachel asked.

I saw her smirking in the rearview mirror again and laughed, hoping it would cover my nerves. "You're enjoying this, aren't you?"

"Maybe."

Tate snorted. "Girlfriend of the century, this one."

"Apparently." I shook my head, focusing on the drive. "To answer your question, Rowan is cute. Tate will think so too."

Rachel's smile dropped. "Now who's enjoying this?" she grumbled.

"You deserved it for playing dirty," Tate said, shifting back to take Rachel's hand and kiss it. I rolled my eyes, but only because I was used to them being disgustingly adorable.

Tate turned up Taylor Swift to amuse Rachel with his mediocre singing while I went over the plan in my head for the hundredth time. Rowan was a church-camp friend. We wouldn't talk about roleplaying or Tide Wars. My friends and girlfriend would like her *almost* as much as I did, and they'd want to see her again. Hopefully I'd explain my secret by the time college started.

Once I parked at the train station, I shifted to look at Tate and Rachel. "Try not to embarrass me too much this weekend. And no more talking about Rowan being hot."

"Boring, but okay," Rachel said, a sweet smile on her face that couldn't be trusted.

"Activating best behavior mode," Tate said in a robotic voice.

"You're so weird," Rachel said, hitting his arm playfully. "Let's go!"

"Gods, save me," I mumbled, knowing I was in trouble if Rachel was excited.

My anxiety kicked in as we entered the station and moved through a small crowd of people, but everything calmed the moment I saw Rowan Davies. Much like seeing her for the first time, everything around me ceased to exist.

Even better? She was holding a box from Stan's Donuts.

A wide smile broke across my face as I ran to her, engulfing her in a hug.

"Excited to see me or something?" Rowan teased, hugging me back with her free arm.

"I'm sorry," I whispered in her ear, needing to get that out before my friends joined us.

"I know." She pulled back after a few seconds, looking like she wanted to say something else, but she stepped around me instead. "You must be Tate. I come bearing gifts."

"You must be Rowan," Tate said, a grin on his face as his eyes scanned the box. "I like you already. But I don't know why you'd come all this way just to see Cass."

"Rude." I nudged him before nodding at Rachel. "This is Rachel."

"Tate's *girlfriend*," Rachel said pointedly, a dangerous smile forming on her lips. "Welcome to Minneapolis."

"Thanks," Rowan said, glancing at Tate. "I obviously came to see you. Cass was just my way in." And then she winked at him.

Rachel's mouth dropped as Tate barked a laugh. "It's official, I definitely like you," he said, taking Rachel's hand to lead them toward the exit. "To the car!"

"To the car!" I echoed before looking at Rowan. "How was the train?"

"Oh, you know, it was the train."

I nodded, knowing what she meant. "Generous of you to brave it for me."

"I live to serve, Captain."

"That's the spirit." I grinned at the nickname, in a daze over this being real. It felt normal having her here. Natural. "Come on, we have some wholesome Minnesota fun planned." I grabbed her suitcase handle and wheeled it after the others.

Rowan laughed, following along. "If you say we're going to church, I'm outing your secret the second we catch up with your friends."

I knew she was joking, but the reminder made my stomach drop. I felt terrible all over again. "No churches, promise."

Rowan sighed dramatically. "Praise be."

We made it to the Crosstrek, and I put Rowan's suitcase in the trunk as she hopped into the passenger seat, the other two already in the back. "So tonight is all planned out," I said as we left the parking lot. "But tomorrow is open until the party. What do you want to do?"

"How touristy is it to go to the Mall of America?" Rowan asked.

"About as touristy as taking pictures at the Bean and seeing the *Ferris Bueller* painting," I said, smirking. "It's a glorified mall with a theme park, LEGO store, aquarium, and movie theater. But we can go."

"Don't forget the Crayola Store," Tate said.

"We're not all five," Rachel teased.

"If Tate's going, I'm there," Rowan said, shifting to look back at them. "Crayonfest for our first date. So romantic."

I sensed Rachel's eye daggers as Tate chuckled. "As much as I'd love to watch you and Tate bond over crayons, they can't make it. But it's settled. We'll go to the mall and see how much time we have after that. There's a little waterfall nearby that I've been meaning to check out in the winter. Some of the water will be frozen, and we can walk behind it."

"It feels like you're in an ice cave," Tate added.

"I love it," Rowan said, opening the Stan's Donuts box. "Let's def do that if there's time. If not, I'll have to come back."

"You say that as if I'm letting you leave," I said, taking the lemon-pistachio doughnut she held out to me.

The sound of Rowan's laugh warmed me. My two best friends had finally met and already had their own inside joke. The ease of the first introduction made me a little less paranoid about Rowan meeting Taylor.

All I had to do was keep my heart eyes to myself, because almost three months apart apparently wasn't long enough to make them go away.

We ate doughnuts and sang along to a playlist I'd put together of Rowan's favorites until I parked in the lot of a large, plain-looking warehouse. "Here we are," I said, grinning at Rowan. "Are you ready?"

Rowan hesitated as she took in the building. "For what? My death?"

Tate snorted. "Damn, you figured us out already," he teased before getting out, Rachel close behind.

"Wait and see," I said. "But I promise it's cool, and not in a death kind of way."

"Don't make me regret this." Her tone was serious, but she

smirked before following the others. We walked through a hall to the check-in area, and her smile grew. "Mini golf?"

I nodded, relieved by her excitement. "You got it! Can Can Wonderland isn't your typical mini-golf course. Each hole was created by a local artist, and they all have different themes, like state fair and grandma's living room."

"And there's good food," Tate added. "It's overpriced, but also worth it."

"And you're not allowed to pay," I told Rowan when she pulled out her wallet. "My turn to treat you."

"I knew my generosity would catch up with me," she groaned dramatically. "Thank you."

We agreed to play first and eat second. The eighteen-hole course went beyond the state fair and grandma's living room. There were designs dedicated to a tornado, squirrels, a giant blue toad with a tongue for a ball ramp, baseball, and a golden toilet. I quickly took last place and never recovered. Tate and Rachel had been on enough mini-golf dates to be pros. And true to her nickname, Rowan played like a champ, coming in first place. Having my two best friends together made it worth them giving me shit for losing. But that didn't stop me from bragging about crushing a single hole that everyone else needed more strokes to finish.

We split a couple of pizzas after, and I made Rowan try the cereal malts. She ordered the Cinnamon Toast Crunch version, and I got Reese's Puffs. Both were a dream.

Hanging out with Rowan in person made me feel less tempted

to check my phone for roleplay stuff, but I took it out during the end of the meal in case Dad got off work early. I'd missed two calls and multiple texts from Taylor.

**Taylor: Hey! Tried calling. Where are you?**

**Taylor: I got done early. The girl who called in decided she wasn't sick lol**

**Taylor: Let me know where you're at, my dad can drop me off**

**Taylor: Hello?**

Shit.

"Everything okay?" Rowan asked.

I looked up to see them all staring at me. "Taylor got off work early, and I missed a bunch of texts from her."

"Oh, damn," Tate said, making a face. I'd seen him on the receiving end of missing Rachel's texts, so he understood. "Good luck with that."

"Yeah, thanks. Be right back." I stepped into the hall to call her.

"I was starting to think you got in an accident or something," Taylor said when she answered, then she gasped. "Wait, you *didn't* get in an accident, did you?"

"No, we're all good," I said, my stomach in knots. Ever since seeing Rowan at the train station, I'd felt relaxed, but now my nerves were on high alert. I felt bad for missing Taylor's texts, and my first thought was her thinking it was intentional. Her being concerned instead made me feel even worse. "We went to Can Can Wonderland after picking up Rowan, and I wasn't paying attention to my phone. I'm sorry."

"It's all good," she said. "What's up now?"

"We're finishing dinner, then I need to drop Tate and Rachel back at school to get his truck. Want to meet at my place after?"

"It'll be too late by then," she said, a finality in her voice. "Let's just meet up tomorrow."

"Yeah." I frowned. "I'm sorry."

"Don't be. What's the birthday plan?"

I knew her tone well enough to know she was more upset than she was letting on, but I was trying. "We're going for brunch, then Rowan wants to check out our massive mall."

Taylor snorted. "Of course she does."

"I know, I know, super touristy," I said, letting out a short laugh. "But I'm allowing it since she's never been here."

"For sure. What about after that?"

"I'm gonna show her the frozen waterfall at Minnehaha. And it's all fair game if you want to join for any of it."

She wasn't a fan of the Mall of America or the cold, but I wanted her to know she was welcome, especially after our fight. I needed her to get to know Rowan and trust that there was nothing to worry about. One-sided feelings weren't exactly fair to anyone, but I was trying to push them away. That had to count for something.

"Thanks, but I'll just see you at your place after, give you some friend time," she said. "We're starting around six?"

"Yep! It'll be us, Rowan, Tate, and Rachel for dinner, and anyone y'all invited will show up around eight."

"I only invited Fynn and June since I know you want to keep it small."

"I appreciate that, thanks," I said, and I knew Dad would too.

"Of course. I'll let you get back to it, but see you tomorrow. Love you!"

"See you!"

She hadn't brought up the *love* conversation again, but I still felt an ache of guilt every time she said it. Like every day spent not loving her would put us that much closer to the end. But she continued to be patient, and I hung on to the hope that I'd get on her level eventually.

Once we parked at my house, we put Rowan's suitcase in the guest room and I gave her the grand tour. I showed her the famous Ursula costume and introduced her to Tuttles, who purred for her instantly.

In my room, Rowan put the doughnut box on the desk and sat in the chair to get a sense of my life while nerding out online. "Can you see Tate's window from here?" she asked, leaning over to open the curtains.

"Yes, creep, I can," I teased. "His window is across from mine. He switched rooms a few months after we'd become friends, so we could talk and throw things back and forth. Only broke a couple windows over the years."

Rowan chuckled. "Do you still do that kind of stuff?"

"No, now we text each other."

"Youths these days. Pure laziness."

"Tell me about it."

"I've only ever lived in apartments," she said after closing the curtains again. "I always wondered if people actually did that kind of stuff like they do in movies."

"Well, I can't speak for the rest of the world, but we do that kind of stuff in the great state of Minnesota."

"What do we do in Minnesota?"

Dad was in the doorway, smiling broadly despite looking exhausted from work.

"I was telling her about the windows Tate and I broke growing up," I said.

"I lost count of how many times we threatened to move you to the other bedroom." He stepped closer, holding a hand out to Rowan. "I'm Marcus, Cassidy's dad."

Rowan hopped up from the chair and shook his hand eagerly. "Rowan Davies. Nice to meet you, Dr. Williams."

"Marcus is fine, or Cool Dad." He shot me a wink before looking back to her. "How's your first day in Minneapolis?"

"It's been amazing," Rowan said enthusiastically. "We went to Can Can Wonderland with Tate and Rachel."

Dad let out a low whistle. "That place is overpriced."

"But also kind of worth it," she said, grinning. She was already one of us.

Dad chuckled. "Exactly. Well, I'll leave you girls to it. Cass, I'm stopping at home before my date tomorrow, but I'll be out of your hair after that. Let me know if you need anything. Same goes for you, Rowan."

"Thanks, Dad," I said, relieved he didn't say anything embarrassing.

"Yeah, thanks," Rowan said. She looked back at me after he left. "Okay, your dad is great. And he *totally* loves that you call him Cool Dad. It's adorable."

"Right?" I laughed a little. "And trying to live up to his name benefits me. I don't hate it."

We changed into pajamas before sitting together on my bed with the remaining two doughnuts, our laptops open. I clicked on Home Base to see a few messages from Holly and Autumn screaming about needing updates.

**Cass:** Rowan made it and it's the best!!!

**Rowan:** She's lying. I'm having a terrible time.

I scoffed, nudging her. Gods, it was amazing being able to nudge her in person. We were officially real best friends hanging out on my bed, our legs touching. And that was it. No other thoughts or feelings entered my head.

None. At. All.

**Cass:** Wow, thanks for that.

**Rowan:** Welcome!

**Autumn:** LOL! What are your plans?

**Rowan:** Tonight was mini golf, food, and meeting friends.
Tomorrow we're going to brunch, the Mall of America, and a waterfall before the party.

**Autumn:** Sounds fun! And happy early birthday, Cass!

**Holly:** I can't believe you're hanging out again! Jealous!

**Rowan:** Same bed, actually ;)

**Holly:** DAMN, GIRL

**Cass:** lolol calm down, she's kidding

**Holly:** A girl can dream. You two have the best RP ship ever!

**Autumn:** Seconded! Roux/Aresha are OTP!

**Holly:** 1,000%! Have the best time, friends!

**Cass:** Will do, thanks!

**Rowan:** Bye, nerds! <3

My eyes lingered on the conversation, my heart racing. How would I survive thirty-six hours with Rowan Davies this close to me? The urge to hold her hand was strong, and some of our more romantic roleplay scenes flashed through my mind.

*Nope, shut it down*, I told myself. *Roleplay life and real life are two separate worlds. You aren't your characters.*

"Should we reply to scenes?" I asked, tucking some hair behind my ear to keep my hand from moving anywhere else.

Rowan was quiet for a beat before closing her laptop. "Nah, it can wait. Let's find something on Netflix."

*It can wait.* The three words escaped her lips with ease, and I envied her. I'd only briefly disappeared from my roleplay world a couple of times, but *It can wait* was hardly a mantra in my day-to-day life. If anything, I was closer to Autumn's always-available mentality. But having Rowan here to balance things out made it easier to stay offline.

"Sounds perfect," I said, setting my laptop aside and turning on the TV. "Important question. Can we agree on something to watch?"

"We better," Rowan said, nudging my leg with hers. "Our friendship is on the line."

"No pressure." I grinned as I moved through the various lists, stopping at *Dumplin'* after a minute. Macy Whittier's fantasy books had my heart, especially Tide Wars, but I was also a sucker for Julie Murphy's contemporary books. She was funny, sassy, and a fellow fat person who didn't hate her body. And the movie adaptation of her *Dumplin'* book was genius. "Have you seen this?"

"No, but it's on my list. You've mentioned it a time or twenty."

"Ha ha," I said dryly. "So is that a yes for watching it?"

"That's a yes. But don't recite the movie or do that thing people do where they say *This part is hilarious* or *Wait until the next scene*!"

I laughed, knowing exactly what she meant. Those people were *the worst* to watch movies with—just like the people who asked a dozen questions when you've never seen the movie. I was neither of those people. Usually. "I'll pretend I'm watching it for the first time."

"That's the spirit."

I started the movie before resting back against the headboard. It was easy to stay quiet during a movie I loved, and I looked at Rowan several times throughout to see if she smiled at the parts I smiled at—she did—and cried when I cried—she did, but she pretended she didn't. Tuttles jumped up halfway through and curled into a purring ball on our legs. We spoiled him with pets, our fingers brushing several times throughout.

*Thirty-four hours.*

"That was a damn good movie," she said once the credits rolled. "The author has other books, right?"

"Yeah," I said, glancing at her. "I own them all if you want to borrow one, but only if I get it back eventually."

"Uh, yes please. Send me home with your favorite one. It'll give me something new to read on the train instead of Tide Wars fanfic."

"You'll read that anyway," I teased, moving Tuttles aside and fetching my signed copy of *Pumpkin* from my bookcase. "They're all my favorites, but I'm obsessed with this one. I read it in a day."

"No pressure. Perfect." She took the book, focusing on it for a moment. "Is it cool if we call it a night? I'm wiped."

"For sure," I said, relieved she'd brought it up. Between school and everything else, I was ready to pass out. And I needed to calm my damn nerves after being close to her. "Do you have everything you need?"

"Yeah, thanks." Tuttles squawked an aggressive-for-him meow as she left the bed, and she stopped in the doorway. "Good night, Captain. See you in the morning."

That look returned, like she had more to say. But same as Taylor, Rowan didn't hold back if it was important. Not that I was comparing her with Taylor. "Good night, Champ," I said, leaving it alone.

I closed the door most of the way behind her, leaving enough room for Tuttles to bail when it suited him, and climbed back into bed. My online best friend was sleeping in my guest room. We got along as perfectly in person as we did online—when I wasn't being the worst. And she made me feel like I wasn't some chaotic person who didn't have her shit together.

Sometimes, life had an interesting way of being exactly what I needed. The rest I'd need to learn to let go of before it ruined everything.

[Unfinished one-on-one scene between Cass and Holly]

**Holly:** "What happens once everything calms down and Girishtova is safe?" Katrin asked, watching the captain with curiosity. "Will you marry Roux?"

**Cass:** "Who's talking about marriage?" Aresha asked, her cheeks feeling warm instantly, something she wasn't used to. "You're getting ahead of yourself."

**Holly:** "Don't care. I knew there was something special about her the day she snuck into our lives. I didn't think the special thing was that she'd convince your heart to beat for reasons beyond revenge, but I'm grateful for it." She knew Allain was grateful for it, too, but try getting a scene with that guy.

**Cass:** ((lol subtle Carina dig))

**Holly:** ((It was there, I went for it))

**Cass:** Aresha hadn't expected that either. "I don't know what will become of us. All I know is that we're here now, and that's more than enough."

**Holly:** Katrin grinned, nudging her. "You are going to marry her. I see it all over your face."

**Cass:** Aresha laughed softly, shaking her head. "Don't tempt me to prove you wrong. Because I would do it, if only to teach you a lesson."

**Holly:** "A lesson in foolishness," Katrin said, grinning. "Don't prove me wrong this time."

**Cass:** "No?" Aresha asked, pausing momentarily to torture the poor girl. Of course she already knew the answer. One day. "Very well."

# EIGHTEEN

We started my birthday morning at Hot Plate—a small '70s-themed diner with odd paintings and vintage figurines littering the walls and shelves. We ate in a booth by paintings of cats, clowns, and, ironically, Jesus. The absurdity of the diner was what made me love it. And the pancakes were swoonworthy.

After stuffing ourselves and drinking a vat of coffee, I drove us to the Mall of America. It was packed with tourists, families, and the occasional swarm of teens who actually liked it there. I agreed to walk the circular layout of every floor to give Rowan the full experience.

We stopped at BoxLunch to fawn over nerdy swag. Rowan bought a mug for her mom at the Minnesot-ah store and socks for her brothers at Alpaca Connection. We ate cannoli from Carlo's Bakery and drank bubble tea from Sencha. Rowan took a picture of us at the Crayola Store for Tate to hype up the joke, and we walked through Nickelodeon Universe to ride the log chute and take pictures with character statues for Home Base.

Once we'd had our fill of being around humans, we drove to Minnehaha Regional Park nearby to see the winter wonderland. Snow covered the surrounding trees and hiking paths, and the creek water that normally flowed toward the Mississippi River was frozen over. The main waterfall was active, but the surrounding water had frozen into an ice cave.

"What do you think?" I asked Rowan once we were inside it.

"It's beautiful," she said, her eyes focused on the ice. "I don't get to see a lot of stuff like this at home. We're always moving fast in the city, or I'm home ignoring the world."

I wanted to say Dad's favorite Ferris Bueller quote about life moving pretty fast, but I noticed a tear rolling down her cheek. "What's wrong?"

"Nothing," she said, quickly wiping under her eyes. "I was thinking about my dad. He would've loved this."

There was no right response. As much as I missed my mom and came across things she'd love, it wasn't the same. "Does it hurt thinking about him?"

"Yes and no." She looked back to the ice, a cold cloud escaping her mouth as she let out a shaky breath. "Seventeen years with him wasn't enough, but it was still seventeen years. And thinking about him helps me remember, you know? I don't want a day to come where I don't know what his laugh sounded like or how his cologne smelled. Or the look he had when I told a clever joke or did something that made him proud."

My eyes were glued to her as she spoke. I hated that I couldn't erase her pain, but I also knew pain was a reminder it had all been real. "Stand closer to the ice," I said, taking out my phone. "We'll capture this moment so you'll always remember how much he would've loved it."

"You just want to capture me looking like a mess," she said, wiping at her cheeks again and sniffling.

"Obviously, but also for unselfish reasons."

Rowan groaned as she stepped closer to the ice wall. "You're an asshole."

"I know," I said in a singsong voice, trying to cheer her up. "Now smile!"

I took a picture of her rolling her eyes. Another of her wiping the last tears away. Another of her lips turned slightly upward.

"Come on, Champ," I said. "You can do better than that."

Another of her flipping me off.

Another of her smiling a little, then a lot.

Another of her laughing.

"Got it." I stepped up to stand beside her. "And now we selfie."

"The ice will melt by the time you're done with this photo shoot," she snarked.

I nudged her. "So dramatic. It's my birthday, and this is what I want."

Rowan let out a deep sigh for added theatrical effect, then flashed a bright smile.

We went through a series of poses before I was satisfied. "These are perfect. Thanks for indulging me." I looked them over for a moment before realizing the time. "We should get back. Don't want to be late for my own party."

"Whatever you say, Captain," Rowan said, grinning and ruffling my hair before walking toward the cave's opening, leaving me with every thought and feeling I couldn't express.

*Seventeen hours.*

Dad was gone by the time we got home, leaving a note saying hamburger meat was thawed in the fridge and to have fun. The shame I felt over not telling him there'd be alcohol was added to the pile with my lies.

I turned on the oven before taking out the meat and other ingredients as Rowan sat at the island. Home Base knew all about my family's Tater Tot hotdish, and I was excited to share it with her. "So it might be my birthday, but you came all this way, and that warrants totdish."

Rowan's eyes lit up. "I was hoping it was totdish! But also, I think you'll stop speaking to me if I hate it, so bold move on your part."

I laughed. "I mean, it *is* the true test to see if my family will keep someone around, but let's not assume the worst yet."

"Like I said—bold move."

Some people made totdish with green beans or cheese, but there was a special place in hell for them. The recipe I grew up on was the only version I liked, and I didn't care how dramatic that sounded. The ingredients were simple: Tater Tots, ground beef, cream-style corn, cream of mushroom soup, and cream of celery soup. Salt and pepper after baking optional. Adding any other flavors ruined it—even cheese, which was one of my favorite foods.

After cooking the meat and combining it with the canned ingredients, I poured it over a layer of tots in a baking dish, then added a top tot layer and put the dish in the oven. It needed an hour to bake, so I led us upstairs to put on makeup and change. I slipped on a knee-length dress with rainbow sequins and a pair of black tights before stepping into the hall. Like me, Rowan was usually a dressed-for-comfort kind of person, but she was wearing a thigh-length black dress with sequin sleeves, and no leggings. We matched without planning it, and she looked . . .

*Fifteen and a half hours.*

"I love the dress," I said, begging my heart to stop being chaotic. "We're sequin twins."

"Oh gods, you're right," she said, giggling and looking me over. "You look awesome! That dress was made for you. We need pics immediately."

My cheeks warmed from the compliment. We found a spot in the hall, and Rowan took pictures of us being adorable and silly. "I'll send a few of these to the group," she said. "Maybe it'll motivate them to join next time."

"I can't wait for a Home Base retreat," I said as I looked through the pictures with her.

"Totally," Rowan said. "They can stay in our dorm."

My stomach dropped at the thought. We'd talked about it, but I'd pushed it out my head after our fight. Living with Rowan would be a constant nerd party. I wouldn't have to explain roleplaying to another roommate, and she'd help me manage my online addiction by threatening to end our ship if I refused to leave the room for class or events.

But would I be able to handle it emotionally? As much as I didn't want to have a crush on her, nothing had changed. "True," I said slowly, knowing that was future Cass's problem if I got accepted to UIC. "But dorms are tiny. We'd need a hotel to fit everyone."

Rowan shrugged, clearly not overthinking it like *some people*. "We'd make it work—get an air mattress or share beds. And Carina won't be there. Even if she wanted to come, how would she explain it to her friends? Imagine the drama."

It was like she was talking about me. "Yeah, also true," I said quietly.

"Shit, I'm sorry," Rowan said, taking my hand. "I promised we wouldn't talk about that, and there I go talking about it. Ignore me."

"Hard to ignore something that's bothering you," I said, frowning. "I know I messed up, but it won't be like this forever. Seeing you around my dad and Tate has really helped, but I'm not ready for everything to come out yet."

"Progress is progress," Rowan said, squeezing my hand. "We're good, okay? Promise."

The warmth of her skin felt like a mitt after taking totdish out of the oven. "Thanks." I smiled like a goof as the doorbell rang, and I checked my phone. Someone was ten minutes early.

Rowan's hand slipped away. "So it begins," she said, grinning. "I'm *so* ready for this."

That made one of us.

We skipped down the stairs, and I opened the door to find Taylor on the other end. "Hey, there she is!"

There. She. Is. What the fuck, Cass?

"Here I am," Taylor said, laughing a little as she walked in. "Happy birthday!" She kissed me, keeping it short, then handed me a wrapped gift as her gaze wandered. "You must be Rowan. I'm Taylor."

"Great to meet you," Rowan said, smiling brightly. "I've heard a lot about you."

"Wish I could say the same. Cass has been pretty quiet. But honestly, church camp is nothing to be embarrassed about. Parents rope kids into all kinds of stuff when they're young."

"They sure do," Rowan said, playing along like the best friend I didn't deserve. "But I'm here now, and I'm an open book."

"Good. Can't wait to get to know you better." Taylor took off her coat to reveal a turquoise velvet suit with a low-cut white top.

Once again, my girlfriend was pulling mad modern Roux vibes. "You look amazing," I said, finding it hard to look away.

"Thanks," Taylor said, taking us both in. "I would've worn something sequin had I gotten the memo."

Rowan chuckled, shaking her head. "Sequins are the go-to for people who don't know how to dress for parties. You're killing the velvet look."

I was forever grateful to Rowan Davies for knowing exactly what to say.

"Thanks," Taylor said again, holding my hand before glancing around the room. "So who's all coming tonight?"

"It'll be us, Tate, Rachel, June, and Fynn," I said. "Tate hasn't mentioned inviting anyone, so that's probably it." My hand felt heavy in hers. I squeezed it quickly before letting go and leading them to the kitchen. "I gotta check on the totdish. Feel free to grab whatever to drink. Tate and Rachel should be here soon."

"Cool," Taylor said as she and Rowan sat at the island. "So tell me more about you two."

"What do you mean?" I asked way too quickly, turning from the oven to face them.

"Well, church camp was a long time ago," Taylor said slowly, raising her eyebrows. "Did you turn into old-school pen pals, or was it all social media?"

I stared back at her. This wasn't part of the plan. I'd wanted Rowan to meet the people in my life, but I didn't want the people in my life asking her questions that would put her in a position to lie. "We messaged online and called each other sometimes," I said before Rowan could answer. It was my lie, after all. What did I have to lose except for *everything*? "Chicago was the first time I'd seen her since camp."

"Seems like a long time to go without hanging out when you're only six hours away."

I blinked at Taylor's response, trying not to get prickly over her innocent attempts at a conversation. But it was hard when it felt like an interrogation. "The world feels bigger when you're young."

"Now that we've hung out again, I'm sure it'll happen more

often," Rowan said with an easy smile, saving the moment yet again. "Especially if we both end up in Chicago for school."

"Exactly," I said. "And now it's like we're real best friends, not camp friends."

Taylor nodded, staring at her phone. "Love that," she said absently, biting her lip after a moment.

"What's up?" I asked, instantly on alert.

She hesitated before looking back at me. "Did you invite Greg?"

I laughed at the mention of my only ex-boyfriend, who was obviously *not* welcome at my house. Me going to his house twice last year was irrelevant. "Uh, no, definitely not," I said, my eyes narrowing. "Why?"

She glanced at her phone again. "Um, he posted about getting ready for your party, saying it was gonna be, and I quote, *so dope*. And a ton of people commented that they're coming too."

I groaned. Had Tate invited his football friends? My Greg Jensen conflict wasn't a *real* conflict anymore, and I didn't have anything against the rest of the team, but still. This was high school. It was one thing to go to a cool party with your cool best friend or cool girlfriend. It was completely different to be the not-cool friend hosting the cool kids. With no warning.

"What do I do?" I asked, looking between them.

"How big of a deal is this?" Rowan asked.

"Not that big," Taylor said, shrugging. "Just . . . unexpected?"

"*So* unexpected," I agreed, my brain already in panic mode. "Should I get more snacks? Tell Tate to buy more alcohol? His older cousin is getting us a few things, but that'll be gone in five minutes if the football team shows up."

Taylor rested her hands on my shoulders. "Relax. I'm sure Tate knows how much alcohol to get."

Funny how anyone would think I'd be capable of relaxing in a moment like this. It was comical. Hysterical. I shook my head and texted Tate as Taylor dropped her hands with a sigh.

**Cass: Greg Jensen is coming tonight? And a ton of other people? WTF, TATE?!**

"What do I do?" I asked again.

"If you trust me with your car, I can run to the store for more snacks," Taylor said. "You already have a good music setup and tons of space. We'll be fine as long as there's more food. Oh, and maybe drinking-game supplies?"

Dad had put money in my bank account for my birthday, and of course this was how I was going to spend it. "Do whatever you think is necessary. I don't want tonight to be terrible."

"I promise it won't be terrible," Taylor said, glancing at Rowan. "Want to come? Cass will need space to yell at Tate when he gets here."

Rowan laughed. "As much as I'd love to watch that, I'm in."

Shit. The party hadn't started yet, and the night was already running away from me. Goodbye, chill night with friends. Goodbye, sanity. I grabbed my debit card and keys, handing both to Taylor. "My party is in your hands. *Thank you.*"

"You're welcome," Taylor said, looking thoughtful. "Take a

deep breath, or ten. It'll be great." She kissed my cheek before heading to the door with Rowan, who saluted me with a grin.

They were both adorable, and it was almost enough to calm me down.

Once the door clicked shut, I swept through the house to check on the totdish, take out snacks, and look at my phone multiple times. I tucked Rowan's suitcase in the guest closet with Ursula before picking up clothes and random items in my room. I secured Tuttles in Dad's room with his food, water, and litter box, locking the door to keep him safe from potential drunken shenanigans. It was the least I could do.

By the time I returned downstairs, Tate and Rachel had let themselves in and were setting several bottles of alcohol on the counter and filling the fridge with beer. Rachel gasped when she saw me. "Cass, I *love* your dress!"

"Thanks," I muttered before walking up to Tate, whose fist was raised for our usual greeting. Instead of bumping it, I punched his arm.

"Ow!" Tate frowned, rubbing his arm. "What the hell, C?"

"No, that's *my* question," I said, my hand gesturing to the alcohol. "Clearly you know about the big party I'm throwing now. Why would you invite your football friends? You know how I feel about Greg Jensen."

"Rachel and I only told a couple people about the party. It may have gotten out of hand after that." Tate smiled sheepishly as Rachel conveniently excused herself to the bathroom. "But it'll be okay! You don't have to talk to Greg or even look at him. There will be enough people here for you to avoid him."

I groaned at the confirmation that people were coming to my house. *A lot* of people. And soon. "I wanted a low-key birthday party, Tate, not a drunkfest of people I'm not friends with," I whined, my shoulders slumped.

Tate rested his hands on my shoulders. "I'm really sorry. I wasn't thinking. If you want, I can turn everyone around when they get here, send them to Greg's or something. Say the word, and it'll be a small group watching movies and building a fire out back. We can make s'mores while we freeze our asses off. It'll be great."

I knew he meant it, but I wouldn't let him do that. I'd promised Rowan a good time. I'd promised *myself* a good time. And something about hosting my first—*and last*—high school party with my friends made me feel more like myself than I'd felt in a long time.

Maybe this was a sign. Like Aresha returning to Girishtova, maybe it was time for me to rebuild my life. Now I just needed to learn how to be as brave as my character.

"Let's have the party," I said, forcing a smile. "It'll be great, like you said."

Tate relaxed instantly. "You'll love it! And if you don't, I'll fix it." He squeezed my shoulders. "Rowan will love it, too. Where is she, by the way?"

"She and Taylor went to get more snacks after the news was dumped on me that I'd need to supply more than a few bags of chips and some cookies," I said pointedly, moving his hands away and swatting his arm. "And seriously, next time you want to party away from Greg's house, run it by me first."

"It won't happen again." Tate grinned, probably because he knew I no longer planned on slapping him. "Happy birthday, by the way. Rachel made space for your gifts on the table."

"Yeah, thanks," I said, assuming the only gifts I'd get would be from the people I'd wanted at the party. I took in the spread of alcohol, reality consuming me all over again. Rowan would see a part of my life that was nothing like my real life, and she would no doubt give me fake shit for it. And look cute doing it. Perfect.

*Fifteen hours.*

Taylor and Rowan returned with more snacks than Dad bought in a month. "A thousand times thank you!" I said, kissing Taylor quickly before looking at Rowan. "You too, Champ. Nice teamwork."

"You got it, Captain," Rowan said before looking at Tate, a light smirk forming. "Hey, boyfriend."

"Sup, girlfriend?" Tate said, before quickly getting side jabbed by Rachel. "Hey!"

I snorted, putting on mitts and opening the oven to take out the totdish.

Taylor stopped beside me. "What's with the Champ and Captain nicknames?" she asked quietly.

And then I almost dropped the totdish. The nicknames had

come out naturally, and I hadn't considered how weird it would sound to literally anyone outside of the roleplay. "Nothing really," I said, laughing off my slip. "Inside joke."

"Oh."

Rowan came to stand by us. "Okay, let's see this famous tot-dish."

Relieved by the distraction, I set the dish on a couple of pot holders and stepped aside so she could see it. Most of it looked like mush, but the top layer of golden tots made up for it. "Your taste buds will never be the same."

"I still say it's boring without cheese," Rachel said. "My family would be appalled by your version, just saying."

"Well, hey, back at your fam," I said, flashing her a smile. We'd had the conversation more than once since she'd started dating Tate.

"Don't listen to her, C," Tate said, stepping up behind Rachel and resting a hand over her mouth playfully. "She knows not what she says."

"Don't!" Rachel whined behind his hand, bumping him with her butt before stepping away. They were both grinning as Tate held his hands up in surrender.

Per usual, I rolled my eyes at their vomitworthy cuteness before glancing at Taylor. She met my eyes with a frown, and I quickly moved away to grab plates and forks as if I hadn't seen her—you know, basically the worst thing I could've done. "Okay, dish up!"

Everyone settled at the table and started to eat, and within seconds Rowan let out a light moan. "This is delicious," she said enthusiastically before taking another big bite.

Tate and I grinned. "Glad you like it," I said, looking at Taylor. "What's the verdict?"

"It's good," she mumbled, finishing her bite before smiling in a way that said she was being kind, not honest.

"There's nothing wrong with wanting cheese on it," Rachel said before I could respond.

She then launched into a fresh debate about food with Tate, and it was like the rest of us weren't there as they grew more and more grossly adorable. I laughed quietly and focused on eating. Taylor barely looked at me the rest of dinner as she poked at my favorite meal, only eating half of her serving.

Rowan ate every bite of totdish and complimented it again. But she didn't say anything else, and the longer we sat there, the more nervous she looked. Did something happen while she and Taylor were shopping? Had Taylor asked an uncomfortable question or Rowan said something that didn't align with my lies? Had I put too much pressure on her to be someone she wasn't?

My nerves were underscored by the fact that Mom wasn't here to make me a cake or embarrass me with her singing or anything else I'd grown up expecting every birthday. Knowing I couldn't do a damn thing about it, I ate my favorite meal in silence. If nothing else, at least I'd always have totdish.

# NINETEEN

Music worthy of a Greg Jensen party played as people arrived. A few of them surprised me by bringing gifts, which somewhat helped ease my fear that my birthday was completely ruined. I escaped to the kitchen for another drink after practically clinging to my friends for the first half hour.

Greg walked in as I mixed together one of Taylor's concoctions from New Year's. "Happy birthday," he said, holding out a poorly wrapped gift. "Thanks for the invite."

"I didn't invite you," I said before I could help it, still a little sour with Tate for accidentally spreading the word. And sour with Greg forever on principle.

"Same as when you show up to my parties, then." He smiled a little, stepping closer as his voice quieted. "And hey, I'm sorry about what happened after you came out. I was mad we'd stopped being friends after breaking up, but that's no excuse. I was an asshole." He rubbed the back of his neck—a nervous tic I remembered from years ago. "It was cool of you to figure out your identity and all that."

Shock from his words pulsed through me. "Look at you talking about *identity*. Did a feminist get to you or something?"

"Yeah, your best friend," he said, dropping his hand. "Tate called me out for how I acted. And it took a long time for it to sink in, but I should've said something sooner. And now that we're about to graduate, I couldn't leave without telling you I'm sorry."

Tate had never mentioned that, but I wasn't surprised. He was my silent hero, and I doubted that was the only time he'd defended me when I wasn't around to do it myself. And he knew I'd do the same for him—you know, if anyone dared speak a word against Saint Tate.

Greg's apology brought back a flood of childhood memories. Dragging our moms to the Mall of America and the zoo too many times to count. Making brownies for school bake sales. Having water-balloon fights in the summer and snowball fights in the winter. I was sure that old friend was still in there somewhere. *Deep down.* "Thanks, Greg. It's been easy hating you, but that speech will make it slightly harder."

"Good, that was the idea," he said, grinning gently. "Anyway, Tate said you might be going to school in Chicago?"

I nodded, holding the gift closer to me after accepting that it wasn't poisonous. "That's the plan, if I get accepted to UIC."

"Solid. I'm aiming for Loyola. Maybe we can hang out some-time? If you officially stop hating me, I mean."

I rolled my eyes because I'd never *truly* hated him—just severely disliked. "Despite my better judgment, I'd like that. But only if we both end up there. I'm not driving six hours to visit your ass."

He barked a laugh, shaking his head. "I'd expect nothing less. But cool, let me know."

"Will do. Now go away before I decide you're a decent person."

"Too late, I think." He winked before grabbing a beer and walking off to join some of the football team, yelling something about getting wasted.

*Gods.*

I was tempted to rip open the present he'd brought, but I added it to the growing pile and made the rounds instead, since people had ventured upstairs. Fortunately, no one had broken anything or gotten into Dad's room. But when I walked into mine, a handful of people were there, and my laptop screen was turned on—a message on display for them to see.

"Hey, Cass!" one girl said, a bright smile on her lips. "Great party."

"Hey, thanks." My eyes shifted from her to the screen. "Did someone use my laptop?"

"What? No?" She looked down. "It must've turned on when I bumped the desk."

"Did you read the message?"

"Wow, paranoid much?" she asked, causing her friends to snicker. "No one read your message, but now I kind of want to."

"Find another room."

I looked at the screen once they'd left to see what could've been discovered.

**Autumn:** Hope you have the best birthday party ever, friend! <3<3

A relieved breath escaped me, and I locked the screen before returning downstairs. Tate and Rachel were playing a drinking game. Taylor's best friends, Fynn and June, were on the couch having an enthusiastic conversation about something. And Rowan was swaying along to the music with a handful of other people.

I knew I should look for Taylor, especially since she was worried about not getting any time together, but Rowan noticed me and my body pulled me to her. "Hey! Having fun?" I asked her.

"I am," Rowan said, laying an arm across my shoulders. "Sway with me."

I laughed but did as she said. "You're drunk."

"Almost. Are *you* having fun, Captain?"

"You know, I think I actually am," I said, smiling genuinely. "I'm honestly surprised this many people showed up."

"Why?"

"This kind of turnout is for the Greg Jensens of the world. I'm more in the loner category at school, and I'd totally be considered a loser if Tate wasn't my best friend."

"Don't talk about my best friend like that," Rowan said. "I saw all those gifts on the table. People came here for you." She rested her drink against my cheek, giggling as I flinched at the cold. "I came here for you."

I laughed, knowing better than to read into that. "You're definitely drunk."

"Maybe." She pulled the can away to drink more, then looked around, recognition forming. "Hey, Taylor! Join us."

My eyes found Taylor's, and I waved for her as Rowan moved her arm from my shoulders. "Where've you been?" I asked once she was closer.

"Hanging out with June and Fynn, and a minute ago I was in the bathroom," she said, looking between us. "Where have *you* been, birthday girl?"

"Oh, here and there." I wasn't as drunk as Rowan, but I felt the small amount I'd had since I rarely drank. "I actually caught up with Greg, of all people."

"That's promising," Taylor said, smiling encouragingly. "I saw him walk in with a present earlier."

"Oh!" Rowan said excitedly. "Maybe it's a zoo pass. You two can hang with the penguins again."

"I could only be so lucky," I said dryly. The things she remembered were wild. I envied her brain.

"What about penguins?" Taylor asked, her eyebrows furrowed.

"Cass and Greg used to make their moms take them to the zoo all the time when they were little," Rowan said. "Penguins were the *it* animal, apparently."

"I didn't know you and Greg were friends before dating," Taylor said.

"Yeah." I shrugged. "It was forever ago. We haven't been friends since middle school."

"Oh."

The discomfort could be cut with a knife. We were all quiet for an awkward amount of time before Rowan clapped her free hand to her drink. "Bathroom. Be right back."

Once she was gone, Taylor and I spoke at the same time.

"Do you want to dance?"

"I'm gonna go."

I blinked. "Wait, what? Why?"

"Because I'm tired and over all the noise," she said as she took out her phone. "But it's cool. My parents are at a friend's house nearby and said they'd pick me up." She glanced at me, smiling a little. "Wait outside with me?"

I might've been the shitty one in our relationship, but I knew when she was holding back. "Yeah, okay."

We put on our coats and boots before sitting on the porch steps outside. "Are you okay?" I asked, already spiraling over what she was thinking.

"I don't know," she said, looking at her hands that were clasped together on her lap. "I feel like you have more fun with other people than you do with me. And the way you and Rowan interact—it's like this secret code way beyond anything we have. And it feels like there's something more going on with her, and it's really hard to be around you two together with that thought blaring in my head."

I stifled a laugh as my nerves jumbled. My private Rowan crush was far from anything Taylor was imagining. "Nothing else is going on."

She shot me a pointed look. "Right."

"You don't believe me?"

"I believe that *you* believe there's nothing going on."

I groaned, hating when people said shit like that. "Maybe we do have a secret-code thing, but it doesn't mean anything. We've just known each other longer. I have that with Tate, too." I paused. "If this is about the love thing, I'm sorry. But I'm here, and I like you. Can that be enough?"

"I'm trying to let it be, and it has been." She looked at me. "But then you sprung Rowan on me. And maybe there's nothing going on and it's all me, but things feel off."

This was all my fault. I'd tried to protect such an innocent part of my life, and this was where it got me. And I needed to fix it. Now. "Taylor—"

"There's something else," she said before I could continue. "I really didn't want to bring it up on your birthday, but then you and Rowan used those Tide Wars nicknames, and I can't stop thinking about it."

I frowned at the memory. "I'm sure it's hard to believe right now considering everything else you're thinking, but they're just our favorite characters."

"It's not that," she said, heaving a sigh. "I finished reading the books. I wanted to get through them before your birthday and hopefully give them all kinds of praise and, I don't know, feel more connected to you. Have something to fangirl over together."

I frowned, knowing where this was going. "But you didn't like them."

Her eyes lingered on me for a few seconds before she shook her head. "No, I didn't. And I'm sorry. I *really* wanted to love them because you do. And seeing how much you and Rowan love them felt like another thing I got wrong."

"You didn't get anything wrong," I said, taking her hand. Of course it hurt that she didn't love the books, but it was hardly a breakup-able offense—especially considering all my faults. "What didn't you like about them?"

Taylor cringed, looking at our hands. "I don't think I should say."

"Try me."

She shifted in place. "Well, it all felt super dramatic, and not in a good way. I had trouble believing the main love story. And the author's writing . . . I don't know, it felt like she was trying too hard."

Taylor's words punched me in the face. I hadn't written the books, obviously, but she was talking about mine and Rowan's characters. We'd worked hard on them and kept them pretty true to the books. "That's . . . too bad," I said slowly. "But it's fine. They're just books." I smiled a little and focused on our hands, trying to stay calm.

It was fine. They were just books.

But they weren't *just books*. Macy Whittier's words changed my life. Tide Wars had been there for me during my lowest time. It was full of inseparable family when mine was being ripped apart, full of love when the person I'd thought loved me the most abandoned me, and full of leadership when I didn't know how to lead myself forward anymore. It gave me my own found family. It helped me breathe and find myself again. And my girlfriend didn't like it.

"Are you okay?"

I met her eyes. "Yeah, all good. Why?"

"You're crying."

As if I wasn't a big enough noodle already. I forced a laugh and wiped under my eyes. "Guess I was in my head."

"We can talk about it," Taylor said, frowning. "That's how the girlfriend thing works, you know. You can tell me things. I *want* you to tell me things."

I couldn't tell her about the roleplay anymore. Tide Wars meant *everything* to me, but to her it was dramatic and unbelievable. And she'd essentially made fun of the character I played, which in a way felt like she was making fun of me. We were allowed to like different things, but this felt lonely.

Carina had been right. Taylor didn't need to know about my second life. No one did. They wouldn't understand. "There's nothing to say," I said, squeezing her hand. "The important thing is that you tried reading them again. That means a lot to me."

"Are you sure? I've felt like shit about it for days."

She looked defeated. And as much as I hated this, I hated more that she was worried about Rowan. No matter what was going on in my head, the reality was that I had a girlfriend who I needed to try harder with and put first for once.

"I'm sure," I said as her dad pulled up. "There's your ride, but I'll see you tomorrow?"

"Yeah," she said, letting out a breath. "Enjoy the rest of your party. And I'm sorry again. Tell Rowan it was nice meeting her?"

"I will," I said, relieved we could end on a somewhat positive note.

After a quick kiss, I watched her go, knowing I needed to get over her not loving Tide Wars, since she knew nothing about why it mattered. And I needed to do something big to make everything else up to her.

Tate found me after I'd gotten another drink and returned to the living room. "Is everything okay?" he asked, his voice laced with concern. "I thought you'd left your own party."

His best friend radar had clearly gone off. And I wanted to tell him everything, but now wasn't the time. I was tipsy and confused and slightly terrified of losing my girlfriend. "Taylor decided to call it early."

"Boring." He snorted, looking around. "Where's Rowan?"

"No idea. That's my next mission. And hey, thanks for offering to cancel the party, but I'm glad you didn't."

He smiled warmly. "Me too. I know you wanted to have a

low-key night, but you deserved this." He leaned closer. "I wanted you to remember there are people who'd give a shit about you if you'd let them."

After everything with my mom, I'd needed to hear that. "That's why I love you," I said, pulling him in for a hug. "Thank you, seriously. It's been a messy, almost glorious birthday."

"Mission accomplished." Tate stepped back after a moment, nodding toward the party. "Found Rowan."

I followed his gaze and saw Rowan playing a drinking game with Rachel and a couple of other people. She already looked victorious with her sparkling dress and winning smile. When she paused to wave at me, my heart did a little dance. "Yeah, she's a natural," I said softly, waving back before looking at Tate. "I'm gonna take some pictures, but can you kick people out for me within the hour?"

Tate had an odd look on his face, and he shook his head, chuckling. "Yeah, consider it done. Have fun with your pictures." He laughed a little more and walked away.

Not knowing what that was about, I shrugged it off and went in the opposite direction with my phone, capturing the only high school party I'd ever host.

Once the crowd thinned, Tate and Rachel helped me half-ass clean before going to Tate's to crash. I locked up, turned off the lights downstairs, and freed Tuttles from Dad's room. Leaning against my bedroom doorway, I saw Rowan sitting on my bed, staring at her phone. I still couldn't believe she was here. In my city. In my house. In my room. In my life.

On my bed.

*Nine hours.*

"Have fun tonight?" I asked.

Rowan looked up, a slightly drunken smile on her lips. "I did. Minneapolis people are pretty cool."

"Yeah, we do all right," I said, sitting next to her. "Taylor wanted me to tell you it was great meeting you."

"Cool, same to her."

She looked back to her phone, her expression unreadable. I watched her for a moment before following her gaze to Home Base on her screen.

> **Holly:** OMG you look killer!!
>
> **Autumn:** Cuuuute! Love the matching dresses.
>
> **Holly:** It's settled. We're going to Chicago next year and living in the dorm for a weekend. Convince your parents, Autumn
>
> **Autumn:** I'll work my magic.
>
> **Holly:** good luck with that
>
> **Autumn:** lol shut up :)

I laughed at their reactions, but my smile faded when I noticed Rowan biting her lip. "What's wrong?"

"I hate this," she said after a pause. "Lying for you. People asked me questions that I didn't know how to answer. I didn't out your secret, obviously, but damn it, I *wanted to*. I'm already keeping in a lot, and adding this to the list is too much."

"What else are you keeping in?" I asked. "I thought you were an open book."

"Not always."

"What, then?"

"I can't tell you."

I frowned. "Why not? We tell each other everything." Almost.

"I know, but this particular thing will mess *everything* up, and I don't want to do that. We've had enough bumps lately."

Now I *needed* to know. "Try me."

Rowan sighed and shut off her screen before looking at me. "I have a thing for you."

I blinked. The alcohol must've gotten to me more than I'd thought. Or she knew my every thought and was messing with me. "You what?"

"I'm into you. You know what I mean."

"I know what that means, yes, but I didn't know—why didn't you tell me you liked girls when I came out to you?"

"Because I didn't know then. It didn't click until recently. I never cared about dating, and for the longest time I couldn't fig-ure out why." She shrugged. "And then I figured it out."

My heart raced. How could this be happening? How could Taylor have seen it while I was oblivious? "When did you realize how you felt?" I asked, my mind whirling as I tried making sense of everything. Tried to figure out what this meant for us, if any-thing.

Rowan grimaced. "Um, in Chicago. When you first told us about dating Taylor, I thought it was friend jealousy at first because having a girlfriend would mean you not being online as much. But then I started thinking about it more and feeling all these feelings I wasn't used to. And when I met you in person, everything fell into place."

I took in her words, thinking about the end of the first Tide Wars book. Roux and Aresha finally confessed their feelings for each other after 300-ish agonizing pages of *yearning*. But unlike Aresha, I already had a girlfriend. And I lacked Aresha's courage. And this was real life.

"Look, it doesn't matter," she continued after I failed to respond. "You're happy with Taylor, and I'm happy for you. Don't let this mess with anything. We're good."

Of course it mattered. But it couldn't matter. I needed to figure things out with Taylor. And despite my feelings, Rowan was my best friend. We ran a roleplay together and were going to be college roommates. I didn't want to risk ruining any of that.

But would I regret it if I didn't try?

I braved taking her hand, squeezing it as I ignored the pain in my chest. "Thank you for telling me. I'm really proud of you for figuring all of this out for yourself. But I need to process."

"I get it," Rowan said. "And don't think you need to do or say anything. I'm not looking for a specific response. But I hate secrets, and this was kind of a huge one."

It was definitely a huge one, and I wasn't sure I'd ever recover from it. "I'm glad you told me. And you didn't ruin anything. We're still us. Nothing will change that, okay?"

"Okay." She paused. "We should probably get some sleep. Early day tomorrow."

I didn't want to leave things like this, but asking her to stay would send mixed signals, and I'd caused enough problems. "Yeah, get some sleep."

She stood, her eyes fixed on mine. "Happy birthday, Captain."

A strained smile fell across my lips. "Thanks, Champ."

Everything moved in slow motion as she left the room. A part of me wanted to go after her, tell her I felt the same, and kiss her, but I'd never do that to Taylor. I'd lied about a lot, but I wasn't a cheater. Taylor and I would either get closer in time and be perfectly happy together, or things would end naturally, but I wouldn't be like my mom.

In the end, I changed, crawled into bed, and stared at my door, letting every little thing Taylor and Rowan had said flood my brain as I hoped for an easy answer that never came.

[Private conversation between Cass and Autumn]

**Autumn:** Hope you and Rowan are having fun!

**Autumn:** Can't wait to see pics

**Autumn:** JK I see some got sent to Home Base :)

**Autumn:** Hope you have the best birthday party ever, friend! <3<3

**Autumn:** Maybe we can have a group scene this week?

**Cass:** Sorry, been a busy couple days. Will send more pics soon. And yes to a group scene! We'll get something posted to the main server.

**Autumn:** Yay, can't wait! And I'm so happy you got to hang with Rowan again.

**Cass:** Thanks, me too. She's the best. :)

# TWENTY

A hangover hit me the next morning, though it didn't compare with the lingering pain in my chest. But I didn't have time to fight it. After making sure Rowan was awake, I threw my hair in a ponytail and changed into leggings and a sweater, feeling far less glamorous than the night before. I missed my gay rainbow dress.

I found Dad at the kitchen table, drinking coffee. "How was the party?" he asked, shooting me a knowing look.

The state of the room confirmed that being drunk last night had made me incapable of cleaning properly. "It was bigger than I'd planned, but fun. And I kind of made up with Greg Jensen, which was nice, I guess."

"There's a name I haven't heard in ages," Dad said. "But good. Did Rowan have fun?"

"I think so," I said, though I honestly wasn't sure at this point. My eyes locked on a pong ball on the other end of the table. We both knew he'd seen it. "I guess some people played beer pong?"

Dad chuckled, shaking his head. "I'm going to let all of this slide as part of your birthday present, and because I haven't gotten more calls from the school about your grades. But let's agree it was your first and last party in this house."

"Deal," I said easily.

"Good. And speaking of presents, your mom sent one. It's with the rest of your pile."

Oh, right. People had brought presents. And Mom . . . nope, future Cass problem. "Okay. I need to take Rowan to the station and meet up with Taylor for brunch, but I promise to do a better job cleaning when I get home. When's dinner?"

"Let's plan on seven," Dad said.

"Perfect. You can tell me all about your date."

"Looking forward to it."

I grinned. If he was willing to share, that meant things were getting serious. I returned upstairs and knocked on the open doorway of the guest room as Rowan packed her suitcase. "Hey, wanted to make sure you're good to leave soon."

"Yeah, almost ready," Rowan said, pausing. "And hey, I'm sorry about everything last night. I was a little drunk."

"We both were," I said, trying to decide whether or not to bring everything back up. "Do you remember what you said?"

"Oh, I remember. And I meant all of it, but I'm still sorry. I know it makes things awkward."

"Don't be sorry. We're good," I said, smiling a little. "Want help with your bag?"

"I got it, thanks. But can we get coffee on the way to the station?"

"Obviously."

*One hour.*

I didn't want her to leave, but I knew it was for the best. Not just because of dreaded *Feelings*, but because she kind of needed to finish high school. I led us downstairs, Tuttles trailing behind after appearing out of nowhere.

"Good morning," Dad said, smiling at Rowan as Tuttles purred against her legs. "Sorry I wasn't really around this weekend, but you're welcome back anytime."

"Thanks, Cool Dad, I'll definitely take you up on that," Rowan said, kneeling to pet Tuttles and say goodbye. She'd been in my city for less than forty-eight hours, and she'd effortlessly made a mark. It wouldn't feel the same without her.

After picking up two coffees and a breakfast sandwich for Rowan, we drove on in silence. I didn't want it to be awkward, and shutting my mouth was the only way to keep it from getting worse. But I couldn't stop thinking about what she'd told me, and what I could've told her.

"We should schedule a group scene once I get home," Rowan said in a purely professional tone.

"For sure," I said, playing along despite feeling tortured. "Autumn actually asked about that, so she'll be happy. I still feel bad for missing that one scene."

"You've had a lot going on. But since you play the ship's captain, you're kind of a big deal."

"And I'm your girlfriend." I immediately regretted my words. "I mean, Aresha—you know what I mean."

"I do."

She was looking out the window. This was exactly why I didn't want to open my mouth. But would roleplaying be weird now? I sighed, twisting the knife I'd plunged into my own back. "Is everything that happened gonna make our scenes awkward? Our writing can get kind of—well, it's not always innocent."

"It'll be fine," she said dismissively. "We're not our characters. At least that's how I see it."

"Same," I said quickly, my cheeks warming. "And good. There's no one else I'd rather ship my character with. You're kind of stuck with me."

"There are worse things than being stuck with you, Cassidy Williams."

Another quick glance showed she was smiling now. Was this flirting? Did it matter? As much as I'd miss her, a little distance would do us good. I could get lost overthinking every single word. Every glance. Every smile. Every time her hand inched closer to mine.

"Back at you," I said as I pulled up in front of the station. "Want me to come in and hang until your train arrives?"

"Thanks, but you have a brunch to get to," she said, her expression calming again.

Right. My birthday brunch. With my real-life girlfriend. "Let me at least get your bag."

"A true chauffeur."

I laughed, hopping out to grab her suitcase. "Text me when you get home, okay?"

"I will." She pulled me in for a hug. "Thanks for a fun weekend. And please try not to overthink everything."

The awkwardness slipped away as I hugged her back, feeling warm and comfortable in her arms. "I'll try. And sorry again for being a shit about roleplay life."

"You're not a shit," Rowan said. "You'll tell people the truth when it feels right. I'm starting to understand that better. Don't tell them because of me or the others. Do it for you."

"Thanks," I said. A weight lifted as I reluctantly let go. "So see you sometime?"

She nodded, grinning. "See you sometime."

I watched her walk away, hating myself all over again for not being everything she deserved. Feelings aside, this weekend had changed us and our friendship. She was stuck with me now, even if she got mad at me again. I wasn't going anywhere.

The drive to brunch with Taylor was quieter than the one with Rowan. The night had ended okay, but sobering up and the light of day changed things. "Sorry about last night," I said after ten grueling minutes of listening to songs from a playlist we normally sang along to while Taylor stared at her phone.

"We were drunk," Taylor said, shrugging. "But let's put that behind us. I want to treat you to a delicious brunch and talk to you about something kind of important."

Important? Oh gods.

"What is it?" I asked, trying and failing to sound chill.

"Nothing terrible, I promise," she said, smirking. "Deep breaths."

"Shut up," I laughed, shaking my head. And then I let out a dramatic deep breath for emphasis. "Better?"

"Better." She took my free hand, holding it for the rest of the drive.

After parking in front of Barbette, a French-style restaurant in Uptown Minneapolis, we secured a table and ordered hot chocolates. "I want to talk about prom," Taylor said once the server left. "I know you don't want to go, but I really hope I can change your mind."

My eyes narrowed. "This is the first time we've talked about prom. I haven't said anything about not wanting to go."

"Right," she said slowly, fidgeting with her napkin. "But Rowan did."

"What are you talking about?"

"I told her I was gonna ask you to prom when we were out buying party snacks, and she said you wouldn't want to go."

As she explained, I remembered telling Rowan all about my prom dilemma in Chicago. And I was going to be proactive and honest for once and tell Taylor about not wanting to go, but then the Rowan fight overshadowed everything else that day and I'd genuinely forgotten.

It also explained why Rowan had acted weird after getting back from shopping with Taylor. And she was right, but still. "I'm sorry she said that," I said, internally slapping myself for not bringing this up yet.

"She wasn't rude about it," she added quickly. "But she said it like it was the most obvious thing it the world. And it made me feel stupid, like I should've known that about you." She sighed, hurt in her eyes. "Why didn't I know that? And why didn't I know about you and Greg being friends when it seemed like an important part of your life? Why don't I know things, Cass?"

"Some things aren't easy for me to talk about," I said after a pause, knowing I needed to try. "My mom really did a number on me when she left. We used to make my costumes and big event dresses together. It was hard wearing the Ursula costume knowing she'd helped with it, but thinking about making my prom dress without her is worse."

Taylor's hand found mine across the table. "You could buy a dress?"

"I know, but it's not the same." I sighed, looking at our hands. "I knew exactly what I wanted to make. It's clear in my mind, and I've never seen anything like it in my size." Floor-length tulle. Seafoam green. Off-the-shoulder neckline. Lace overlay on top.

"I'm sure we can find something like it," Taylor said.

"Not in my size," I said firmly. This wasn't something she had to think about. But it wasn't just about the size. It was the Mom part more than anything.

"Then we don't have to go," she said after a pause. "We can stay in and watch Netflix, or I could go with a friend and you can stay in. You choose."

That was the obvious solution—ignore it. But this was my chance to put her first, make up for all my failures, and prove to her that she was the girl I wanted to date. "No. We're going to prom. I'll make the dress. It'll be hard, but worth it. Proof that you're not the only one who can make pretty things, Miss Cross-Stitch."

She laughed, squeezing my hand. "Hey, those movie coupons you made for Valentine's Day were perfection."

I snorted, shaking my head. "Yeah, art at its finest."

Taylor smiled more, nudging my foot under the table. "Thanks for indulging me. I know it's silly, but it means a lot to me."

"That's what girlfriends are for," I said, taking her other hand. Maybe it wouldn't make up for keeping my Rowan feelings and roleplay life from her, but it was something.

The server returned with drinks and took our order, saving me from having to overthink every detail for a while longer.

I stopped to buy prom dress materials on the way home. Dad was at the hospital for a few more hours, giving me free rein to blast music and give the house a proper cleaning and start laundry. After everything was back to normal, I brought my gifts upstairs to unwrap with Tuttles. He hadn't forgiven me for locking him up during the party, but he loved murdering wrapping paper, so he made an exception.

Tate's gift was a Star Wars–themed waffle maker and a card that read, *Don't you dare make these without me.* Rachel gave me a new fantasy book I'd eyed a couple of times when out with her and Tate.

Rowan gifted a couple of Tide Wars art prints that came from an online shop we both fangirled over frequently, including a print of our two characters. Her card read, *Now you can put me on your wall, Captain! XoXo Champ.* My stomach did a flip.

Greg's wrapping was tragic, but the gift was surprisingly perfect. Along with a Barnes & Noble gift card, he gave me a massive bag of chocolate-covered almonds. His card read, *My mom used to always buy these almonds because you loved them. Hope that's still true. Happy birthday!*

On top of brunch, Taylor's gift was a handmade rainbow scarf and coupons for unlimited Spyhouse Coffee drinks until graduation. Her card read, *Here's to hoping you stay warm and energized. I love you!* She'd also included the Tide Wars books she'd borrowed, but I quickly pushed them aside, not wanting to think about what she'd said.

After opening a few more gifts, I stared down at the last one.

I didn't want to open it. No gift would make up for Mom leaving us or how things went down on Valentine's Day. But I found myself untying the ribbons and handing them to Tuttles before tearing through the wrapping paper and opening the box. Inside was a dress, a small jewelry box, and a note.

*Cassidy,*

*I hate how our last conversation ended, and I understand where you're coming from. It was unfair of me to assume you'd let me in after what I did, and I'm so very sorry for how everything has affected you. You deserved better, and I acted selfishly. I'd like a chance to make it up to you. And I'd love for you to meet Colin one day, if you're open to it. Despite everything, I really think you'd like him.*

*I made the dress for your graduation party. You'll recognize the necklace as the one your grandma gave me when I graduated high*

*school. I hope you'll wear both on the big day. I also hope I'm invited,
but that's your decision. I won't show up again or push you, but I'd
love another chance at being the mom you deserve when you're ready.*

*Happy birthday, my sweet girl. I love you.*

*Mom*

I read the letter a few times before the ink started to run from
tears, and I set it aside to open the gifts. The satin, knee-length
dress was royal blue with short sleeves and a mesh strip near the
bottom. The necklace was a simple string of pearls that were far
too fancy for my taste, but I could make them work.

The apology was everything I'd needed on Valentine's Day—
and back in October. Mom wasn't one to throw out apologies
lightly, so I knew she meant it. And while it didn't instantly make
up for everything else, it was a start. I texted her after putting the
gifts back in the box.

**Cass: I'm not ready to talk yet, but thanks for the dress and
necklace. They're beautiful.**

I sent a thank-you message to everyone else who'd brought
presents before opening the chocolate-covered almonds and turning on my laptop to respond to roleplay scenes and catch up on
weekend homework before dinner.

For the first time in a long time, switching to school stuff after
a few scene replies felt like a natural groove. I had a long way to go,
but like with Mom's apology, it was a start.

[One-on-one scene between Cass and Autumn]

**Autumn:** "I'm worried about Allain," Hypernia said as she played with the fabric of her dress nervously. "Ever since we returned to Girishtova, he's been acting different. Distant. I'm not sure he loves me anymore."

**Cass:** "Of course he loves you," Aresha said, frowning. Hypernia was like a sister to her, and it wrecked her that she doubted something so serious. "Being home is difficult for him. Give him time."

**Autumn:** "I will," Hypernia said. "But I fear no amount of time will change the fact that he's running from old ghosts that will always haunt him."

**Cass:** Aresha nodded, understanding that more than she'd dare admit. But she had to believe Allain would figure it out and heal. "Give him time," she said again, forcing a smile.

# TWENTY-ONE

A couple of weeks and several borderline panic attacks passed before college application results started arriving. Roleplaying was all I could do to prevent me from losing my mind over the unknowns of my future. But considering it was also the reason I was on edge over college acceptance and graduation, I understood the irony.

Taylor got accepted to the University of Minnesota and would join Tate in becoming a Gopher. To no one's surprise, Rachel was accepted to every school she'd applied to, but we all knew she was heading to Berkeley. Greg got a few acceptance emails and chose Loyola.

By the time my UIC result came in, I'd somehow gotten accepted to every other school on my list—except U of M, of course. I was still beating myself up over missing that application date, but at least I had options.

I sat at my desk to check my email for the fifth time that day, and there it was. My result. My fate. I stared at it for a full minute before opening it. The words *congratulations* and *our pleasure* were on the screen, and I blinked several times to make sure it was real.

By some miracle, I'd pulled it off. I got in.

I read the email again before jumping from the chair with my phone, warmth filling me. I knew exactly who I wanted to tell first, but they were already calling me. My heart skipped a beat as I answered.

"Are we going to UIC?" I asked, already knowing the answer.

"Yes, we are!" Rowan said, her excitement clear from four hundred miles away. "I knew you'd get in! Congratulations!"

"I didn't!" I laughed in shock, pacing the room with Tuttles at my heels. "And congratulations to you too! Now we can apply to be roommates. And roleplay in the same room! And have Autumn and Holly visit. It'll be perfect."

I didn't bother including Carina. She'd replied only once in the last month to wish me a belated happy birthday in our private server, saying nothing about her absence or when she'd be back. She also hadn't replied to roleplay scenes in almost two months, which was enough proof that she was either over it or too busy to come back.

"I can't wait," Rowan said. "I need to go tell my mom and everyone else, but I had to tell you first."

I knew the feeling. "I should probably tell people too. And I'll message Home Base."

"Sounds good. And Captain?"

"Yeah?"

"I'm really happy about this."

I didn't think it was possible to smile more. "Me too, Champ."

Dad deserved an in-person update after work, so I focused on everyone else. Tate was sad I wasn't staying in the area, but we made plans to celebrate the next day, because obviously he was happy for me. Greg was *stoked*—his word—about going to the same city. I texted Taylor since she was at work before clicking on Home Base.

**Cass:** Your dreams of visiting Rowan and me in Chicago will officially come true. We got accepted to UIC!

**Autumn:** OMG, CONGRATULATIONS!

**Holly:** Love that journey for you two! Congrats!

**Rowan:** She seriously thinks we'll be roommates. Nice try.

**Cass:** Shut up! You know it'll be amazing.

**Rowan:** I know, I know. :)

**Holly:** Chicago, here we come!

**Autumn:** Yesss! Hopefully Cari can come too.

**Rowan:** The day Carina reads this message is the day she's invited.

**Holly:** So she probably won't get invited lol

**Autumn:** UGH! :(

My heart forever ached for Autumn. Her ship partner had jumped ship. Aresha and Allain were siblings, so I understood her frustration. It was hard writing around the big plots without playing Allain for her, which I refused to do. His absences had to make sense, and there had to be room for him to pop back in if Carina reappeared. She didn't realize how inconsiderate it was to ghost regularly—or worse, she did and didn't care.

We'd understand if she couldn't commit anymore, but she needed to tell us that and move on instead of leaving Autumn hanging for weeks or months at a time. Even if it wasn't real life, it mattered to us. And more important than that, we missed her.

I sent Autumn a private message.

**Cass:** Hey! Making sure you're okay. Here if you want to talk.

**Autumn:** Thanks. Things have been rough at home lately, and Cari disappearing hasn't helped. It's like I'm losing my only outlet, and there's nothing I can do about it.

**Autumn:** And I'm starting to feel like the background friend of our group.

I frowned, having zero idea what she meant. My phone buzzed before I could reply.

**Taylor: Congrats!! Want to celebrate? I'm wrapping up at work and can come over after.**

I stared at her words, torn. I *did* want to celebrate, but Autumn was clearly going through something. Celebrations would have to wait.

**Cass: Despite the great news, I'm not feeling great. Rain check?**

**Taylor: Sure thing. Feel better!**

World's worst girlfriend? Check.

I returned to my private server with Autumn.

**Cass:** What do you mean?

**Autumn:** Ever since Cari stopped being active in the RP, I feel like everything has been about you and Rowan. Your ship. Hanging out in person. College. And Holly has other RP friends and tons of plots, but I don't. I relied on Cari too much, and now I'm stuck in a corner and don't know how to fix it. I don't know where I fit anymore.

**Autumn:** And I know it's not fair to be upset when you're all going through stuff and have lives. The RP is all I have, but sometimes it feels like I'm losing you too.

**Autumn:** And home sucks. My parents are talking about moving into a camper or something, so I'd basically be homeschooled from a box. And since they won't let me get a car, I'm always stuck here with them and their friends.

**Autumn:** And I haven't wanted to bring it up, but something weird seems to be going on with you and Rowan. It's not our business, but Holly and I are worried.

Every time I started to type, she sent another message, each one adding another layer of guilt logs to the fire. Carina ghosting had done a number on her, and we hadn't helped by making jokes about it or not checking in on her more. I'd been a terrible friend, but the last part hit on a personal level. Our friends were catching on to our drama, and that was the last thing I wanted.

**Cass:** I'm sorry about your parents! If you ever need a

change of scenery, I know a Cool Dad who will miss having a daughter around next year. He'd happily host you. And you'll always be welcome in Chicago.

**Cass:** Also, I'm sorry for not being a better friend. This year has been really shitty and weird, and it's made me less aware of everything else going on. But that's no excuse. You totally matter to us! You're the heartbeat of this RP and our friend group. You're our Hypernia! This RP wouldn't be a success without you.

A few agonizing minutes went by before she replied.

**Autumn:** Thanks for saying that, and sorry for getting upset. It's mostly the parent stuff and Cari, but all those little things kept building into a bigger thing. And I really am happy for you with college and Taylor and everything. You deserve good things!

**Cass:** Thank you, and I know you are. Let me know if I can do anything to help with the Cari stuff or anything else. I mean it.

**Autumn:** Thanks <3

**Autumn:** What about you and Rowan? Is everything okay?

**Cass:** It's complicated

**Autumn:** Want to talk about it?

Yes. No. Ugh, I didn't know. If I could confess to anyone, it was someone who knew us both well. Someone I trusted who wasn't my girlfriend.

**Cass:** It needs to stay between us

**Autumn:** Promise

**Cass:** When Rowan was here, she told me she has feelings for me. And I don't know what to do about it. I can't
really talk to anyone here about it because they all
know Taylor, and I don't want them thinking something
happened when it didn't, you know?

Autumn started typing. Stopped. Continued. Stopped. Long
pause. Continued. My heart raced as I waited.

**Autumn:** I get it. Holly thought it was feelings related. Ro
got all weird when you started dating Taylor.

**Cass:** I don't know what to do. She's one of my most
favorite people in the world, but I have a girlfriend. And
I really messed up in Chicago. Rowan found out that no
one in my life knows about RP life. They think she's a
church-camp friend from forever ago. She played along
when she was here, but she didn't want to.

**Autumn:** Are you ashamed of us?

**Cass:** No! It's def not that, promise.

And then I typed out a long explanation similar to what I'd
told Rowan. Parents not trusting the internet. Mom leaving us for
an internet person. The *Sims* addiction. Tate not knowing because
he'd worry and tell my parents. Taylor not liking Tide Wars and
dragging Aresha and Roux. All of it.

**Cass:** It felt like everything was working against me. I
didn't want to lose y'all, but it was wrong, and I'm sorry.

**Autumn:** It's okay! That's a lot to deal with. But it must've been hard for Ro to hear.

**Cass:** It was. I don't want to hurt her or for things to be
weird at college. She deserves better, but I still want her
in my life.

The doorbell rang as Autumn typed a reply, and I realized we'd
been slowly chatting for over an hour while I responded to scenes
and made progress on homework. I went downstairs, finding Taylor on the other side of the door. "Hey!" I laughed in surprise.
"Sorry, did I miss a text?"

"No, but I was worried and thought you might want some soup
and tea," Taylor said as she walked in. "Are you feeling better? You
sound okay."

Oh, right. I was supposed to be sick. "Sorry, it's a stomach
thing."

Cool, another lie. Nothing to be proud of, Cass, you literal
garbage person.

"That's the worst," Taylor said, making a face. "I can go if you
want, but I thought we could watch something and relax."

I needed to get back to Autumn, but I wouldn't kick my
thoughtful girlfriend out. And relaxing with a movie did sound
nice. "Don't go. My dad's at work, so we can hang out down here.
Thanks for the care package."

"You're welcome." Taylor took off her shoes and plopped down
on the couch. "I don't know about you, but I'm feeling Marvel.
First-date vibes."

I smiled at the memory of our judging costumes together on

Halloween, for once stopping at the fun part. "A solid choice," I said as I sat beside her, pulling up the app. "*Thor: Ragnarok*?"

"Considering it's the best one, yes," Taylor said. "Valkyrie is a babe."

"Totally. And it's pre-fat-jokes Thor. Very important."

"Um, yeah. What the hell, Marvel?"

I laughed, glancing at her. "Did we just agree on something to watch without you having to use a coupon?"

"I think we did," Taylor said, giggling. "Look at us. Who woulda thought?"

"Not me," I said, grinning as I looked back to the TV, starting the movie.

How had we not bonded over *Thor: Ragnarok* yet? There was probably a lot I hadn't let us bond over, always too in my own head to let her in. But it was fine—I was working on that.

After finishing the soup and half the tea, I laid down and rested my head on Taylor's lap, her fingers moving to my hair for a massage. One second Valkyrie was dragging Thor, and the next I woke up to Thor fighting Hela near the end of the movie. Taylor's warm lap was replaced with a throw pillow, but her shoes by the door confirmed she was still there. After checking the kitchen and bathroom, I headed upstairs.

I found her in my room. Sitting at my desk. Looking at my laptop. No, *reading* something on my laptop. "What are you doing?" I asked, panic brain on high alert.

Taylor turned toward me, confusion flooding her face. "What's all this?"

My Discord server with Autumn was still up, and a single click would take Taylor to a number of other roleplay servers. "Why are you looking at my stuff?"

She narrowed her eyes. "I came up here to get a sweatshirt, and Tuttles was batting at your water cup. It was hard to miss all this when moving him."

I couldn't call bullshit because Tuttles knocked my stuff over constantly. "I can explain."

"I fucking hope so," Taylor said. "Why didn't you tell me Rowan has feelings for you?"

Shit. She'd definitely read the messages.

"I knew it would upset you," I said, but of course that was only part of it.

"Obviously it would upset me," Taylor said, her voice laced with anger. "What about Autumn's last question?"

I looked at the conversation to see what was sent after the doorbell rang.

**Autumn:** Do you think something might happen with her?

I know it's complicated because you have a girlfriend,

but she won't be in Chicago. Ro will be your roommate.

Double shit.

"Nothing is gonna happen with Rowan," I said. "We're friends."

"So you keep saying," Taylor said. "What about the other servers?"

There it was—the conversation I'd buried. I was prepared to

die on the hill of her never finding out, and this was what I'd gotten for it. "Rowan and I moderate a Tide Wars roleplay. It's like fan fiction, but you're writing with other people."

Taylor's eyes bored into me. "And Rowan isn't from church camp."

So she'd read the *entire* conversation. Perfect. "No. I met her when I started roleplaying. But I did really go to a church camp. That part was true."

"Oh, thank god," she said dryly, rolling her eyes. "How can I trust you after all this?"

"I'm sorry," I said, terrified of where the conversation was going. But I couldn't hide anymore. I had to let it all out. "I wanted to tell you about the roleplay, but then on Halloween you said you didn't like Tide Wars, and I froze. And I was excited when you'd decided to read the books again, but then you didn't like them."

"So because I didn't react how you wanted me to, I didn't deserve to know about this big part of your life?" Taylor said, her voice raising a little. "I'd tried to like something *for you*, to connect with you on *something*. Why was that not good enough?"

"I'm sorry," I said again, flailing for words. "I really did want to tell you, but Tide Wars means a lot to me, and you not liking it was hard to swallow. And that's obviously not your fault. We're allowed to like different things. But I didn't know how to tell you everything after that."

Taylor looked at me, and I hated that I couldn't read her expression anymore. I'd been shut out, and I had a feeling I wouldn't be let back in. "What's really going on with Rowan?"

"I thought she was straight," I said. "Truly, I didn't know she had feelings for me until after the birthday party had ended, and I didn't want to make a thing about it."

"Did anything else happen while you two were drunk?"

"Of course not," I said quickly, feeling like my entire body was on fire. "I'd never do that to you."

Taylor shook her head. "I don't believe you."

"I'm telling you the truth! I'm not my mom, Taylor."

That seemed to soften her, but only for a moment. "Then answer me this. Do you have feelings for her? And don't you dare lie to me."

I stared back at her, the truth not aligning with what I wished was the truth. But I wouldn't lie to her again. "Yes," I said quietly as my hands clutched together nervously. "I promise nothing happened. She doesn't even know how I feel."

"Why not?" Taylor asked.

"Because I'm dating you, and I'm not trying to change that. I mean, I feel like we just had a breakthrough downstairs. And we're going to prom together. Do you think that was easy for me to agree to? I did that for *you*."

Taylor looked at the space between us, biting her lip. "I wish that was enough," she said after a pause, her now teary eyes finding mine again. "I can't be with you anymore, Cass. This is too much, and I don't trust you anymore."

"Don't say that," I said, stepping closer, for once having to force myself not to touch her. "I know I've been the worst, but I never lied to hurt you."

"That doesn't mean you didn't hurt me," she said, her voice shaking. "And it's more than the lying and Rowan. You don't love me. You basically turn to stone whenever I try getting close. And I feel like I'm always walking on eggshells around you." She let out a ragged breath. "Be honest. Why do you want to be with me?"

I looked back at her, willing the right answer to come. But it didn't. Having a crush on someone who reminded me of a fictional character wasn't enough. Having things in common wasn't enough. Her being funny and cool and cute and smart and everything else didn't matter if I didn't actually *feel* something. "I'm really sorry, Taylor," I said. She deserved better, and I needed to let her go so she could find it.

Tears crept down her cheeks as she nodded. "Me too. But thanks for finally being honest. I guess I'll see you at school or whatever."

She was gone before I could form words.

[One-on-one scene between Cass and Rowan]

**Cass:** "I am the queen of Girishtova!" Aresha yelled, her temper flaring as she glared at Roux. "I will decide what's best!"

**Rowan:** "Can you say that again a little louder?" Roux said, her eyes narrowed. She wouldn't remind Aresha that she wasn't officially the queen yet. "I don't think all of Shiibka heard you."

**Cass:** "Don't speak to me like that," Aresha said, standing taller. "That's an order."

**Rowan:** Roux let out a slow breath, knowing one of them had to maintain a cool temper. Apparently, it was her turn. "When the captain I know and love comes back, let me know. Until then, stay out of my sight." And then she left.

**Cass:** Aresha watched her go before sinking to her knees in the middle of the throne room. What had she done?

# TWENTY-TWO

What had I done?

I paced the main floor of the house as I tried calling and texting Taylor—like I could somehow fix my colossal mistake. But she didn't answer.

She was serious. We were done.

The fact that I didn't cry made me feel officially convinced there was something wrong with me. What kind of person got dumped by her girlfriend and didn't even shed a tear? That had to mean something, right?

The worst part was I'd created an image of the perfect girlfriend in my head, but the fantasy never landed. And none of that was Taylor's fault. She wasn't *actually* Roux, and I was nothing like Aresha. And I hated that it took hurting her to realize it.

I couldn't bring myself to go back upstairs. Talking to Autumn meant telling her what had happened—telling *all of them* what had happened. Instead of facing it, I returned to the couch and restarted *Thor: Ragnarok*, hoping Valkyrie would help me feel better.

Spoiler alert: She didn't.

Dad walked in from work as the movie ended. His parent radar, which had improved over the last six months, went off as he frowned. "What's up, kid?"

I shifted to make room for him on the couch. "Today was a lot."

Neither of us was a fan of big conversations, but we always survived them. And we both knew one was coming on now. "Then we'll figure out dinner and talk about it," he said as he sat. "What sounds good? Go out? Stay in?"

"Definitely stay in. And comfort food."

"Ah, it's *that kind* of conversation. I'll order Chinese."

I smiled weakly. "Thanks, Cool Dad. That's exactly what I want."

"It cures all ailments. And tomorrow we can make totdish."

The usual relief of those words fell flat. Totdish would always remind me of my birthday. Taylor hating it should've been enough of a sign we were doomed, but thinking that wasn't fair to her when I was the one who'd messed it all up. And I couldn't tell Dad that or he'd never make it again out of solidarity. "Sounds perfect," I said instead.

He called in our usual order before focusing on me. "Okay, let's talk."

I nodded, deciding to start with the good news. "I got accepted to UIC."

"Hey, congratulations!" Dad beamed, pulling me in for a hug. "I'm so proud of you."

A light smile crept up on my lips as I hugged him back. "Thanks. I'm shocked. Rowan got in too."

"That's great. And I'm not surprised. Your ACT score was impressive, and your GPA averaged out fine. As long as you don't miss any finals this round, you'll be good to go."

"Ha ha," I said dryly, nudging him. "But thanks."

He nodded, quiet for a moment. "So, assuming you're not upset about going to your top-choice college with your friend, what's going on?"

I made a face, wishing I'd started with the bad news. "Taylor and I broke up."

Dad's proud smile faded. "I'm sorry to hear that. What happened?"

"It'll make me look pretty bad if I tell you the full story. And you'll be really disappointed in me for some of it—maybe mad."

Dad leaned back against the couch, his arm resting across my shoulders, no doubt thinking I was incapable of anything terrible. *Dads.* "Try me."

After what had happened with Taylor, I knew I couldn't lie anymore. "I was chasing after something that wasn't there, and that was on me, not her. But also, I hid something really big from her—the same thing I've been keeping from you for almost two years." I turned to better face him, the ache in my chest growing. "You know how I'm online a lot?"

"I'm familiar with you being glued to technology, yes," he said, his eyebrows furrowed. "Are you back on the *Sims* train?"

"No, not exactly," I said, clasping my hands together to keep them from shaking. "I found this online group of Tide Wars fans, and we started roleplaying." I let out a breath. No matter what happened next, I was relieved the words were finally coming out of my mouth. "It's like writing a story, but with other people. You pick characters and write scenes together."

"So it's like fan fiction?"

My eyes widened. "How do you know about fan fiction?"

"One of my patients told me about it, and because I'm cool," he said, shrugging. "So you write stories with people online. Continue."

"Honestly, there's not much more to say about it. I just feel really bad for keeping it a secret from you."

"Why *did* you keep it from me?" Dad asked.

I couldn't tell if he really wasn't picking up on the problem or if me explaining everything was part of my punishment. Either way, I looked down at my hands as I explained, not sure I could get everything out looking at him.

"Everyone in the roleplay was a stranger when I started writing with them, and I knew how you and Mom felt about that and gaming-type stuff in general. And then Mom moving in with a guy from the internet made it worse. But before then, when you two started fighting, I needed an escape, and it helped. And the friends I made along the way . . . well, I wouldn't have gotten through these past six months without them."

When Dad didn't respond, I looked up to meet his eyes. There was a sadness there, but something told me it had nothing to do with my secret. "Say something," I said, tears threatening to spill.

"I won't pretend I love hearing all of this," Dad said after a pause, resting a hand over my shaking ones. "But your mom and I should be sorry, not you. We let our issues affect you, and I never wanted that. It wasn't fair to you—neither was her leaving you."

"It wasn't," I agreed. "But don't be sorry. You stayed and made sure I was okay. And that's obviously what parents *should* do, but it means a lot that we've been able to get closer lately. I'm just sorry I ruined it with this secret."

"You didn't ruin anything," he said, smiling gently. "If anything, I'm confused why this secret caused your breakup. I might know about fan fiction, but the modern teenage brain is a bit out of my scope."

I let out a breath, relieved he didn't sound disappointed. "It was too many secrets and lies piled on top of each other. And sometimes I'd make excuses for not being able to hang out when really I was at home roleplaying."

"Ah," Dad said. "That's a factor."

"Yeah. Like today, Taylor wanted to come over to celebrate college stuff, but one of my roleplay friends was going through a crisis, and I wanted to be there for her. And because Taylor didn't know anything about my online life, I told her I was sick. Then she came by anyway and ended up finding all my roleplay stuff on my laptop."

"Oh, kid."

"I know!" I slumped against the couch cushions. "And then she found out I was lying about Rowan, too, because she's not from church camp."

"Obviously."

My eyebrows shot up. "You *knew*?"

"Of course I knew," he said, grinning gently. "Just because I wasn't around as much when you were growing up doesn't mean I'd forget about you forming a bond with someone and keeping up the friendship for years. Give me a little credit."

"Why didn't you say anything?" I asked, feeling beyond stupid. "She could've been some stalker person that you willingly let into the house."

"I wasn't worried about that."

"Why not?"

"Because I trust you. I know you wouldn't have someone spend the weekend if they weren't the real deal. Also, the internet is forever. After you asked about her coming to stay, I found her Instagram." He shot me a pointed look. "Funny, I don't recall you mentioning seeing a friend in Chicago."

My eyes widened. "You've seriously been sitting on this information for over a month? Why didn't you say something sooner?"

"I wanted to hear it from you," Dad said. "I've been pretty relaxed with you this year because of everything going on, but I hope you understand how hard it was realizing you'd lied to me. Between the online stuff and school, it's a lot."

"I'm really sorry," I said, my cheeks warming. "And there's actually more to the whole Taylor breakup story."

"Now, that I didn't know," Dad said. "Go on."

Did my dad need to know what I was about to tell him? No. But we'd grown so close lately, and I didn't want to keep anything from him again. "Okay, so Taylor thought Rowan and I had some kind of *thing* going on. We don't, but I did find out that Rowan likes me. And I like her, too, but she doesn't know that. But now Taylor knows because, you guessed it, another uncovered lie. So again, the breakup is all my fault, and I doubt she'll ever speak to me again."

Dad was quiet for a moment before nodding. "I think I'm following, and that's a lot of lying, kid. Sounds very out of character for you."

"I know," I groaned. "The whole relationship was a mess. Not just because of the lies, but she'd asked me out right after Mom left, and I jumped into it without thinking. And we never got on the same page, and I didn't know how to talk to her. Maybe it's better she hates me. It's what I deserve."

Dad looked thoughtful. "You know, your mom is painted as the villain because she was the one to do something about our problems, but we stopped working long before that. Her mistakes didn't make me hate her, and they didn't make me a saint. She's human, and she deserves to be happy. So do you. Don't let this Taylor thing eat you up."

I hadn't thought about it that way. I was too busy being mad at Mom and feeling sorry for Dad to consider anything else. "Thanks, Dad. But there's one more thing."

"Isn't there always?"

I nodded, looking down at my hands again as I prepared for a fresh shame spiral. "You probably figured this out by now, but I got addicted to roleplaying, which contributed to my grades being terrible. I'd sleep in sometimes because I was up late roleplaying, and I'd skip classes or cancel plans. Basically any time I was staring at my phone, I was in that world. I could give you a dozen more examples, but the point is that I'm a huge disappointment, and I understand if you want to ground me until college or take away my phone and laptop again."

I met Dad's eyes finally, convinced I'd broken his heart. He took my hands again as he spoke. "We've already worked through the school stuff, so I'm not going to ground you or take anything away, especially because I can see how important those friends are to you," he said, his voice calm. "And I'm sorry for not noticing any of this. I won't pretend you didn't mess up, but I'm the parent. I should've seen there was more going on and been there for you."

"You've been there plenty," I said dismissively, my eyes narrowing in thought. "Are you really not mad about the internet stuff? I was positive you'd at least take away my laptop."

Dad shrugged. "I obviously want you to be safe online, but after meeting Rowan, I'm not worried about that. As long as you keep me posted on your test scores and sign off by ten on school nights, we're good." He paused. "But more important than that, I hope you'll be more honest with me moving forward. And if you're addicted or get worried about going down that path again, talk to me. I can't help you if I don't know what's going on."

"I have a handle on it now," I said, feeling sure of it. There would be nights when a group scene was going strong and it would be hard to sign off, but I knew that if I needed the push, my friends would be there, and now Dad. "Thanks for being *you* about this. Your plan is more than fair."

"You got it. And as for Taylor, don't give up on her yet. It'll take some time, but you two would make good friends."

"I won't," I said, smiling a little. "Thanks—again."

"You're welcome, kid," Dad said, standing. "Also, if you turn into a chronic liar, I *won't* pay for college." He ruffled my hair.

"Hey!" I shoved his hand away, giggling. "I'm done with the lies. Promise."

"Good. I guess I'll do what I can to prevent an agonizing student-loan bill. Don't want you living in this house until you're forty."

"Wow. Good one, Cool Dad," I said, nudging him before going to the kitchen to set the table for dinner, feeling like I'd been released from the pit of my own making.

After eating dinner, I returned to my room to face Home Base. I wasn't ready, but they deserved the truth, starting with Autumn.

**Cass:** Sorry, I'm here! Taylor showed up without notice and things exploded, and then I hung out with my dad for a while

**Autumn:** Hope everything is okay!

**Cass:** Thanks! I'll explain in HB, but I wanted to apologize again for being a bad friend. I should've noticed you weren't doing great. I promise to be better. And I really do hope you can come visit sometime!

**Autumn:** Thanks, that means a lot. I'll find a way to Chi-cago! <3

I relaxed at her words, hoping she felt a little better. I couldn't do anything about her parents or Carina, but I could be a better friend.

I clicked on the Home Base server.

**Cass:** Second life update of today: Taylor broke up with me.

**Holly:** OMG WHAT?! I'm so sorry!

**Autumn:** Noooo, I'm sorry, Cass!

**Holly:** What happened?

**Cass:** I kept RP life a secret from her, and everyone in my life. But she and my dad know now, and I'll tell Tate tomorrow. I'm really sorry for not telling y'all. I feel terrible.

**Holly:** Damn, girl, I had no idea! And don't be sorry! This shit is hard to explain to people. I mean, I told everyone in my life about it immediately because they already knew I was a Macy Whittier stan, so no one was surprised, but I get it.

**Cass:** lol thanks

**Cass:** Rowan, sorry again about making you pretend you're from church camp.

**Holly:** CHURCH CAMP!? LOLOLOL

**Rowan:** You know how I feel about the lord, Cassidy Williams.

**Rowan:** Sorry about Taylor

**Autumn:** Proud of you Cass <3

**Holly:** You're being really chill about this, Autumn

**Autumn:** I found out earlier today

**Holly:** WOW. I see where I rate.

**Rowan:** Drama queen

**Holly:** Always!!

I grinned, not knowing what I'd do without them. They were my family, and I couldn't imagine ever keeping them a secret again.

After replying to a few scenes, I changed into pajamas and curled up in bed with Tuttles, who cuddled close and purred, so generously acting as an emotional support animal for once. Sticking with the Marvel theme, I started *Captain Marvel*.

Rowan called twenty minutes in, and my heart skipped a beat.

"What's up, Champ?" I said as if I was totally chill and had no idea why she'd be calling.

"Hey, Captain. Are you actually okay?"

I smiled a little at the sound of her voice. "I'm actually okay. Obviously the breakup sucked, and I feel like shit for hurting Taylor, but it's for the best. Talking to Cool Dad helped."

"Good. But how did she find out about it?"

I retold the story from lying about being sick, to Taylor surprising me, to her finding out about Rowan and the roleplay, to the breakup. Not knowing what to do about my own feelings, I left that part out. Because even though it felt different, a part of me worried that my Rowan heart eyes were like my Taylor heart eyes—a fantasy that wouldn't land in reality. Like I wasn't cut out for the real deal. Like I didn't deserve it.

"So Autumn knows everything, too," Rowan said after taking it all in. "Does Holly?"

"No, and Autumn promised she wouldn't say anything. Are you mad?"

"Not mad, no," Rowan said after a pause. "But it's kind of embarrassing. I wouldn't have hated keeping it between us."

I frowned. "Why is it embarrassing?"

"Because the feelings are one-sided," she said pointedly. "You're obviously my best friend, always, but everything has been harder since your birthday. And having other people know about it twists the knife."

"I'm sorry," I said, feeling like I was being backed toward my doom pit again. "I shouldn't have said anything."

Rowan huffed a sigh. "Honestly, it's better than more lies, so I think we can get past it."

"Yeah, I guess that's true."

"But I'm still sorry about the breakup. Even if it wasn't gonna work out and you kind of had it coming."

I blinked at her words, not expecting that. "What do you mean, I had it coming?"

"All those lies weren't great, but you obviously weren't that into her. And that's okay, but it was shitty to lead her on."

"Um, I didn't lead her on?"

"No?"

I sighed. "Okay, I didn't *intentionally* lead her on. I was trying to figure out my feelings."

"How long would you have dated her hoping your feelings would eventually change?"

"What's this *really* about, Rowan?" I asked, having no answer to that question.

"This is about exactly what I'm getting at," Rowan said, her voice raising slightly. "When you first told Home Base about her, it was like she was this real-life version of Roux, appearance and everything. Dating her sounded perfect, but when you actually started dating she wasn't right, because the version you'd dreamed up wasn't real. And while you tried figuring that out, you lied to her about all kinds of shit—like you were punishing her for not being what you wanted. But what did you expect?"

"I don't know!" I said, my voice now louder than hers. I usually loved how easily she knew and understood me, but I didn't love this. "But it's none of your damn business. I'm sorry I didn't react how you wanted me to that night, but don't call me if all you're gonna do is give me shit for being flawed." I groaned. "And you know what? You shouldn't have told me you were into me, because obviously it *is* messing with everything."

"Oh, believe me, I'm starting to regret it," Rowan said. "And I hope you get assigned a shitty roommate at UIC, because you can count me out."

She hung up before I could yell anything back that would've no doubt been rude and an in-the-moment lie. I threw my phone at Tuttles's empty cat bed as tears spilled like a flood from my eyes.

# TWENTY-THREE

Tate came over the next morning for Star Wars waffles and bacon, which were so aggressively needed. I didn't try reaching out to Rowan or Taylor again, knowing I wouldn't be able to fix either situation anytime soon. My only pathetic solace was reading some of my favorite Aresha and Roux one-on-one scenes.

"Hey, C," Tate said as he set down a fruit platter that his mom no doubt insisted he bring. "Ready to celebrate our futures?"

"Almost." The bacon splattered like an omen, and I poured the first of the batter into the waffle maker. "I need to talk to you about something important first."

"If it's to tell me I'll be fine without you next year while you're in Chicago and I'm stuck here being a football star, don't worry, I already know."

"When you say it like that, I almost pity you," I said, rolling my eyes. "But also, Taylor and I broke up."

"What?" he asked, nearly spilling the juice he was pouring. "Why?"

"We weren't right for each other, which you probably knew," I said, narrowing my eyes.

Tate held his hands up. "Hey, she was your first girlfriend, and she's good people. And I've been wrong once or twice in my life. I wasn't going to tell you what to do."

"Only once or twice?" I teased, shaking my head. "But yeah, I also kind of messed everything up."

Tate snorted. "Doubt it. You don't mess up." And then his eyes widened. "Oh, shit, girl! Was it Rowan? What happened?"

My mouth opened to immediately deny something that would end up being a lie. "It wasn't Rowan . . . directly. Why would you say that?"

"I don't know. It felt like there was a little somethin' somethin' going on there." He wiggled his eyebrows.

I swatted him with the spatula. "I was lying to Taylor long before Rowan came to visit."

"What were you lying about?"

"My secret life."

"Okay, stealth mode," he said, his tone full of doubt.

"I'm being serious." I flipped the bacon as I explained the concept of roleplaying.

"I know what roleplaying is," he said when I finished.

Shock flooded my face. "You do?"

He shrugged. "Okay, I've heard the term. I thought it was a sex thing."

I scrunched my nose. "Ew, Tate! Of course you did." I sighed.

"Anyway, I got addicted to it. That's why my grades started to suck and why I'm always staring at my phone. Honestly, you're probably better off without me."

Tate scoffed. "I'm not better off. You're my best friend. No shady sex writing will change that."

"It's not sex writing!" I swatted him again. "And you really mean that?"

"For sure! You were there for me when I moved here and was scared to start at a new school. A friendship like that never dies. But why didn't you tell me about it sooner?"

"Because I knew you'd get all worried and go to my dad—which, valid. And I didn't want him taking all that away."

"Ah, yes, *Sims*gate, I'm following," Tate said, nudging me. "And you're right, I would've been really fucking worried, but we could've talked through it and found a solution together. But you clearly overthought the situation—like you do."

"I know, I know," I said, frowning. "I'm really sorry."

Tate nodded as his eyes narrowed. "But it wasn't just all that, was it?"

"No, it wasn't," I said. "Maybe I'm not over my mom leaving, and everything before that. The roleplay was a good escape, and I made some great friends along the way."

"Like Rowan?" He was grinning now and practically bouncing on his heels.

"Not you too," I laughed, thinking about my dad. "How did you know?"

"I didn't, but that church-camp story was weak sauce. And you never lie to me, so I didn't read too far into it." He poked my arm. "There were also the Tide Wars nicknames on your birthday. Don't think I didn't pick up on that."

Gods. At least I knew never to try making it as a secret agent. "So then I guess you also picked up on her having feelings for me, boy genius," I said. "Because I didn't. I literally found out after the party."

Tate's smile was the biggest I'd ever seen it. Considering how wide it usually was, the look was borderline terrifying. "And you have feelings for her," he said.

"Yes." I sighed, hating how obvious it was to him. "I realized it a while ago. And obviously it didn't help the Taylor situation, but it really had nothing to do with the breakup." I paused. "Also, Rowan doesn't know."

Now, *that* surprised him. "Wait, why the hell not?" he asked.

"Because I was dating someone!" I laughed, shaking my head. "And I still had it in my head that Taylor and I could work out, so I didn't say anything. I didn't want to complicate everything."

"I think everything is already complicated, C," Tate said, his tone softening. "But hey, you're single now. You deserve to be happy. And Rowan deserves to know."

"I hear you. I really do," I said. "But I'm not ready. I have enough to worry about with school, and I don't want to jump into another relationship."

Tate's shoulders sagged. "Okay, fair, but promise me you'll go for it before it's too late?"

"I promise," I said, smiling a little. The idea of confessing feelings to Rowan made a chill run down my spine. I needed to stop thinking about this for now. "Anyway, thanks for being cool about this. It was a harmless lie that grew too big."

"It's all good C, really," he said, looking at me for a moment. "But also?"

"Yeah?" I said, waiting for the other shoe to drop.

"Check your waffle."

"Shit!" I hustled over and opened the lid, finding an almost-black Death Star.

Tate snorted. "At least it looks realistic?"

"Shut up," I whined. "Okay, you finish the bacon and I'll fix this mess."

I threw attempt one in the garbage and started a second waffle. Once everything was ready and not burned, we sat at the table to devour breakfast.

"So, what about prom?" Tate asked a few bites in.

"What about it?" I mumbled, my mouth full of food.

"I assume you're not going with Taylor anymore. And Rowan doesn't seem like an option just yet, which annoys me, but I'll get over it."

I rolled my eyes. "Both of those things are one thousand percent accurate. What's your point?"

"I know you don't *need* a date, but I bet Greg would love to go with you if you want. He keeps gushing about you like you're besties now. I'm almost jealous."

I laughed at the visual. Imagining going to prom with Greg Jensen was even more comical than Taylor. "Doesn't he have, like, four girls wanting to go with him?"

"At least, but he's currently dateless. Want me to ask him about it?"

"Absolutely not," I said quickly. "I'm not going to prom."

"Okay," he said slowly. "But if you change your mind, I think you'd have fun together. Or you could go solo and hang out with me and Rachel."

"I love you, Tate, but I'm not getting in the way of your senior prom with Rachel. She'd murder us both."

He snorted. "Yeah, you're probably right. But think about going at least."

"Sure," I said, knowing I wouldn't. Prom wasn't something I was mad about missing, and I could wear the dress I'd started another time. And I'd still go to Tate's house that night to take pictures and embarrass him with his mom.

But he didn't need to know that.

Similar to when I'd gotten a girlfriend, I'd expected chaos at school the Monday after we broke up. And again, no one gave a shit—at least not most people. Fynn and June shot eye daggers at me across the room during lunch while Taylor sat with her back to me. She'd also made a point to look away the couple of times I'd seen her. Just like that, I was back to riding solo through the halls.

Relief came as the final bell rang and I went to Mr. Blake's room. He'd continued to get on my case about assignments, but his lectures decreased as my grades improved. If I wanted to share my UIC news with anyone at school, it was him—even if only to gloat a little.

"I have college news," I said as his last class cleared out.

He nodded, like he already had a speech prepared. "I've told other students this, Miss Williams. There's no shame in starting at a smaller state school. Minnesota has many promising colleges to choose from, and you can always transfer later."

"Last I checked, Chicago wasn't in Minnesota."

He blinked, his mouth opening slightly. "You got in to UIC?"

"I did." I showed him the acceptance email to prove it.

"Damn," he said after glancing at it, a smile forming on his lips. "Congratulations. I guess all my grief kicked you into gear."

*Of course* he'd congratulate himself first. "Yeah, it was all you."

"Give me fifteen percent of the credit—the rest was all you," he said, standing. "You've come a long way, and I'm proud of you. Keep putting in the effort and you'll go far in college."

My gloating plan disappeared at his sincerity. Someone choosing to believe in me and push me to do better when they didn't have to meant more than I could express. And I wasn't going to try when neither of us wanted to deal with something as gross as sentiment. "Thanks, Mr. Blake. That means a lot. And I'm proud of you for putting up with me."

"Someone had to," he teased. "But good. Let my vast wisdom drive you when I'm not around to give you hell in person."

I snorted. He definitely wanted more than 15 percent of the credit. "I will."

"And don't forget about the test on Wednesday," he said, his eyes boring into me. "It might not be the final, but it's a decent chunk of your grade. No slippery slopes."

The next roleplay group scene wasn't until Thursday night, and I didn't have a girlfriend anymore. There wasn't room to mess the test up. "No slippery slopes," I echoed. "I won't forget."

The day took a bizarre turn when Greg called me after dinner. I hadn't seen him at school, so his Taylor commentary would apparently come from a personal call. Super.

"Sorry to hear about your breakup," he said when I answered.

"Hey, thanks. I'm over here ruining lives. The usual." I sighed. "What did you hear?"

"You know, for once I didn't ask anyone for details."

I was beyond shocked. "Wow, that's growth. Good for you."

"Yeah, it's like I'm almost an adult or something."

"Don't get carried away," I said, smiling a little.

"Too late. But seriously, are you okay?"

He was the first person to ask me that today, and it made me feel like less of a scaly monster and more like an imperfect human teenager. "I'm okay, thanks."

"For sure," he said, pausing. "Also, this is going to seem random, but I don't have a date to prom yet, and I assume you don't either. I mean, unless you have a list of ladies on reserve or something."

I was going to kill Tate. "You know me," I said dryly. "But no, no date."

"Well, maybe we could go together—as friends, obviously."

Confirmed: Tate Larson was a dead man. "I appreciate that, but don't let Tate talk you into going to your senior prom with a pity date."

"What does Tate have to do with this?"

"He didn't talk you into asking me?"

"Uh, no?" He scoffed. "I came up with this one on my own, thanks. I mean, I *obviously* have options, but I don't want any girls thinking it's like a *date* date. I want to go with a friend. And we're friends now, right?"

"Yes, we're friends now." The idea of going to prom with him was as ridiculous as when Tate had mentioned it. But also, it was kind of sweet. "You really want to go with me?"

"I really want to go with you," he said, his voice genuine. "And if I end up making out with someone, you won't get jealous. Best of both worlds."

*There he was.* How did "straight" Cass ever think Greg was a good option for a boyfriend? "You're such a freak. But okay."

"Okay?"

"We can go to prom together."

"Hell yes!" he yelled. I could practically hear him fist pumping through the phone. "It's gonna be *so* dope. You'll get everything that comes with a legit prom experience—except the hotel room, of course."

I laughed. I'd always thought that the whole hotel thing was a movie myth. Maybe it was and Greg was just being Greg. Also, I had a lot to teach him about how to talk to other humans. College would be fun. "You know how much I love a free meal."

"That's the spirit! Speaking of food, I need to do that. See you at school tomorrow, prom date."

"Yeah, okay, see you."

Reality hit as we hung up. I was going to prom with my only ex-boyfriend, who I'd despised until recently. What the *hell* was my life?

[Private conversation between Cass and Holly]

**Holly:** This is your casual reminder that prom night is the best time to find a rebound. It's scientifically proven.

**Cass:** LOL! Thanks, but no rebounds. I'm fine.

**Holly:** Uh-huh. My comment stands. Also, send me a butt pic of your date. I stalked his Insta and he's SO HOT!!!

**Cass:** I'm not going anywhere near his butt!

**Holly:** Just a pic!

**Cass:** Wow, so thirsty. I'll see what I can do.

**Holly:** LOVE YOU!

# TWENTY-FOUR

I never thought I'd go to prom. First because I didn't want to, then because my girlfriend broke up with me. But now that I was going for real, I vowed to make some solid memories.

Creating the dress from scratch without Mom resulted in several mistakes and a lot of tears, but I managed to finish it the night before prom. In the end, I hadn't needed Mom's help to make it, and I didn't need a girlfriend to wear it. This dress was for me and me alone.

Dad and I were almost to Tate's house for pictures when Greg jumped out of his SUV in the driveway, whistling. "Damn, Williams! Look at you!"

"Hey, Greg," I said, smirking. "You remember my dad, right?"

Greg cleared his throat as if just noticing I wasn't alone. "Of course. Good evening, Dr. Williams. Nice to see you again, sir."

"Hello, Gregory," Dad said in a stern dad tone that I'd heard maybe twice my entire life, and that was being generous. "Were you objectifying my daughter?"

"No, sir, I would never," Greg said, his face paling. "I'm excited about prom, that's all. Sir."

"Uh-huh." Dad shot him another warning glare before winking at me and ringing the doorbell.

I grinned, nudging him and glancing at Greg. He wore a black tuxedo with a seafoam bow tie, having insisted we match. "You look nice too, pal."

"Thanks," he said, smirking down at himself. "Only the best for my prom date."

"Are your parents not joining us, Gregory?" Dad asked.

Greg's expression instantly turned serious again. "No, sir. They're in Austin for work."

"That's too bad. I'll send them some pictures."

"Thank you, sir. They'd appreciate that."

I snickered at his forced politeness as Tate's mom opened the door, greeting us with a warm smile. "Marcus! Cassidy! Come on in." Her eyes locked on Greg, narrowing. "*Gregory*. You won't be causing any problems for my boy tonight, will you?"

"No, ma'am," Greg said, standing rod-straight as he followed us inside. "Only a good, respectable time."

"Uh-huh." She closed the door before walking to the stairs, yelling up toward Tate's room. "Enough making out up there! Your friends are here."

Tate and Rachel were downstairs within seconds. Rachel's dress had golden rhinestones and a long slit up one side, and more than half her back was exposed. Tate was wearing a midnight-blue suit with a tie that matched Rachel's dress. They didn't look like two people who'd been making out. When Tate's smile didn't reach his eyes, I knew something was wrong.

"We weren't making out, Mom," he said before taking me in, a genuine smile finally forming as we bumped fists. "I can't believe you made a dress that fast. You look awesome."

"Thanks," I said, looking between him and Rachel. "You two look perfect, of course."

"Thank you, Cass," Rachel said politely before looking at Tate's mom. "I think pictures on the stairs and by the fireplace are our best options."

"I think you're right," Tate's mom said. "Stairs first. Line up, kids."

Greg clapped his hands together and was the first person on the stairs. "Let's go, prom date! I've got my best angles ready."

"Gods, help me," I muttered to Tate before going to stand as directed.

Next came the nitpicky comments from Tate's mom about how to stand and where you put your hands. Greg kept asking to look at the pictures, claiming his mom told him to be sure he wasn't making a ridiculous face when really he liked checking himself out. Tate, the most patient friend on the planet, looked relieved by the time we wrapped up.

As a treat for Holly, I successfully snapped a picture of Greg's butt and texted it to her without anyone noticing. He would've happily obliged if I'd asked, but I didn't want him thinking *too* highly of himself this early in the evening. Or asking if Holly was single.

Through it all, I wished Rowan were there. Even if we went only as friends, I wanted all my big memories to be with her. My stomach twisted at the reminder that I wasn't her favorite person right now, and I shoved the thoughts down as Dad pulled me in for a tight hug.

"Have fun tonight, but don't make too many questionable choices," he said. "And call if you need a ride later."

"I will, thanks," I said, grinning. "And I'm sure my most questionable choice tonight will be my prom date."

Dad glanced at Greg, who was commenting on his picture angles to Rachel, and he laughed under his breath. "You're probably right about that."

After saying goodbye to the parents, we drove to Martina for dinner. Rachel rode with Tate in his truck, and Greg played up his prom date role by chauffeuring me around. "So, what actually happened with you and Taylor?" he asked after an agonizing silence of me not knowing what to talk about.

"What if it's personal and not your business?" I asked, more amused than upset by the blunt question.

"Then I'll shut up about it. But I should get credit for not listening to the gossip. And I can't *not* ask. I've been curious for weeks!"

I chuckled, rolling my eyes. Gods, he was the worst sometimes. "What happened was that I wasn't a good girlfriend and we weren't right for each other."

"What does that mean?"

"Like, she said she loved me after two months, and I never said it back. And I lied to her about how I know Rowan, the friend who was at my birthday, among other things."

"Oh yeah, I remember her. She's really hot."

"Not the point, Greg."

"Right, right, of course. So how *do* you know her?"

I never thought my life would reach a point where I was telling Greg Jensen about roleplaying, but in a way it made sense. We'd be hanging out at college together, hopefully with Rowan, and he'd been there during *Sims*gate. He was actually the one who'd told me about the game, so really this was all his fault.

Greg was quiet after I finished my rambling explanation, like he was pondering a deep thought. "I thought roleplaying was some kind of sex thing," he finally said.

"That's what Tate said!" I groaned, hitting his arm. "You both suck."

"I'm disappointed it's not a sex thing, that's all." He smirked and held up his free arm to avoid another hit. "Kidding! You get on with your nerdy self, Williams."

"I will, thanks," I said, relaxing a little. "Maybe when we're in Chicago you can make sure I'm not glued to my laptop all the time. Drag me to a party every now and then."

"Deal. Between the two of us, we'll dominate the Chicago college scene."

I strongly doubted that. He'd join a frat, and I'd be in some kind of nerd club. Our circles wouldn't be the same, but we'd figure it out.

Eating at a nice restaurant with someone who wasn't a *date* date was strange and comical, but being there with friends made it worth it. I tried my first oyster and was obsessed, and the Parmesan gnocchi made my mouth water long after we'd left. And Tate and Rachel acted more like themselves, making all the difference. Whatever was going on, the last thing I wanted was for prom to suck for them.

Greg and I spent the drive to prom singing along to a playlist someone from our grade had curated for the night. By the time we entered the main event, I felt calmer than I had the entire year. I was out with friends, not tempted to hide in a corner and get lost in roleplay scenes. Progress.

"What should we do first?" I asked after Rachel pulled Tate away. "Dance? Drinks? Say hi to your friends?"

"I can talk to them later," Greg said, shrugging. "I came here to hang with you. Let's go crush that dance floor, if you think you can keep up."

"Oh, I can keep up," I said, taking his hand and walking through the crowd to the middle of it. My moves put half the room to shame, because Midwest. And Greg—well, he didn't fall.

We made the rounds after almost an hour of dancing. Hanging out with one of the football stars apparently meant people wanted to talk to me and compliment my dress, and I was having too much fun to be awkward about it.

When Greg started getting nostalgic with the football team, I disappeared to the bathroom. As I left the stall, I saw Taylor reapplying lipstick at one of the mirrors. I'd been dreading this moment ever since the breakup.

"You look really nice," Taylor said after noticing me in the mirror.

"Thanks, so do you." I stepped up to the sink next to hers to wash my hands, my nerves fraying. "You're here with June?"

"Yeah. She was gonna go with Fynn, but he ended up getting a real date, and it all kind of came together after that."

"That's great," I said genuinely. "I'm glad you were able to come."

"I'm surprised you're here, and with Greg Jensen."

"No one is more surprised than me," I said, laughing nervously. Despite washing my hands, I was sure they were clammy. "I'm sorry. I shouldn't be here. This was your big event."

"Hardly," Taylor said. "You're allowed to go to prom, Cass."

"I get that. I'm just really sorry about everything."

"I know, but tonight is about having fun, so don't worry about apologizing and whatever else you're panicking over. But I need to get back out there." She walked to the door before looking back at me, amused. "You can stop washing your hands now."

"Right," I said, my cheeks warming as I realized I'd been doing that the entire time. "Have a good night."

"Thanks," she said, her smile growing. "I think I will."

I took a minute to calm down after she left; then I found Greg to dance more, needing the distraction. "Thanks for being a good prom date," I said as we swayed to a slower song. "I probably would've roleplayed all night otherwise, but I'm glad I didn't."

"Me too." He pulled out his phone after a moment, groaning. "Shit, it's almost eleven. I need to head out. You coming?"

The one compromise that came along with going to prom with Greg was that he was hosting the after-party. I hadn't committed to it yet, given my skepticism about the human race, but after facing Taylor, I was feeling optimistic. "Yeah, let's go."

Greg fist pumped—which I pretended to ignore—before texting his football friends to nudge people toward his house. We were steps from the exit when Rachel and Tate walked inside. I hadn't seen them leave, but I *did* notice how annoyed Rachel looked by my presence.

"What?" she snapped, like we'd been spying on them.

"Um, nothing. We're heading to Greg's for the party," I said, feeling uncomfortable about whatever was going on. And worried. "You coming?"

"I don't know about Tate, but *I'm* staying here," Rachel said. "I have pictures to take with the girls."

Tate stared after her as she walked off, his hand outstretched slightly as if it could bring her back. He looked like he was going to throw up. "I'm calling it a night," he said after a beat, barely glancing at us before heading toward the exit.

I watched him retreat. "I better make sure he gets home okay,"

I said to Greg. "Do you mind?"

Greg shook his head. "All good, Williams. Tell him to call me tomorrow if he wants to go for a run or something."

That was bro code for *have a moment*. "Will do," I said. "And thanks again for tonight. Hope you find someone awesome to make out with or whatever."

"Oh, girl, you know I will!" he said, holding his hand up for a high five.

I reluctantly indulged him before running outside after Tate, relieved that I'd decided to wear flats. "Wait up!"

"Go to the party, C," Tate said, not stopping. "I'm fine."

"You're obviously not." I linked our arms after reaching him. "Give me your keys. I'll drive us home."

Tate wordlessly handed them over as we got to his truck. He'd always been up-front about everything in his life. The day he'd moved in next door, he'd said, "My parents got a divorce, so my mom and I are gonna live here now." His silence now terrified me, but I knew he'd open up when he was ready.

We were almost home before he spoke. "Rachel and I had a fight earlier today, and another one before you saw us."

"What did you fight about?" I asked.

"*Everything*. Graduation. College. She got accepted to some precollege workshop, but it means going to California early, like a few days after graduation. And the only reason I found out about it tonight was because her mom mentioned it when I picked her up." His voice started to shake. "She'd planned to tell me soon, but she didn't want to mess up prom. And I'm obviously upset, but I understand, you know? She deserves it."

"Yeah," I said gently, taking his hand with my free one. "I'm sorry, Tate."

"It's okay."

And then his sniffles turned into sobs, and he broke.

I stopped the truck in front of our neighborhood park and pulled him in for a tight hug. He cried into my shoulder as I held him, wishing I could take the pain away. It was hard to picture Tate without Rachel. They'd been together for years. Even with huge changes on the horizon, this moment confirmed my belief that childhood was over. "What can I do?" I asked once his sobs returned to sniffles and his grip on me loosened.

"I don't know." He sat back, wiping under his eyes. "We didn't break up, but it's inevitable at this point. I won't be able to visit her much between school and football, and she won't come home except for big holidays. That won't be enough." He huffed out a breath. "So I think we'll stay together until she leaves for California. At least I hope we do. I'm not ready to let her go yet. I'll never meet anyone like her again."

"You won't," I said honestly, taking his hand again. "She's one of a kind, and you have something very special together. But that doesn't mean you'll never have something special with someone else. It'll just be special in a different way. And it'll probably happen randomly and knock you off your feet, because that's who you are. Something good gets thrown your way, and you drink in every ounce of it. And I *love* that about you."

"Thanks, C," he said, squeezing my hand. "And thanks for being here."

"You know I'll always choose you over a Greg Jensen party."

He choked out a laugh, nodding. "Yeah, I know. That's why you're the best."

"I try." I let go of his hand and started driving again. "Want to sleep over tonight?"

"Only if you catch me up on roleplay life," he said. "I need all the dirt on Girishtova."

I laughed, hearting him for knowing the name of Aresha's homeland. Ever since my confession, he'd been very invested in Tide Wars shenanigans. "Deal."

After parking Tate's truck in his driveway, we split up to change and talk to our parents. Dad was waiting on the couch when I walked in. I'd miss this trend at college.

"Hey, you're back early," he said, setting down the book he'd been reading. "How was prom?"

"It was surprisingly fun, and Greg was surprisingly the perfect date," I said as I took off my shoes and grabbed my phone from my purse. "But Tate's having a rough night, so we skipped the after-party. Is it okay if he sleeps over?"

"Of course," Dad said, knowing he had nothing to worry about there. "Is he okay?"

"Thanks, and he will be," I said. "But I need to get out of this dress. Send him up when he gets here?"

"Will do." He smiled a little. "I'm glad you had a good time, kid."

It was such a simple response, but it warmed my heart. Dad wasn't able to help me pick out fabrics or sew a dress, but his support made me feel like I'd won the parent lottery, especially after everything that had happened lately. "Me too. See you in the morning."

I went upstairs to change and get ready for bed. Tate's light in his room was still on after I finished, so I hopped on my laptop to see what I'd missed from roleplay life. Apart from a couple of scene replies, things were quiet. I stared at my scene with Rowan that she hadn't replied to since before our fight. After everything Tate had gone through tonight, I felt a pull to check in on my other best friend.

I messaged her before the courage disappeared.

**Cass:** Hey, Champ. I know things aren't great between us right now, but I wanted to make sure you're okay. I'm really sorry about our fight. You trusted me with your feelings, and I threw them back in your face. I get why we're not talking, but I hate it.

I didn't expect a reply anytime soon, but she started typing within a minute.

**Rowan:** I'm sorry I said you had your breakup coming. But I need more time with the other stuff. I can't turn off my feelings and don't want our friendship to suck because of that.

**Cass:** Understood, take your time. But know that I miss you.

**Rowan:** I miss you too, Captain.

A chill went up my spine at the nickname, which was proof enough that everything would be okay. I typed out *I wish you'd been my prom date* but quickly deleted it. Our situation was too fragile for a comment I wasn't ready to explain. Despite my feelings, which were still very much there, the last thing I wanted was to make our situation harder.

I shut my laptop and turned on *Schitt's Creek*. Tate and I had seen it enough times that it could serve as background noise while we talked and fell asleep.

Tate crawled into bed next to me a couple of minutes later, resting his head on my lap. "Okay, tell me about the roleplay. What's new?"

I smiled at his enthusiasm. My fingers moved to his head, massaging it like Taylor had done for me and Roux did for Aresha, thinking on what I'd told him last. "So things have started to come together in Shiibka, and Aresha is preparing to host her first royal ball. . . ."

[Tide Wars main server message]

*Attention, nerds!*

*We'd like to get in another group scene before finals take over. Please vote which dates you're free by Friday. Have your characters dust off their fancy clothes and get ready for some shenanigans, because Aresha is hosting a ball at the palace!*

*Also, a word to the wise: Don't forget to study for finals! They're the worst, but they're also kind of a big deal. We want you all to succeed, graduate high school (if you're a senior), and stay excellent.*

*XoXo Rowan and Cass*

# TWENTY-FIVE

"We need to mail out your graduation invitations," Dad said on Sunday morning. "And I don't care what the kids are doing these days. A mass invite online isn't good enough."

"Can I wake up first?" I sat across from him and took a sip of the coffee he'd set out for me. "Why aren't you at work?"

"Believe it or not, I have today off, which is why we need to finish these." He slid his laptop over. "Let me know if anyone is missing from this list."

I nodded and scanned the names and addresses, impressed. Dad had included almost everyone I wanted to invite, and some extended family members I knew were begrudgingly invited. Dad had crushed it.

And then I saw Mom's address. No, Mom and *Colin's* address. "Can we not invite Mom and Colin?" I asked, smiling hopefully.

"Not an option," he said.

I groaned. "But it'll be awkward!"

"No doubt, but we'll survive it together."

I sighed, shaking my head. "I don't want them to come, Dad. I'm serious."

Dad looked borderline annoyed, which was as close to mad as he'd ever gotten with me. "Put the last six months aside for a moment. Your mom raised you while I was working. She taught you how to read, ride a bike, bake, make costumes—basically everything. She's responsible for a lot of your favorite things. And she gave up a lot for us for a long time."

"I know, but I can't ignore what she did," I said, starting to match his annoyance, mainly in an attempt not to cry over her yet again.

Dad nodded. "I understand you're mad at her, and that's valid. But from what you said about the birthday card, she's trying. Talking to her again will be hard, but this party is a safe space to test the waters. If it gets to be too much, I'll ask them to leave. But I want you to at least try, okay?"

I took in his words, knowing he was right. And she *did* apologize, which was what I'd wanted. But none of that instantly made up for everything, and that was only part of the problem.

"I don't know how to act around her anymore," I said. "When she showed up on Valentine's Day, it was like she'd gone back in time. And I can't play pretend with her. I won't."

"I know. She went about it wrong, but she wouldn't have come all that way if she hadn't missed you. She could've told you about the wedding on the phone." Dad took my hand, squeezing it. "And she *does* love you. We have thousands of pictures and videos and memories to prove it. Don't wash all that away forever because of one mistake."

"It was a damn big mistake," I mumbled.

"Huge," he agreed. "But we all slip sometimes—like your role-play situation. Your friends didn't cut you out when they found out you were keeping secrets."

I shot him a pointed look. "No, but Taylor broke up with me over it." Among other reasons.

"She'll come around. And when she does, you'll figure out how to be something different. Like I did with your mom."

Okay, that was news. "You did *what*?"

"How do you think I got her address for the invite?" he asked.

I frowned. "You didn't have to do that for me."

"I didn't, at least not only for you. I hate resentment. The end of our marriage was messy, but our future doesn't need to be." He laughed quietly. "I mean, I don't see us hanging out without you or going on family trips together, but I won't spend the rest of my life feeling bitter. And I'm moving on. You know that."

I perked up at the last part. He'd finally given me the name and a couple of details about the woman he'd started dating seriously. "Speaking of moving on, why isn't Elaine on this list?"

"Because you haven't met her yet," Dad said, smiling sheepishly. "I didn't want to assume anything."

I rolled my eyes. "Sure, invite *Colin* of all people, but not the woman who sounds perfect for you from the little you've told me about her. Got it."

"You really want to meet her?" he asked.

"Um, yes!" I said loudly. "I've been waiting for you to stop keeping her to yourself and confirm she's a real person."

Dad laughed, shaking his head. "Yes, drama queen, Elaine is very real. I'll find time for us to have dinner."

"Only if I can make totdish," I said, grinning. "She needs to try it so we know if she can hang with this family or not."

"Good idea. If she hates it, she might not be the one for me."

My brain immediately went to Taylor barely touching the totdish on my birthday, while Rowan ate every bite on her plate. "Exactly."

After adding a couple more names to the invite list, I slid the laptop back to Dad. Inviting Mom and Colin would either end up being cathartic or a total disaster, but I was grateful to have a dad who was willing to be the bigger person. And he was right—we'd survive it together.

Elaine came over the next weekend for games and totdish, which she *loved*. And she kicked our asses playing Sequence. Three times. I let it slide because I liked her immediately. I learned that she and Dad had met at a local conference. She was a family-practice physician at a different hospital, and she had two daughters ages eight and ten. She agreed to bring them over next time to meet me. I was basically obsessed with her.

I signed online to update Home Base after Elaine left. My eyes widened as I saw a new message from Carina.

**Carina:** Hi, all! Life got busy, but I'm back and will send scene replies soon.

Autumn had no doubt read the message by now and was probably debating between what she *wanted* to say and her usual polite cinnamon-roll response. I started typing to get there first.

**Cass:** Welcome back! I wouldn't worry about replying to past scenes since they're dated by now and we've had a few group scenes.

Holly private messaged me almost instantly.

**Holly:** OMG, THANK YOU! I've been staring at this for five minutes trying to figure out what to say. I thought she was gone for good!

**Cass:** You're not the only one

I clicked back to Home Base.

**Carina:** Thanks, but I had some good scenes going so I'll pick them up.

**Holly:** We've hardly heard from you this year

**Carina:** I've had a lot going on.

**Holly:** We've all had a lot going on, like how Cass took your advice to keep RP life and Rowan a secret, and then Taylor found out and broke up with her. Not that you care.

**Carina:** I obviously care. And sorry to hear, Cass, but I didn't tell you to keep Rowan a secret? If one of you came here to visit, I'd tell people how I know you.

**Holly:** I find that hard to believe.

**Rowan:** Me too. You've barely talked to us for months. We're not exactly a priority anymore. And that sucks, but just own up?

**Carina:** I wouldn't have come back if I'd known I'd get attacked like this. We're supposed to be friends.

**Holly:** EXACTLY

I groaned. I didn't mind Holly bringing up the breakup or anything else they were saying, but things were escalating quickly. None of us wanted Carina to leave, but we also knew her coming back was temporary.

**Cass:** We're not trying to attack you, Cari. We understand people get busy. I think we're all just hoping for a little better communication in the future? It's hard to be in an RP and have one of our main characters and friends disappear.

**Carina:** You know this isn't real, right? More important stuff is going on in the world.

**Rowan:** Obvi, but it's the life we all share since we can't hang in person. And you've ghosted on our "hang time" for months.

**Holly:** Yeah! Life happens, we get it, but characters have been at a standstill since you've been gone and that's not fair to them. And your friendships have been at a standstill, which makes us feel shitty.

**Carina:** Wow, okay

**Carina:** Is that how you feel, Autumn?

Autumn didn't owe some big response to Carina, but I couldn't protect her. This was her thing to handle. The minutes ticked by in agony while we waited.

**Autumn:** Yes, I agree with the others. Hypernia has been almost completely on hold for months, and I've missed out on big plots because I didn't want to end our ship.

And you're my best friend, but we've hardly talked in months. Not trying to make you feel guilty, but it hurts. And it would be nice to feel like we mattered on some level instead of being ignored.

Damn, Autumn. I smiled, beyond proud of our sweet summer child. Leaning forward, I stared at the screen, hoping Autumn's words would get through to Carina.

**Carina:** I didn't ask anyone to hold their characters. I'm sorry if you missed out on some big plots or whatever, but that was your choice. It's just a game.

An ache formed in my chest at the lack of accountability. I bit at the inside of my cheek as Autumn typed.

**Autumn:** But our friendship isn't. You haven't asked how any of us are doing or replied to any of the stuff going on in our real lives. You don't even answer when we check in to make sure you're okay. Those aren't RP things. They're friendship things.

**Carina:** I didn't come back to be berated. It's pretty clear I'm not wanted anymore.

"Okay, fuck that," I said, responding quickly before Autumn felt obligated to handle all of this herself.

**Cass:** No one is saying that. Of course we want you around. But it wouldn't kill you to acknowledge Autumn's feelings so we can move past this.

**Carina:** I obviously felt bad for not being around, but I don't have time for all this drama. I have a life, so thanks for giving me a reason to stop wasting my time.

I blinked, my heart feeling four times heavier after I clicked to the list of members and saw Carina was no longer there.

That was *not* how I'd expected the conversation to go. Granted, I hadn't expected Carina to come back at all, but the others were right. Our friendships were real, and it was valid to be affected by her actions. But no matter who was right or wrong, Carina was gone.

**Holly:** WTF just happened??!

**Autumn:** She just left like none of it mattered. Like we didn't matter.

**Autumn:** This is all my fault

**Holly:** Don't you dare blame yourself, you precious cinnamon roll!

**Rowan:** She was on her way out and wanted an excuse. None of this is your fault.

**Autumn:** Promise you aren't mad?

**Rowan:** At her? Furious! At you? Never.

**Holly:** Seconded

**Cass:** Thirded! Proud of you for being honest. You okay?

**Autumn:** I'm crying tbh, but it's for the best. Thanks for having my back.

**Holly:** Sweet baby angel! Don't cry for her.

**Rowan:** She didn't give us a chance to talk through it. That's on her, and her ghosting is on her.

**Autumn:** Ugh, you're right. I guess I can finally move on with Hypernia. But I don't know what to do about Allain. They were my favorite ship in the books. I love writing them.

**Holly:** DIBS! I'll play Allain.

**Autumn:** You will?

**Holly:** Girl, yes! I would've played him originally, but Cari had already claimed him. And you know I love writing with you. <3

**Autumn:** omg I love you!!! You're the best. <3

**Holly:** Make sure to tell the others that frequently.

**Autumn:** Done!

**Cass:** This is awesome! But I'm also low-key sad we aren't killing off Allain. I would've loved Aresha getting a huge pity party and making everyone comfort her.

**Holly:** LOL, too bad! ;)

**Rowan:** Shame. Roux is the best at comforting.

**Cass:** Honestly she deserves medals

**Rowan:** Roux and I will take a best-friend roommate at college instead.

I stared at her response. Was she serious? She wouldn't say it to the others if she wasn't, especially when they didn't know about our most recent fight.

**Cass:** Aresha and I accept, always :)

A comfort swept through me that I hadn't felt in gods knew how long. Losing Carina would stay with us for a while, but at least the four of us had each other.

[One-on-one scene between Cass and Rowan]

**Cass:** "I'm nervous," Aresha admitted, her heart racing. "What if something goes wrong?"

**Rowan:** "Nothing will go wrong," Roux said. "You walk down the aisle, recite the vows of your ancestors, get a crown placed on your head, and become the queen of Girishtova. It's simple, unless you trip on your gown."

**Cass:** Aresha groaned, nudging her. "I should've left you on the ship."

**Rowan:** Roux rolled her eyes, taking Aresha's hands. "Nothing will stop me from seeing this moment. You could lock me in dungeon or make me walk the plank. I'd still find a way back to you."

**Cass:** Aresha laughed to hide her emotions, knowing she needed to remain calm. "Remind me to never make an enemy of you, Champ."

**Rowan:** "As if you could, Captain," Roux said, grinning wickedly.

# TWENTY-SIX

Graduation day arrived, and I was sure I'd throw up before the end of it. Enough movies and books had informed me of the many ways it could go wrong, and now I could think about little else. But at least I'd passed all my classes with a few As, including government. Mr. Blake was for sure congratulating himself.

When Mom accepted the invitation, Tate talked me through several scenarios until I stopped feeling like a giant ball of nerves. One way or another, we'd all survive. We had to. The second option was spontaneous combustion, and I wasn't about that Charles Dickens life.

I clicked on Home Base so I wasn't flailing alone.

**Cass:** I leave for graduation soon and I'm panicking

**Holly:** Hells yes you do! No panics allowed

**Autumn:** Yay Cass!

**Rowan:** Congrats, Cassidy Williams!

**Rowan:** Also, don't trip when accepting your diploma.

**Cass:** That's very supportive, thanks.

**Rowan:** I believe in you!

I rolled my eyes and grinned, my heart feeling full at their words. After signing off, I changed into the blue dress Mom had made and put on my grandma's pearl necklace.

Dad knocked as I finished curling my hair. "Hey, kid. Your mom is here. Thought I'd check before sending her up."

Was it too late to fake my own death? Or maybe I could literally run away from my problems. I had a good pair of flats for it. It was doable.

Instead, I swallowed my nerves. "So it begins," I said, forcing a smile. "Yes, I guess you can send her up."

Dad nodded, a small grin forming. "You look great. Like a high school graduate."

I laughed. "I hope so, otherwise today will be awkward. And thanks. You look like the parent of a high school graduate."

Dad chuckled before leaving the room, and I let out the deepest of breaths. The bar was low—I needed today to go better than Valentine's Day. I held my hands together tightly until Mom stopped in the doorway, Tuttles at her heels.

"Hi there," she said, a hesitant smile on her lips. "Can I come in?"

"Yeah." I watched as she stepped closer and closer until her arms were around me. I begrudgingly returned the hug, because damn those social norms. "Thanks for coming."

"Thanks for inviting me." She stepped back to look at me, resting a hand over my hair as her smile widened. "You wore the dress. And the pearls."

"I needed a dress, so," I said, trying to sound casual despite her making a dress meaning a lot to me. And I was already trying not to cry, which took a lot of energy. "Where's Colin?"

"Downstairs talking to your dad and his girlfriend. She seems nice."

"She is." I'd seen Elaine a couple of times since meeting her, and it amazed me how easily Dad and I fell into a routine with her and her daughters. "I'm glad he's moving on."

"Me too." Mom paused before sitting on my bed, and Tuttles jumped up to join her. "I know it's been an inexcusable amount of time, but I'm truly sorry for how everything went down last year. I should've considered you more in my decision, or at least offered to bring you with me. I know you wouldn't have come, but I should've asked. And I'm sorry if I made you feel like I didn't want you around when that couldn't be further from the truth. I guess the more time that passed, the harder it was to make things right. And I don't know if they can be made right, but I hope you're willing to give me another chance. I'll do whatever it takes."

She was rambling. And crying. And rambling some more. And holding her hands together tightly while playing with her thumbs. At least I knew where I got that trait from. Did that mean she had anxiety too? I guess there was a lot I didn't know about her.

Her words made me realize how she'd handled leaving was

similar to how I'd handled my roleplay secret and relationship with Taylor. As more time passed, being honest became harder. It wasn't nearly as bad as what Mom had done, but it still clicked how much I was like her. We were avoiders, and we didn't like the hard conversations. But we *needed* to have them if we were going to heal and move forward.

"I don't know if it can be made right either," I said as I sat next to her and started petting Tuttles. "But we can try. I mean, coming home will take priority when I have college breaks, but we can figure all that out."

"Of course," Mom said easily, relieved I hadn't immediately shut her down. "Whatever you want."

I nodded, quiet for a beat. "When's your wedding?"

"October," Mom said. "Colin keeps reminding me of the date because I'm making my dress, and he's worried I won't finish it in time."

"I'll have to tell him about your talent for making things beautiful under pressure."

"I tried telling him that, but of course he has doubts."

"Rude of him." I paused again. I never needed my parents to stay married or for Mom to live in Minneapolis forever. All I'd needed was for her to understand where I was coming from, take my pain seriously, and apologize. Now that she had, I knew what I needed to do next. "If you really want me in the wedding, I'll be there."

Her expression quickly changed as she beamed, pulling me in

for another hug. "Oh, sweetie, I would love that! Thank you."

I hugged her back, feeling less forced. "Don't start crying again. This dress is new."

She laughed, pulling away to wipe under her eyes. "You should probably get going."

Right. Graduation. I checked my phone to see the time and stood at the realization that I'd most likely be late. "Yeah, gotta go. I'll see you after."

I hustled downstairs, where Dad was standing with Elaine and a man with ginger hair and a broad smile. Gods, he was Mom's type. I'd never known what that was, considering she'd only ever been with Dad, but something about it clicked, the same way it had for Dad and Elaine. Oddly enough, all of it made sense, even if it came with a little pain first.

Okay, *a lot* of pain.

"Nice to meet you, Colin. I'm Cass," I said, giving his hand a quick shake. "Sorry to meet and bail, but I'm late. Talk more after the ceremony!" I grabbed my things and ran out to the Crosstrek without waiting for a response.

I was hopeful I'd get through graduation without feeling emotions, but of course that didn't happen. Sitting at the ceremony, it hit me that I wouldn't see most of these people again. Part of me would genuinely miss it. Seeing the same faces every day in the halls. Mediocre-at-best lunches. Laughing at other people's shenanigans. Mr. Blake giving me shit. Nostalgia hit hard as my classmates walked across the stage in alphabetical order to say goodbye to one chapter and hello to another.

As Taylor accepted her diploma with a wide, confident smile, I knew I'd be forever grateful to the girl who'd made me realize no secret was worth keeping from the people who cared about you.

When it was Greg's turn, he grinned like he was going to cause a scene but collected himself at the last second and accepted his diploma with as much grace as possible. I couldn't believe we'd gone to prom together, and I was excited for our adventures in Chicago.

Tate was a completely different story. I'd never been prouder of a person than I was watching him on that stage. He'd be a famous football player one day—I could feel it. And him looking at me with a fist raised after accepting his diploma was what caused me to break down in tears. I raised mine back and cheered extra loud.

When my name was called, I walked across the stage, relieved I'd survived the last couple of years to get to this day. I made out the voices of people I loved through the noise, and my heart was full. And it should also be noted that I made it back to my seat without tripping.

After tossing my cap and hugging too many people to count, I rushed to get home before the party guests. Tate and I had decided to combine our backyards for one big event. I didn't care if I wouldn't know everyone there—Tate was my family, so his people were my people.

Tuttles bolted the second I opened the front door, but I was having too good of a day to run after him. And I knew he'd stay close for attention and food scraps.

Inside, chaos unfolded. Dad had hired a local catering company to make the food, and you'd think a wedding was about to happen. (It wasn't, for the record.) A few people looked up from their work to offer their congratulations, and I thanked them before setting my cap and gown aside and walking out back, where Tuttles was already sunning himself on a chair, looking like an absolute prince.

Tate appeared a minute later, resting his arm across my shoulders. "You know, I could've sworn I saw you crying when I was onstage."

"Shut up," I whined, nudging him. "I maybe had a human moment for, like, ten seconds. Don't make a thing of it."

"Hey, I'm not judging you. I think it's sweet that you cried over fond memories of your best friend. It's touching, really."

"Don't give yourself too much credit. I was thinking about everyone—yes, including *you*. But after today, that's it. We'll obviously see each other, but the lives we've had up until this moment are done. We're different people now."

"That's deep for someone who plays a pirate on the internet."

"It's more than that!" I groaned. "Let me have a moment."

"Have as many moments as you want, but don't weep for our youth too long. I for one am looking forward to the whole *what comes next* part of my life. You know, football star and all that. Maybe I'll play for the Vikings one day."

"Uh-huh, sure. Cheers to the future."

"Come on, C. Eat a sandwich. Get nostalgic. Dance a little."

"Talk to my ex-girlfriend."

"What?"

I nodded toward where Taylor had entered the party with Rachel, my stomach dropping.

This wasn't awkward *at all*.

Tate's eyes followed mine. "Would it be weird for you if we hung out at college?"

"No," I said easily. "You should totally be friends."

"And you should totally go talk to her," he said, nudging me in Taylor's direction.

I sighed, knowing he was right. But that didn't mean I wasn't nervous as hell. "Yeah, I'll see you later. Have fun with your girl-friend."

Tate saluted and jogged ahead to meet up with Rachel as Taylor made her way to me. "Congratulations on surviving high school," she said, a small smile on her lips.

"You too," I said, my heart racing. "I don't mean this in a rude way, but what are you doing here? I was the worst girlfriend."

She giggled. We both knew she couldn't deny it. "Maybe in the end, but I knew long before you did that it wasn't working. I wish I could blame it on Rowan, but it wasn't her."

"Really?" I asked, my eyebrows furrowed.

"Really. I kept trying because I really wanted us to be right for each other, but holding on was just as wrong as you keeping things from me. So stop punishing yourself for what happened. I don't hate you—not even close."

I still felt bad, but it helped knowing she didn't hate me. "Thanks." I glanced around the party and saw Dad looking at us with an encouraging smile, and I remembered our talk. "Maybe when I come home for school breaks we can get together?" I asked, looking back at Taylor.

Taylor's smile grew, and I pushed down that part of me that had long crushed on the curve of her lips. "I'd like that." She looked toward the street, then back at me. "I should go, but let's not wait that long. Text me when you're free next?"

"Yeah, for sure." We hesitated before hugging, and I felt a massive weight lift. "Thanks for coming, and for being a great girlfriend."

"You're welcome, Ursula. See ya soon."

"See ya, Link."

I watched her walk off, laughing quietly at how strange and sweet the world could be. And at how right Dad had been.

"Who was that?"

I turned to see Mom and Colin. They'd definitely seen the hug. Could I die now? "Um, Taylor. Ex-girlfriend."

"Oh, *that's* Taylor," Mom said as if she'd heard all about her from me. Thanks a lot, Cool Dad. "Did you make up?"

"Yeah, as friends," I said before focusing on Colin. "Sorry for the quick bail earlier. I was embarrassingly late."

"No worries," Colin said in a smooth English accent, his broad smile from earlier returning. "It's wonderful to meet you. I hear you'll be celebrating our wedding with us."

"Yes, and I'll make sure Mom's dress is ready in time," I said, looking between them.

Colin chuckled. "Thank you. I hate to admit my list of concerns includes a dress, but here we are."

"Here we are," I echoed, amused by how funny he was.

"I know you have a lot of people to talk to," Mom said. "But we're staying in the area for a week. I hope you have some time to catch up."

"Yeah, we'll find a day," I said, genuinely wanting to.

Mom smiled more and nodded, pulling me in for a quick hug before walking off with Colin to talk to other people she knew. I had to give her credit for acting so casual after leaving the man who was hosting the party. But at least Dad was happy. I would've found a way to disinvite her if he wasn't.

# TWENTY-SEVEN

The party went late into the evening. As it wound down and the remaining guests trickled out, I sat at the abandoned bonfire to make a well-deserved s'more. I had my marshmallow on a stick when Tate walked out, sitting next to me with a deep sigh. The light from the flames danced on his face enough for me to make out the exhaustion, and my best-friend radar went off. "What's up?"

His eyes met mine. "Rachel and I broke up."

"Oh gods." I set the stick down, trying to think of a good reply. But there was none. "Come here."

We stood, engulfing each other in a tight hug. "I'm okay," he said after a moment.

I pulled back to look at him. "Are you sure? You were pretty wrecked about it at prom, and you haven't wanted to talk about it since. It's okay if you're not okay."

"I know." He sat again, picking up a stick to prep a marsh-mallow. "I had a lot of time to think. And as much as it sucks, it's right. We'd never be able to make long distance work, and dragging it out until the last second would've hurt more."

I repositioned my chair closer to his and sat, watching him for a moment. "I'm surprised how chill you're being about this."

He laughed quietly, shaking his head. "Me too. But I don't want to have any regrets in life. Rachel and I went for it, and it was perfect for a long time. But we're starting new chapters or whatever, and they don't line up. We still love each other, and we'll talk and hopefully hang out when she comes home for breaks, but the relationship part is done."

We roasted marshmallows while he talked. My heart hurt for him, but I was also proud. "That makes sense," I said gently, taking his free hand. "And someone else will come along when the time is right. Until then, you'll be your usual charming self and crush school and football and life."

"That's the plan," Tate said, a small smile on his lips. "Thanks, C."

"Anytime." I squeezed his hand before focusing on the task ahead. In typical fashion, I obsessively rotated my marshmallow until it was a perfect shade of brown, and Tate impatiently set his on fire, blowing it out after it was black.

"Just how I like it," he said before sandwiching it between two graham squares and a layer of chocolate.

"Uh-huh." I grinned, doing the same with mine once it was ready.

A comfortable silence took over as we ate and watched the

fire, and I thought about the last year. I'd managed to raise my grades enough to graduate. I'd gotten into UIC. I'd more or less made up with Taylor. Mom was back in my life, though that relationship would take time to mend. Her fiancé was nice. Dad had an amazing girlfriend to keep him busy after I left for college. The roleplay was going strong despite Carina's departure. I had the world's greatest friends, and I'd soon be living with one of them.

Living with Rowan Davies. In a few months, we'd be sleeping across from each other, roleplaying in the same room, helping each other study, and staying up late watching Netflix and eating doughnuts. It was a dream that I hadn't fully let sink in until now. But something about it was off—like a piece of the puzzle was missing.

"My turn to ask what's wrong."

I looked at Tate, seeing a knowing grin on his lips. "Nothing," I said, smiling a little. "All good."

"Bullshit," he said loudly, nudging my foot. "Out with it. Does it have to do with Taylor? You looked surprised to see her at the party."

"I *was* surprised. Running into each other at prom didn't make us friends. But I think we're okay now." I shrugged. "And it sounds like she's over the whole Rowan thing, which is a huge relief."

A knowing expression crossed his face. "So this is about Rowan."

My eyes fixed on the fire. "Of course it's about Rowan."

"Spill," he said eagerly. "And you *have to* tell me because I'm sad."

"You're the worst," I said, pausing. "We're going to be room-mates at college, and that just . . . doesn't feel right anymore."

"Uh, yeah," Tate laughed. "If you both have a thing for each other, and you *still haven't told her*, by the way, I'd say being room-mates isn't the best idea."

I groaned, looking at him. "I can't tell her, Tate. Our roleplay group is so close, and every fight we've had has made things weird for everyone. And if we were to date and break up, it would proba-bly end the roleplay. And what if I just *think* I like her, but it's this stupid fantasy in my head like it was with Taylor?"

"Sounds like you're grasping at excuses," Tate said gently.

"They aren't excuses." I sighed, trying to think of how to best explain it. "She's my best friend—next to you, of course. We tell each other everything. She confided in me when her dad died. I told her everything about my mom. We've visited each other and shared a ton of great memories. Our roleplay characters have this *amazing* chemistry. And she makes me feel brave—like I can do anything. I don't want to risk losing all of that."

"Are you done?" Tate asked, his smile softening. "Can I tell you what I think?"

I made a face, not realizing I'd been rambling. "Yes, fine."

"I think you're in love with her."

I blinked, knowing I'd heard that wrong. "Uh, no?"

Tate gave me a pointed look. "Come on, C. I've known you basically forever. You've always been on the reserved side, and that doubled when your parents started fighting. Taylor only knew things when she had to, and she was your *girlfriend*. But you let Rowan in because you *wanted to*."

"Letting someone in doesn't equal love."

"No, but I knew there was something there the second you saw each other in the train station. She brought you doughnuts because she knows you love them. Your face did a thing, and you *ran* to her. You *hate* running."

I couldn't argue that. "Why didn't you say anything?" I asked.

"Because you were dating Taylor, like you said, and you clearly didn't want to accept what was really going on. And maybe it's not love yet, but there's something there worth fighting for. And if you'd stop overthinking every damn way it could go wrong, you'd see how it could go right."

My brain bolted through memories of banter, flirting disguised as banter, the way I'd felt when I first saw her in person, the way I'd felt when our fingers brushed while petting Tuttles, the times I'd cried over her but not Taylor, her love of totdish, the online jokes, our characters. Gods, *our characters*.

Tate was *so* fucking right. How I felt about Rowan Davies went far beyond anything I'd felt for Taylor, and I was the world's biggest goof for not realizing it months ago. I'd been too busy fighting it and making excuses. "I don't know what to do," I said, shifting in my chair to face him. "What do I do?"

A mischievous smirk formed on his lips "The drive to Chicago isn't too long."

I snorted. "You're such a romantic, Tate Larson. I can't drive to Chicago and—what? Tell her I like her and want to be together and live happily ever after?"

"Don't be ridiculous. Happily ever after is a dated concept manufactured by Disney—even I know that. But yes to the rest of it. Start with college and go from there. And maybe don't be roommates if you're all into each other and shit."

I nudged him for the last comment—but also, fair, that part needed to change. My brain moved a million miles, for once considering the ways it could go *right*. And then I spiraled back to uncertainty. "Can I actually do this?"

"You said she makes you feel brave," Tate said. "So be brave."

Damn him for using my words against me. "Are you sure? You shouldn't be alone right now. I could call her instead."

He shook his head. "Nope, you're not getting out of this one. And to make sure of it, I'm coming with you. You'll need me to keep you going when you inevitably panic every fifteen minutes."

Tate would forever know me too well. I thought back to Chicago and how I'd been all in that day because of Rowan Davies. And whatever came next, it was time to be all in again. "Okay, deal," I said.

"Yes!" Tate cheered, clapping his hands together and standing. "Meet me at the Crosstrek in ten minutes. And grab some snacks."

My eyebrows raised. "Wait, we're going *right now*?"

"Hell yes, we are!" He took my hands to pull me up. "Let's go!"

My body was on fire, and the flames in front of me had nothing to do with it. I was going to drive to Chicago with my best friend to tell my other best friend I had feelings for her. "You're the worst, but also the best. Thank you."

"You can thank me properly with a deep-dish pizza after you get your girl," he said, nudging me toward my house. "Go on now, get!"

"I'm getting!" I said, panicking all the way to the house.

After grabbing essentials and explaining things to Cool Dad—who was, of course, thrilled for me and in full support of my mission—Tate and I were on the road. We'd get to Rowan's house sometime after six in the morning.

Most of the drive was spent singing along to playlists and talking about summer plans and college. We wanted to go camping before I left for Chicago. Tate wanted to get tattoos together, but I kept my answer at a safe "We'll see" for now. Thousands of needle pricks sounded almost as terrifying as confessing my feelings to Rowan. Almost.

We made it to Madison for gas and a bathroom break before I could allow myself to accept that I should actually have some sort of speech prepared. "So how exactly do I talk to Rowan about all of this?" I asked Tate, who was now driving.

He shrugged. "Well, the easy part is done. You already know she's into you."

"Yeah, but I don't know if it's a little crush or if she's, like, in love with me," I said.

"Who cares? She's into you. All you need to do is show up and tell her how you feel. Let the fact that you drove six hours for her speak to the romance element."

I frowned. "What if she doesn't want me anymore?"

Tate laughed tiredly. "If I know anything about people, it's that they can't control how they feel. If she was into you at your birthday party, she's into you now. You don't shut that shit off because you get rejected or things don't work out. It lingers."

I knew exactly what he was talking about. "I'm sorry we're on a romantic-gesture road trip right after your breakup."

He poked my arm. "Don't be sorry. I'm not. I've been waiting forever for you to feel this way about someone. And Rowan is badass. *And* this is a great distraction." He glanced at me. "But no matter how she reacts, you're still your own damn hero. Got it?"

So. Did. Not. Deserve. Him. "Yeah, I got it."

Tate was right. Even if Rowan didn't want me back, I was my own damn hero for putting myself out there. And I'd come too far to give up now.

We turned onto Rowan's street as the sun rose, parking in an open spot a few brownstones down from hers. My heart threatened to explode, but an encouraging smile and fist bump from Tate got me out of the Crosstrek. I slowly approached the address I'd sent cards and packages to over the last couple of years, taking out my phone to call Rowan.

"Hey, graduate," she said after a few rings, her morning voice slightly raspy.

"Hey, almost graduate," I said, rubbing a hand over my chest in the hope that it would calm the fuck down. No such luck. "Hope I didn't wake you."

"You didn't. I'm drinking my weight in coffee and making breakfast with my mom while she talks to herself about the state of the world. The usual Sunday."

I smiled a little as I heard her mom defend herself in the background. "I love it. Can you do me a favor and go outside? Need your help with something."

"Um, okay," Rowan said, laughing quietly. "Do I need to go somewhere specific? Like my balcony or the front steps?"

"Sure, front steps," I said, trying to sound casual.

"Okay, hang on."

The sounds of her breathing and skipping down the stairs came through the phone, and it took everything in me not to make a run for it. The door opened, and her eyes locked on mine as she looked more taken aback than I'd ever thought possible. Rowan Davies wasn't the kind of girl who surprised easily.

"Oh my gods!" she yelled, leaping off the few remaining stairs and engulfing me in a tight hug.

"Surprise!" I took in her warmth and the smell of coffee—one of my favorites.

"This is the *best* surprise." She pulled back to look at me, her eyes scanning my face. "What are you doing here?"

"I came to see you, and to tell you something."

"Must be a big something to come all this way," she teased.

"Yeah," I said, giggling nervously. "It's just that—"

Her eyebrows raised as I lost my words. "What is it?" she asked.

"I love you," I said quickly, loudly. And my heart swelled. Oh gods, I loved her. I really *loved* her. And now she knew.

"You love me," she said slowly, staring back at me. "I don't understand. Is this a joke?"

"No, of course not," I said, though considering everything I didn't blame her for asking. "You said you had a thing for me, and it's fine if it's nothing more than that. But gods, Rowan, I love you. I didn't think I knew what that word meant, but then it hit me like an oar to the face. You're everything people describe in movies and books that I used to roll my eyes at, but you're more than that. You're the person I tell all my big and little stuff to. You make me feel brave. I wouldn't even be here right now if you didn't do the kinds of things you do to me. And I know I've messed up a lot, and I haven't always been a good friend, but—"

"Cass?" Rowan said.

"Yeah?"

"Shut up."

I blinked. "What?"

"I said shut up." She stepped up to me, her hands moving to my cheeks. "I love you too."

"You do?" I asked, hoping to gods I wasn't dreaming. "You

mean it? Even after everything I've put us through?"

Rowan smiled gently. "Even after all that, I mean it. And I'm gonna kiss you now."

"Okay," I said quietly, forcing myself to stop speaking.

And then she kissed me. It wasn't fire or raging storms or the clash of swords, or any other nonsense that I'd read in a thousand stories. We were coffee breath and memories and the promise of something more. My chaotic mind shut down in that kiss, and my heart hummed for a whole new reason. I could build a life with this feeling.

I pressed my forehead against hers after, taking in the feel of our bodies against each other as an early-morning breeze brushed against us. "You know we can't be roommates now, right?" I asked. "Living together would obviously be amazing, but we should probably figure us out and, like, date a while first."

A laugh escaped her lips that fit perfectly with mine. "Agreed. We'll figure it out."

"Cool," I said, so many thoughts flooding me at once. "Tate's here, too. We can't stay too long, but I promised him Chicago-style pizza."

Rowan nodded, unfazed by this. Tourists. "Then we'll take him to Lou Malnati's for lunch, and you can get doughnuts for your drive home." She tucked some loose hair behind my ear, those stunning gray eyes locked on mine. "Y'all can meet my mom first, and we'll figure out the morning. Maybe check out campus before lunch?"

"That sounds perfect," I said, leaning in this time to kiss her, an unspoken promise forming between us. Whatever came next, we'd figure it out.

"Go get your friend," she mumbled against my lips after a moment.

"Right," I said, pulling away with a laugh. I took a few steps before turning back to her. "Hey, Rowan Davies?"

"Yes, Cassidy Williams?" she said.

"I'm so glad we met on the internet."

Her smile lit up my entire world. "Me too, Captain. Me too."

[Roleplay scene between Cass and Rowan]

**Rowan:** Roux started to feel less foolish over the dress Aresha had chosen for the ball. It was almost comfortable, but nothing compared to her sea clothes. She eyed a couple dancing next to them before looking back at Aresha, needing a distraction. "What are you thinking about?"

**Cass:** Aresha met Roux's eyes, smiling warmly. "I think it's time we return to the ship."

**Rowan:** Roux was sure she'd misheard her. "Why? You fought for years to get home."

**Cass:** "I fought to make Girishtova safe, to fill the streets of Shiibka with hope and joy again. We've done that." She smiled a little. "Do you really want to stay here forever, living like a princess and wearing gowns regularly?"

**Rowan:** Roux, decidedly, did not. She was made for the sea. And after becoming one with the tides, so was Aresha. "Who will rule over Girishtova?"

**Cass:** "I'll figure that out." Aresha twirled Roux before pulling her close again. She wanted Allain and Hypernia to come with them, but that was their decision to make. "But don't think about that. Do you want to return to the ship?"

**Rowan:** Roux laughed in disbelief. She'd planned to never board a large vessel again, but of course it hadn't been what she wanted. "You know I do," she said, pausing. "You're doing this for me, aren't you?"

**Cass:** "And me." Aresha shrugged, grinning. "But yes, mostly for you."

**Rowan:** "I love you," Roux said before kissing her, unable to wait another second.

**Cass:** Aresha felt the tides shift in their kiss. Whatever came next, she was ready to face it together. "I love you too. Until my last sunset."

# ACKNOWLEDGMENTS

If anyone had told teenage me that my online roleplaying obsession would turn into a YA novel, I would've laughed in their face—in and out of character. But here we are, and what a ride it's been! *Out of Character* (*OOC*) wouldn't exist without so many incredible people, and I wouldn't be where I am today without so many more. I'm beyond honored to be thanking them below.

Thank you to my agent, Mike Whatnall, for believing in me and this story of my heart. You helped me take *OOC* to the next level and find the perfect publisher for it. Your support is beyond anything I could've imagined, and I'm so thrilled to be on this journey together. Roleplay nerds forever! Thank you to Michael Bourret, Andrew Dugan, and the rest of the Dystel, Goderich & Bourret team for doing what you do every day to bring stories into the world.

Thank you to my editor, Alyssa Miele, for being so enthusiastic about *OOC* from the beginning. Your brilliant vision and thoughtfulness are appreciated beyond words, and I'm thankful every day that you helped me and *OOC* find a home at Quill Tree. Cool Dad Club united!

Thank you to the editorial, marketing, and publicity teams at Quill Tree/HarperCollins who helped make *OOC* shine both on and off the page, specifically to Laura Harshberger, Annabelle Sinoff, Lisa Calcasola, and Anna Ravenelle.

Thank you to Nicole Rifkin and David DeWitt for turning *OOC* into a masterpiece with your cover art and design. Y'all gave me the cover of my dreams, and I'm forever in awe of your talents.

Thank you to Janice Davis for being my fiercest advocate and greatest friend. Between meeting online in 2005, roleplaying together for years, reading each other's books, and adventuring IRL, you've been here through it all. And if you hadn't bullied me to read and write Young Adult, I don't know where I'd be. *Thank you* will never be enough.

Thank you to my other best friends, Brian and Amanda, whose pep talks and encouragement pushed me to believe in myself and follow this dream. And thank you for still being my friends after the countless times I roleplayed on my phone while hanging out.

Thank you to my sister and original roleplay partner, Julia, for inventing worlds with me as kids and for asking to read every book draft. Thank you to the Brubakens for listening to me ramble about every writing-life detail and keeping me sane through it all. And thank you to the rest of my family for supporting me on this journey.

Thank you to my Author Mentor Match family, including Kalie Holford and Emily Miner, my first online critique partners who became dear friends and two of *OOC*'s biggest champions. Thank you to my mentor, Haley Neil, whose editorial vision, guidance, and support was essential to getting *OOC* ready for querying. And a major thank you to Team Trash (Andy Perez, Crystal Seitz, Elle Tesch, Jenna Voris, Mallory Jones, Melody Robinette, Michelle Milton,

Monica Gribouski, Nat Lockett, Nina Grauer, and SJ Whitby) for being the best feral raccoons a SoftJ could ever need. Your feedback is immensely appreciated, and your friendship means everything to me.

Thank you to my other incredibly talented writing friends whose stories inspire me and support drives me: Zoulfa Katouh, M.K. Lobb, Shelly Page, Jenny Perinovic, Ash Nouveau, Cat Bakewell, A. J. Sass, Meredith Tate, Elle Gonzalez Rose, Edward Underhill, Courtney Kae, Amelia Diane Coombs, and Christen Young.

Thank you to the Madcap Retreats crew for sprinting and flailing together, and teaching me so much about craft, writing tools, publishing, and movies I need to watch.

While the characters in this book are fictional, Cass's Home Base represents the very special nerd community I found online. *OOC* is a love letter to the original ride or dies who stayed long after the role-play scenes wrapped, who continue to be more than roleplay friends, and who I wouldn't be here without. Janice, Catz, Abbey, Alyssa, and Kelsey, I'm so glad we met on the internet.

I wrote Cass as a happily out lesbian nerd who loves her body because it's what anyone in her shoes deserves and something that took me far too long to realize for myself. To anyone who's figuring themselves out or doesn't feel comfortable in their body or feel safe/ready to come out, I see you. You're valid, and you deserve to be seen and have your voice heard. This story is for you. Thank you for reading.